TEENAGE WRITINGS

JANE AUSTEN was born in 1775 in the village of Steventon, Hampshire, the daughter of an Anglican clergyman. The Austens were cultured but not at all rich, though one of Austen's brothers was adopted by a wealthy relative. Other brothers followed professional careers in the church, the Navy, and banking. With the exception of two brief periods away at school, Austen and her elder sister Cassandra, her closest friend and confidante, were educated at home. Austen's earliest surviving work, written at Steventon while still in her teens, is dedicated to her family and close female friends. Between 1801 and 1809 Austen lived in Bath, where her father died in 1805, and in Southampton. In 1809, she moved with her mother, Cassandra, and their great friend Martha Lloyd to Chawton, Hampshire, her home until her death at Winchester in 1817. During this time, Austen published four of her major novels: *Sense and Sensibility* (1811), *Pride and Prejudice* (1813), *Mansfield Park* (1814), and *Emma* (1816), visiting London regularly to oversee their publication. Her two final novels, *Persuasion* and *Northanger Abbey*, were published posthumously in 1818.

KATHRYN SUTHERLAND is Professor of Bibliography and Textual Criticism at the University of Oxford. Her recent publications include *Jane Austen's Textual Lives: From Aeschylus to Bollywood* (2005) and, with Marilyn Deegan, *Transferred Illusions: Digital Technology and the Forms of Print* (2009). She is the editor of *Jane Austen's Fiction Manuscripts: A Digital Edition* (2010). In the World's Classics series she has also published editions of Walter Scott's *Redgauntlet*, of Adam Smith's *An Inquiry into the Nature and Causes of the Wealth of Nations*, and of James Edward Austen-Leigh's *A Memoir of Jane Austen and Other Family Recollections*.

FREYA JOHNSTON is University Lecturer and Tutorial Fellow in English at St Anne's College, Oxford. She is the author of *Samuel Johnson and the Art of Sinking, 1709–1791* (2005) and general editor of The Cambridge Edition of the Novels of Thomas Love Peacock (2016–).

OXFORD WORLD'S CLASSICS

For over 100 years Oxford World's Classics have brought readers closer to the world's great literature. Now with over 700 titles—from the 4,000-year-old myths of Mesopotamia to the twentieth century's greatest novels—the series makes available lesser-known as well as celebrated writing.

The pocket-sized hardbacks of the early years contained introductions by Virginia Woolf, T. S. Eliot, Graham Greene, and other literary figures which enriched the experience of reading. Today the series is recognized for its fine scholarship and reliability in texts that span world literature, drama and poetry, religion, philosophy, and politics. Each edition includes perceptive commentary and essential background information to meet the changing needs of readers.

OXFORD WORLD'S CLASSICS

JANE AUSTEN

Teenage Writings

Edited with an Introduction and Notes by
KATHRYN SUTHERLAND
and
FREYA JOHNSTON

OXFORD
UNIVERSITY PRESS

OXFORD
UNIVERSITY PRESS

Great Clarendon Street, Oxford, OX2 6DP,
United Kingdom

Oxford University Press is a department of the University of Oxford.
It furthers the University's objective of excellence in research, scholarship,
and education by publishing worldwide. Oxford is a registered trade mark of
Oxford University Press in the UK and in certain other countries

© Editorial material Kathryn Sutherland and Freya Johnston 2017

The moral rights of the authors have been asserted

First Edition published in 2017
Impression: 2

Published in the United States of America by Oxford University Press
198 Madison Avenue, New York, NY 10016, United States of America

British Library Cataloguing in Publication Data
Data available

Library of Congress Control Number: 2017933151

ISBN 978-0-19-873745-2

Printed in Great Britain by
Clays Ltd, St Ives plc

Links to third party websites are provided by Oxford in good faith and
for information only. Oxford disclaims any responsibility for the materials
contained in any third party website referenced in this work.

ACKNOWLEDGEMENTS

JUDITH LUNA suggested a new edition of Jane Austen's teenage writings. We are grateful to her, first and last, for her advice and her enthusiasm for the project. Work towards the edition was generously funded by the Leverhulme Trust and by the English Faculty of the University of Oxford. Our thanks go to Daniel Sperrin for a map of Great Britain and to Professor Paul Luna for help with the design of the Textual Notes. Medallion portraits of kings and queens by Cassandra Austen in 'The History of England', *Volume the Second*, are reproduced by kind permission of the British Library, London.

CONTENTS

VOLUME THE FIRST

VOLUME THE SECOND

VOLUME THE THIRD

FAMILY CONTINUATIONS TO
VOLUME THE THIRD

Note: Jane Austen was inconsistent in her styling of the titles of individual stories in the three teenage notebooks, with small discrepancies between the form in which they are listed on the Contents pages of each notebook and the titles that accompany the actual stories. In the Introduction and editorial apparatus to this edition, we have adopted the policy of following, in every instance, the titles as laid out on the three Contents pages. This means that the story widely known as 'Love and Freindship' is referred to throughout as 'Love and Friendship', its title having been amended to the less distinctive spelling on the Contents page of *Volume the Second*. No attempt, however, has been made to standardize Austen's text: the discrepancies remain.

INTRODUCTION

'THE letter which I have this moment received from you has diverted me beyond moderation. I could die of laughter at it, as they used to say at school. You are indeed the finest comic writer of the present age.'[1] With these words, Jane Austen began her reply on 1 September 1796 to her sister Cassandra. It is one of only a handful of her letters to survive from the 1790s. Jane was 20 years old and staying with her brother Edward and his wife, Elizabeth, at their home in Kent. Five years earlier, the circumstances of Edward and Elizabeth's courtship and marriage had prompted the short story 'The three Sisters',[2] dedicated to Edward and inserted towards the end of Jane Austen's first notebook collection of teenage writings. Edward Austen's engagement to Elizabeth Bridges was announced on 1 March 1791. That same year, Elizabeth's two elder sisters, Fanny and Sophia, also became engaged, and on 27 December 1791 Edward and Elizabeth and Sophia and William Deedes shared a double wedding.[3] While these details are matters of fact, 'The three Sisters' is a work of fiction. Written as a series of letters from Mary Stanhope and her sister Georgiana to their female correspondents, the story explores Mary's dilemma over an offer of marriage from 'quite an old Man, about two & thirty' (p. 52). If she marries him, she will be well settled before her sisters; if she refuses him, he will turn his attention in their direction, and she cannot run the risk that one of them might beat her to the altar. She dislikes him; but she longs to spend his fortune. Despite signs that he is as obstinate as she, Mary's confidence in her youth and beauty to bend her future husband to her will remains unshaken; on it depend the new carriages, jewels, fine clothes, and trips to the theatre that make up her fantasy of married life:

[1] *Jane Austen's Letters*, ed. Deirdre Le Faye, 4th edn (Oxford: Oxford University Press, 2011) (hereafter *Letters*), 5.

[2] Here and throughout, the titles of the individual teenage writings are standardized to the forms in which they appear on the Contents pages of the notebooks; the titles at the head of the stories sometimes differ.

[3] See Deirdre Le Faye, *Jane Austen: A Family Record*, 2nd edn (Cambridge: Cambridge University Press, 2004), 70; and Jon Spence, *Becoming Jane Austen: A Life* (London and New York: Hambledon and London, 2003), 62.

'And Remember I am to have a new Carriage hung as high as the Duttons', & blue spotted with silver; and I shall expect a new Saddle horse, a suit of fine lace, and an infinite number of the most valuable Jewels.' (p. 58)

The characters in 'The three Sisters' are thinly painted, their psychology is brittle, and the story's comedy unsophisticated, yet its social preoccupations and gender relations are recognizably those of Jane Austen's adult fiction, in all of which courtship and marriage continue to define a woman's life.

In October 1796, only a month after the date of the letter to Cassandra, Austen began drafting the novel eventually published in 1813 as *Pride and Prejudice*.[4] In *Pride and Prejudice*, the teenage flirt Lydia Bennet, described by the narrator as having 'a sort of natural self-consequence' (ch. 9), regards the world with the same blithe egotism as Mary Stanhope and shapes her conduct accordingly:

In Lydia's imagination, a visit to Brighton comprised every possibility of earthly happiness. She saw with the creative eye of fancy, the streets of that gay bathing place covered with officers. She saw herself the object of attention, to tens and to scores of them at present unknown. (ch. 41)

Among Austen's adult creations, Lydia Bennet is the most prone to laughter, which is described in much the same terms as those her creator conjures for her own younger laughing self. 'Lord! how I laughed! . . . I thought I should have died', Lydia exclaims to her sisters; and, a few paragraphs later, 'I was ready to die of laughter' (ch. 39). To the reader, whether teenage or adult, of the mature fiction, the comparison between a hysterically giggling Jane Austen and wilful, silly Lydia Bennet may be disturbing. But looked at another way, the teenage writings promote the kind of experimental freedom, with life and with fiction, that the later novels bury deep or even appear to condemn. The absurdities and nonsense of her early stories help us to recover the disruptive voices that Austen never completely silenced. Here is the world according to Lydia Bennet.

Long before she was a published novelist, the young Jane Austen was an indiscriminate and precocious reader. She devoured pulp

---

[4] We know this from the list Cassandra Austen made of the dates of composition of the six published novels. 'First Impressions', the original draft of *Pride and Prejudice*, was written between October 1796 and August 1797; see Jane Austen, *Minor Works*, ed. R. W. Chapman (1954), rev. B. C. Southam (Oxford: Oxford University Press, 1969), facing 242.

fiction and classic literature alike: the multi-volume novels of Samuel Richardson (*Sir Charles Grandison* was a favourite) and the latest Gothic adventures and sentimental romances. What she read, she soon began to imitate and parody. Three notebooks survive containing early short works in a variety of genres (stories, dramatic sketches, verses, moral fragments). The notebooks are inscribed on their front covers *Volume the First*, *Volume the Second*, and *Volume the Third*, in conscious imitation of the publishing format of a contemporary novel. The bookmaking joke, which is hardly a joke to the modern reader—rather, something inevitable and pleasingly prophetic of the three-volume novels she would eventually publish—is strengthened by physical evidence. The three quarto notebooks are similar to one another in size and appearance and have been filled with comparable care and attention. Entries in *Volume the First*, in particular, consciously imitate the display features of the printed page and, in a series of inversions of usual protocols—chapters of only a sentence in length, ridiculously truncated and unfinished tales, extravagant dedications—constitute a kind of mock book.[5] The earliest pieces probably date from 1786 or 1787, around the time that Jane, aged 11 or 12, and Cassandra, three years older, left the Abbey House School in Reading. Writing to Cassandra in 1796, Jane reminds her of those days. The latest dated entry in any of the three notebooks is 'June 3d 1793', when Jane Austen was 17. Two of the notebooks, *Volume the Second* and *Volume the Third*, are among the treasures of the British Library; *Volume the First* is held in the Bodleian Library, Oxford. Unlike the six printed novels by which she became known, the teenage writings are unique drafts, written in her own hand, their physical structures as notebooks contributing to their meaning and status.

All three have come down to us as manuscripts, but that does not mean they were intended only for the author's private use. Rather, they were written and prepared for sociable reading and for circulation and performance among family and friends.[6] Unlike many teenage

[5] Mock book formatting is a particular feature of *Volume the First*. The present edition offers modern print equivalents by representing as closely as possible the formal layout of dedications, titles, and letter salutations. For detailed physical descriptions of the notebooks and other visual features, see the headnote to each manuscript in *Jane Austen's Fiction Manuscripts: A Digital Edition*, ed. Kathryn Sutherland (2010), <http://www.janeausten.ac.uk> [hereafter *JA's Fiction Manuscripts*].

[6] See Donald Reiman, *The Study of Modern Manuscripts: Public, Confidential, and Private* (Baltimore and London: Johns Hopkins University Press, 1993), 39, where he

writings, then and now, these are not secret or agonized confessions entrusted to a private journal and for the writer's eyes alone. Rather, they are stories to be shared and admired by a named audience, to whom with only one exception ('Edgar & Emma') they are directly addressed, and extending to an even wider community of friendly readers. To this end, they are filled with allusions to shared jokes and events that imply a coterie of sympathetic readers. There is a particular aptness to many of the dedications, even in their very inappropriateness. Two stories inscribed to Austen's youngest brother, Charles, 'Sir William Mountague' and 'Mr Clifford', involve heroes whose adventures—seduction, partridge shooting, murder, more seduction, and a passion for fancy carriages and distant travel—appear even more absurd when we discover Charles's age at the time; they were probably written and dedicated when he was no more than nine years old. But, as in traditional tales, the ending makes all right when Mr Clifford's inconsequential journeying across southern England returns him eventually to the familiar places of Overton and Dean Gate, within a child's walking distance of the Austens' home at Steventon.[7] The dedications are dropped like anchors, securing texts that in some instances are less substantial than their moorings. Several are later additions, as witnessed by changes in handwriting or the cramped space into which they have been squeezed.[8] All solicit patronage; all emphasize their texts' sociability and the work of a precocious young writer showing off her talents. Uniting the three notebooks are the repeated dedications to Cassandra (four in all), 'the finest comic writer of the present age', illustrator of the spoof 'History of England' in the second notebook, and, we sense, Jane's close collaborator since schooldays.[9] The thirteen miniature images of monarchs that Cassandra

describes such manuscripts as 'confidential' publications, 'addressed to a specific group of individuals all of whom either are personally known to the writer or belong to some predefined group that the writer has reason to believe share communal values with him or her'.

[7] Christine Alexander notes how '[i]n children's writing there is no contradiction between the literal and the fantastic', in Christine Alexander and Juliet McMaster (eds.), *The Child Writer from Austen to Woolf* (Cambridge: Cambridge University Press, 2005), 18.

[8] Dedications to 'Jack & Alice' and 'Mr Harley' in *Volume the First* were evidently added later. See the original notebook (pp. 22, 104) in *JA's Fiction Manuscripts*, <http://www.janeausten.ac.uk/manuscripts/blvolfirst/22.html>.

[9] Cassandra is the dedicatee of 'The beautifull Cassandra' and 'Ode to Pity' in *Volume the First*, of 'The History of England' in *Volume the Second*, and of 'Kitty, or the Bower' in *Volume the Third*.

contributed to 'The History of England' provide some of the strongest evidence to support the family inspiration behind the teenage writings. Not only are Cassandra's kings and queens decked out in modern dress, they appear in several instances to be modelled on Austen family and friends.[10] All three notebooks show signs of heavy wear, which suggests that they were passed around and frequently read. Perhaps their mini-plays and dramatic stories were acted out in the style of the amateur theatricals staged by Jane's elder brother James.[11] Appropriately enough, after Austen's death in 1817, the notebooks descended to Cassandra and were dispersed only after her death in 1845. Cassandra bequeathed *Volume the First* to their little brother Charles, writing on a scrap of paper attached to its front pastedown: 'I think I recollect that a few of the trifles in this Vol: were written expressly for his amusement.' She left *Volume the Second* to their brother Francis; by now Vice-Admiral Austen, he is mentioned in 'The History of England' as the equal of the great sixteenth-century navigator Sir Francis Drake. *Volume the Third* went to their nephew James Edward Austen-Leigh, who as a teenager had written continuations to the two stories within this final notebook.[12]

* * *

Jane Austen is our great interpreter of domestic life among the gentry around the year 1800. Although her novels are acutely conscious of the finest gradations of rank within society,[13] their persistently high standing is evidence of a capacity to transcend the specifics of time and place; they belong to our world too. From the outset, her readers felt they knew her characters; she appeared to work in a new way, at the intersection between art and life. In particular, her heroines and

[10] For the recent identification of the likenesses, see Annette Upfal, introduction to *Jane Austen's 'The History of England' & Cassandra's Portraits*, ed. Annette Upfal and Christine Alexander (Sydney: Juvenilia Press, 2009).

[11] The eldest of the eight Austen children, James (1765–1819) was actor–manager for family theatricals at Steventon parsonage. Between 1782 and 1790, he adapted contemporary plays, adding his own prologues and epilogues, for amateur performance. Some of these survive, along with notes of the roles taken by family members and friends. Jane dedicated her own play 'The Visit' in *Volume the First* to James. See Paula Byrne, *Jane Austen and the Theatre* (London and New York: Hambledon and London, 2002), 6–24.

[12] For more information on their provenance, see the headnotes to each notebook in *JA's Fiction Manuscripts*, <http://www.janeausten.ac.uk>.

[13] See Thomas Keymer, 'Rank', in Janet Todd (ed.), *Jane Austen in Context* (Cambridge: Cambridge University Press, 2005), 387–96.

heroes, unlike those of Daniel Defoe or Henry Fielding before her
and of Charlotte and Emily Brontë or Thomas Hardy after her, are
not transgressors or rebels; they do not break the social rules in any
but the subtlest ways. Instead, their stories play out within the realms
of probable reality and within the ordinary lives of women, where fiction and fantasy are held in check. They explore what it means for
a woman to make a home in a space that is both private and public,
bounded and exposed, where opportunities and amusements are fleet-
ing and precious, and where she is always on show or on trial. Novel
by novel, Austen assembles little worlds filled with everyday social
and moral pitfalls that her heroines must identify and overcome, and
where pleasing oneself, even when possible, entails complex negoti-
ation with the needs and expectations of others. Austen's subjects are
not only courtship and marriage, but the false expectations we have of
love, of ourselves and others; always implied, just beneath the romantic surface that both softens and complicates things, are the harsh facts
of a material and financial reality. Money matters; a comfortable house
matters; marriage is essential to secure these things. The laughter that
lies in wait for the unmarried older woman, dependent on others' charity and herself the object of ridicule, is far different from the comedy
that overwhelms Austen's rebellious teenagers. As Elizabeth Watson
remarks to her younger sister in the unfinished early novel *The Watsons*:

'—but you know we must marry.—I could do very well single for my own
part—A little Company, & a pleasant Ball now & then, would be enough
for me, if one could be young for ever, but my Father cannot provide for us, &
it is very bad to grow old & be poor & laughed at.'[14]

But look deeper still, and these probable romances are littered with
characters from a far more sensational kind of fiction. Some are way-
ward figures, sacrificial victims to the heroine's happy ending: adul-
terous Maria Bertram, banished to the country with shrewish Aunt
Norris at the close of *Mansfield Park*; giddy Lydia Bennet, hastily married to rascally Wickham and packed off to Newcastle. Others, like
Colonel Brandon's first love, the seduced and abandoned Eliza and
her daughter (another seduced Eliza) in *Sense and Sensibility*, and the
mysterious Mrs Smith, Anne Elliot's invalided friend in *Persuasion*,

---

[14] *The Watsons* in *JA's Fiction Manuscripts*, <http://www.janeausten.ac.uk/manuscripts/
pmwats/4.html>.

emerge like ghosts from the machine of the naturalistic novel, their improbable stories used to extricate the heroine from the clutches of a melodramatic plot. The adult Jane Austen called such contrivances 'thorough novel slang',[15] but she was not beyond learning from and using them. As a young reader, she relished novel slang; it sparked her imagination. In the teenage writings novel slang marks the place where reading and writing, consumption and creation, fuse.

Discovering the teenage fiction, as perhaps all readers do, only after the adult novels, is a revelation. They turn everything we think we know about Austen inside out and upside down. Virginia Woolf, one of her best critics, described the experience as seeing Jane Austen 'practising'.[16] Devices operating by stealth in the adult fiction run riot openly and exuberantly across the teenage page, where the very codes and standards of humane society are under attack. The mininovels that make up the bulk of *Volume the First* take a swipe at fashionable novels of sensibility, moral tales designed to move the reader to pity, and even tears, at the world's callousness and the melancholy fates of its victims. For compassion and fellow feeling these stories substitute anarchy and self-gratification, and in their abrupt and broken forms they mirror the hectic behaviour of their subjects: female drunkenness, brawling, sexual misdemeanour, theft, and even murder prevail in the nonsense villages of Crankhumdunberry and Pammydiddle. In defiance of social hierarchy, these disordered societies relish the joke by which a gentleman might marry his cook or the landlady of the local pub. Strapped for cash, as heroines at least since the days of Defoe's Moll Flanders have tended to be, Eliza, of 'Henry & Eliza', supplies her needs with a banknote for £50, stolen from her 'inhuman Benefactors'; emboldened, she follows this up by stealing the fiancé of the daughter of her next protector, the 'Dutchess of F.' (pp. 27–9). Eliza is a survivor who acts on instinct and on impulse, but so too do all around her: the Harcourts, her benefactors, alternately smile upon or 'cudgel' their workers; the Dutchess imprisons her; her children eat two of her fingers (pp. 27, 30). In 'Jack & Alice' and 'The beautifull

[15] *Letters*, 289 (to Anna Austen, 28 Sept. 1814).

[16] Virginia Woolf, 'Jane Austen Practising', *New Statesman*, 19 (15 July 1922), 419–20; reprinted in Andrew McNeillie (ed.), *The Essays of Virginia Woolf*, iii (London: Hogarth Press, 1988), 331–5 (a review of *Volume the Second*, published as *'Love and Freindship' and Other Early Works* (London: Chatto and Windus; New York: Fredrick A. Stokes, 1922), with a preface by G. K. Chesterton).

Cassandra', lawlessness and indiscriminate violence extend to such familiar Austen locations as Bath and London's Bond Street.

This first notebook also suggests a writer training herself in the parts and rules of fiction, playing with its various elements—story, character, plot, motive—and testing how sparely and cryptically a piece of fiction might be assembled and retain the elements necessary for comprehension. Who is Jack of 'Jack & Alice'? Must a named figure (even a hero) appear in his own story? The brief, inconsequential chapters that make up 'The beautifull Cassandra' expose the random plot trajectory in contemporary novels of adventure. In 'Amelia Webster', the first of Austen's mini-novels-in-letters, the reader discovers an unsuspected briskness that challenges the prolix master of the form, Samuel Richardson. His sentimental letter-writers took volumes to speak their minds. Amelia, on the contrary, finds her paper (and so her thoughts) is used up after only a sentence:

Dear Maud
Beleive me I'm happy to hear of your Brother's arrival. I have a thousand things to tell you, but my paper will only permit me to add that I am y^r affec.^{t} Freind

Amelia Webster (p. 41)

Where knockabout humour dominates the first notebook, *Volume the Second* offers more extended studies of female character and motive. The target is manuals of instruction, or conduct books, as they were called, standard schoolroom fare, like Hester Mulso Chapone's *Letters on the Improvement of the Mind, Addressed to a Young Lady*. A popular and lucrative category of the late eighteenth-century book market, conduct books fused a variety of genres: works of devotion, educational tracts (lessons in history, geography, and home economics), recipe books, and advice on female accomplishments. The entries in *Volume the Second* calculatedly distort this formula to mock the limits it imposed on female education and the behaviour expected of a daughter, wife, or mother (the only roles for which well-born teenage girls were trained). The sustained parody achieves a more unified design without sacrificing any of the comedy of *Volume the First*. *Volume the Second* has a good claim to be Jane Austen's funniest work.

First published in 1773, two years before Jane Austen's birth, Chapone's *Letters* had been reprinted in individual editions at least sixteen times by the end of the century and was regularly bundled with other similar manuals to form small 'Ladies' Libraries' of improving texts. Chapone's book is addressed by an aunt to her niece in her 'fifteenth year',[17] Austen's exact age when she embarked on the first of the 'educational' pieces assembled in the second notebook, the sentimental novels 'Love and Friendship' and 'Lesley-Castle'. Five 'Scraps', among them the single act of a comic play, conclude the volume and form a matching book-end to the mini-anthology of 'Miscellanious Morsels' or 'Detached peices' in *Volume the First*. Dedicated to her first-born niece, Fanny Austen (as those inserted at a slightly later date into the closing pages of *Volume the First* are to her second-born niece, Anna Austen), these 'Scraps' satirize the restrictive educational diet proposed for young ladies and the role of moral guide laid down for aunts, as the comparison of Chapone's opening address to her niece with that of Aunt Jane to Fanny shows:

My dearest niece,

Though you are so happy as to have parents, who are both capable and desirous of giving you all proper instruction, yet I, who love you so tenderly, cannot help fondly wishing to contribute something, if possible, to your improvement and welfare:– And, as I am so far separated from you, that it is only by pen and ink I can offer you my sentiments, I will hope that your attention may be engaged, by seeing on paper, from the hand of one of your warmest friends, Truths of the highest importance, which, though you may not find new, can never be too deeply engraven on your mind.[18]

My dear Neice

As I am prevented by the great distance between Rowling & Steventon from superintending Your Education Myself, the care of which will probably on that account devolve on your Father & Mother, I think it is my particular Duty to prevent your feeling as much as possible the want of my personal instructions, by addressing to You on paper my Opinions & Admonitions on the conduct of Young Women, which you will find expressed in the following pages.—(p. 151)

By announcing herself an authority 'on the conduct of Young Women', Austen turns the tables on the adult world, setting up the teenager as

---

[17] Hester Chapone, *Letters on the Improvement of the Mind, Addressed to a Young Lady*, 2nd edn, 2 vols. (London, 1773), i, 3.

[18] Chapone, *Letters on the Improvement of the Mind*, i, 1–2.

instructor. As a whole and in its parts, *Volume the Second* is best appreciated as a perverse conduct manual, a girls' guide to behaving badly. As for the addressee of the 'Scraps', Fanny (like baby Anna in *Volume the First*) was only weeks old when the dedication was penned. The message is clear: if teenage aunts might turn instructors, then it is never too early for little girls to begin to disregard the rules.

The composite character of the ideal young lady of the conduct book is ruthlessly dismantled in sentimental egomaniacs Laura and Sophia of 'Love and Friendship'; in food-obsessed Charlotte Lutterell and the spiteful socialite Susan Lesley of 'Lesley-Castle'; in the boldly revisionist 'partial, prejudiced, & ignorant Historian' of the spoof 'History of England'; and in the 'Collection' of five letters that parodies the dilemmas facing a young woman as she enters adult society. Where the conventional conduct book proposes the letter form as a vehicle for moral instruction, in the hands of the satirical author the novel-in-letters becomes the virtuoso performance of a series of exhibitionist egos, who, possessing no social filters, quickly disclose their true natures and squander any credibility. 'I hate Scandal and detest Children', Lady Susan Lesley confides to Charlotte Lutterell (p. 107), while Laura's absurd response to the sight of an overturned carriage suggests a grossly mangled exercise in juvenile philosophy: ' "What an ample subject for reflection on the uncertain Enjoyments of this World, would not that Phaeton & the Life of Cardinal Wolsey afford a thinking Mind!" said I to Sophia as we were hastening to the field of Action' (p. 87). Without discretion, modesty, or self-regulation, Laura, Sophia, Charlotte, and Susan are the very reverse of a feminine ideal. It is as if the young Jane Austen has strategically animated and empowered a whole regiment of teenage girls in open contention, in their anti-social and undisciplined behaviour, with the educational models of the classroom and the drawing room. Having read the pieces in *Volume the Second*, Woolf's conclusion was that 'at seventeen she had few illusions about other people and none about herself'.[19]

Although there is no simple and straightforward chronology for the entries in the three notebooks, a general sense of development emerges from one to the next.[20] Inscribed on the inside front cover of the third and

[19] Woolf, 'Jane Austen Practising', *The Essays of Virginia Woolf*, iii, 334. Austen was 17 years old when she wrote the final items in *Volume the Second*.

[20] See 'Chronology of the Teenage Writings', pp. xxxvi–xxxvii.

last are the words 'Effusions of Fancy By a very Young Lady Consisting of Tales In a Style entirely new'.[21] The contents page is dated May 6th 1792 and it lists only two stories: 'Evelyn' and 'Kitty, or the Bower', which is separately dated, in its dedication to Cassandra, to August 1792, when Austen was 16. Neither story is finished in her hand. 'Evelyn' is an absurd and oddly surreal tale, a study of bizarre generosity and innocent greed whose angular morality and humour quickly break down. In its abstraction, it reads like an attempt to pare back the sentimental narrative to see how its elements fit together: do characters need motive or psychology? How does plot relate to character? These are issues grappled with in *Volume the First*. By contrast, 'Kitty', filling ninety-four pages in Austen's hand, is her most sustained piece of writing to date. In its realistic presentation of domestic life through the eyes of a teenage girl (both its writer and its protagonist, Kitty) it foreshadows themes that will emerge in the adult fiction. 'Kitty, or the Bower', beyond any other of the teenage writings, is recognizably a novel by Jane Austen. It is also openly, and unusually, a political story.

'Kitty' is addressed to Cassandra in a dedication that links the work to two others 'Encouraged by your warm patronage': 'The beautifull Cassandra', a tale of arbitrary female assertiveness, and 'The History of England', a sweeping and absurd survey of tyranny and incompetence in the guise of brief biographies of kings and queens. Now Cassandra's support is solicited for a more nuanced study of sexual politics. 'Kitty' is political in its harsh criticism of the economic constraints on female opportunity and the social injustice by which 'a Girl of Genius & Feeling' can be married off to a man she scarcely knows, 'who may be a Tyrant, or a Fool or both', simply because she is poor (p. 178). Kitty Peterson, who voices the novel's critique, is an apt heroine for the 1790s, a period when the exposure of social inequalities was linked to constitutional reform and arguments for an extension of political rights, and when male and female writers were exploring the novel as a vehicle for comment and change.[22] Kitty values education over mere accomplishments, but she is also keenly alert

---

[21] It has been suggested that the hand is that of Jane Austen's father, the Revd George Austen (*Family Record*, 78). But the letter shapes are also consistent with the hands of both Jane and Cassandra Austen.

[22] Mary Wollstonecraft, Charlotte Smith, Robert Bage, and William Godwin were all writing political novels of this kind through the 1790s, making Austen's 'Kitty' in 1792 an early contribution to the form.

to the fact that, as the daughter of a merchant, her social standing is below that of her well-connected friend, the empty-headed Camilla Stanley. Camilla's brother Edward, an unexpected visitor 'returned from France', brings into their confined female world the hint of danger, which is acted out when he dances and flirts with Kitty. Edward's breaches of social etiquette may not be apparent to the modern reader, but they are severe—sharing a carriage, unchaperoned, with Kitty, and leading her, in defiance of rank, to the head of the line of dancers. As in his connection to France, a country torn apart in 1792 by revolution, his disregard for the rules of polite society injects a further political dimension into the tale's domestic events. This is emphasized through relations between Kitty's aunt, who is her guardian, and Edward and Camilla's father, Mr Stanley, a Member of Parliament in William Pitt's government. Both are political creatures; national politics is the lens through which they see the world. Convinced that an English revolution is imminent, Kitty's aunt is, in her febrile state, 'tremblingly alive to every alarm'. She obsessively patrols her niece's behaviour, interpreting any relaxation of her own rigid social code as a sign of utter moral collapse, summed up in her refrain that 'every thing is going to sixes & sevens and all order will soon be at an end throughout the Kingdom' (p. 199).

Kitty is a typical Austen heroine, caught up in a battle of wills with her elders. Like Elizabeth Bennet after her, she is both impressionable and critical, weighing traits, even in those to whom she is attracted, with every appearance of detachment, and persuading herself (if no one else) of her keen penetration and wisdom, as in this passage of reflection on Edward Stanley's character:

The more she had seen of him, the more inclined was she to like him, & the more desirous that he should like *her*. She was convinced of his being naturally very clever and very well disposed, and that his thoughtlessness & negligence, which tho' they appeared to *her* as very becoming in *him*, she was aware would by many people be considered as defects in his Character, merely proceeded from a vivacity always pleasing in Young Men, & were far from testifying a weak or vacant Understanding. Having settled this point within herself, and being perfectly convinced by her own arguments of it's truth, she went to bed in high spirits, determined to study his Character, and watch his Behaviour still more the next day. (pp. 201–2)

Although the story remains tantalizingly unfinished, the reader's interest in Kitty is secure—beyond her love life and any future relationship with Edward Stanley. We care about Kitty in and for herself; we care about her capacity to distinguish true from false friends and to learn from her mistakes; and we hope that she might learn these lessons without losing either her openness to experience or her keen sense of justice. 'Kitty, or the Bower' sets the stage for Jane Austen the professional novelist, but she will never again write with such candour about social and sexual politics.

* * *

Volume the Third marks a close to the teenage writings, as far as we know them. But habits established in the three notebooks continued in two particular ways. For the rest of her life, Jane Austen would maintain the practice of amateur composition to amuse family and friends alongside her writing for the printing press. Home-centred pieces, such as her occasional verses and the comic 'Plan of a Novel, according to hints from various quarters', probably written in early 1816 soon after the publication of *Emma*, grow out of and thrive upon the opinions and reception of a circle of family and friends reading, laughing over, and commenting upon the author's performance.[23] There is also evidence, provided by the substantial continuations to both stories in *Volume the Third*, that this notebook became, in time, a different kind of shared space—a space for family writing as well as reading. Critics have long recognized that these continuations, inserted more than twenty years after the initial composition of the stories, are in the hands of Anna Lefroy and her younger half-brother, James Edward Austen, the children of Jane's eldest brother James.

Anna and James Edward grew up close to Aunt Jane, moving into her old home of Steventon parsonage after their father took over clerical duties there when his own father, George Austen, retired with his wife and daughters to Bath in 1801. Even earlier, Anna (who, christened Jane Anna Elizabeth Austen, was her aunt's namesake) had been brought, as a 2-year-old, to live at Steventon with Jane and Cassandra after the death of her mother. Earlier still, she became the

---

[23] Austen referred to the family 'improvement' of her occasional poetry in a letter of 29 Nov. 1812 to Martha Lloyd (*Letters*, 205). She openly acknowledges family advice in the marginal display of sources on the manuscript pages of the 'Plan of a Novel', available to view in *JA's Fiction Manuscripts*, <http://www.janeausten.ac.uk/manuscripts/pmplan/1.html>.

unwitting 6-week-old dedicatee of the 'Detached peices' towards the close of *Volume the First*. There is ample evidence that Anna was Aunt Jane's willing pupil throughout her childhood and teenage years, and that habits of shared composition began early between them. Anna's unfinished continuation to 'Evelyn' is written on four leaves of varying sizes, loosely inserted at the end of *Volume the Third* and signed with the initials '*JAEL*' (Jane Anna Elizabeth Lefroy), indicating that it does not pre-date November 1814, when, aged 21, she married Ben Lefroy.[24] Long after Austen's death, Anna would attempt a continuation of her aunt's final manuscript, *Sanditon*.[25]

Like his sister, the teenage James Edward tried his hand at short stories and novels, portions of which survive, sending them, on occasion, for comment and approval to Aunt Jane.[26] His conclusion to 'Evelyn' is written directly into *Volume the Third*, taking up the story where Austen broke it off; he also attempted a continuation to 'Kitty, or the Bower' within the notebook. Significantly, too, he undertook to make some bold revisions to 'Kitty' as originally written by his aunt. These have only recently been attributed to him, and the recognition of his revising hand alters considerably any appreciation of the story. Many small local revisions to the notebook, including such important details as the change of title from 'Kitty, or the Bower' to 'Catharine, or the Bower', and the renaming of Kitty Peterson as Catharine Percival, assumed by previous editors to be Austen's own, were introduced by James Edward. These alterations, all tending to gentrify or upgrade the tone of the story, diminish its political thrust as it was originally written in 1792, a time when championship of wider civil rights and educational opportunities was linked to a reappraisal of vernacular English. The cultural and political resonances of the straightforwardly English name Kitty Peterson, for example, accord with the story's realism; the restyled Catharine Percival appears, by contrast, a figure

---

[24] Anna Lefroy's four leaves are digitized and transcribed in *JA's Fiction Manuscripts*, <http://www.janeausten.ac.uk/manuscripts/blvolthird/21a.html>.

[25] For Anna Austen's collaborations with her aunt, see Kathryn Sutherland, *Jane Austen's Textual Lives: From Aeschylus to Bollywood* (Oxford: Oxford University Press, 2005), 224–5, 246–8.

[26] *Letters*, 337 (to James Edward, 16 Dec. 1816), 339–40 (to Caroline Austen, 23 Jan. 1817). Portions survive from several of James Edward Austen's teenage manuscript fictions in Winchester, Hampshire Record Office, MS 23M93/86/6/1–5. Some are datable by hand and by paper to 1812–17, when he was aged 13 to 18.

cloaked in the chivalric flattery of romance.[27] The text presented here offers the reader the first opportunity, other than that granted to Jane Austen's immediate family, to read her story as she wrote it—and before the next generation set about its revision and amelioration.[28]

Many of these revisions can be dated, either by internal reference or by hand. For example, two alterations in 'Kitty' were possible only in or after 1809. The first, Camilla Stanley's reference to a 'new Regency walking dress' (replacing an original reference to a 'Pierrot'), must postdate the Regency Act (5 February 1811).[29] The second, the deletion of an allusion to 'Seccar's explanation of the Catechism' (Thomas Secker's *Lectures on the Catechism of the Church of England* (1769)) and substitution of 'Coelebs in Search of a Wife', must be later than December 1808, when Hannah More's novel of that title was published. But it is most likely, given similarities of hand with his other teenage stories, that James Edward was writing into his aunt's notebook in 1815 or 1816, when he was aged 16 or 17. In allowing niece and nephew to try their hands at continuations to the stories in *Volume the Third* and even permitting James Edward to edit 'Kitty, or the Bower', Jane Austen confirmed for the next generation of scribbling Austens the original function of the notebooks: to nurture authorship within family life.

* * *

Austen described her family as 'great Novel-readers & not ashamed of being so', even in a period when the novel's status was proverbially low.[30] Countless tales of adventure, mystery, and intrigue, featuring exotic locations and creaky, sensational plots, were published during her early years. Take Agnes Maria Bennett's *Anna; or Memoirs of a Welch Heiress, interspersed with Anecdotes of a Nabob* (1785), a four-volume blockbuster of which one reviewer commented that 'In some

---

[27] Kathryn Sutherland, 'From Kitty to Catharine: James Edward Austen's Hand in *Volume the Third*', *Review of English Studies*, new series, 66 (2014), 124–43; and Olivia Smith, *The Politics of Language, 1791–1819* (Oxford: Oxford University Press, 1984).

[28] Anna Lefroy's and James Edward Austen's continuations appear separately at the end of the text of *Volume the Third* in this edition. James Edward's revisions are stripped out of Jane Austen's texts and are all noted within the Textual Notes as they occur, allowing readers to make comparison between original and revision.

[29] Jenny McAuley, ' "A Long Letter Upon a Jacket and a Petticoat": Reading Beneath some Deletions in the Manuscript of "Catharine, or The Bower" ', *Persuasions: The Jane Austen Journal*, 31 (2009), 191–8.

[30] *Letters*, 27 (to Cassandra Austen, 18–19 Dec. 1798).

parts of it the incidents are scarcely within the verge of probability; and the language is generally incorrect'; however, 'We have seen many worse novels'.[31] Evidence of the Austens' love of such outlandish fiction is stamped all over the teenage writings; it survives in romantic, fanciful names, such as Elfrida, heroine of the capsule novel with which *Volume the First* opens. Austen might have come across it in *Elfrida; or Paternal Ambition. A Novel* (1786); or she could have known of another Elfrida in *Beatrice, or The Inconstant. A Tragic Novel* (1788). There is yet another Elfrida in the later *Agatha; or, A Narrative of Recent Events. A Novel* (1796). The name also crops up in Frances Burney's *Cecilia; or, Memoirs of an Heiress* (1782). We know that Austen read Burney avidly, so this may be where she discovered an Elfrida for the first time. But in view of her omnivorous taste for novels, other and long-forgotten titles are plausible contenders too.

The influence of Richardson's epistolary fiction, as well as that of his imitators, is everywhere apparent in the teenage works—and not only in the formal sense that many of the pieces Austen writes are letters. In 'Jack & Alice', for example, the intolerably handsome Charles Adams descends from the peerless paragon of Richardson's final novel, *Sir Charles Grandison*. Delivering a lengthy eulogy on himself—'I am certainly more accomplished in every Language, every Science, every Art & every thing than any other person in Europe. My temper is even, my virtues innumerable, my self unparalelled' (p. 20)—Adams takes to its natural conclusion the praise heaped on Richardson's heroes and heroines and in turn repeated by them or by others in their letters. Adams, however, prides himself on his looks and abilities rather than on his charity or kindness, and Austen thereby perverts as well as honours her literary model. The teenage writings take gleeful aim at exemplary figures of all kinds, and therefore at their instructive value. When Mr Gower (in 'Evelyn') blithely exclaims, moments after meeting Mrs Willis, 'Amiable Woman . . . What would I not give to be your Neighbour, to be blessed with your Acquaintance, and with the farther knowledge of your virtues! Oh! with what pleasure would I form myself by such an example!' (p. 161), he is echoing novels that present their characters as models on whom readers might base their own conduct—as, indeed, do other characters within the fiction itself. The heroine of the epistolary novel *Female Stability: or, The*

---

[31] *Critical Review, or, Annals of Literature*, 59 (1785), 476.

History of Miss Belville (1780) writes: 'I often think, when I am going to do any thing material, would Augustus have acted thus? and endeavour to form myself by his excellent example.'[32]

The logical consequence of such pervasive copying would be a world populated by duplicates or automatons. This is the world of the teenage writings. Austen replays and accentuates the symmetrical gestures and mirrored emotions that, like coincidences, pepper sentimental novels of the late eighteenth century. She appears to have digested and regurgitated novelistic mechanisms so quickly as to make herself feel giddy—fainting is among her favoured comic scenarios—and the early works are best approached as a variety of fan fiction. Duplication is funny in itself, perhaps especially to two sisters of whom their mother reportedly said 'if Cassandra's head had been going to be cut off, Jane would have her's cut off too'.[33] The varieties of rehashing that occur at the culinary level, in some tales, play out with equally skilled economy at the literary level. (The parallel nature of these female activities is brought home by the fact that the same kind of stationer's quarto notebook was used by Jane Austen's close friend Martha Lloyd to jot down recipes as was employed by Austen to copy out her teenage experiments in fiction.) Good housekeeping, a key principle of female upbringing, is both sent up and exemplified in the way Austen deploys and redeploys her sources. Take her reference to 'making a Curry' for the ailing Maria in 'A beautiful description' (p. 64). The culinary aspect of the quip is that this spicy dish will hardly suit the delicate stomach of an invalid. But Austen is also flipping a joke made in 'The Visit' (p. 47), in which a soothing drink, fit for an invalid, is served up to a young, healthy woman. Such neat, efficient reversals are a form of recycling; they also show how quickly Austen learnt the rules of comic writing. What cuts one way cuts the other. This rule applies to gender as well as to cooking and jokes: the teenage skits contain some striking, wilful exchanges of male and female behaviour. In 'Edgar & Emma' (p. 25), Thomas the footman is cast in the role of a female confidante for Emma, while 'The History of England' imagines Lambert Simnel as the widow of Richard III

---

[32] Miss Palmer, *Female Stability: or, The History of Miss Belville*, 5 vols. (London, 1780), iii, 158.

[33] See J. E. Austen-Leigh, *A Memoir of Jane Austen and Other Family Recollections*, ed. Kathryn Sutherland, Oxford World's Classics (Oxford: Oxford University Press, 2002), 160.

(p. 124). Women rather than men pass around the bottle and drink with cheery abandon (p. 48), and Hamlet's celebrated speech 'What a piece of work is a man!' is parodically recast as 'Oh! what a silly Thing is Woman!' (p. 202).

* * *

Jane Austen's early writings are concerned with people and events that manifestly do or manifestly do not merit our interest. Time and again, they narrate either an excess of action and accomplishment, or the complete absence of both. In *Volume the First*, we are told of the hero of 'Jack & Alice', who fails to appear in the story, that he 'never did anything worth mentioning' (p. 20). In *Volume the Second*, we learn in passing that tragedy is 'not worth reading' (p. 124). Austen describes 'Frederic & Elfrida' as a 'little production', a word that implies dramatic exhibition as well as the product of writing (p. 2). Later in the same volume, the prose fiction 'Sir William Mountague' is billed, with a similar theatrical flourish, as 'an unfinished perform-ance' (p. 34). Austen writes with an awareness of being watched, and she creates parts for characters who, without having anything much to show or tell, long for an audience.

The solemn rites of induction into authorship, as well as the related condition of being celebrated, are always in this writer's mind. 'Kitty, or the Bower' shows a sophisticated awareness of how novels were puffed to their prospective readers; the dedication mentions Cassandra Austen's 'warm patronage of The beautiful Cassandra, and The History of England, which through your generous support, have obtained a place in every library in the Kingdom' (p. 169). That phras-ing echoes the terms in which contemporary fiction was advertised. The title page of *Edward and Harriet, or The Happy Recovery; A Sentimental Novel* (1788), states that the work 'may be had at every Circulating Library in the Kingdom', while Charles Dibdin's *The Younger Brother: A Novel* (1793) includes a bookseller, Mr Allen, who boasts: 'look at this drawer: full, chuck full—all novels—I supply every library in the kingdom'.[34] In the dedication to her brother James of 'The Visit', Austen refers to what may be lost works of her own, or possibly his, or perhaps just titles of works they dreamt up between

[34] *Edward and Harriet, or The Happy Recovery; A Sentimental Novel*, 2 vols. (London, 1788); Charles Dibdin, *The Younger Brother: A Novel*, 3 vols. (London, 1793), iii, 138.

them: 'those celebrated Comedies called "The school for Jealousy" & "The travelled Man"' (p. 44). Such titles place her squarely in the dramatic, anti-sentimental company of Richard Brinsley Sheridan and Oliver Goldsmith. Henry Tilney twits Catherine in *Northanger Abbey* with his reference to 'the easy style of writing for which ladies are so generally celebrated' (ch. 3). But, in celebrating her own works in this arch manner—if that is indeed what she is up to—the young Jane Austen is also setting herself apart from them. Ladies were not typically celebrated for writing comedies. Not long before Austen began her teenage skits, Burney was composing and then reluctantly suppressing her satirical drama *The Witlings* (written 1778–9).[35]

As a 15-year-old, Burney dedicated the account in her journal of 'my wonderful, surprising & interesting adventures' to 'Nobody'. In choosing to do so, she was well aware that namelessness appears to cancel out, or at least radically to compromise, our ability to celebrate anyone. But anonymity—a convention of eighteenth-century novels— also licenses storytelling.[36] Part of the apparatus of mock reality, this sham decorum is intended to suggest that the tale we are reading originated in real life. Hence Austen's glancing references to a 'Miss XXX' in 'The three Sisters' (p. 54) and to 'M.' and 'F.' in 'Henry & Eliza' (p. 28), which imitate the practice of abbreviating or concealing the names of characters as if they were real people. 'The beautifull Cassandra' is, we are told, 'the Daughter and the only Daughter of a celebrated Millener in Bond Street' (p. 38). No name is supplied, although we have the address. Other names are cryptically represented: 'the Dutchess of —'s Butler' (p. 38); 'the Countess of —' (p. 38). The heroine encounters an otherwise unidentified Viscount, 'a young Man, no less celebrated for his Accomplishments & Virtues, than for his Elegance & Beauty' (p. 38). Contributing to this joke about namelessness is the sheer banality of the terms of praise; in late eighteenth-century novels, 'Accomplishments' and 'Virtues', like 'Elegance' and 'Beauty', are as briskly circulated as is the bottle of gooseberry wine in 'The Visit'. 'The beautifull Cassandra', like 'The

[35] See Pat Rogers, 'Burney, Frances (1752–1840)', *Oxford Dictionary of National Biography*, Oxford University Press, 2004; online edn, May 2015, <http://www.oxforddnb. com/view/article/603>, accessed 19 Feb. 2016.

[36] *The Early Journals and Letters of Fanny Burney*, i: *1768–1773*, ed. Lars E. Troide (Kingston and Montreal: McGill-Queen's University Press, 1988), 1–2.

Mystery'—a playlet in which the cast of whispering characters apparently understand one another perfectly, but we never find out what
they are discussing—contains important fuss about something that
may add up to nothing at all.

* * *

Alongside schoolroom histories and conduct books, Francis Grose's
Classical Dictionary of the Vulgar Tongue (1785), which combines the
pedagogical form of a lexicon with thieves' cant and low language, is
one likely inspiration for the mock-authoritative quality of Austen's
teenage writings. The revised title of Grose's *Classical Dictionary*, when
it reappeared in expanded form in 1811, was *A Dictionary of Buckish
Slang, University Wit, and Pickpocket Eloquence*, emphasizing a strain
of male undergraduate humour that had been there from the beginning. The new title gestures more clearly towards a certain type of
minor character in the works of Jane Austen—idle, well off, not very
bright young men at the university. Through her brothers, who were
students at Oxford in the late 1780s, she could have encountered plenty
of drawling loungers and loiterers like John Thorpe in *Northanger
Abbey*, the type to enjoy innuendo and dirty jokes such as those Austen
makes about King James's 'keener penetration' in her 'History of
England' (p. 132)—punning that is carried over into Mary Crawford's
infamous 'Rears and Vices' quip in *Mansfield Park* (ch. 6). The teenage Austen was writing for a boisterous audience. She may well have
been producing and performing her early works for a group including
young male lodgers, since her father took in boys for tutoring as a way
to supplement his income (this is how Cassandra's fiancé, Thomas
Fowle, was introduced to the Austen family).[37] It is easy to see how
such a domestic arrangement could prove congenial to highly charged,
flirtatious performances, and that it might prompt hysterical laughter
whenever a hint of sexual impropriety emerged. Take the phrase 'family of Love', which crops up in 'Jack & Alice'. It originates as the name
of a sixteenth-century religious sect; by the eighteenth century, however, it is commonly deployed in novels and without any religious implication to describe a happy, virtuous household. In *Edward. A Novel*

---

[37] See *Family Record*, 26, 41–2. By 1779, Thomas Fowle's elder brother Fulwar Craven
Fowle was a boarding pupil of the Revd George Austen; he was one of four boys (not
including Jane Austen's brothers) living at the rectory at that time.

(1774), James Wharton declares: 'there is not so enchanting a society as that of a well-regulated family, a family of love'.[38] But the phrase had a far less reputable connotation that may also have been in Austen's mind; in Grose's *Classical Dictionary*, 'FAMILY OF LOVE' is said to mean 'lewd women'. Language can serve both to disguise and uncover bad behaviour, like the masks and costumes sported at masquerades. As a teenager, Austen leapt upon words and phrases that could be pressed to accommodate the full range of virtue and vice.

Under- and overstatement, like other measures of insufficiency or excess, are the engines of her comedy; they are partly responses to conduct books and to any models of decorum and restraint. One of the keywords in the teenage writings is the busy, unobtrusive 'too'—as in 'too high', 'too much', 'too small', 'too great'. Time and again, what is striking about the geography and pace of the three volumes is that things are made to go excessively fast, or comically slowly; that places are too far away, or too close to one another, for the time spent in getting to them to be credible. As is shown from her revisions, Austen tended to make these jokes more extreme when she had the chance to reconsider them. There is a wider, and a wilder, range of places in the teenage writings than in the mature novels. In middle age, Austen advised her niece Anna not to travel in fiction where she had not been in life, but she did not follow that counsel in her own early works.[39] *Volume the Second* reflects a craze for Scottish travel, landscape, and music, and takes in Gretna Green, Edinburgh, Sterling, Aberdeen, Perth, and Dunbeath. As in the mature novels, and as in the pulp fiction Austen would have been reading, the fashionable streets and pleasure grounds of central London play a key role—Portland Place, Queen's Square, Brook Street, Bond Street, Bloomsbury Square, Portman Square, Sackville Street, Grosvenor Street, Vauxhall, and Ranelagh Gardens—as well as the less respectable Holborn, King's Bench Prison, and Newgate Prison.[40] A few entirely fictional locations appear in the teenage writings—Crankhumdunberry, Pammydiddle, Chetwynde, and Evelyn—but two of these are located in or near real places, Chetwynde near Exeter and Evelyn in Sussex. Characters in these miniature books not only travel oddly across the landscapes

---

[38] *Edward. A Novel*, 2 vols. (London, 1774), ii, 82.
[39] *Letters*, 280 (to Anna Austen, 18 Aug. 1814).
[40] For a full list, see the map of London on p. lviii.

in which they feature—in one tale, running and hopping sweatily
alongside a galloping pony—they also know startlingly little about
where anything is. When, in 'Kitty', Camilla Stanley imagines 'a delightful voyage to Bengal or Barbadoes', the locations are paired simply
because they begin with 'B' (p. 178). In 'Love and Friendship', Edward
remarks:

My Father's house is situated in Bedfordshire, my Aunt's in Middlesex,
and tho' I flatter myself with being a tolerable proficient in Geography,
I know not how it happened, but I found myself entering this beautifull
Vale which I find is in South Wales, when I had expected to have reached
my Aunts. (p. 73)

* * *

Henry Austen remarked of his sister that she became 'at a very early
age . . . sensible to the charms of style, and enthusiastic in the cultivation of her own language'.[41] The teenage writings allow us to chart the
progress of that early, acute attention to high and low style and language. Any reasonably well-educated girl of the 1780s and 1790s could
be expected to show familiarity with Samuel Johnson and Alexander
Pope—the most celebrated prose-writer and the most celebrated poet
of the century—whether that was through reading their works in
their entirety, or via anthologies of 'beauties' and 'elegant extracts'.
Austen owned one such anthology and passed it on to her novel-writing
niece, Anna.[42] The habit of excerpting is itself presented as something
of a joke in a passing reference to 'Sentiments of Morality' ('The
female philosopher' (p. 151)), and in the dedication of 'Collection
of Letters', a work described as 'this Clever Collection of Curious
Comments, which have been Carefully Culled, Collected & Classed
by your Comical Cousin' (p. 134).

Johnsonian syntax and snatches of Pope contribute to the 'Style
entirely new' of Austen's teenage writings, as celebrated on the inside
cover of *Volume the Third*. As befits the mock-heroic register of these
works, in which, as Pope phrased it in 1714, 'mighty Quarrels rise from

---

[41] 'Biographical Notice of the Author' (1818), in Austen-Leigh, *Memoir*, 137.
[42] *Elegant Extracts: or useful and entertaining Passages in Prose* (London: Charles Dilly,
n.d.), an anthology much in use in late eighteenth-century schoolrooms. The Austen
family copy, inscribed to Anna, 'the gift of her Aunt Jane', is now in Jane Austen's House
Museum, Chawton.

trivial Things'[43] and vanishingly slight subjects are yoked to the most lavish praise, Austen can allude to her productions as 'interesting' and '*complete*', while virtually in the same breath calling them 'short', 'little' and 'unfinished', 'Scraps' and 'Morsels'. The reference in 'Frederic & Elfrida' to 'Patches, Powder, Pomatum & Paint' (p. 5) loudly and clearly echoes the most celebrated list in eighteenth-century literature: 'Puffs, Powders, Patches, Bibles, Billet-doux'.[44] Austen sometimes employs syllepsis, or zeugma, whereby one verb governs two different, incongruous objects—as in 'Jack & Alice', where 'cruel Charles' is said 'to wound the hearts & legs of all the fair' (p. 18). It is a technique she probably learned from Pope's *Rape of the Lock*, in which Queen Anne's dignity is vaguely compromised when she is said to 'take' both 'Counsel' and '*Tea*'.[45]

Henry Austen noted that his sister's 'favourite moral writer' in prose was Samuel Johnson; their lives overlapped by nine years.[46] Unlike the figure of Pope, that of Johnson bulks as large at the biographical level as he does at the level of style, and several characters in the teenage writings bear his surname (in 'A Tour through Wales', the character Elizabeth Johnson is named after his wife). In his lifetime and for decades thereafter, partly thanks to the continuing popularity of James Boswell's *Life of Samuel Johnson* (1791), this towering author was both praised and attacked for the gravity, symmetry, and parallelism of his writing, as exemplified in a sentence from *Rambler* no. 29: 'Evil is uncertain in the same degree as good, and for the reason that we ought not to hope too securely, we ought not to fear with too much dejection.'[47] Each member of the antithetical pair (evil / good; hope / fear) is equally weighted. As a result, the assertion feels at once succinct and comprehensive, like an aphorism, and in its general yet sympathetic handling of human nature it possesses dignity and solemnity. These unmistakable stylistic features—which Johnson himself was capable of spoofing—are parodied in Austen's description of Lady Williams ('Jack & Alice') and in a comparison of Bath with Southampton ('Love and Friendship'):

---

[43] Alexander Pope, *The Rape of the Lock. An Heroi-Comical Poem* (London, 1714), canto 1, line 2.   [44] Pope, *Rape of the Lock*, canto 1, line 138.

[45] Pope, *Rape of the Lock*, canto 3, line 8.

[46] Austen-Leigh, *Memoir*, 141. Austen was born in 1775; Johnson died in 1784.

[47] Samuel Johnson, *Rambler* no. 29 (1750), in *The Rambler*, 6 vols. (London, 1752), i, 254.

Tho' Benevolent & Candid, she was Generous & sincere; Tho' Pious & Good, she was Religious & amiable, & Tho, Elegant & Agreable, she was Polished & Entertaining. (pp. 10–11)

Beware of the unmeaning Luxuries of Bath & of the Stinking fish of Southampton. (p. 71)

In the first example, the balanced pairs of adjectives lead us to expect that a series of antitheses is about to be presented—although Lady Williams was this, she was (contrastingly) that. But the syntactic structures that promise contradiction and opposition turn out to yield nothing but sameness. In the second example, the conventional (and morally disapproving) abstraction of 'unmeaning Luxuries' collides, startlingly, with the low reality of 'Stinking fish', to which it is yoked by an '&' that makes us expect a comparable level of abstraction in the second half of the sentence. The joke is brought home by the Johnsonian parallelism. In the first example, we expect difference, and meet with sameness; in the second instance, we expect sameness, and meet with difference. Once again, Austen shows that what cuts one way cuts the other. As in 'Edgar & Emma' and 'The Visit'—in which apparently wealthy families live in needlessly harsh conditions or eat cheap, coarse food—high collides with low. Here Austen reverses the premiss of James Townley's *High Life Below Stairs* (1759), a farce performed by her family in winter 1788, in which a group of servants impersonate aristocrats. In doing so, she enlists Johnson as an agent of bathos, a term given its comic sense of 'Ludicrous descent from the elevated to the commonplace in writing or speech; anticlimax' by Pope in his prose treatise, *Peri Bathos* (1727).[48]

So Pope and Johnson both help the young Austen to engineer comic flops, to stage a series of triumphant verbal and syntactic letdowns. In addition to his stylistic donations, Johnson's travels to the Highlands contribute to the Scottish flavour of *Volume the Second*. The passage in which Laura remembers how she and Sophia

sate down by the side of a clear limpid stream to refresh our exhausted limbs. The place was suited to meditation—. A Grove of full-grown Elms sheltered us from the East—. A Bed of full-grown Nettles from the West—. (p. 86)

---

[48] See *OED*, 'bathos', sense 2.

comically recalls and accentuates the 'rudeness' of *A Journey to the Western Islands of Scotland*, a work published in the year of Austen's birth:

> I sat down on a bank, such as a writer of romance might have delighted to feign. I had indeed no trees to whisper over my head, but a clear rivulet streamed at my feet. The day was calm, the air soft, and all was rudeness, silence, and solitude.[49]

'Lesley-Castle' echoes various descriptions of isolated, rock-bound castles in Johnson's *Journey* and in Boswell's *Journal of a Tour to the Hebrides*—a text published ten years after Johnson's account of the same visit to Scotland and by way of a dress rehearsal for the full-length biography (in a letter of 1798, Austen mentions that her father has bought a copy of Boswell's *Journal*, and that they 'are to have' his *Life of Johnson*).[50] In chapter 14 of *Northanger Abbey*, Johnson is invoked on the basis of his overwhelming lexicographical authority— his *Dictionary of the English Language* was published in 1755—while chapter 39 of *Mansfield Park* invokes his 'celebrated judgment' on matrimony and celibacy. Both ways of thinking about Johnson are entirely conventional in this period. He is quotable, and he is the definitive point of reference as far as linguistic correctness is concerned. Austen is neither cowed by nor resentful of such authority; rather, she feels licensed, even as a teenager, to play with it, to make it serve her own creative purposes.[51]

Pedagogical guides to language, such as John Trusler's *The Distinction Between Words Esteemed Synonymous* (1776)—the first English thesaurus to be published—and Hester Lynch Piozzi's *British Synonymy* (1794), suggest, as Austen's writing does, the necessity of adjudicating between words that might appear to be exactly the same. Austen certainly knew Piozzi's work well—she cites it in her *Letters*—because of Piozzi's close friendship with Johnson, on whom she published a collection of biographical anecdotes in 1789.[52] The ways in which

[49] Samuel Johnson, *A Journey to the Western Islands of Scotland* (London, 1775), 61.

[50] *Letters*, 23 (to Cassandra Austen, 25 Nov. 1798).

[51] See also Freya Johnston, 'Johnson and Austen', in Greg Clingham and Philip Smallwood (eds.), *Samuel Johnson After 300 Years* (Cambridge: Cambridge University Press, 2009), 225–45.

[52] 'So much for Mrs Piozzi.—I had some thoughts of writing the whole of my letter in her stile, but I believe I shall not' (*Letters*, 46, to Cassandra Austen, 11 June 1799); ' "But all this, as my dear Mrs Piozzi says, is flight & fancy & nonsense—for my Master has his great Casks to mind, & I have my little Children" ' (*Letters*, 162, to Cassandra Austen, 9 Dec. 1808).

Trusler and Piozzi, on their title pages, style the proper art of speaking as a form of learned discrimination, propriety, and regulation have obvious and immediate applicability to social and moral spheres, as they do in Austen. We might categorize her description of Lady Williams in 'Jack & Alice' as reversing the aims of Trusler's thesaurus in eliciting the synonymity between words esteemed distinct. But *Sense and Sensibility* takes us back to Trusler again, dwelling on the need to distinguish between 'like', 'esteem', and 'love', terms that Mrs Dashwood prides herself on confounding:

'It is enough,' said she; 'to say that he is unlike Fanny is enough. It implies everything amiable. I love him already.'

'I think you will like him,' said Elinor, 'when you know more of him.'

'Like him!' replied her mother, with a smile. 'I can feel no sentiment of approbation inferior to love.'

'You may esteem him.'

'I have never yet known what it was to separate esteem and love.' (ch. 3)

Mrs Dashwood thinks it a positive virtue not to separate esteem and love. But her author implicitly regards this as evidence of linguistic, emotional, and moral confusion. Differences in vocabulary stand for differences of feeling and call for appropriate differences in conduct. In other words, Elinor's mother should recognize and act on the distinction between 'like', 'esteem', and 'love'. The early works show us how Jane Austen schooled herself in such niceties of verbal and stylistic discrimination, and in the forms of behaviour they license and curb. She tests the boundaries between words, sometimes by playfully exaggerating them, sometimes by refusing to acknowledge that any boundaries exist at all.

The teenage writings face in two directions, poised as they are between childhood and adulthood, between the fiction of sensibility and the realistic novel, and between suspicion and celebration of imaginative freedom. Sometimes a single word, such as 'enthusiastic' (in 'Kitty, or the Bower'), can bring such mixed feelings into very clear view. Enthusiasm was a positive and negative attribute in Austen's lifetime. In his *Dictionary*, Johnson defines the word (negatively) as 'A vain belief of private revelation; a vain confidence of divine favour or communication' and 'Heat of imagination; violence of passion; confidence of opinion', but also (more positively) as 'Elevation of Fancy;

exaltation of ideas'. In her 'warm' rather than heated imagination, and in her cultivation of 'Fancy' (p. 170), Kitty seems to hover between the second and third senses of the word and therefore to anticipate both the outdoor 'rambling fancy' of Fanny Price (*Mansfield Park*, ch. 22) and the more culpable activities of Emma Woodhouse, an 'imaginist . . . on fire with speculation and foresight' (*Emma*, ch. 39).

Austen's early works stand on the edge of imaginative flight from a domestic schoolroom environment into the wider vistas of fiction, with their different but related forms of adjudication. For now, she was reckoning with the judgement of a highly literate family audience. Mary Stanhope, in 'The three Sisters', mirrors Laura, antiheroine of 'Love and Friendship', in soliciting the eyes of the world and basking in performance—even when it reflects very badly on her. This aspect of her character, like that of Lydia Bennet, seems to reflect the collaborative origins of Austen's early works and their reception at home:

The subject being now fairly introduced and she found herself the object of every one's attention in company, she lost all her confusion & became perfectly unreserved & communicative.

'I wonder you should never have heard of it before for in general things of this Nature are very well known in the Neighbourhood.'

'I assure you said Jemima I never had the least suspicion of such an affair. Has it been in agitation long?'

'Oh! yes, ever since Wednesday.'

They all smiled particularly Mr Brudenell.

'You must know Mr Watts is very much in love with me, so that it is quite a match of Affection on his side.'

'Not on his only, I suppose' said Kitty.

'Oh! when there is so much Love on one side there is no occasion for it on the other. However I do not much dislike him tho' he is very plain to be sure.'

Mr Brudenell stared, the Miss Duttons laughed & Sophy & I were heartily ashamed of our Sister. (pp. 60–1)

That moment, in its light and excruciating hilarity, might sum up Austen's teenage writings, concerned as they are with proper introductions, attention seeking, and company. They revel in the sort of unreserved communication that makes people stare, and then laugh.

CHRONOLOGY OF THE TEENAGE WRITINGS

Titles are as they appear on the Contents page of each volume of the notebooks; dates and other annotations in italics within the parentheses are those provided by Jane Austen.

Volume the First

1787–90 'Frederic & Elfrida', 'Jack & Alice', 'Edgar & Emma', 'Henry & Eliza', 'Mr Harley', 'Sir William Mountague', 'Mr Clifford', 'The beautifull Cassandra', 'Amelia Webster', 'The Visit', 'The Mystery'

The first eleven items are the earliest written and in most cases cannot be dated more precisely.

'Jack & Alice' and 'Mr Harley' are dedicated to JA's fifth brother, Francis, 'Midshipman on board his Magesty's ship the Perseverance'; Francis Austen held this rank on HMS *Perseverance* from December 1789 to November 1791, but since the dedications were inserted after the inscription of the tales, these dates can be no precise guide to either composition or inscription.

'Henry & Eliza' may date from December 1787 or 1788, when Henry, JA's fourth brother, and their cousin Eliza de Feuillide were involved together in family theatricals at Steventon.

'Sir William Mountague' may be dated to late 1788. In that year 1 September fell on a Monday, which coincides with a reference in the text to 'Monday . . . the first of September'.

'The beautifull Cassandra' may be dated after summer 1788, when Mr and Mrs Austen took JA and Cassandra on a trip to London and Kent. The story is set in central London.

'The Visit' must post-date June 1789, as it is dedicated to 'the Revd James Austen', JA's eldest brother, who was ordained priest in that month.

Volume the Second

1790 'Love and Friendship' (dated at the end: *June 13ᵗʰ1790*)

The date is the earliest given by JA in the notebooks, though several writings in *Volume the First* clearly pre-date 1790. JA deleted 'Sunday' before the date, 'June 13ᵗʰ', though 13 June did fall on a Sunday in 1790.

1791 'The History of England' (dated at the end: *Saturday Nov: 26ᵗʰ 1791*)

Volume the First

1791 'The three Sisters'

'The three Sisters' may date from December 1791, when JA's third brother, Edward, to whom the story is dedicated, married one of three sisters.

Volume the Second

1792 'Lesley-Castle' (letters in the story are dated from *Janʳy 3ᵈ 1792* to *April 13ᵗʰ [1792]*)

Henry Austen, JA's fourth brother, took his BA at Oxford in spring 1792. JA may have dedicated this tale to him in order to mark the occasion.

'Collection of Letters'

The letters may date to autumn 1792, when Jane Cooper, their dedicatee, was staying at Steventon and before her marriage that December.

Volume the Third

1792 (contents page signed and dated: *May 6ᵗʰ 1792*)

'Evelyn'

'Kitty, or the Bower' (dedication dated: *August 1792*)

Volume the Second

1793 (early) 'Scraps'

These are dedicated to JA's niece Fanny Catherine Austen, the daughter of JA's third brother, Edward, and his wife, Elizabeth Bridges. Fanny was born 23 January 1793.

Volume the First

1793 'Detached peices' (dedication dated: *June 2ᵈ 1793*)

The dedicatee—another niece, Jane Anna Elizabeth Austen, the daughter of JA's eldest brother, James, and his wife, Anne Mathew—was born 15 April 1793.

'Ode to Pity' (annotated at the end *End of the first volume. June 3ᵈ 1793*)

NOTE ON THE TEXT

UNLIKE modern editions of Jane Austen's famous six novels, which are prepared from printed texts issued in or soon after her lifetime, editions of her teenage writings are based on unique copies of manuscript versions in her own hand: *Volume the First*, in the Bodleian Library, Oxford (MS Don. e.7), and *Volume the Second* and *Volume the Third*, in the British Library, London (respectively Add. MS 59874 and Add. MS 65381). In fact, all the works collected here were left unpublished at Austen's death in 1817 and therefore derive directly from handwritten sources. Printed editions of the teenage writings began to be issued only in the twentieth century. (For a list of the major editions, see 'Editions' in the Select Bibliography.) Modern editors, therefore, can choose either to follow the textual choices made by previous editors in transforming manuscript into print or, like us, to turn afresh to the original manuscript forms and make new decisions on how far to attempt to retain the trace of the written hand, recognizing of course that this is not always possible. Handwriting, unlike print, accommodates itself to individual mechanical quirks—of hand and pen; it can even seem a window onto the personality of the writer; and it changes over time. Since, in her teenage writings especially, Austen paid arch attention to the act of writing itself and to its differences from print, it seems desirable to try to represent those distinctive features that print might suppress or regularize but which appear to enrich her manuscript texts meaningfully. This, of course, is a matter of interpretation over which different editors will reach different decisions.

For this new edition, no changes have been made to Austen's spellings, capitalization, paragraphing, or punctuation, all features that stamp her writings as her own or of her time. We have preserved Austen's characteristic use of capitalized initial letters for common nouns occurring in mid-sentence, a use that extends in some cases to adjectives. Capitalizations of this kind are sprinkled liberally across all her manuscript pages from *Volume the First* to *Sanditon*, the novel she was writing in 1817 in the last months of her life. But she was by no means consistent in her practice: sometimes in a single sentence the initial letter of one common noun is capitalized and another is not; and where initial letters often hover ambiguously between what print must determine as either upper-case (capital) or lower-case forms, editors must interpret the evidence one way or the other. This shifting between capitalization and non-capitalization gives a slightly irregular and more expressive feel to the text when translated into print. The long-tailed 's', still in use in the handwriting of Austen's contemporaries (William Wordsworth and John Keats, for example), contributes nothing to meaning and might merely impede the enjoyment of the modern reader; we have therefore taken the decision not to retain it.

By contrast, and in a departure from other modern editions, we have retained Austen's use of ampersand (&) as a variation upon 'and'. Ampersands are sprinkled liberally over *Volume the First* and *Volume the Second* in particular, acting as the connector of choice for the truncations, distortions, and elisions of the many teasing and frantic performances that make up these two anthologies. The clear preference for 'and' in *Volume the Third*, especially in linking phrases and clauses, reads like a change of pace—a sign, like the lengthier paragraphs, that Austen's writing is striding out—and the measure of a new belief in her imaginative stamina to sustain a story. By regularly expanding '&' to 'and' in print versions of all three notebooks, previous editors of the teenage writings have suppressed what we believe is a significant distinction between the two uses. We have also retained other contractions and abbreviations, such as 'Compts' for 'Compliments', 'Capt.' for 'Captain', as contributing to the air of naturalism and even colloquialism achieved by several of the texts collected here. In abbreviations, Austen, like her contemporaries, used raised final letters, writing 'M^r', 'M^{rs}', 'Rev^d', and 'S^t', which we represent as 'Mr', 'Mrs', 'Revd', 'St'; but we have preserved her use of raised letters in some instance, like 'Esqre', '1st'.

Austen's floating or absent apostrophes in the so-called Saxon genitive, 'its'' / 'it's', and the contracted forms 'sha'nt' / 'shan't' / 'shant', 'wo'nt' / 'won't' / 'wont' are a challenge; they also seem, like the variations in her spelling (for which see Note on Spelling), peculiarly characteristic of her style, though unlike her distinctive spellings they probably represent no more than a kind of casualness or carelessness in pointing her text. Where she does not include an apostrophe ('shant', 'wont'), we do not supply it. Elsewhere, we have regularized her floating apostrophe to the modern standard ('shan't', 'won't'). There are major differences between Austen's paratactic punctuation (with its resemblance to the pauses made by the speaking voice) and the syntactic punctuation of twenty-first-century printed prose. We have resisted intervening to 'correct' what is merely different, most notably by not peppering the pages with those extra commas that the modern reader has come to expect but which are not there in Austen's text. In her day, for example, conventions for recording direct speech in novels were still experimental and slightly different from modern usage. Austen's own treatment of written speech changes from item to item within the teenage notebooks, and we have respected and reproduced those differences. So, while we have standardized her double quotation marks around speeches to single, in line with modern British style, we have retained the normal late eighteenth-century conventions of either not marking off the speaker from her spoken words or, on occasion, setting brackets around a speaker's name; in this we have followed precisely the various systems Austen herself sets in play, intruding into the text in only a very few instances to insert opening or closing quotation marks where they have been accidentally omitted. We do not believe that Austen's lighter punctuation (a feature of print, too, at that time) will confuse the reader. On the other hand, it will give the modern reader a better sense of the young writer's use of her notebooks as a trial ground for presenting her work. One particular punctuation mark is worth notice since it is not reproducible in print: that is her occasional combination of an exclamation mark with a comma or semi-colon, piling the two on top of each other; the printed edition can render these only serially, as '!;' or '!,'.

One of the most distinctive aspects of the teenage notebooks is their mimicry of bibliographic or print conventions: these are mock books, in which the apprentice author can be seen relishing her experiments with layout and *mise en page* and imitating what she finds in the volumes she is reading—presentational features as well as subject matter and language—whether they be anthologies of elegant extracts suitable for young ladies or the latest pulp fiction. Austen's borrowed or parodied formatting features include the layout of dedications, printer's rules that mark off titles and chapter numbers, conventions for setting out letters, and the representation of dramatic dialogue and of conversations in novels, like the use of running inverted commas down the side of the page to punctuate speech (for example, in 'Jack & Alice')—a typographic convention in novels of sensibility in the late eighteenth century.[1] We believe that these display features contribute meaningfully to Austen's stories and constitute a significant aspect of her purpose in the teenage notebooks; our edition accordingly restores many that have slipped from other modern editions or tries to find print equivalents to give the reader a flavour of the visual appearance of the notebooks.

In presenting this new edition of the manuscript materials we have made the following minor decisions: words and phrases underlined for emphasis are printed in italics; we have reduced paragraph indentations to a single length and restricted the range of the dash (Austen uses many different lengths for both); within each story or short work, we have standardized chapter and letter numbers to the most common form (for example, where Austen may within a single piece write on one occasion 'Chapter the First' and on another 'Chapter the second', or 'Letter the first' and 'Letter the Second'); we have left as they occur within the text any slight differences in the spelling of names of characters (hence, on p. 28 the reader finds 'Mrs Willson' and 'Mrs Wilson', and on p. 29 'Lady Hariet' and 'Lady Harriet', and on p. 103 the 'Lutterell' sisters but on p. 106 the 'Luttrell' sisters) since they do not impede the reader's comprehension, and are an aspect of Austen's swift or careless style that marks her earliest and latest writings. All Austen's revisions, deletions, and additions are recorded in the Textual Notes at the end of the volume. This edition is based upon work undertaken for the digital edition of Jane Austen's fiction manuscripts published electronically in 2010. Through digitization, many new readings have been recovered. The reader interested in testing our readings, in inspecting how Jane Austen worked, and in comparing the actual manuscripts with our print interpretations can do so at <http//www.janeausten.ac.uk>.

Finally, previous editors have attributed to changes in Jane Austen's hand over time some revisions in the teenage notebooks (specifically in 'Kitty, or the Bower' in *Volume the Third*) that are, in fact, in the hand of her nephew James Edward Austen. For argument and evidence, we refer readers to the Introduction and the appropriate places in the Textual Notes.

---

[1] See Vivienne Mylne, 'The Punctuation of Dialogue in Eighteenth-Century French and English Fiction', *The Library*, 6th series, 1 (1979), 43–61.

NOTE ON SPELLING

WHILE spelling in printed texts exhibited greater stability from the later eighteenth century, the same did not hold for the written language, and especially not for forms unintended for publication, where there could be significant divergence between public and private usage, between print and manuscript. Even among educated people of the period, spelling continued to retain, like handwriting itself, a more expressive and individual stamp. In these circumstances, variations in the appearance of a word, between different authors or between different works by the same author, and even within a single document, should not be viewed as incorrect.[1]

Jane Austen's spelling requires no apology or excuse; no serious editor since Victorian times has attempted to amend it. At the same time, it carries for the modern reader the stamp of her personality; variations in her spelling within manuscripts, between manuscripts over time, and in revision may be significant. Variation may suggest a timescale within which certain pieces were written or revised, or it may point to the introduction of a different hand and thus offer evidence for reattribution, as we argue is the case in the revision of 'Kitty, or the Bower' in *Volume the Third*, with its different spellings 'Catherine' / 'Catharine' and 'amiable' / 'aimiable'.

Because non-standard spelling is among the effects contributing to the reader's enjoyment of the resistant texture of Jane Austen's teenage writings—their flavour of anarchy or disconnection from a norm—it is tempting, but probably wrong, to argue that this was part of the writer's intention. Her various attempts to name Sir Arthur Hampton in the short play 'The Visit' (*Volume the First*) appear at first sight to pun upon similarities, to eye and ear, between 'Author' and 'Arthur' (pp. 44, 224). But it is more likely that the confusion is a clue to Austen's pronunciation, with 'Author' sounding in her Hampshire accent not unlike 'Arthur', and so 'Author', a word she gleefully inscribes as often

---

[1] See 'Spelling and Punctuation in *Lady Susan*', in *Lady Susan*, ed. Christine Alexander and David Owen (Sydney: Juvenilia Press, 2009), 102. For a similar argument, see N. E. Osselton, 'Informal Spelling Systems in Early Modern English: 1500–1800' (1984), repr. in *A Reader in Early Modern English*, ed. Mats Rydén, Ingrid Tieken-Boon van Ostade, and Merja Kytö (Frankfurt am Main: Peter Lang, 1998), 33–45.

as possible in these early works, instructed her in how to spell 'Arthur': she originally wrote 'Sir Author' and (several times) 'Authur', though on each occasion she corrected the text to the conventional spelling.

The use and disappearance, or even replacement, across the teenage notebooks of some characteristic variant forms may be a clue to dating. For example, at the beginning of *Volume the First* Austen wrote 'extream' (p. 20) and 'extreamly' (pp. 26, 45), but by the time, several years later, that she inscribed 'The three Sisters' into its pages, she wrote 'extremely' (pp. 52 and 55), and 'extreme' / 'extremely' remain her standard spelling thereafter. Moreover, at some point she returned to p. 26 to alter 'extreamly' to 'extremely', though the spellings at p. 20 and p. 45 remain unchanged. Similarly, the forms 'compleat', 'compleatly', and 'compleated' figure prominently in the earlier sections of *Volume the First* (pp. 20, 23, 37, 38), with the shift to 'completed' at 'The three Sisters' (p. 59). But 'compleat' is in use in 'Love and Friendship' in the early pages of *Volume the Second* (pp. 79, 81), to be replaced by 'complete' at p. 135 (in 'Collection of Letters'), and this remains her spelling through the subsequent fiction manuscripts. It offers a tiny further clue, if we needed it, that 'The three Sisters' was inscribed into *Volume the First* after 'Love and Friendship' into *Volume the Second*.

Some forms unique to the early entries in the teenage notebooks are best described as childish errors: 'dispaired', 'speek', 'Desease', and 'Mistery' subsequently corrected to 'Mystery' (*Volume the First*, pp. 30, 31, 37, 49). The young Austen had trouble determining between 'g' and 'j', favouring the spelling 'Magesty' and 'magestic' (*Volume the First*, pp. 10, 33, 37; *Volume the Second*, pp. 86, 132), which she returned to correct at *Volume the Second*, p. 106 ('unmagestic' > 'unmajestic'), and only settled to spelling conventionally, as we might expect, in the course of 'The History of England' ('Magesty', p. 122; but 'Majesty', p. 124; with a wobble at p. 132, where line 18 has 'Magesty' and line 21 'Majesty's'). Her coining of the forms 'diminushed' (p. 101) and 'diminushing' (p. 103) (from 'Diminution', p. 101), perhaps the confusion of 'emminent' with 'imminent' at p. 99 ('emminent Danger'), and the spelling 'Dissapointment' (p. 98), all in 'Lesley-Castle', may also fall into the same category of childish error.

Austen shares with a range of contemporary writers, including Walter Scott, other common variant forms, like her youthful preference for consonant doubling. The 'full' suffix in words such as 'beautifull', 'chearfull', 'delightfull', 'dreadfull', wonderfull', and the double

medial 'll' in 'Wellcome', 'wellfare', 'alltho'' is largely confined to
Volume the First and *Volume the Second*, though even here there are
signs of standardization in chronologically later entries. The hand
that enters into the closing pages of *Volume the First* the short piece
'A beautiful description of the different effects of Sensibility on different Minds' (p. 63) does so after 2 June 1793, though it is not possible to date precisely the correction found at *Volume the Second*,
p. 92, deleting 'Beautifull' and inserting above the line 'delightful'.

Austen's preference for a fairly consistent series of digraphs, as in
'beleive', 'cheif', 'greif', 'neice', 'peice', 'veiw', 'yeild', has come to
be seen as a hallmark of her style. The 'ei' form of these words is in
regular use from *Volume the First* through to her final adult writings,
regardless of an intention to print. Interestingly, the form 'freind'
(a spelling favoured by Scott too), which we might wish to include in
this list, is less likely to be used in the post-teenage writings.

Variation in spelling the proper names of characters is evident
early and late: in Mrs Willson / Wilson and Lady Hariet / Harriet of
'Henry & Eliza' in *Volume the First* (pp. 28, 29); in 'Lesley-Castle',
Volume the Second, where the 'Lutterell' sisters (p. 96 onwards) subsequently become the 'Luttrell' sisters (p. 106 onwards). This slight
carelessness of hand, found too in Scott's fiction manuscripts, is no
more than a failure to look back through the pages and check the
chosen form; it may explain the naming in print of Sir Thomas
Bertram's butler as 'Baddeley' and 'Baddely' in *Mansfield Park*.[2] By
contrast, the shift from 'Catherine' to 'Catharine' in 'Kitty, or the
Bower' is significantly atypical and strongly suggests that all seven
instances of 'Catharine' are non-authorial.[3]

Austen is consistent in favouring the spellings 'agreable' and 'disagreable', for two of her most regularly employed adjectives. The spellings 'excercise' (*Volume the First*, p. 36), 'irrisistable' (*Volume the
Second*, p. 118) and 'irresistable' (*Volume the Third*, p. 171), 'simpathy'
(pp. 74, 147) and 'travellor' are also distinctive. *Volume the First* corrects 'travellors' to 'travellers' (p. 33), and *Volume the Second* has
'travellers' (p. 90); but *Volume the Third* has 'Travellor' (p. 164), and

---

[2] *Mansfield Park* (1814), ed. Kathryn Sutherland (1996; reissued London: Penguin,
2003), 168, 299 ('Baddeley'), 318 ('Baddely'); and see Walter Scott, *Waverley*, ed. P. D.
Garside (Edinburgh: Edinburgh University Press, 2007), 399–400.

[3] Kathryn Sutherland, 'From Kitty to Catharine: James Edward Austen's Hand in
Volume the Third', *Review of English Studies*, new series, 66 (2014), 124–43.

she is still using this form in her last manuscript, *Sanditon*, in 1817, the year of her death. Occasional non-standard spellings may point to Austen's pronunciation: 'attrack' for 'attract' (*Volume the First*, p. 16); 'pracure' altered to 'procure' (*Volume the First*, p. 21); 'extroidinary' (*Volume the Second*, pp. 102, 109).[4]

Some inconsistencies in spelling found in Austen's fiction manuscripts broadly characterize print of the early nineteenth century: not only the first published forms of her six novels, but also the printed works of her contemporaries share many of Austen's variant spellings. In general, we should be wary of attaching significance to individual variability and to lack of uniformity within a single text; rather, we should see variation as a sign of the flexibility of the standard or norm within the public printed text as in private usage.[5] In this category might be placed the use of both '-ise' and '-ize' endings, as in 'surprise' / 'surprize', 'realise' / 'realize', 'recognise' / 'recognize'; and the mixing of older and newer forms, as in 'chuse' / 'choose', 'shew' / 'show', 'croud' / 'crowd', 'encrease'/ 'increase', 'cloathes' / 'clothes', 'sopha' / 'sofa'. In some instances, the manuscripts suggest that Austen favoured one spelling over another. For example, 'surprize' appears only in the teenage writings, and thereafter, she prefers 'surprise'; 'choose' is also confined to the teenage manuscripts, while elsewhere she favours 'chuse'; 'shew' is preferred throughout her writings, as is 'cloathes'; 'encrease' appears to be a youthful preference; while 'sopha' / 'sofa' are used indiscriminately, both forms appearing in *Volume the First* and in *Sanditon*, her last work. While it is tempting to try to argue that changes between Austen's teenage and post-teenage manuscripts demonstrate a later tendency to favour print norms, in fact, there appears no overriding predilection for either older or normalized forms in the range of manuscript evidence available to us.

---

[4] Compare the printer's query about 'arra-root' in setting *Emma* in type, which Jane Austen relays with some amusement to Cassandra, writing on 26 Nov. 1815 as she corrects proofs: 'I am advanced in vol. 3 to my <u>arra</u>-root, upon which peculiar style of spelling, there is a modest <u>qu</u>:ᵅ? in the Margin' (*Letters*, 313).

[5] Systemic variability was a normal feature of both printers' and authors' style well into the nineteenth century. See Philip Gaskell, *From Writer to Reader: Studies in Editorial Method* (Oxford: Clarendon Press, 1978), 7–8; Lynda Mugglestone, 'English in the Nineteenth Century', in *The Oxford History of English*, ed. Mugglestone (Oxford: Oxford University Press, 2006), 274–88. See too the examination of inconsistencies in spelling in and between manuscript and first-edition print versions of Walter Scott's *Waverley* (1814), in *Waverley*, ed. Garside, 399–400.

SELECT BIBLIOGRAPHY

Editions

'Love and Freindship' and Other Early Works, with a preface by G. K. Chesterton (London: Chatto and Windus; New York: Fredrick A. Stokes, 1922) [an edition of Volume the Second].

Volume the First, ed. R. W. Chapman (Oxford: Clarendon Press, 1933; repr. London: Athlone Press, 1984) [a transcription of the manuscript].

Volume the Third, ed. R. W. Chapman (Oxford: Clarendon Press, 1951) [a transcription of the manuscript].

Minor Works, vol. vi of The Works of Jane Austen, ed. R. W. Chapman (1954), rev. B. C. Southam (Oxford: Oxford University Press, 1969).

Volume the Second, ed. B. C. Southam (Oxford: Clarendon Press, 1963) [a transcription of the manuscript].

The Juvenilia of Jane Austen and Charlotte Brontë, ed. Frances Beer (Harmondsworth: Penguin, 1986) [a selected edition with major omissions of 'Lesley-Castle', 'The History of England', and 'Evelyn'].

Catharine and Other Writings, ed. Margaret Anne Doody and Douglas Murray, Oxford World's Classics (Oxford: Oxford University Press, 1993; repr. 2009) [the first edition with full textual and explanatory notes].

Juvenilia, ed. Peter Sabor, The Cambridge Edition of the Works of Jane Austen (Cambridge: Cambridge University Press, 2006).

Jane Austen's Fiction Manuscripts: A Digital Edition, ed. Kathryn Sutherland (2010), <http://www.janeausten.ac.uk> [the surviving adult manuscripts, as well as the three teenage notebooks, available as full photographic images with transcriptions, descriptions, and accounts of their provenance].

Volume the First, with an introduction by Kathryn Sutherland (Oxford: Bodleian Library, 2013) [a photofacsimile of the manuscript and its notebook].

Love and Freindship and Other Youthful Writings, ed. Christine Alexander (London: Penguin, 2014).

Textual Studies

McAuley, Jenny, ' "A Long Letter Upon a Jacket and Petticoat": Reading Beneath some Deletions in the Manuscript of "Catharine, or The Bower" ', Persuasions: The Jane Austen Journal, 31 (2009), 191–8.

Marshall, Mary Gaither, 'Jane Austen's Manuscripts of the Juvenilia and Lady Susan: A History and Description', in J. David Grey (ed.), Jane Austen's Beginnings: The Juvenilia and Lady Susan (Ann Arbor, Mich., and London: University of Michigan Research Press, 1989), 107–21.

Sabor, Peter, 'James Edward Austen, Anna Lefroy, and the Interpolations to Jane Austen's "Volume the Third" ', *Notes and Queries*, new series, 47 (2000), 304–6.

Southam, B. C., 'Interpolations to Jane Austen's "Volume the Third" ', *Notes and Queries*, new series, 9 (1962), 185–7.

Southam, B. C., 'The Manuscript of Jane Austen's "Volume the First" ', *The Library*, 5th series, 17 (1962), 231–7.

Southam, B. C., 'Jane Austen's Juvenilia: The Question of Completeness', *Notes and Queries*, new series, 11 (1964), 180–1.

Southam, B. C., *Jane Austen's Literary Manuscripts: A Study of the Novelist's Development through the Surviving Papers* (1964); rev. edn (London: Athlone Press, 2001).

Sutherland, Kathryn, *Jane Austen's Textual Lives: From Aeschylus to Bollywood* (Oxford: Oxford University Press, 2005).

Biography

Jane Austen's Letters, ed. Deirdre Le Faye, 4th edn (Oxford: Oxford University Press, 2011).

Austen-Leigh, J. E., *A Memoir of Jane Austen and Other Family Recollections*, ed. Kathryn Sutherland, Oxford World's Classics (Oxford: Oxford University Press, 2002).

Byrne, Paula, *The Real Jane Austen: A Life in Small Things* (London: HarperPress, 2013).

Le Faye, Deirdre, *Jane Austen: A Family Record*, 2nd edn (Cambridge: Cambridge University Press, 2004).

McAleer, John, 'What a Biographer Can Learn about Jane Austen from Her Juvenilia', in J. David Grey (ed.), *Jane Austen's Beginnings: The Juvenilia and Lady Susan* (Ann Arbor, Mich., and London: University of Michigan Research Press, 1989), 7–27.

Modert, Jo, *Jane Austen's Manuscript Letters in Facsimile* (Carbondale and Edwardsville, Ill.: Southern Illinois University Press, 1990).

Shields, Carol, *Jane Austen* (London: Weidenfeld and Nicolson, 2001).

Criticism

Daffron, Eric, 'Child's Play: A Short Publication and Critical History of Jane Austen's Juvenilia', in Laura Cooner Lambdin and Robert Thomas Lambdin (eds.), *A Companion to Jane Austen Studies* (Connecticut and London: Greenwood Press, 2000), 191–7.

Gilson, David J., and J. David Grey, 'Jane Austen's Juvenilia and *Lady Susan*: An Annotated Bibliography', in J. David Grey (ed.), *Jane Austen's Beginnings: The Juvenilia and Lady Susan* (Ann Arbor, Mich., and London: University of Michigan Research Press, 1989), 243–62.

These surveys of early criticism are supplemented by later on-line resources, such as *Persuasions On-Line*, which since vol. 22 (Winter 2001) provides regularly updated bibliographies (<http://www.jasna.org/persuasions/on-line/index.html>).

Alexander, Christine, and Juliet McMaster (eds.), *The Child Writer from Austen to Woolf* (Cambridge: Cambridge University Press, 2005) [includes Margaret Anne Doody, 'Jane Austen, that Disconcerting "Child"', 101–21; and Rachel M. Brownstein, 'Endless Imitation: Austen's and Byron's Juvenilia', 122–37].

Barker, Gerard A., *Grandison's Heirs: The Paragon's Progress in the Late Eighteenth-Century English Novel* (Newark: University of Delaware Press; and London: Associated University Presses, 1985).

Brophy, Brigid, 'Jane Austen and the Stuarts', in B. C. Southam (ed.), *Critical Essays on Jane Austen* (London: Routledge & Kegan Paul, 1968), 21–38.

Byrne, Paula, *Jane Austen and the Theatre* (London and New York: Hambledon and London, 2002).

Doody, Margaret Anne, 'Jane Austen's Reading', in J. David Grey, A. Walton Litz, and Brian Southam (eds.), *The Jane Austen Companion* (New York: Macmillan, 1986) (published in the UK as *The Jane Austen Handbook* (London: Athlone Press, 1986)), 347–63.

Doody, Margaret Anne, 'The Early Short Fiction', in Edward Copeland and Juliet McMaster (eds.), *The Cambridge Companion to Jane Austen*, 2nd edn (Cambridge: Cambridge University Press, 2011), 72–86.

Epstein, Julia, 'Jane Austen's Juvenilia and the Female Epistolary Tradition', *Papers on Language and Literature*, 21 (1985), 399–416.

Gay, Penny, *Jane Austen and the Theatre* (Cambridge: Cambridge University Press, 2002) [ch. 1 discusses her early experience of the theatre].

Gilbert, Sandra M., and Gubar, Susan, 'Shut Up in Prose: Gender and Genre in Austen's Juvenilia', in *The Madwoman in the Attic: The Woman Writer and the Nineteenth-Century Literary Imagination* (New Haven, Conn., and London: Yale University Press, 1979), 107–45.

Harris, Jocelyn, *Jane Austen's Art of Memory* (Cambridge: Cambridge University Press, 1989) [Appendix 2, '*Sir Charles Grandison* in the Juvenilia', addresses allusions in the teenage writings to Samuel Richardson's *Sir Charles Grandison*].

Johnston, Freya, 'Jane Austen's Past Lives', *Cambridge Quarterly*, 39 (2010), 103–21.

Kent, Christopher, 'Learning History with, and from, Jane Austen', in J. David Grey (ed.), *Jane Austen's Beginnings: The Juvenilia and Lady Susan* (Ann Arbor, Mich., and London: University of Michigan Research Press, 1989), 59–72.

Litz, A. Walton, *Jane Austen: A Study of Her Artistic Development* (London: Chatto and Windus, 1965).

Litz, A. Walton, 'Jane Austen: The Juvenilia', in J. David Grey (ed.), *Jane Austen's Beginnings: The Juvenilia and Lady Susan* (Ann Arbor, Mich., and London: University of Michigan Research Press, 1989), 1–6.

McMaster, Juliet, 'The Juvenilia: Energy versus Sympathy', in Laura Cooner Lambdin and Robert Thomas Lambdin (eds.), *A Companion to Jane Austen Studies* (Connecticut and London, Greenwood Press, 2000), 173–89.

McMaster, Juliet, 'Your sincere Freind, The Author', *Persuasions On-Line*, 27 (Winter 2006), <http://www.jasna.org/persuasions/on-line/vol27no1/mcmaster.htm>.

McMaster, Juliet, 'Young Jane Austen: Author', in Claudia L. Johnson and Clara Tuite (eds.), *A Companion to Jane Austen* (Chichester: Wiley-Blackwell, 2009), 81–90.

Sutherland, Kathryn, 'From Kitty to Catharine: James Edward Austen's Hand in *Volume the Third*', *Review of English Studies*, new series, 66 (2014), 124–43.

Tuite, Clara, *Romantic Austen: Sexual Politics and the Literary Canon* (Cambridge: Cambridge University Press, 2002) [ch. 1 discusses the historical context of the teenage writings].

Upfal, Annette, introduction to *Jane Austen's 'The History of England' & Cassandra's Portraits*, ed. Annette Upfal and Christine Alexander (Sydney: Juvenilia Press, 2009).

Woolf, Virginia, 'Jane Austen Practising', *New Statesman*, 19 (15 July 1922), 419–20; repr. in Andrew McNeillie (ed.), *The Essays of Virginia Woolf*, iii (London: Hogarth Press, 1988), 331–5 (a review of '*Love and Freindship*' and *Other Early Works* (1922)).

A CHRONOLOGY OF JANE AUSTEN

	Life	*Historical and Cultural Background*
1775	(16 Dec.) born in Steventon, Hampshire, seventh child of Revd George Austen (1731–1805), Rector of Steventon and Deane, and Cassandra Austen, née Leigh (1739–1827)	American War of Independence begins.
1776		American Declaration of Independence; James Cook's third Pacific voyage.
1778		France enters war on side of American revolutionaries. Frances Burney, *Evelina*
1779	Birth of youngest brother, Charles (1779–1852); eldest brother, James (1765–1819), goes to St John's College, Oxford; distant cousin Thomas Knight II and wife, Catherine, of Godmersham in Kent, visit Steventon and take close interest in brother Edward (1767–1852)	Britain at war with Spain; siege of Gibraltar (to 1783); Samuel Crompton's spinning mule revolutionizes textile production.
1781	Cousin Eliza Hancock (thought by some to be natural daughter of Warren Hastings) marries Jean-François Capot de Feuillide in France	Warren Hastings deposes Raja of Benares and seizes treasure from Nabob of Oudh.
1782	Austens put on first amateur theatricals at Steventon	Frances Burney, *Cecilia*; William Gilpin, *Observations on the River Wye*; William Cowper, *Poems*
1783	JA, sister Cassandra (1773–1845), and cousin Jane Cooper are tutored by Mrs Cawley in Oxford then Southampton until they fall ill with typhoid fever; death of aunt Jane Cooper from typhoid; brother Edward formally adopted by the Knights; JA's mentor, Anne Lefroy, moves into neighbourhood	American independence conceded at Peace of Versailles; Pitt becomes Prime Minister.

	Life	Historical and Cultural Background
1784	Performance of Sheridan's *The Rivals* at Steventon	India Act imposes some parliamentary control on East India Company; Prince Regent begins to build Brighton Pavilion; death of Samuel Johnson.
1785	Attends Abbey House School, Reading, with Cassandra	William Cowper, *The Task*
1786	Brother Francis (1774–1865) enters Royal Naval Academy, Portsmouth; brother Edward on Grand Tour (to 1790); JA and Cassandra leave school for good	William Gilpin, *Observations, Relative Chiefly to Picturesque Beauty . . . particularly the Mountains, and Lakes of Cumberland, and Westmoreland*
1787	Starts writing stories collected in three notebooks (to 1793); cousin Eliza de Feuillide visits Steventon; performance of Susannah Centlivre's *The Wonder* at Steventon	American constitution signed.
1788	JA and Cassandra taken on a trip to Kent and London; *The Chances* and *Tom Thumb* performed at Steventon; brother Henry (1771–1850) goes to St John's College, Oxford; brother Francis sails to East Indies on HMS *Perseverance*; cousins Eliza de Feuillide and Philadelphia Walter attend Hastings's trial	Warren Hastings impeached for corruption in India; George III's first spell of madness.
1789	James and Henry in Oxford produce periodical, *The Loiterer* (to Mar. 1790); JA begins lifelong friendship with Martha Lloyd and sister Mary when their mother rents Deane Parsonage	Fall of the Bastille marks beginning of French Revolution.
1790	(June) completes 'Love and Friendship'	Edmund Burke, *Reflections on the Revolution in France*; [Mary Wollstonecraft], *Vindication of the Rights of Men*
1791	Brother Charles enters Royal Naval Academy, Portsmouth; (Nov.) completes 'The History of England'; Edward marries Elizabeth Bridges and they live at Rowling, Kent	Parliament rejects bill to abolish slave trade. James Boswell, *Life of Johnson*; Ann Radcliffe, *The Romance of the Forest*

Life	Historical and Cultural Background
1792 Writes 'Lesley-Castle' and 'Evelyn', and begins 'Kitty, or the Bower'; Lloyds leave Deane to make way for James and first wife, Anne Mathew; cousin Jane Cooper marries Capt. Thomas Williams, RN; sister Cassandra engaged to Revd Tom Fowle	France declared a republic; Warren Hastings acquitted. Mary Wollstonecraft; *Vindication of the Rights of Woman*; Clara Reeve, *Plans of Education*
1793 Birth of eldest nieces, Fanny and Anna, daughters of brothers Edward and James; writes last of entries in the teenage notebooks; brother Henry joins Oxford Militia	Execution of Louis XVI of France and Marie Antoinette: revolutionary 'Terror' in Paris; Britain declares war on France.
1794 Probably working on *Lady Susan*; cousin Eliza de Feuillide's husband guillotined in Paris	Suspension of Habeas Corpus; 'Treason Trials' of radicals abandoned by government when juries refuse to convict; failure of harvests keeps food prices high. Uyedale Price, *Essays on the Picturesque*; Ann Radcliffe, *The Mysteries of Udolpho*
1795 Writes 'Elinor and Marianne' (first draft of *Sense and Sensibility*); death of James's wife; JA flirts with Tom Lefroy, as recorded in first surviving letter	George III's coach stoned; Pitt's 'Two Acts' enforce repression of radical dissent.
1796 Visits Edward at Rowling; (Oct.) begins 'First Impressions'; subscribes to Frances Burney's *Camilla*	Frances Burney, *Camilla*; Regina Maria Roche, *Children of the Abbey*; Jane West, *A Gossip's Story*
1797 Marriage of James to Mary Lloyd; (Aug.) completes 'First Impressions'; Cassandra's fiancé dies of fever off Santo Domingo; begins revision of 'Elinor and Marianne' into *Sense and Sensibility*; George Austen offers 'First Impressions' to publisher Cadell without success; Catherine Knight gives Edward possession of Godmersham; marriage of Henry and Eliza de Feuillide	Napoleon becomes commander of French army; failure of French attempt to invade by landing in Wales; mutinies in British Navy, leaders hanged. Ann Radcliffe, *The Italian*

	Life	Historical and Cultural Background
1798	Starts to write 'Susan' (later *Northanger Abbey*); visits Godmersham; death in driving accident of cousin Lady Williams (Jane Cooper)	Irish Rebellion; defeat of French fleet at Battle of the Nile; French army lands in Ireland; further suspension of Habeas Corpus. Elizabeth Inchbald, *Lovers' Vows*, translation of play by Kotzebue.
1799	Visit to Bath; probably finishes 'Susan'; aunt, Mrs Leigh-Perrot, charged with theft and imprisoned in Ilchester Gaol	Napoleon becomes consul in France. Hannah More, *Strictures on the Modern System of Female Education*; Jane West, *A Tale of the Times*
1800	Stays with Martha Lloyd at Ibthorpe; trial and acquittal of Mrs Leigh-Perrot	French conquer Italy; British capture Malta; food riots; first iron-frame printing press; copyright law extended to Ireland. Elizabeth Hamilton, *Memoirs of Modern Philosophers*
1801	Austens move to Bath on George Austen's retirement; James and family move into Stevenson Rectory; first of series of holidays in West Country (to 1804), during one of which thought to have had brief romantic involvement with a man who later died; Henry resigns from Oxford Militia and becomes banker and Army agent in London	Slave rebellion in Santo Domingo led by Toussaint L'Ouverture; Nelson defeats Danes at Battle of Copenhagen; Act of Union joins Britain and Ireland. Maria Edgeworth, *Belinda*
1802	Visits Godmersham; accepts, then the following morning refuses, proposal of marriage from Harris Bigg-Wither; revises 'Susan'	L'Ouverture's slave rebellion crushed by French; Peace of Amiens with France; founding of William Cobbett's *Political Register*
1803	With brother Henry's help, 'Susan' sold to publishers Crosby & Co. for £10	Resumption of war with France.
1804	Starts writing *The Watsons*; (Dec.) death of Anne Lefroy in riding accident	
1805	(Jan.) death of George Austen; stops working on *The Watsons*	Battle of Trafalgar. Walter Scott, *The Lay of the Last Minstrel*

	Life	Historical and Cultural Background
1806	Austens leave Bath; visit relations at Adlestrop and Stoneleigh; Martha Lloyd becomes member of Austen household after death of her mother; brother Francis marries Mary Gibson; JA, Cassandra, and Mrs Austen take lodgings with them in Southampton	French blockade of continental ports against British shipping; first steam-powered textile mill opens in Manchester. Lady Morgan, *The Wild Irish Girl*
1807	Brother Charles marries Fanny Palmer in Bermuda	France invades Portugal; slave-trading by British ships outlawed. George Crabbe, *Poems*
1808	JA visits Godmersham; death of Edward's wife Elizabeth after giving birth to eleventh child	France invades Spain; beginning of Peninsular War. Debrett, *Baronetage* (*Peerage* first published 1802); Hannah More, *Coelebs in Search of a Wife*; Walter Scott, *Marmion*
1809	(Apr.) attempts unsuccessfully to make Crosby publish 'Susan', writing under pseudonym 'Mrs Ashton Dennis' ('M.A.D.'); visits Godmersham; (July) moves, with Cassandra, Martha, and Mrs Austen, to house owned by Edward at Chawton, Hampshire	British capture Martinique and Cayenne from France.
1810	Publisher Egerton accepts *Sense and Sensibility*	British capture Guadeloupe, last French West Indian colony; riots in London in support of parliamentary reform. Walter Scott, *The Lady of the Lake*
1811	(Feb.) begins *Mansfield Park*; stays with Henry and Eliza in London to correct proofs of *Sense and Sensibility*; (Oct.) *Sense and Sensibility*, 'by a Lady', published on commission; revises 'First Impressions' into *Pride and Prejudice*	Prince of Wales becomes Regent; Ludditte anti-machine riots in North and Midlands. Mary Brunton, *Self-Control*
1812	Copyright of *Pride and Prejudice* sold to Egerton for £110; Edward's family take name of Knight at death of Catherine Knight	United States declare war on Britain; French retreat from Moscow; Lord Liverpool becomes Prime Minister after assassination of Spencer Perceval.

	Life	*Historical and Cultural Background*
1813	(Jan.) *Pride and Prejudice* published to great acclaim; JA stays in London to nurse Eliza; death of Eliza; in letter, expresses her hatred for Prince Regent; (June) finishes *Mansfield Park*; second editions of *Sense and Sensibility* and *Pride and Prejudice*	British invasion of France after Wellington's success at Battle of Vittoria. Byron, *The Giaour, The Bride of Abydos*; Robert Southey, *Life of Nelson*
1814	(21 Jan.) begins *Emma*; (Mar. and Nov.) visits brother Henry in London, sees Kean play Shylock; (May) Egerton publishes *Mansfield Park* on commission, sold out in six months; death of Fanny Palmer Austen, brother Charles's wife, after childbirth; marriage of niece Anna Austen to Ben Lefroy	Napoleon defeated and exiled to Elba; George Stevenson builds first steam locomotive; Edmund Kean's first appearance at Drury Lane. Mary Brunton, *Discipline*; Frances Burney, *The Wanderer*; Byron, *The Corsair*; Maria Edgeworth, *Patronage*; Walter Scott, *Waverley*
1815	(29 Mar.) completes *Emma*; (Aug.) begins *Persuasion*; invited to dedicate *Emma* to the Prince Regent; visits Henry in London; (Dec.) *Emma* published by Murray	Napoleon escapes; finally defeated at Battle of Waterloo and exiled to St Helena; Humphry Davy invents miners' safety lamp.
1816	'Susan' bought back from Crosby and revised as 'Catherine'; failure of Henry's bank; second edition of *Mansfield Park*; (Aug.) JA completes *Persuasion*; health beginning to fail	Post-war slump inaugurates years of popular agitation for political and social reform.
1817	(Jan.–Mar.) works on *Sanditon*; (Apr.) makes her Will; moves, with Cassandra, to Winchester, to be closer to skilled medical care; (15 July) composes last poem 'When Winchester Races'; (18 July, 4.30 a.m.) dies in Winchester; buried in Winchester Cathedral; (Dec.) publication (dated 1818) of *Northanger Abbey* and *Persuasion*, together with brother Henry's 'Biographical Notice'	Attacks on Prince Regent at opening of Parliament; death of his only legitimate child, Princess Charlotte.

Map of Great Britain according to the Teenage Jane Austen

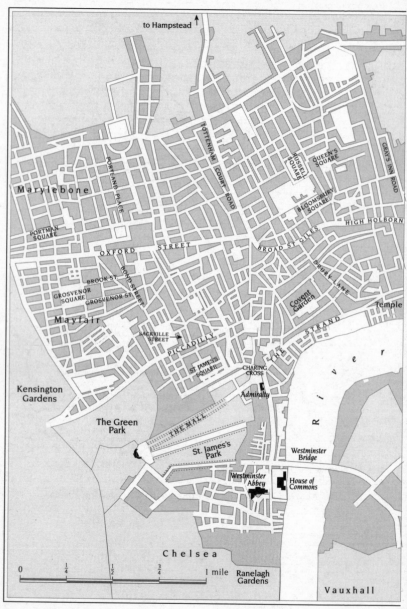

Map of London according to the Teenage Jane Austen

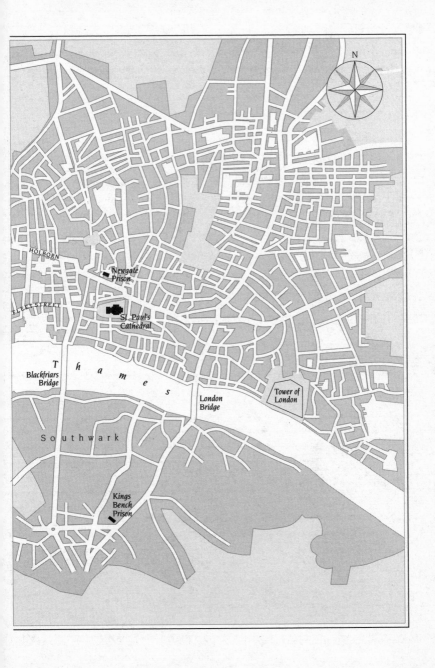

VOLUME THE FIRST

CONTENTS*

My dear Martha

    As a small testimony of the gratitude I feel for your late generosity to me in finishing my muslin Cloak,* I beg leave to offer you this little production* of your sincere Freind

The Author

Frederic & Elfrida

a novel*

Chapter the First

The Uncle of Elfrida was the Father of Frederic; in other words, they were first cousins by the Father's side.*

Being both born in one day & both brought up at one school,* it was not wonderfull that they should look on each other with something more than bare politeness.* They loved with mutual sincerity but were both determined not to transgress the rules of Propriety* by owning their attachment, either to the object beloved, or to any one else.

They were exceedingly handsome and so much alike,* that it was not every one who knew them apart.—Nay even their most intimate freinds* had nothing to distinguish them by, but the shape of the face, the colour of the Eye, the length of the Nose & the difference of the complexion.

Elfrida had an intimate freind to whom, being on a visit to an Aunt, she wrote the following Letter.

To Miss Drummond

'Dear Charlotte'
    'I should be obliged to you, if you would buy me, during your stay'
'with Mrs Williamson, a new & fashionable Bonnet, to suit the'
'complexion* of your'

'E. Falknor'

Charlotte, whose character was a willingness to oblige every one, when she returned into the Country, brought her Freind the wished-for Bonnet, & so ended this little adventure, much to the satisfaction of all parties.

On her return to Crankhumdunberry (of which sweet village* her father was Rector) Charlotte was received with the greatest Joy by Frederic & Elfrida, who, after pressing her alternately to their Bosoms,* proposed to her to take a walk in a Grove of Poplars* which

led from the Parsonage to a verdant Lawn enamelled with a variety of
variegated flowers* & watered by a purling Stream, brought from the
Valley of Tempé* by a passage under ground.

In this Grove they had scarcely remained above 9 hours, when they
were suddenly agreably surprized by hearing a most delightfull voice
warble the following stanza.

Song

> That Damon was in love with me
> I once thought & beleiv'd
> But now that he is not I see,
> I fear I was deceiv'd.*

No sooner were the lines finished than they beheld by a turning in
the Grove 2 elegant young women leaning on each other's arm, who
immediately on perceiving them, took a different path & disappeared
from their sight.

=======

Chapter the Second

=======

As Elfrida & her companions, had seen enough of them to know that
they were neither the 2 Miss Greens, nor Mrs Jackson & her Daughter,
they could not help expressing their surprise at their appearance; till at
length recollecting, that a new family had lately taken a House not far
from the Grove, they hastened home, determined to lose no time in
forming an acquaintance with 2 such amiable & worthy Girls, of which
family they rightly imagined them to be a part.

Agreable to such a determination, they went that very evening to
pay their respects to Mrs Fitzroy & her two Daughters. On being shewn
into an elegant dressing room, ornamented with festoons of artificial
flowers,* they were struck with the engaging Exterior & beautifull
outside of Jezalinda* the eldest of the young Ladies; but e'er they had
been many minutes seated, the Wit & Charms which shone resplendant
in the conversation of the amiable Rebecca,* enchanted them so much
that they all with one accord jumped up & exclaimed.

'Lovely & too charming Fair one,* notwithstanding your forbidding Squint, your greazy tresses & your swelling Back,* which are more frightfull than imagination can paint or pen describe, I cannot refrain from expressing my raptures, at the engaging Qualities of your Mind, which so amply atone for the Horror, with which your first appearance must ever inspire the unwary visitor.'

'Your sentiments so nobly expressed on the different excellencies of Indian & English Muslins, & the judicious preference you give the former, have excited in me an admiration of which I can alone give an adequate idea, by assuring you it is nearly equal to what I feel for myself.'

Then making a profound Curtesy* to the amiable & abashed Rebecca, they left the room & hurried home.

From this period, the intimacy between the Families of Fitzroy, Drummond, and Falknor, daily encreased till at length it grew to such a pitch, that they did not scruple to kick one another out of the window on the slightest provocation.*

During this happy state of Harmony, the eldest Miss Fitzroy ran off with the Coachman* & the amiable Rebecca was asked in marriage by Captain Roger of Buckinghamshire.

Mrs Fitzroy did not approve of the match on account of the tender years of the young couple, Rebecca being but 36 & Captain Roger little more than 63.* To remedy this objection, it was agreed that they should wait a little while till they were a good deal older.

Chapter the Third

In the mean time the parents of Frederic proposed to those of Elfrida, an union between them,* which being accepted with pleasure, the wedding cloathes were bought & nothing remained to be settled but the naming of the Day.*

As to the lovely Charlotte, being importuned with eagerness to pay another visit to her Aunt, she determined to accept the invitation & in consequence of it walked to Mrs Fitzroys to take leave of the amiable Rebecca, whom she found surrounded by Patches, Powder, Pomatum & Paint* with which she was vainly endeavouring to remedy the natural plainness of her face.

'I am come my amiable Rebecca, to take my leave of you for the fortnight I am destined to spend with my aunt. Beleive me this separation is painfull to me, but it is as necessary as the labour which now engages you.'

'Why to tell you the truth my Love, replied Rebecca, I have lately taken it into my head to think (perhaps with little reason) that my complexion is by no means equal to the rest of my face & have therefore taken, as you see, to white & red paint which I would scorn to use on any other occasion as I hate art.'

Charlotte, who perfectly understood the meaning of her freind's speech, was too goodtemper'd & obliging to refuse her, what she knew she wished,—a compliment; & they parted the best freinds in the world.

With a heavy heart & streaming Eyes did she ascend the lovely vehicle† which bore her from her freinds & home; but greived as she was, she little thought in what a strange & different manner she should return to it.

On her entrance into the city of London which was the place of Mrs Williamson's abode, the postilion,* whose stupidity was amazing, declared & declared even without the least shame or Compunction, that having never been informed he was totally ignorant of what part of the Town, he was to drive to.

Charlotte, whose nature we have before intimated, was an earnest desire to oblige every one, with the greatest Condescension* & Good humour informed him that he was to drive to Portland Place,* which he accordingly did & Charlotte soon found herself in the arms of a fond Aunt.

Scarcely were they seated as usual, in the most affectionate manner in one chair,* than the Door suddenly opened & an aged gentleman with a sallow face & old pink Coat,* partly by intention & partly thro' weakness was at the feet of the lovely Charlotte, declaring his attachment to her & beseeching her pity in the most moving manner.

Not being able to resolve to make any one miserable, she consented to become his wife; where upon the Gentleman left the room & all was quiet.

Their quiet however continued but a short time, for on a second opening of the door a young & Handsome Gentleman with a new blue

---

† a post-chaise.*

coat,* entered & intreated from the lovely Charlotte, permission to pay to her, his addresses.

There was a something in the appearance of the second Stranger, that influenced Charlotte in his favour, to the full as much as the appearance of the first: she could not account for it,* but so it was.

Having therefore agreable to that & the natural turn of her mind to make every one happy, promised to become his Wife the next morning, he took his leave & the two Ladies sat down to Supper on a young Leveret, a brace of Partridges, a leash of Pheasants* & a Dozen of Pigeons.

Chapter the Fourth

It was not till the next morning that Charlotte recollected the double engagement* she had entered into; but when she did, the reflection of her past folly, operated so strongly on her mind, that she resolved to be guilty of a greater,* & to that end threw herself into a deep stream which ran thro' her Aunts pleasure Grounds in Portland Place.*

She floated to Crankhumdunberry where she was picked up & buried; the following epitaph, composed by Frederic Elfrida & Rebecca, was placed on her tomb.

Epitaph

Here lies our freind who having promis-ed
That unto two she would be marri-ed
Threw her sweet Body & her lovely face
Into the Stream that runs thro' Portland Place

These sweet lines, as pathetic as beautifull* were never read by any one who passed that way, without a shower of tears, which if they should fail of exciting in you, Reader, your mind must be unworthy to peruse them.

Having performed the last sad office to their departed freind, Frederic & Elfrida together with Captain Roger & Rebecca returned to Mrs Fitzroy's at whose feet they threw themselves with one accord & addressed her in the following Manner.

'Madam'

'When the sweet Captain Roger first addressed the amiable Rebecca, you alone objected to their union on account of the tender years of the Parties. That plea can be no more, seven days being now expired, together with the lovely Charlotte,* since the Captain first spoke to you on the subject.'

'Consent then Madam to their union & as a reward, this smelling Bottle which I enclose in my right hand, shall be yours & yours forever; I never will claim it again. But if you refuse to join their hands in 3 days time, this dagger* which I enclose in my left shall be steeped in your hearts blood.'

'Speak then Madam & decide their fate & yours.'

Such gentle & sweet persuasion could not fail of having the desired effect. The answer they received, was this.

'My dear young freinds'

'The arguments you have used are too just & too eloquent to be withstood; Rebecca in 3 days time, you shall be united to the Captain.'

This speech, than which nothing could be more satisfactory, was received with Joy by all; & peace being once more restored on all sides, Captain Roger intreated Rebecca to favour them with a Song, in compliance with which request having first assured them that she had a terrible cold, she sung as follows.

Song

when Corydon went to the fair
He bought a red ribbon for Bess,
with which she encircled her hair
& made herself look very *fess*.*

Chapter the Fifth

At the end of 3 days Captain Roger and Rebecca were united and immediately after the Ceremony set off in the Stage Waggon* for the Captains seat in Buckinghamshire.

The parents of Elfrida, alltho' they earnestly wished to see her married to Frederic before they died, yet knowing the delicate frame of her mind could ill bear the least excertion & rightly judging that naming her wedding day would be too great a one, forebore to press her on the subject.*

Weeks & Fortnights flew away without gaining the least ground; the Cloathes grew out of fashion & at length Capt. Roger & his Lady arrived, to pay a visit to their Mother & introduce to her their beautifull Daughter of eighteen.

Elfrida, who had found her former acquaintance were growing too old & too ugly to be any longer agreable, was rejoiced to hear of the arrival of so pretty a girl as Eleanor with whom she determined to form the strictest freindship.

But the Happiness she had expected from an acquaintance with Eleanor, she soon found was not to be received, for she had not only the mortification of finding herself treated by her as little less than an old woman, but had actually the horror of perceiving a growing passion in the Bosom of Frederic for the Daughter of the amiable Rebecca.

The instant she had the first idea of such an attachment, she flew to Frederic & in a manner truly heroick, spluttered* out to him her intention of being married the next Day.

To one in his predicament who possessed less personal Courage than Frederic was master of, such a speech would have been Death; but he not being the least terrified boldly replied,

'Dammé Elfrida *you* may be married tomorrow but *I* wont.'

This answer distressed her too much for her delicate Constitution. She accordingly fainted & was in such a hurry to have a succession of fainting fits, that she had scarcely patience enough to recover from one before she fell into another.*

Tho', in any threatening Danger to his Life or Liberty, Frederic was as bold as brass yet in other respects his heart was as soft as cotton* & immediately on hearing of the dangerous way Elfrida was in, he flew to her & finding her better than he had been taught to expect, was united to her Forever—.

Finis

Jack & Alice

a novel

Is respectfully inscribed to Francis William Austen Esq[r], Midshipman on board his Magesty's Ship the Perseverance* by his obedient humble Servant

The Author

Chapter the First

Mr Johnson* was once upon a time about 53; in a twelvemonth afterwards he was 54, which so much delighted him that he was determined to celebrate his next Birth day by giving a Masquerade* to his Children & Freinds. Accordingly on the Day he attained his 55th year* tickets* were dispatched to all his Neighbours to that purpose. His acquaintance indeed in that part of the World were not very numerous as they consisted only of Lady Williams, Mr & Mrs Jones, Charles Adams & the 3 Miss Simpsons, who composed the neighbourhood of Pammydiddle* & formed the Masquerade.

Before I proceed to give an account of the Evening, it will be proper to describe to my reader, the persons and Characters of the party introduced to his acquaintance.

Mr & Mrs Jones were both rather tall* & very passionate,* but were in other respects, good tempered, well behaved People. Charles Adams* was an amiable, accomplished & bewitching young Man; of so dazzling a Beauty that none but Eagles could look him in the Face.*

Miss Simpson was pleasing in her person, in her manners & in her Disposition; an unbounded ambition was her only fault. Her second sister Sukey* was Envious, Spitefull & Malicious. Her person was short, fat & disagreable. Cecilia (the youngest) was perfectly handsome but too affected to be pleasing.

In Lady Williams every virtue met. She was a widow with a handsome Jointure* & the remains of a very handsome face. Tho' Benevolent

& Candid, she was Generous & sincere; Tho' Pious & Good, she was Religious & amiable, & Tho, Elegant & Agreable, she was Polished & Entertaining.*

The Johnsons were a family of Love,* & though a little addicted to the Bottle & the Dice,* had many good Qualities.

Such was the party assembled in the elegant Drawing Room* of Johnson Court, amongst which the pleasing figure of a Sultana* was the most remarkable of the female Masks.* Of the Males a Mask representing the Sun,* was the most universally admired. The Beams that darted from his Eyes were like those of that glorious Luminary tho' infinitely superior. So strong were they that no one dared venture within half a mile of them; he had therefore the best part of the Room to himself, its size not amounting to more than 3 quarters of a mile in length & half a one in breadth. The Gentleman at last finding the feirceness of his beams to be very inconvenient to the concourse by obliging them to croud together in one corner of the room, half shut his eyes by which means, the Company discovered him to be Charles Adams in his plain green Coat,* without any mask at all.

When their astonishment was a little subsided their attention was attracted by 2 Domino's* who advanced in a horrible Passion; they were both very tall, but seemed in other respects to have many good qualities. 'These said the witty Charles, these are Mr & Mrs Jones.' and so indeed they were.

No one could imagine who was the Sultana! Till at length on her addressing a beautifull Flora* who was reclining in a studied attitude* on a couch, with 'Oh Cecilia, I wish I was really what I pretend to be', she was discovered by the never failing genius of Charles Adams, to be the elegant but ambitious Caroline Simpson, & the person to whom she addressed herself, he rightly imagined to be her lovely but affected sister Cecilia.

The Company now advanced to a Gaming Table where sat 3 Dominos (each with a bottle in their hand) deeply engaged; but a female in the character of Virtue* fled with hasty footsteps from the shocking scene, whilst a little fat woman representing Envy, sate alternately on the foreheads of the 3 Gamesters. Charles Adams was still as bright as ever; he soon discovered the party at play to be the 3 Johnsons, Envy to be Sukey Simpson & Virtue to be Lady Williams.

The Masks were then all removed & the Company retired to another room, to partake of an elegant & well managed Entertainment,* after which the Bottle being pretty briskly pushed about by the 3 Johnsons, the whole party not excepting even Virtue were carried home, Dead Drunk.

Chapter the Second

For three months did the Masquerade afford ample subject for conversation to the inhabitants of Pammydiddle; but no character at it was so fully expatiated on as Charles Adams. The singularity of his appearance, the beams which darted from his eyes, the brightness of his Wit, & the whole *tout ensemble** of his person had subdued the hearts of so many of the young Ladies, that of the six present at the Masquerade but five had returned uncaptivated. Alice Johnson was the unhappy sixth whose heart had not been able to withstand the power of his Charms. But as it may appear strange to my Readers, that so much worth and Excellence as he possessed should have conquered only hers, it will be necessary to inform them that the Miss Simpsons were defended from his Power by Ambition, Envy, & Self-admiration.

Every wish of Caroline was centered in a titled Husband; whilst in Sukey such superior excellence could only raise her Envy not her Love, & Cecilia was too tenderly attached to herself to be pleased with any one besides. As for Lady Williams and Mrs Jones, the former of them was too sensible, to fall in love with one so much her Junior* & the latter, tho' very tall & very passionate was too fond of her Husband to think of such a thing.

Yet in spite of every endeavour on the part of Miss Johnson to discover any attachment to her in him; the cold & indifferent heart of Charles Adams still to all appearance, preserved its native freedom; polite to all but partial to none,* he still remained the lovely, the lively, but insensible* Charles Adams.

One evening, Alice finding herself somewhat heated by wine (no very uncommon case) determined to seek a releif for her disordered Head & Love-sick Heart in the Conversation of the intelligent Lady Williams.

She found her Ladyship at home as was in general the Case, for she was not fond of going out, & like the great Sir Charles Grandison scorned to deny herself when at Home,* as she looked on that

fashionable method of shutting out disagreable Visitors, as little less
than downright Bigamy.*

In spite of the wine she had been drinking, poor Alice was uncommonly out of spirits;* she could think of nothing but Charles Adams,
she could talk of nothing but him, & in short spoke so openly that
Lady Williams soon discovered the unreturned affection she bore
him, which excited her Pity & Compassion so strongly that she
addressed her in the following Manner.

'I perceive but too plainly my dear Miss Johnson, that your Heart'
'has not been able to withstand the fascinating Charms of this young'
'Man & I pity you sincerely. Is it a first Love'?

'It is.'

'I am still more greived to hear *that*; I am myself a sad example of'
'the Miseries, in general attendant on a first Love & I am determined'
'for the future to avoid the like Misfortune. I wish it may not be too'
'late for you to do the same; if it is not endeavour my dear Girl to'
'secure yourself from so great a Danger. A second attachment is seldom'
'attended with any serious consequences;* against *that* therefore I have'
'nothing to say. Preserve yourself from a first Love & you need not'
'fear a second.'

'You mentioned Madam something of your having yourself been'
'a sufferer by the misfortune you are so good as to wish me to avoid.'
'Will you favour me with your Life & Adventures?'*

'Willingly my Love.'

Chapter the Third

'My Father was a gentleman of considerable Fortune in Berkshire;'
'myself & a few more his only Children. I was but six years old when'
'I had the misfortune of losing my Mother & being at that time'
'young & Tender, my father instead of sending me to School, procured'
'an able handed Governess to superintend my Education at Home.'*
'My Brothers were placed at Schools suitable to their Ages & my'
'Sisters being all younger than myself, remained still under the Care'
'of their Nurse.'

'Miss Dickins was an excellent Governess. She instructed me in'
'the Paths of Virtue; under her tuition I daily became more amiable, &'

'might perhaps by this time have nearly attained perfection, had not'
'my worthy Preceptoress been torn from my arms, e'er I had attained'
'my seventeenth year. I never shall forget her last words. "My dear'
'Kitty* she said, Good night t'ye." I never saw her afterwards,'
'continued Lady Williams wiping her eyes, She eloped with the Butler'
'the same night.'

'I was invited the following Year by a distant relation of my Father's'
'to spend the Winter with her in town.* Mrs Watkins was a Lady of'
'Fashion, Family & fortune; she was in general esteemed a pretty'
'Woman, but I never thought her very handsome, for my part. She had'
'too high a forehead, Her eyes were too small & she had too much'
'colour.'*

'How can *that* be?' interrupted Miss Johnson reddening with'
'anger; 'Do you think that any one can have too much colour?'

'Indeed I do, & I'll tell you why I do my dear Alice; when a person'
'has too great a degree of red in their Complexion, it gives their face'
'in my opinion, too red a look.'*

'But can a face my Lady have too red a look'?

'Certainly my dear Miss Johnson & I'll tell you why. When a face'
'has too red a look it does not appear to so much advantage as it'
'would were it paler.'

'Pray Ma'am proceed in your story.'

'Well, as I said before, I was invited by this Lady to spend some'
'weeks with her in town. Many Gentlemen thought her Handsome'
'but in my opinion, Her forehead was too high, her eyes too small &'
'she had too much colour.'

'In that Madam as I said before your Ladyship must have been'
'mistaken. Mrs Watkins could not have too much colour since no one'
'can have too much.'

'Excuse me my Love if I do not agree with you in that particular.'
'Let me explain myself clearly; my idea of the case is this. When'
'a Woman has too great a proportion of red in her Cheeks, she must'
'have too much colour.'

'But madam I deny that it is possible for any one to have too great'
'a proportion of red in their Cheeks.'

'What my Love not if they have too much colour?'

Miss Johnson was now out of all patience, the more so perhaps
as Lady Williams still remained so inflexibly cool. It must be
remembered however that her Ladyship had in one respect by far

the advantage of Alice; I mean in not being drunk, for heated with wine & raised by Passion, she could have little command of her Temper—.

The Dispute at length grew so hot, on the part of Alice that,
'From Words she almost came to Blows'*
When Mr Johnson luckily entered & with some difficulty forced her away from Lady Williams, Mrs Watkins & her red cheeks.

Chapter the Fourth

My Readers may perhaps imagine that after such a fracas, no intimacy could longer subsist between the Johnsons and Lady Williams, but in that they are mistaken for her Ladyship was too sensible to be angry at a conduct which she could not help perceiving to be the natural consequence of inebriety & Alice had too sincere a respect for Lady Williams & too great a relish for her Claret,* not to make every concession in her power.

A few days after their reconciliation Lady Williams called on Miss Johnson to propose a walk in a Citron Grove* which led from her Ladyship's pigstye to Charles Adams's Horsepond. Alice was too sensible* of Lady Williams's kindness in proposing such a walk & too much pleased with the prospect of seeing at the end of it, a Horsepond of Charles's, not to accept it with visible delight. They had not proceeded far before she was roused from the reflection of the happiness she was going to enjoy, by Lady Williams's thus addressing her.

'I have as yet forborn my dear Alice to continue the narrative of my'
'Life from an unwillingness of recalling to your Memory a scene'
'which (since it reflects on you rather disgrace than credit) had better'
'be forgot than remembered.'

Alice had already begun to colour up & was beginning to speak, when her Ladyship perceiving her displeasure, continued thus.

'I am afraid my dear Girl that I have offended you by what I have'
'just said; I assure you I do not mean to distress you by a retrospection'
'of what cannot now be helped; considering all things I do not think'
'you so much to blame as many People do; for when a person is'
'in Liquor, there is no answering for what they may do.'

'Madam, this is not to be borne; I insist—'

'My dear Girl dont vex yourself about the matter; I assure you'
'I have entirely forgiven every thing respecting it; indeed I was not'
'angry at the time, because as I saw all along, you were nearly dead'
'drunk I knew you could not help saying the strange things you did.'
'But I see I distress you; so I will change the subject & desire it may'
'never again be mentioned; remember it is all forgot—I will now'
'pursue my story; but I must insist upon not giving you any description'
'of Mrs Watkins; it would only be reviving old stories & as you never'
'saw her, it can be nothing to you, if her forehead *was* too high, her'
'eyes *were* too small, or if she *had* too much colour.'

'Again! Lady Williams: this is too much'—

So provoked was poor Alice at this renewal of the old story, that
I know not what might have been the consequence of it, had not their
attention been engaged by another object. A lovely young Woman
lying apparently in great pain beneath a Citron-tree, was an object too
interesting not to attract their notice. Forgetting their own dispute
they both with simpathizing Tenderness advanced towards her &
accosted her in these terms.

'You seem fair Nymph* to be labouring under some misfortune'
'which we shall be happy to releive if you will inform us what it is.'
'Will you favour us with your Life & adventures?'*

'Willingly Ladies, if you will be so kind as to be seated.' They took
their places & she thus began.

Chapter the Fifth

'I am a native of North Wales & my Father is one of the most capital'
'Taylors* in it. Having a numerous family, he was easily prevailed'
'on by a sister of my Mother's who is a widow in good circumstances'
'& keeps an alehouse in the next Village to ours, to let her take me &'
'breed me up at her own expence. Accordingly I have lived with her'
'for the last 8 years of my Life, during which time she provided me'
'with some of the first rate Masters, who taught me all the accom-'
'plishments requisite for one of my sex and rank. Under their instruc-'
'tions I learned Dancing, Music, Drawing & various Languages, by'
'which means I became more accomplished than any other Taylor's'
'Daughter in Wales.* Never was there a happier creature than I was,'

'till within the last half year—but I should have told you before that'
'the principal Estate in our Neighbourhood belongs to Charles'
'Adams, the owner of the brick House, you see yonder.'

   'Charles Adams!' exclaimed the astonished Alice; 'are you acquainted'
'with Charles Adams?'

   'To my sorrow madam I am. He came about half a year ago to'
'receive the rents of the Estate* I have just mentioned. At that time'
'I first saw him; as you seem ma'am acquainted with him, I need'
'not describe to you how charming he is. I could not resist his'
'attractions;'—

   'Ah! who can,' said Alice with a deep sigh.

   'My aunt being in terms of the greatest intimacy with his cook,'
'determined, at my request, to try whether she could discover, by'
'means of her freind if there were any chance of his returning my'
'affection. For this purpose she went one evening to drink tea with'
'Mrs Susan,* who in the course of Conversation mentioned the good-'
'ness of her Place* & the Goodness of her Master; upon which my'
'aunt began pumping her* with so much dexterity that in a short time'
'Susan owned, that she did not think her Master would ever marry,'
' "for (said she) he has often & often declared to me that his wife," '
' "whoever she might be, must possess, Youth, Beauty, Birth, Wit," '
' "Merit, & Money. I have many a time (she continued) endeavoured" '
' "to reason him out of his resolution & to convince him of the improb-" '
' "ability of his ever meeting with such a Lady; but my arguments" '
' "have had no effect & he continues as firm in his determination as" '
' "ever." You may imagine Ladies my distress on hearing this; for'
'I was fearfull that tho' possessed of Youth, Beauty, Wit & Merit, &'
'tho' the probable Heiress of my aunts House & business, he might'
'think me deficient in Rank, & in being so, unworthy of his hand.'

   'However I was determined to make a bold push & therefore wrote'
'him a very kind letter, offering him with great tenderness my hand &'
'heart.* To this I received an angry & peremptory refusal, but think-'
'ing it might be rather the effect of his modesty than any thing else,'
'I pressed him again on the subject. But he never answered any more'
'of my Letters & very soon afterwards left the Country. As soon as'
'I heard of his departure I wrote to him here, informing him that'
'I should shortly do myself the honour of waiting on him at Pammydiddle,'
'to which I received no answer; therefore choosing to take, Silence'
'for Consent, I left Wales, unknown to my aunt, & arrived here after'

'a tedious Journey this Morning. On enquiring for his House I was'
'directed thro' this Wood, to the one you there see. With a heart elated'
'by the expected happiness of beholding him I entered it & had'
'proceeded thus far in my progress thro' it, when I found myself'
'suddenly seized by the leg & on examining the cause of it, found that'
'I was caught in one of the steel traps* so common in gentlemen's'
'grounds.'

'Ah cried Lady Williams, how fortunate we are to meet with you;'
'since we might otherwise perhaps have shared the like misfortune'—

'It is indeed happy for you Ladies, that I should have been a short'
'time before you. I screamed as you may easily imagine till The woods'
'resounded again & till one of the inhuman Wretch's servants came'
'to my assistance & released me from my dreadfull prison, but not'
'before one of my legs was entirely broken.'

Chapter the Sixth

At this melancholy recital the fair eyes of Lady Williams, were suf-
fused in tears & Alice could not help exclaiming,

'Oh! cruel Charles to wound the hearts & legs of all the fair.'

Lady Williams now interposed & observed that the young Lady's
leg ought to be set without farther delay. After examining the fracture
therefore, she immediately began & performed the operation with
great skill which was the more wonderfull on account of her having
never performed such a one before.* Lucy, then arose from the
ground & finding that she could walk with the greatest ease, accompanied them to Lady Williams's House at her Ladyship's particular
request.

The perfect form, the beautifull face, & elegant manners of Lucy
so won on the affections of Alice that when they parted, which was not
till after Supper, She assured her that except her Father, Brother,
Uncles, Aunts, Cousins & other relations, Lady Williams, Charles
Adams & a few dozen more of particular freinds, she loved her better
than almost any other person in the world.

Such a flattering assurance of her regard would justly have given
much pleasure to the object of it, had she not plainly perceived that
the amiable Alice had partaken too freely of Lady Williams's claret.

Her Ladyship (whose discernment was great) read in the intelligent countenance of Lucy her thoughts on the subject & as soon as Miss Johnson had taken her leave, thus addressed her.

'When you are more intimately acquainted with my Alice you will' 'not be surprised, Lucy, to see the dear Creature drink a little too' 'much; for such things happen every day. She has many rare & charm-' 'ing qualities, but Sobriety is not one of them. The whole Family are' 'indeed a sad drunken set. I am sorry to say too that I never knew' 'three such thorough Gamesters as they are, more particularly Alice.' 'But she is a charming girl. I fancy not one of the sweetest tempers' 'in the world; to be sure I have seen her in such passions! However she' 'is a sweet young Woman. I am sure you'll like her. I scarcely know any' 'one so amiable.—Oh! that you could but have seen her the other' 'Evening! How she raved! & on such a trifle too! She is indeed a most' 'pleasing Girl! I shall always love her!'

'She appears by your ladyship's account to have many good' 'qualities', replied Lucy. 'Oh! a thousand,' answered Lady Williams;' 'tho' I am very partial to her, and perhaps am blinded by my affection,' 'to her real defects.'*

Chapter the Seventh

The next morning brought the three Miss Simpsons to wait on Lady Williams, who received them with the utmost politeness & introduced to their acquaintance Lucy, with whom the eldest was so much pleased that at parting she declared her sole *ambition* was to have her accompany them the next morning to Bath,* whither they were going for some weeks.

'Lucy, said Lady Williams, is quite at her own disposal & if she' 'chooses to accept so kind an invitation, I hope she will not hesitate,' 'from any motives of delicacy on my account. I know not indeed how' 'I shall ever be able to part with her. She never was at Bath & I should' 'think that it would be a most agreable Jaunt* to her. Speak my Love,' 'continued she, turning to Lucy, what say you to accompanying these' 'Ladies? I shall be miserable without you—t'will be a most pleasant' 'tour to you—I hope you'll go; if you do I am sure t'will be the Death' 'of me—pray be persuaded'——

Lucy begged leave to decline the honour of accompanying them, with many expressions of gratitude for the extream politeness of Miss Simpson in inviting her.

Miss Simpson appeared much disappointed by her refusal. Lady Williams insisted on her going—declared that she would never forgive her if she did not, and that she should never survive it if she did, & inshort used such persuasive arguments that it was at length resolved she was to go. The Miss Simpsons called for her at ten o'clock the next morning & Lady Williams had soon the satisfaction of receiving from her young freind, the pleasing intelligence of their safe arrival in Bath.

It may now be proper to return to the Hero of this Novel,* the brother of Alice, of whom I beleive I have scarcely ever had occasion to speak; which may perhaps be partly oweing to his unfortunate propensity to Liquor, which so compleatly deprived him of the use of those faculties Nature had endowed him with, that he never did anything worth mentioning. His Death happened a short time after Lucy's departure & was the natural Consequence of this pernicious practice. By his decease, his sister became the sole inheritress of a very large fortune, which as it gave her fresh Hopes of rendering herself acceptable as a wife to Charles Adams could not fail of being most pleasing to her—& as the effect was Joyfull the Cause could scarcely be lamented.

Finding the violence of her attachment to him daily augment, she at length disclosed it to her Father & desired him to propose a union between them to Charles. Her father consented & set out one morning to open the affair to the young Man. Mr Johnson being a man of few words his part was soon performed & the answer he received was as follows—

'Sir, I may perhaps be expected to appear pleased at & gratefull' 'for the offer you have made me: but let me tell you that I consider' 'it as an affront. I look upon myself to be Sir a perfect Beauty—' 'where would you see a finer figure or a more charming face. Then,' 'sir I imagine my Manners & Address to be of the most polished kind;' 'there is a certain elegance a peculiar sweetness in them that I never' 'saw equalled & cannot describe—. Partiality aside, I am certainly' 'more accomplished in every Language, every Science, every Art &' 'every thing than any other person in Europe. My temper is even, my' 'virtues innumerable, my self unparalelled.* Since such Sir is my'

'character, what do you mean by wishing me to marry your Daughter?'
'Let me give you a short sketch of yourself & of her. I look upon you'
'Sir to be a very good sort of Man in the main; a drunken old Dog to'
'be sure, but that's nothing to me. your daughter sir, is neither suffi-'
'ciently beautifull, sufficiently amiable, sufficiently witty, nor suffi-'
'ciently' rich for me——. I expect nothing more in my wife than my wife'
'will find in me—Perfection. These sir, are my sentiments & I honour'
'myself for having such. One freind I have* & glory in having but'
'one——. She is at present preparing my Dinner, but if you choose to'
'see her, she shall come & she will inform you that these have ever'
'been my sentiments.'

Mr Johnson was satisfied: & expressing himself to be much obliged
to Mr Adams for the characters he had favoured him with of himself &
his Daughter, took his leave.

The unfortunate Alice on receiving from her father the sad account
of the ill success his visit had been attended with, could scarcely
support the disappointment—She flew to her Bottle & it was soon
forgot.*

Chapter the Eighth

While these affairs were transacting at Pammydiddle, Lucy was
conquering every Heart at Bath. A fortnight's residence there had nearly
effaced from her remembrance the captivating form of Charles—The
recollection of what her Heart had formerly suffered by his charms &
her Leg by his trap, enabled her to forget him with tolerable Ease,
which was what she determined to do; & for that purpose dedicated
five minutes in every day to the employment of driving him from her
remembrance.

Her second Letter to Lady Williams contained the pleasing intelligence of her having accomplished her undertaking to her entire satisfaction; she mentioned in it also an offer of marriage she had received
from the Duke of——an elderly Man of noble fortune whose ill health
was the cheif inducement of his Journey to Bath. 'I am distressed (she'
'continued) to know whether I mean to accept him or not. There are'
'a thousand advantages to be derived from a marriage with the Duke;'
'for besides those more inferior ones of Rank & Fortune it will procure'

'me a home, which of all other things is what I most desire. Your'
'ladyship's kind wish of my always remaining with you, is noble &'
'generous but I cannot think of becoming so great a burden on one'
'I so much love & esteem. That One should receive obligations only'
'from those we despise, is a sentiment instilled into my mind by'
'my worthy aunt, in my early years, & cannot in my opinion be too'
'strictly adhered to. The excellent woman of whom I now speak, is'
'I hear too much incensed by my imprudent departure from Wales,'
'to receive me again—. I most earnestly wish to leave the Ladies'
'I am now with. Miss Simpson is indeed (setting aside ambition)'
'very amiable, but her 2^d Sister the envious & malvolent Sukey is'
'too disagreable to live with.—I have reason to think that the'
'admiration I have met with in the circles of the great at this Place,'
'has raised her Hatred & Envy; for often has she threatened, &'
'sometimes endeavoured to cut my throat.—Your Ladyship will'
'therefore allow that I am not wrong in wishing to leave Bath, & in'
'wishing to have a home to receive me, when I do. I shall expect'
'with impatience your advice concerning the Duke & am your most'
'obliged'

&c. &c. 'Lucy.'

Lady Williams sent her, her opinion on the subject in the following
Manner.

'Why do you hesitate my dearest Lucy, a moment with respect to'
'the Duke? I have enquired into his Character & find him to be an'
'unprincipaled, illiterate Man. Never shall my Lucy be united to'
'such a one! He has a princely fortune, which is every day encreasing.'
'How nobly will you spend it!; what credit will you give him in the'
'eyes of all!; How much will he be respected on his Wife's account!'
'But why my dearest Lucy, why will you not at once decide this affair'
'by returning to me & never leaving me again? Altho' I admire your'
'noble sentiments with respect to obligations, yet, let me beg that'
'they may not prevent your making me happy. It will to be sure be'
'a great expence to me, to have you always with me—I shall not be able'
'to support it—but what is that in comparison with the happiness'
'I shall enjoy in your society?—t'will ruin me I know—you will not'
'therefore surely, withstand these arguments, or refuse to return to'
'yours most affectionately – &c. &c.'

'C. Williams'

Chapter the Ninth

What might have been the effect of her Ladyship's advice, had it ever been received by Lucy, is uncertain, as it reached Bath a few Hours after she had breathed her last. She fell a sacrifice to the Envy & Malice of Sukey who jealous of her superior charms took her by poison from an admiring World at the age of seventeen.

Thus fell the amiable & lovely Lucy whose Life had been marked by no crime, and stained by no blemish but her imprudent departure from her Aunts, & whose death was sincerely lamented by every one who knew her. Among the most afflicted of her freinds were Lady Williams, Miss Johnson & the Duke; the 2 first of whom had a most sincere regard for her, more particularly Alice, who had spent a whole evening in her company & had never thought of her since. His Grace's affliction may likewise be easily accounted for, since he lost one for whom he had experienced during the last ten days, a tender affection & sincere regard. He mourned her loss with unshaken constancy for the next fortnight at the end of which time, he gratified the ambition of Caroline Simpson by raising her to the rank of a Dutchess. Thus was she at length rendered compleatly happy in the gratification of her favourite passion. Her sister the perfidious Sukey, was likewise shortly after exalted in a manner she truly deserved, & by her actions appeared to have always desired. Her barbarous Murder was discovered & in spite of every interceding freind she was speedily raised to the Gallows*—. The beautifull but affected Cecilia was too sensible of her own superior charms, not to imagine that if Caroline could engage a Duke, she might without censure aspire to the affections of some Prince—& knowing that those of her native Country were cheifly engaged,* she left England & I have since heard is at present the favourite Sultana of the great Mogul*—.

In the mean time the inhabitants of Pammydiddle were in a state of the greatest astonishment and Wonder, a report being circulated of the intended marriage of Charles Adams. The Lady's name was still a secret. Mr & Mrs Jones imagined it to be, Miss Johnson; but *she* knew better; all *her* fears were centered in his Cook, when to the astonishment of every one, he was publicly united to Lady Williams—

Finis

Edgar and Emma

a tale*

Chapter the first

'I cannot imagine,' said Sir Godfrey* to his Lady, 'why we continue' 'in such deplorable Lodgings as these, in a paltry Market-town,'* 'while we have 3 good Houses of our own situated in some of the' 'finest parts of England, & perfectly ready to receive us!'

'I'm sure Sir Godfrey,' replied Lady Marlow, 'it has been much' 'against my inclination that we have staid here so long; or why we' 'should ever have come at all indeed, has been to me a wonder as' 'none of our Houses have been in the least want of repair.'

'Nay my dear,' answered Sir Godfrey, 'you are the last person who' 'ought to be displeased with what was always meant as a compliment' 'to you; for you cannot but be sensible of the very great inconvenience' 'your Daughters & I have been put to during the 2 years we have' 'remained crowded in these Lodgings in order to give you pleasure.'

'My dear,' replied Lady Marlow, 'How can you stand & tell such' 'lies, when you very well know that it was merely to oblige the Girls &' 'you, that I left a most commodious House situated in a most delight-' 'full Country & surrounded by a most agreable Neighbourhood, to live' '2 years cramped up in Lodgings three pair of Stairs high,* in' 'a smokey & unwholesome town, which has given me a continual' 'fever & almost thrown me into a Consumption.'*

As, after a few more speeches on both sides, they could not determine which was the most to blame, they prudently laid aside the debate, & having packed up their Cloathes & paid their rent, they set out the next morning with their 2 Daughters for their seat in Sussex.

Sir Godfrey & Lady Marlow were indeed very sensible people & tho' (as in this instance) like many other sensible People, they sometimes did a foolish thing, yet in general their actions were guided by Prudence & regulated by discretion.

After a Journey of two Days & a half they arrived at Marlhurst* in good health & high spirits; so overjoyed were they all to inhabit again a place, they had left with mutual regret for two years, that they ordered the bells to be rung & distributed ninepence among the Ringers.*

Chapter the second

The news of their arrival being quickly spread throughout the Country, brought them in a few Days visits of congratulation from every family in it.

Amongst the rest came the inhabitants of Willmot Lodge a beautifull Villa* not far from Marlhurst. Mr Willmot was the representative of a very ancient Family & possessed besides his paternal Estate, a considerable share in a Lead mine & a ticket in the Lottery.* His Lady was an agreable Woman. Their Children were too numerous to be particularly described; it is sufficient to say that in general they were virtuously inclined & not given to any wicked ways. Their family being too large to accompany them in every visit, they took nine with them alternately. When their coach* stopped at Sir Godfrey's door, the Miss Marlow's Hearts throbbed in the eager expectation of once more beholding a family so dear to them. Emma* the youngest (who was more particularly interested in their arrival, being attached to their eldest Son) continued at her Dressing-room window in anxious Hopes of seeing young Edgar* descend from the Carriage.

Mr & Mrs Willmot with their three eldest Daughters first appeared—Emma began to tremble—.* Robert, Richard, Ralph, & Rodolphus* followed—Emma turned pale—. Their two youngest Girls were lifted from the Coach—Emma sunk breathless on a Sopha.* A footman came to announce to her the arrival of Company; her heart was too full to contain its afflictions. A confidante* was necessary— In Thomas she hoped to experience a faithfull one—for one she must have & Thomas was the only one at Hand. To him she unbosomed herself without restraint & after owning her passion for young Willmot, requested his advice in what manner she should conduct herself in the melancholy Disappointment under which she laboured.

Thomas, who would gladly have been excused from listening to her complaint, begged leave to decline giving any advice concerning it, which much against her will, she was obliged to comply with.

Having dispatched him therefore with many injunctions of secrecy, she descended with a heavy heart into the Parlour, where she found the good Party seated in a social manner* round a blazing fire.

Chapter the third

Emma had continued in the Parlour some time before she could summon up sufficient courage to ask Mrs Willmot after the rest of her family; & when she did, it was in so low, so faltering a voice that no one knew she spoke. Dejected by the ill success of her first attempt she made no other, till on Mrs Willmots desiring one of the little Girls to ring the bell for their Carriage, she stepped across the room & seizing the string said in a resolute manner.

'Mrs Willmot, you do not stir from this House till you let me know'
'how all the rest of your family do, particularly your eldest son.'

They were all greatly surprised by such an unexpected address & the more so, on account of the manner in which it was spoken; but Emma, who would not be again disappointed, requesting an answer, Mrs Willmot made the following eloquent oration.

'Our children are all extremely well but at present most of them'
'from home. Amy is with my sister Clayton. Sam at Eton.* David'
'with his Uncle John. Jem & Will at Winchester.* Kitty at Queen's'
'Square.* Ned with his Grandmother. Hetty & Patty in a convent at'
'Brussells.* Edgar at college,* Peter at Nurse,* & all the rest (except'
'the nine here) at home.'

It was with difficulty that Emma could refrain from tears on hearing of the absence of Edgar; she remained however tolerably composed till the Willmot's were gone when having no check to the overflowings of her greif, she gave free vent to them, & retiring to her own room, continued in tears the remainder of her Life.

Finis

Henry and Eliza*

a novel

Is humbly dedicated to Miss Cooper* by her obedient Humble Servant
The Author

———

As Sir George and Lady Harcourt were superintending the Labours of their Haymakers, rewarding the industry of some by smiles of approbation,* & punishing the idleness of others, by a cudgel,* they perceived lying closely concealed beneath the thick foliage of a Haycock,* a beautifull little Girl not more than 3 months old.*

Touched with the enchanting Graces of her face & delighted with the infantine tho' sprightly answers she returned to their many questions, they resolved to take her home &, having no Children of their own, to educate her with care & cost.

Being good People themselves, their first & principal care was to incite in her a Love of Virtue & a Hatred of Vice, in which they so well succeeded (Eliza having a natural turn that way herself) that when she grew up, she was the delight of all who knew her.

Beloved by Lady Harcourt, adored by Sir George & admired by all the world, she lived in a continued course of uninterrupted Happiness, till she had attained her eighteenth year, when happening one day to be detected in stealing a bank-note of 50£, she was turned out of doors by her inhuman Benefactors.* Such a transition to one who did not possess so noble & exalted a mind as Eliza, would have been Death, but she, happy in the conscious knowledge of her own Excellence, amused herself, as she sate beneath a tree with making & singing the following Lines.

Song

Though misfortunes my footsteps may ever attend
I hope I shall never have need of a Freind
as an innocent Heart I will ever preserve
and will never from Virtue's dear boundaries swerve.

Having amused herself some hours, with this song & her own pleasing reflections, she arose & took the road to M.* a small market town of which place her most intimate freind kept the red Lion.*

To this freind she immediately went, to whom having recounted her late misfortune, she communicated her wish of getting into some family in the capacity of Humble Companion.*

Mrs Willson,* who was the most amiable creature on earth, was no sooner acquainted with her Desire, than she sate down in the Bar & wrote the following Letter to the Dutchess of F, the woman whom of all others, she most Esteemed.

'To the Dutchess of F.'

'Receive into your Family, at my request a young woman of'
'unexceptionable Character, who is so good as to choose your Society'
'in preference to going to Service. Hasten, & take her from the arms'
'of your'

'Sarah Wilson.'

The Dutchess, whose freindship for Mrs Wilson would have carried her any lengths, was overjoyed at such an opportunity of obliging her & accordingly sate out immediately on the receipt of her letter for the red Lion, which she reached the same Evening.* The Dutchess of F. was about 45 & a half; Her passions were strong, her freindships firm & her Enmities, unconquerable. She was a widow & had only one Daughter who was on the point of marriage with a young Man of considerable fortune.

The Dutchess no sooner beheld our Heroine than throwing her arms around her neck, she declared herself so much pleased with her, that she was resolved they never more should part. Eliza was delighted with such a protestation of freindship, & after taking a most affecting leave of her dear Mrs Wilson, accompanied her grace the next morning to her seat in Surry.

With every expression of regard did the Dutchess introduce her to Lady Hariet, who was so much pleased with her appearance that she besought her, to consider her as her Sister, which Eliza with the greatest Condescension promised to do.

Mr Cecil, the Lover of Lady Harriet, being often with the family was often with Eliza. A mutual Love took place & Cecil having declared his first, prevailed on Eliza to consent to a private union,* which was easy to be effected, as the dutchess's chaplain* being very much in love with Eliza himself, would they were certain do anything to oblige her.

The Dutchess & Lady Hariet being engaged one evening to an assembly, they took the opportunity of their absence & were united by the enamoured Chaplain.

When the Ladies returned, their amazement was great at finding instead of Eliza the following Note.

'Madam'
    'We are married & gone.'
                      'Henry & Eliza Cecil.'

Her Grace as soon as she had read the letter, which sufficiently explained the whole affair, flew into the most violent passion & after having spent an agreable half hour, in calling them by all the shocking Names her rage could suggest to her, sent out after them 300 armed Men, with orders not to return without their Bodies, dead or alive; intending that if they should be brought to her in the latter condition to have them put to Death in some torturelike manner, after a few years Confinement.

In the mean time Cecil & Eliza continued their flight to the Continent,* which they judged to be more secure than their native Land, from the dreadfull effects of the Dutchess's vengeance, which they had so much reason to apprehend.

In France they remained 3 years, during which time they became the parents of two Boys, & at the end of it Eliza became a widow without any thing to support either her or her Children. They had lived since their Marriage at the rate of 18,000£ a year,* of which Mr Cecil's estate being rather less than the twentieth part,* they had been able to save but a trifle, having lived to the utmost extent of their Income.

Eliza, being perfectly conscious of the derangement in their affairs, immediately on her Husband's death set sail for England, in a man of War of 55 Guns,* which they had built in their more pros- perous Days. But no sooner had she stepped on Shore at Dover, with a Child in each hand, than she was seized by the officers of the Dutchess, & conducted by them to a snug little Newgate* of their Lady's, which she had erected for the reception of her own private Prisoners.

No sooner had Eliza entered her Dungeon than the first thought which occurred to her, was how to get out of it again.

She went to the Door; but it was locked. She looked at the Window; but it was barred with iron; disappointed in both her expectations, she dispaired of effecting her Escape; when she fortunately perceived in a Corner of her Cell, a small saw & a Ladder of ropes. With the saw she instantly went to work & in a few weeks had displaced every Bar but one to which she fastened the Ladder.

A difficulty then occurred which for sometime, she knew not how to obviate. Her Children were too small to get down the Ladder by themselves. nor would it be possible for her to take them in her arms, when *she* did. At last she determined to fling down all her Cloathes, of which she had a large Quantity, & then having given them strict Charge not to hurt themselves, threw her Children after them.* She herself with ease descended by the Ladder, at the bottom of which she had the pleasure of finding Her little boys in perfect Health & fast asleep.

Her wardrobe she now saw a fatal necessity of selling, both for the preservation of her Children & herself. With tears in her eyes, she parted with these last reliques of her former Glory, & with the money she got for them, bought others more usefull, some play things for her Boys and a gold Watch for herself.*

But scarcely was she provided with the above-mentioned necessar- ies, than she began to find herself rather hungry, & had reason to think, by their biting off two of her fingers, that her Children were much in the same situation.

To remedy these unavoidable misfortunes, she determined to return to her old freinds, Sir George & Lady Harcourt, whose generos- ity she had so often experienced & hoped to experience as often again.

She had about 40 miles to travel before she could reach their hospitable Mansion, of which having walked 30 without stopping,* she
found herself at the Entrance of a Town, where often in happier times,
she had accompanied Sir George & Lady Harcourt to regale themselves with a cold collation* at one of the Inns.

The reflections that her adventures since the last time she had partaken of these happy *Junkettings*,* afforded her, occupied her mind,
for some time, as she sate on the steps at the door of a Gentleman's
house. As soon as these reflections were ended, she arose & determined to take her station at the very inn, she remembered with so
much delight, from the Company of which, as they went in & out, she
hoped to receive some Charitable Gratuity.*

She had but just taken her post at the Inn yard, before a Carriage
drove out of it, & on turning the Corner at which she was stationed,
stopped to give the Postilion an opportunity of admiring the beauty
of the prospect. Eliza then advanced to the carriage & was going to
request their Charity, when on fixing her Eyes on the Lady, within it,
she exclaimed,

'Lady Harcourt!'

To which the lady replied,

'Eliza!'

'Yes Madam it is the wretched Eliza herself.'

Sir George, who was also in the Carriage, but too much amazed to
speek, was proceeding to demand an explanation from Eliza of the
Situation she was then in, when lady Harcourt in transports of Joy,
exclaimed.

'Sir George, Sir George, she is not only Eliza our adopted Daughter,'
'but our real Child.'*

'Our real Child! What Lady Harcourt, do you mean? You know you'
'never even was with child. Explain yourself, I beseech you.'

'You must remember Sir George that when you sailed for America,'
'you left me breeding.'

'I do, I do, go on dear Polly.'*

'Four months after you were gone, I was delivered of this Girl, but'
'dreading your just resentment at her not proving the Boy you wished'
'I took her to a Haycock & laid her down. A few weeks afterwards, you'
'returned, & fortunately for me, made no enquiries on the subject.'
'Satisfied within myself of the wellfare of my Child,* I soon forgot'
'I had one, insomuch that when, we shortly after found her in the'

'very Haycock, I had placed her, I had no more idea of her being my'
'own, than you had, & nothing I will venture to say would have recalled'
'the circumstance to my remembrance, but my thus accidentally'
'hearing her voice, which now strikes me as being the very counterpart'
'of my own Child's.'

'The rational & convincing Account you have given of the whole'
'affair, said Sir George, leaves no doubt of her being our Daughter &'
'as such I freely forgive the robbery she was guilty of.'

A mutual Reconciliation then took place, & Eliza, ascending the Carriage with her two Children returned to that home from which she had been absent nearly four years.

No sooner was she reinstated in her accustomed power at Harcourt Hall, than she raised an Army, with which she entirely demolished the Dutchess's Newgate, snug as it was, and by that act, gained the Blessings of thousands, & the Applause of her own Heart.

Finis

The adventures of Mr Harley

a short, but interesting Tale, is with all imaginable Respect inscribed To Mr Francis Willm Austen Midshipman on board his Magestys Ship the Perseverance* by his Obedient Servant

The Author

———

Mr Harley* was one of many Children. Destined by his father for the Church & by his Mother for the Sea,* desirous of pleasing both, he prevailed on Sir John to obtain for him a Chaplaincy on board a Man of War. He accordingly, cut his Hair & sailed.

In half a year* he returned & sat-off* in the Stage Coach* for Hogsworth Green,* the seat of Emma. His fellow travellers were, A man without a Hat, Another with two, An old maid & a young Wife.

This last appeared about 17 with fine dark Eyes & an elegant Shape; inshort Mr Harley soon found out, that she was his Emma & recollected he had married her a few weeks before he left England.

———

Finis

Sir William Mountague*

an unfinished performance*
is humbly dedicated to Charles John
Austen Esqre,* by his most obedient humble
Servant

The Author

===

Sir William Mountague was the son of Sir Henry Mountague, who was the son of Sir John Mountague, a descendant of Sir Christopher Mountague, who was the nephew of Sir Edward Mountague, whose ancestor was Sir James Mountague a near relation of Sir Robert Mountague, who inherited the Title & Estate from Sir Frederic Mountague.*

Sir William was about 17 when his Father died, & left him a handsome fortune, an ancient House & a Park well stocked with Deer.* Sir William had not been long in the possession of his Estate before he fell in Love with the 3 Miss Cliftons of Kilhoobery Park.* These young Ladies were all equally young, equally handsome, equally rich & equally amiable—Sir William was equally in Love with them all,* & knowing not which to prefer, he left the Country & took Lodgings in a small Village near Dover.

In this retreat, to which he had retired in the hope of finding a shelter from the Pangs of Love, he became enamoured of a young Widow of Quality, who came for change of air to the same Village, after the death of a Husband, whom she had always tenderly loved & now sincerely lamented.

Lady Percival* was young, accomplished & lovely. Sir William adored her & she consented to become his Wife. Vehemently pressed by Sir William to name the Day in which he might conduct her to the Altar, she at length fixed on the following Monday, which was the first of September.* Sir William was a Shot* & could not support the idea of losing such a Day, even for such a Cause. He begged her to delay the Wedding a short time. Lady Percival was enraged & returned to London the next Morning.

Sir William was sorry to lose her, but as he knew, that he should have been much more greived by the Loss of the 1ˢᵗ of September, his Sorrow was not without a mixture of Happiness, & his Affliction was considerably lessened by his Joy.

After staying at the Village a few weeks longer, he left it & went to a freind's House in Surry. Mr Brudenell was a sensible Man, & had a beautifull Neice with whom Sir William soon fell in love. But Miss Arundel was cruel; she preferred a Mr Stanhope:* Sir William shot Mr Stanhope; the lady had then no reason to refuse him; she accepted him, & they were to be married on the 27ᵗʰ of October. But on the 25ᵗʰ Sir William received a visit from Emma Stanhope the sister of the unfortunate Victim of his rage. She begged some recompence, some atonement for the cruel Murder of her Brother. Sir William bade her name her price. She fixed on 14s.* Sir William offered her himself & Fortune. They went to London the next day & were there privately married.* For a fortnight Sir William was compleatly happy, but chancing one day to see a charming young Woman entering a Chariot* in Brook Street,* he became again most violently in love. On enquiring the name of this fair Unknown, he found that she was the Sister of his old freind Lady Percival, at which he was much rejoiced, as he hoped to have, by his acquaintance with her Ladyship, free access to Miss Wentworth. . . . . . .

Finis

To Charles John Austen Esqre

Sir,

Your generous patronage of the unfinished tale, I have already taken the Liberty of dedicating to you, encourages me to dedicate to you a second, as unfinished as the first.

I am Sir with every expression
of regard for you & y^r noble
Family,* your most obed^t
&c. &c. . . .

The Author

Memoirs of Mr Clifford

an unfinished tale—

Mr Clifford lived at Bath; & having never seen London, set off one monday morning determined to feast his eyes with a sight of that great Metropolis. He travelled in his Coach & Four,* for he was a very rich young Man & kept a great many Carriages of which I do not recollect half. I can only remember that he had a Coach, a Chariot, a Chaise,* a Landeau,* a Landeaulet,* a Phaeton,* a Gig,* a Whisky,* an italian Chair,* a Buggy,* a Curricle* & a wheel barrow.* He had likewise an amazing fine stud* of Horses. To my knowledge he had six Greys, 4 Bays,* eight Blacks & a poney.*

In his Coach & 4 Bays Mr Clifford sate forward about 5 o'clock on Monday Morning the 1st of May. for London. He always travelled remarkably expeditiously & contrived therefore to get to Devizes* from Bath, which is no less than nineteen miles, the first Day. To be sure he did not get in till eleven at night & pretty tight work it was as you may imagine.

However when he was once got to Devizes he was determined to comfort himself with a good hot Supper and therefore ordered a whole Egg to be boiled for him & his Servants. The next morning he pursued his Journey & in the course of 3 days hard labour reached Overton,* where he was seized with a dangerous fever the Consequence of too violent Excercise.

Five months did our Hero remain in this celebrated City under the care of its no less celebrated Physician,* who at length compleatly cured him of his troublesome Desease.

As Mr Clifford still continued very weak, his first Day's Journey carried him only to Dean Gate,* where he remained a few Days & found himself much benefited by the change of air.

In easy Stages he proceeded to Basingstoke.* One day Carrying him to Clarkengreen, the next to Worting,* the 3^d to the bottom of Basingstoke Hill, and the fourth, to Mr Robins's*. . . .

Finis

The beautifull Cassandra

a novel in twelve Chapters

dedicated by permission to Miss Austen.*

Dedication

Madam

You are a Phoenix.* Your taste is refined, your Sentiments are noble, & your Virtues innumerable. Your Person is lovely, your Figure, elegant, & your Form, magestic. Your manners, are polished, your Conversation is rational & your appearance singular. If therefore the following Tale will afford one moment's amusement to you, every wish will be gratified of

your most obediant
humble Servant
The Author

The beautifull Cassandra

a novel, in twelve Chapters

Chapter the first

Cassandra was the Daughter and the only Daughter of a celebrated Millener in Bond Street.* Her father was of noble Birth, being the near relation of the Dutchess of——'s Butler.

Chapter the 2ᵈ

When Cassandra had attained her 16ᵗʰ year, she was lovely & amiable & chancing to fall in love with an elegant Bonnet, her Mother had just compleated bespoke by the Countess of——she placed it on her gentle Head & walked from her Mother's shop to make her Fortune.

Chapter the 3ᵈ

The first person she met, was the Viscount of——a young Man, no less celebrated for his Accomplishments & Virtues, than for his Elegance & Beauty. She curtseyed & walked on.

Chapter the 4ᵗʰ

She then proceeded to a Pastry-cooks where she devoured six ices,* refused to pay for them, knocked down the Pastry Cook & walked away.

Chapter the 5th

She next ascended a Hackney Coach* & ordered it to Hampstead,* where She was no sooner arrived than she ordered the Coachman to turn round & drive her back again.

Chapter the 6th

Being returned to the same spot of the same Street she had sate out from, the Coachman demanded his Pay.*

Chapter the 7th

She searched her pockets over again & again; but every search was unsuccessfull. No money could she find. The man grew peremptory. She placed her bonnet on his head* & ran away.

Chapter the 8th

Thro' many a Street she then proceeded & met in none the least Adventure till on turning a Corner of Bloomsbury Square,* she met Maria.

Chapter the 9th

Cassandra started & Maria seemed surprised; they trembled, blushed, turned pale & passed each other in a mutual silence.

Chapter the 10th

Cassandra was next accosted by her freind the Widow, who squeez-
ing out her little Head thro' her less window,* asked her how she did?
Cassandra curtseyed & went on.

Chapter the 11th

A quarter of a mile brought her to her paternal roof in Bond Street
from which she had now been absent nearly 7 hours.

Chapter the 12th

She entered it & was pressed to her Mother's bosom by that worthy
Woman. Cassandra smiled & whispered to herself 'This is a day well
spent.'

Finis

Amelia Webster

an interesting & well written Tale

is dedicated by Permission
to
Mrs Austen*
by
Her humble Servant

The Author

Letter the first

To Miss Webster

My dear Amelia

You will rejoice to hear of the return of my amiable Brother from abroad. He arrived on thursday, & never did I see a finer form, save that of your sincere freind

Matilda* Hervey

Letter the 2ᵈ

To H. Beverley* Esqʳᵉ

Dear Beverley

I arrived here last thursday & met with a hearty reception from my Father, Mother & Sisters. The latter are both fine Girls— particularly Maud,* who I think would suit you as a Wife well enough. What say you to this? She will have two thousand Pounds* & as much more as you can get. If you dont marry her you will mortally offend

George Hervey

Letter the 3ᵈ

To Miss Hervey

Dear Maud

Beleive me I'm happy to hear of your Brother's arrival. I have a thousand things to tell you, but my paper will only permit me to add* that I am yʳ affec.ᵗ Freind

Amelia Webster

Letter the 4th

To Miss S. Hervey*

Dear Sally

I have found a very convenient old hollow oak to put our Letters in; for you know we have long maintained a private Correspondence.* It is about a mile from my House & seven from yours. You may perhaps imagine that I might have made choice of a tree which would have divided the Distance more equally—I was sensible of this at the time, but as I considered that the walk would be of benefit to you in your weak & uncertain state of Health, I preferred it to one nearer your House, & am y^r faithfull

Benjamin Bar

Letter the 5th

To Miss Hervey

Dear Maud

I write now to inform you that I did not stop at your house in my way to Bath last Monday.—I have many things to inform you of besides; but my Paper, reminds me of concluding;* & beleive me y^{rs} ever &c &c

Amelia Webster.

Letter the 6th

To Miss Webster

Madam   Saturday

An humble Admirer now addresses you—I saw you lovely Fair one as you passed on Monday last, before our House in your way to Bath. I saw you thro' a telescope,* & was so struck by your Charms that from that time to this I have not tasted human food.

George Hervey.

Letter the 7th

To Jack

As I was this morning at Breakfast the Newspaper was brought me, & in the list of Marriages I read the following.

'George Hervey Esqre to Miss Amelia Webster'
'Henry Beverley Esqre to Miss Hervey'
&
'Benjamin Bar Esqre to Miss Sarah Hervey'.

yours, Tom.

Finis

The Visit

a comedy in 2 acts

Dedication
To the Revd James Austen*

Sir,

The following Drama, which I humbly recommend to your Protection & Patronage, tho' inferior to those celebrated Comedies called 'The school for Jealousy' & 'The travelled Man',* will I hope afford some amusement to so respectable a *Curate** as yourself; which was the end in veiw when it was first composed* by your

Humble Servant the Author.

Dramatis Personae

Sir Arthur Hampton	Lady Hampton
Lord Fitzgerald	Miss Fitzgerald
Stanly	Sophy Hampton
Willoughby, Sir Arthur's nephew	Cloe* Willoughby

The scenes are laid in
Lord Fitzgerald's House.

Act the First

Scene the first. a Parlour—

enter Lord Fitzgerald & Stanly

Stanly. Cousin your servant.

Fitzgerald. Stanly, good morning to you. I hope you slept well last night.

Stanly. Remarkably well, I thank you.

Fitzgerald. I am afraid you found your Bed too short.* It was bought in my Grandmother's time, who was herself a very short woman &

made a point of suiting all her Beds to her own length, as she
never wished to have any company in the House, on account of an
unfortunate impediment in her speech, which she was sensible of
being very disagreable to her inmates.

Stanly. Make no more excuses dear Fitzgerald.

Fitzgerald. I will not distress you by too much civility—I only beg
you will consider yourself as much at home as in your Father's
house. Remember, 'The more free, the more Wellcome.'*

(exit Fitzgerald)

Stanly. Amiable Youth!
 Your virtues could he imitate
 How happy would be Stanly's fate!

(exit Stanly)

Scene the 2^d.

Stanly & Miss Fitzgerald, discovered.*

Stanly. What Company is it you expect to dine with you to Day,
Cousin?

Miss F. Sir Arthur & Lady Hampton; their Daughter, Nephew &
Neice.

Stanly. Miss Hampton & her Cousin are both Handsome, are they not?

Miss F. Miss Willoughby is extreamly so. Miss Hampton is a fine
Girl, but not equal to her.

Stanly. Is not your Brother attached to the Latter?

Miss F. He admires her I know, but I beleive nothing more. Indeed
I have heard him, say that she was the most beautifull, pleasing, &
amiable Girl in the world, & that of all others he should prefer her
for his Wife. But it never went any farther I'm certain.

Stanly. And yet my Cousin never says a thing he does not mean.

Miss F. Never. From his Cradle he has always been a strict adherent
to Truth.*

(Exeunt Severally)*

End of the First Act.

Act the Second

Scene the first. The Drawing Room.

Chairs set round in a row.* Lord Fitzgerald,
Miss Fitzgerald & Stanly seated.

Enter a Servant.

Servant. Sir Arthur & Lady Hampton. Miss Hampton, Mr & Miss
Willoughby.

(exit Servant)

Enter the Company.

Miss F. I hope I have the pleasure of seeing your Ladyship well.
Sir Arthur your servant. Y^rs Mr Willoughby. Dear Sophy, Dear
Cloe,—
(They pay their Compliments alternately.)

Miss F. Pray be seated.

(They sit)

Bless me! there ought to be 8 Chairs & there are but 6. However,
if your Ladyship will but take Sir Arthur in your Lap, & Sophy,
my Brother in hers, I beleive we shall do pretty well.*

Lady H. Oh! with pleasure . . .

Sophy. I beg his Lordship would be seated.

Miss F. I am really shocked at crouding you in such a manner, but my
Grandmother (who bought all the furniture of this room) as she
had never a very large Party, did not think it necessary to buy more
Chairs than were sufficient for her own family and two of her
particular freinds.

Sophy. I beg you will make no apologies. Your Brother is very light.

Stanly, aside) What a cherub is Cloe!

Cloe, aside) What a seraph* is Stanly!

Enter a Servant.

Servant. Dinner is on table.

They all rise.

Miss F. Lady Hampton, Miss Hampton, Miss Willoughby.
  Stanly hands Cloe, Lord Fitzgerald, Sophy, Willoughby, Miss
    Fitzgerald, and Sir Arthur, Lady Hampton.

(Exeunt.)

Scene the 2^d

The Dining Parlour.

Miss Fitzgerald at top. Lord Fitzgerald at bottom.*
Company ranged on each side.

Servants waiting.

———

Cloe. I shall trouble Mr Stanly for a Little of the fried Cow heel &
  Onion.*
Stanly. Oh Madam, there is a secret pleasure in helping so amiable
  a Lady—.
Lady H. I assure you my Lord, Sir Arthur never touches wine; but
  Sophy will toss off a bumper* I am sure to oblige your Lordship.
Lord F. Elder wine or Mead,* Miss Hampton?
Sophy. If it is equal to you Sir, I should prefer some warm ale with
  a toast and nutmeg.*
Lord F. Two glasses of warmed ale with a toast and nutmeg.
Miss F. I am afraid Mr Willoughby you take no care of yourself. I fear
  you dont meet with any thing to your liking.
Willoughby. Oh! Madam, I can want for nothing while there are red
  herrings* on table.
Lord F. Sir Arthur taste that Tripe.* I think you will not find it
  amiss.
Lady H. Sir Arthur never eats Tripe; 'tis too savoury for him you
  know my Lord.
Miss F. Take away the Liver & Crow* & bring in the Suet pudding.*

(a short Pause.)

Miss F. Sir Arthur shant I send you a bit of pudding?
Lady H. Sir Arthur never eats suet pudding Ma'am. It is too high
  a Dish for him.

Miss F. Will no one allow me the honour of helping them?
Then John take away the Pudding, & bring the Wine.

(Servants take away the things and bring in the Bottles & Glasses.)

Lord F. I wish we had any Desert* to offer you. But my Grandmother
in her Life time, destroyed the Hot house* in order to build a receptacle
for the Turkies with it's materials; & we have never been able to
raise another tolerable one.
Lady H. I beg you will make no apologies my Lord.
Willoughby. Come Girls, let us circulate the Bottle.*
Sophy. A very good motion Cousin; & I will second it with all my
Heart. Stanly you dont drink.
Stanly. Madam, I am drinking draughts of Love from Cloe's eyes.
Sophy. That's poor nourishment truly. Come, drink to her better
acquaintance.

(Miss Fitzgerald goes to a Closet & brings out a bottle)

Miss F. This, Ladies & Gentlemen is some of my dear Grandmother's
own manufacture. She excelled in Gooseberry Wine.* Pray taste it
Lady Hampton?
Lady H. How refreshing it is!
Miss F. I should think with your Ladyship's permission, that Sir
Arthur might taste a little of it.
Lady H. Not for worlds. Sir Arthur never drinks any thing so high.
Lord F. And now my amiable Sophia condescend to marry me.

(He takes her hand & leads her to the front)

Stanly. Oh! Cloe could I but hope you would make me blessed—
Cloe. I will.

(They advance.)

Miss F. Since you Willoughby are the only one left, I cannot refuse
your earnest solicitations—There is my Hand.—
Lady H. And may you all be Happy!

Finis

The Mystery

an unfinished Comedy

Dedication
To the Revd George Austen*

Sir

I humbly solicit your Patronage to the following Comedy, which tho' an unfinished one, is I flatter myself as *complete* a *Mystery* as any of its kind.

> I am Sir your most Hum.^{le}
> Servant
> The Author

The Mystery

a Comedy—

Dramatis Personae

Men	Women
Colonel Elliott	Fanny Elliott
Sir Edward Spangle*	Mrs Humbug
Old Humbug*	and
Young Humbug	Daphne*—
and	
Corydon*	

Act the First

Scene the 1st

A Garden.

Enter Corydon.

———

Cory.) But Hush! I am interrupted.

(Exit Corydon)

Enter Old Humbug & his Son, talking.

Old Hum:) It is for that reason I wish you to follow my advice. Are
you convinced of its propriety?

Young Hum:) I am Sir, and will certainly act in the manner you have
pointed out to me.

Old Hum:) Then let us return to the House.

(Exeunt)

Scene the 2^d

A Parlour in Humbug's house

Mrs Humbug & Fanny, discovered at work.*

Mrs Hum:) You understand me my Love?

Fanny) Perfectly ma'am. Pray continue your narration.

Mrs Hum:) Alas! it is nearly concluded, for I have nothing more to
say on the Subject.

Fanny. Ah! here's Daphne.

Enter Daphne.

Daphne) My dear Mrs Humbug how d'ye do? Oh! Fanny t'is all over.

Fanny) Is it indeed!

Mrs Hum:) I'm very sorry to hear it.

Fanny) Then t'was to no purpose that I. . . .

Daphne) None upon Earth.

Mrs Hum:) And what is to become of?. . . .

Daphne) Oh! thats all settled.   (whispers* Mrs Humbug)

Fanny) And how is it determined?

Daphne) I'll tell you.   (whispers Fanny)

Mrs Hum:) And is he to?. . . .

Daphne) I'll tell you all I know of the matter.   (whispers Mrs
Humbug & Fanny)

Fanny) Well! now I know every thing about it, I'll go away.

Mrs Hum: ⎫
Daphne   ⎬ And so will I.

(Exeunt)

Scene the 3ᵈ

The Curtain rises and discovers Sir Edward Spangle
reclined in an elegant Attitude* on a Sofa, fast asleep.

Enter Colonel Elliott.

Colonel) My Daughter is not here I see . . . there lies Sir Edward . . .
Shall I tell him the secret? . . . No, he'll certainly blab it . . . But he
is asleep and wont hear me . . . So I'll e'en venture.
(Goes up to Sir Edward, whispers him, & Exit)

End of the 1ˢᵗ Act.

Finis

To Edward Austen Esqre*

The following unfinished Novel
is respectfully inscribed
by
His obedient Hum.^{ble} Servt

The Author

The Three Sisters

a novel.

═══════════

Letter 1st

Miss Stanhope to Mrs——

My dear Fanny

I am the happiest creature in the World, for I have just received an offer of marriage from Mr Watts. It is the first I have ever had & I hardly know how to value it enough. How I will triumph over the Duttons! I do not intend to accept it, at least I beleive not, but as I am not quite certain I gave him an equivocal answer & left him. And now my dear Fanny I want your Advice whether I should accept his offer or not, but that you may be able to judge of his merits & the situation of affairs I will give you an account of them. He is quite an old Man, about two & thirty,* very plain *so* plain that I cannot bear to look at him. He is extremely disagreable & I hate him more than any body else in the world. He has a large fortune & will make great Settlements on me; but then he is very healthy.* In short I do not know what to do. If I refuse him he as good as told me that he should offer himself to Sophia & if *she* refused him to Georgiana, & I could not bear to have either of them married before me. If I accept him I know I shall be miserable all the rest of my Life, for he is very ill tempered & peevish extremely jealous, & so stingy* that there is no living in the house with him. He told me he should mention the affair to Mama, but I insisted upon it that he did not for very likely she would make me marry him whether I would or no; however probably he *has* before now, for he never does anything he is desired to do. I believe I shall have him. It will be such a triumph to be married before Sophy, Georgiana & the Duttons; And he promised to have a new Carriage on the occasion, but we almost quarrelled about the colour, for I insisted upon its being blue spotted with silver, & he declared it should be a plain Chocolate;* & to provoke me more said it should be just as low as his old one.* I wont have him I declare. He said he should come again tomorrow & take my final answer, so I beleive I must get him while I can. I know the Duttons will envy me & I shall be able to chaprone* Sophy & Georgiana to all the Winter Balls.* But then what will be the use of that when very likely he wont let me go myself, for I know he hates dancing & what he hates himself he has no idea of any other person's liking; & besides he talks a great deal of Women's always staying at home & such stuff. I beleive I shant have him; I would refuse him at once if I were certain that neither of my Sisters would accept him, & that if they did not, he would not offer to the Duttons. I cannot run such a risk, so, if he will promise to have the Carriage ordered as I like, I will have him, if not he may ride in it by himself for me. I hope you like my determination; I can think of nothing better;

> And am your ever affec.^{te}
>
> Mary Stanhope*

From the Same to the Same

Dear Fanny

I had but just sealed my last letter to you when my Mother came up & told me she wanted to speak to me on a very particular subject.

'Ah! I know what you mean; (said I) That old fool Mr Watts has told you all about it, tho' I bid him not. However you shant force me to have him if I dont like it.'

'I am not going to force you Child, but only want to know what your resolution is with regard to his Proposals, & to insist upon your making up your mind one way or t'other, that if *you* dont accept him *Sophy* may.'

'Indeed (replied I hastily) Sophy need not trouble herself for I shall certainly marry him myself.'

'If that is your resolution (said my Mother) why should you be afraid of my forcing your inclinations?'

'Why, because I have not settled whether I shall have him or not.'

'You are the strangest Girl in the World Mary. What you say one moment, you unsay the next. Do tell me once for all, whether you intend to marry Mr Watts or not?'

'Law* Mama how can I tell you what I dont know myself?'

'Then I desire you will know, & quickly too, for Mr Watts says he wont be kept in suspense.'

'That depends upon me.'

'No it does not, for if you do not give him your final answer tomorrow when he drinks Tea* with us, he intends to pay his Addresses to Sophy.'

'Then I shall tell all the World that he behaved very ill to me.'

'What good will that do? Mr Watts has been too long abused by all the World to mind it now.'

'I wish I had a Father or a Brother because then they should fight him.'*

'They would be cunning if they did, for Mr Watts would run away first; & therefore you must & shall resolve either to accept or refuse him before tomorrow evening.'

'But why if I don't have him, must he offer to my Sisters?'

'Why! Because he wishes to be allied to the Family & because they are as pretty as you are.'

'But will Sophy marry him Mama if he offers to her?'

'Most likely. Why should not she? If however she does not choose it, then Georgiana must, for I am determined not to let such an opportunity escape of settling one of my Daughters so advantageously. So, make the most of your time; I leave you to settle the Matter with yourself.' And then she went away. The only thing I can think of my dear Fanny is to ask Sophy & Georgiana whether they would have him were he to make proposals to them, & if they say they would not I am resolved to refuse him too, for I hate him more than you can imagine. As for the Duttons if he marries one of *them* I shall still have the triumph of having refused him first. So, adeiu my dear Freind—

Y^rs ever M. S.

Miss Georgiana Stanhope to Miss XXX*

My dear Anne   Wednesday

Sophy & I have just been practising a little deceit on our eldest Sister, to which we are not perfectly reconciled, & yet the circumstances were such that if any thing will excuse it, they must. Our neighbour Mr Watts has made proposals to Mary; Proposals which she knew not how to receive, for tho' she has a particular Dislike to him (in which she is not singular) yet she would willingly marry him sooner than risk his offering to Sophy or me which in case of a refusal from herself, he told her he should do, for you must know that the poor Girl considers our marrying before her as one of the greatest misfortunes that can possibly befall her, & to prevent it would willingly ensure herself everlasting Misery by a Marriage with Mr Watts. An hour ago she came to us to sound our inclinations respecting the affair which were to determine hers. A little before she came my Mother had given us an account of it, telling us that she certainly would not let him go farther than our own family for a Wife. 'And therefore (said she) If Mary wont have him Sophy must, & if Sophy wont Georgiana *shall*.' Poor Georgiana!—We neither of us attempted to alter my Mother's resolution, which I am sorry to say is generally more strictly kept than rationally formed. As soon as she was gone however I broke silence to assure Sophy that if Mary should refuse Mr Watts I should not expect her to sacrifice *her* happiness by becoming his Wife from a motive of Generosity to me, which I was afraid her Good nature and Sisterly affection might induce her to do.

'Let us flatter ourselves (replied She) that Mary will not refuse him. Yet how can I hope that my Sister may accept a Man who cannot make her happy.'

'*He* cannot it is true—but his Fortune his Name, his House, his Carriage will and I have no doubt but that Mary will marry him; indeed why should she not? He is not more than two & thirty; a very proper age for a Man to marry at; He is rather plain to be sure, but then what is Beauty in a Man; if he has but a genteel figure & a sensible looking Face it is quite sufficient.'

'This is all very true Georgiana but Mr Watts's figure is unfortunately extremely vulgar & his Countenance is very heavy.'

'And then as to his temper; it has been reckoned bad, but may not the World be deceived in their Judgement of it. There is an open Frankness in his Disposition which becomes a Man; They say he is stingy; We'll call that Prudence. They say he is suspicious. *That* proceeds from a warmth of Heart always excusable in Youth, & inshort I see no reason why he should not make a very good Husband, or why Mary should not be very happy with him.'

Sophy laughed; I continued,

'However whether Mary accepts him or not I am resolved. My determination is made. I never would marry Mr Watts were Beggary the only alternative. So deficient in every respect! Hideous in his person and without one good Quality to make amends for it. His fortune to be sure is good. Yet not so very large! Three thousand a year.* What is three thousand a year? It is but six times as much as my Mother's income. It will not tempt me.'

'Yet it will be a noble fortune for Mary' said Sophy laughing again.

'For Mary! Yes indeed it will give *me* pleasure to see *her* in such affluence.'

Thus I ran on to the great Entertainment of my Sister, till Mary came into the room to appearance in great agitation. She sate down. We made room for her at the fire. She seemed at a loss how to begin & at last said in some confusion

'Pray Sophy have you any mind to be married?'

'To be married! None in the least. But why do you ask me? Are you acquainted with any one who means to make me proposals?'

'I—no, how should I? But mayn't I ask a common question?'

'Not a very *common* one Mary surely.' (said I). She paused & after some moments silence went on—

'How should you like to marry Mr Watts Sophy?'

I winked at Sophy & replied for her. 'Who is there but must rejoice to marry a man of three thousand a year?'

'Very true (she replied) That's very true. So you would have him if he would offer, Georgiana. & would *you* Sophy?'

Sophy did not like the idea of telling a lie & deceiving her Sister; she prevented the first & saved half her conscience by equivocation.

'I should certainly act just as Georgiana would do.'

'Well then said Mary with triumph in her Eyes, *I* have had an offer from Mr Watts.' We were of course very much surprised; 'Oh! do not accept him said I, and then perhaps he may have me.'

In short my scheme took & Mary is resolved to do *that* to prevent our supposed happiness which she would not have done to ensure it in reality. Yet after all my Heart cannot acquit me & Sophy is even more scrupulous. Quiet our Minds my dear Anne by writing & telling us you approve our conduct. Consider it well over. Mary will have real pleasure in being a married Woman, & able to chaprone us, which she certainly shall do, for I think myself bound to Contribute as much as possible to her happiness in a State I have made her choose. They will probably have a new Carriage, which will be paradise to her, & if we can prevail on Mr W. to set up his Phaeton she will be too happy. These things however would be no consolation to Sophy or me for domestic Misery. Remember all this & do not condemn us.

Friday.

————

Last night Mr Watts by appointment drank tea with us. As soon as his Carriage stopped at the Door, Mary went to the Window.

'Would you beleive it Sophy (said she) the old Fool wants to have his new Chaise just the colour of the old one, & hung as low too. But it shant—I *will* carry my point. And if he wont let it be as high as the Duttons, & blue spotted with Silver, I wont have him. Yes I will too. Here he comes. I know he'll be rude; I know he'll be illtempered & wont say one civil thing to me! nor behave at all like a Lover.' She then sate down & Mr Watts entered.

'Ladies your most obedient.'* We paid our Compliments & he seated himself.

'Fine Weather Ladies.' Then turning to Mary, 'Well Miss Stanhope I hope you have *at last* settled the Matter in your own mind; & will be so good as to let me know whether you will *condescend* to marry me or not.'

'I think Sir (said Mary) You might have asked in a genteeler way than that. I do not know whether I *shall* have you if you behave so odd.'

'Mary!' (said my Mother) 'Well Mama if he will be so cross. . . . .'

'Hush, hush, Mary, you shall not be rude to Mr Watts.'

'Pray Madam do not lay any restraint on Miss Stanhope by obliging her to be civil. If she does not choose to accept my hand, I can offer it else where, for as I am by no means guided by a particular preference to you above your Sisters it is equally the same to me which I marry of the three.' Was there ever such a Wretch! Sophy reddened with Anger, & I felt *so* spiteful!

'Well then (said Mary in a peevish Accent) I *will* have you if I *must*.'

'I should have thought Miss Stanhope that when such Settlements are offered as I have offered to you there can be no great violence done to the inclinations in accepting of them.'

Mary mumbled out something, which I who sate close to her could just distinguish to be 'What's the use of a great Jointure if Men live forever?' And then audibly 'Remember the pin money;* two hundred a year.'

'A hundred & seventy five Madam.'

'Two hundred indeed Sir' said my Mother.

'And Remember I am to have a new Carriage hung as high as the Duttons', & blue spotted with silver; and I shall expect a new Saddle horse,* a suit of fine lace,* and an infinite number of the most valuable Jewels. Diamonds such as never were seen! and Pearls, Rubies, Emeralds, and Beads out of number.* You must set up your Phaeton which must be cream coloured with a wreath of silver flowers round it, You must buy 4 of the finest Bays in the Kingdom & you must drive me in it every day. This is not all; You must entirely new furnish your House after my Taste, You must hire two more Footmen to attend me, two Women to wait on me, must always let me do just as I please and make a very good husband.'

Here she stopped, I beleive rather out of breath.

'This is all very reasonable Mr Watts for my Daughter to expect.'

'And it is very reasonable Mrs Stanhope that your daughter should be disappointed.' He was going on but Mary interrupted him

'You must build me an elegant Greenhouse* & stock it with plants. You must let me spend every Winter in Bath, every Spring in Town,* Every Summer in taking some Tour,* and every autumn at a Watering Place,* and if we are at home the rest of the year (Sophy & I laughed) You must do nothing but give Balls and Masquerades. You must build a room on purpose & a Theatre to act Plays in.* The first Play we have shall be *Which is the Man** and I will do Lady Bell Bloomer.'*

'And pray Miss Stanhope (said Mr Watts) What am I to expect from you in return for all this?'

'Expect? why you may expect to have me pleased.'

'It would be odd if I did not. Your expectations Madam are too high for me, & I must apply to Miss Sophy who perhaps may not have raised her's so much.'

'You are mistaken Sir in supposing so, (said Sophy) for tho' they may not be exactly in the same Line, yet my expectations are to the full as high as my Sister's; for I expect my Husband to be good tempered & Chearful; to consult my Happiness in all his actions, & to love me with Constancy & Sincerity.'

Mr Watts stared. 'These are very odd Ideas truly Young Lady. You had better discard them before you marry, or you will be obliged to do it afterwards.'

My Mother in the meantime was lecturing Mary who was sensible that she had gone too far, & when Mr Watts was just turning towards me in order I beleive to address me, she spoke to him in a voice half humble, half sulky.

'You are mistaken Mr Watts if you think I was in earnest when I said I expected so much. However I must have a new Chaise.'

'Yes Sir, you must allow that Mary has a right to expect that.'

'Mrs Stanhope, I *mean* & have always meant to have a new one on my Marriage. But it shall be the colour of my present one.'

'I think Mr Watts you should pay my Girl the compliment of consulting her Taste on such Matters.'

Mr Watts would not agree to this, & for some time insisted upon its being a Chocolate colour, while Mary was as eager for having it blue with silver Spots. At length however Sophy proposed that to please Mr W. it should be a dark brown & to please Mary it should be hung rather high & have a silver Border.* This was at length agreed to, tho' reluctantly on both sides, as each had intended to carry their point entire. We then proceeded to other Matters, & it was settled that they should be married as soon as the Writings* could be completed. Mary was very eager for a Special Licence & Mr Watts talked of Banns.* A common Licence* was at last agreed on. Mary is to have all the Family Jewels which are very inconsiderable I beleive & Mr W. promised to buy her a Saddle horse; but in return she is not to expect to go to Town or any other public place for these three Years. She is to have neither Greenhouse, Theatre or Phaeton; to be contented with one Maid without an additional Footman. It engrossed the whole Evening to settle these affairs; Mr W. supped with us & did not go till twelve. As soon as he was gone Mary exclaimed 'Thank Heaven! he's off at last; how I do hate him!' It was in vain that Mama represented to her the impropriety she was guilty of in disliking him who was to be her Husband, for she persisted in declaring her aversion to him & hoping she might never see him again. What a Wedding will this be! Adeiu my dear Anne – Y^r faithfully Sincere

Georgiana Stanhope

From the Same to the Same

Dear Anne   Saturday

Mary eager to have every one know of her approaching Wedding & more particularly desirous of triumphing as she called it over the

Duttons, desired us to walk with her this Morning to Stoneham. As we had nothing else to do we readily agreed, & had as pleasant a walk as we could have with Mary whose conversation entirely consisted in abusing the Man she is soon to marry & in longing for a blue Chaise spotted with Silver. When we reached the Duttons we found the two Girls in the dressing-room with a very handsome Young Man, who was of course introduced to us. He is the son of Sir Henry Brudenell of Leicestershire. Mr Brudenell is the handsomest Man I ever saw in my Life; we are all three very much pleased with him. Mary, who from the moment of our reaching the Dressing-room had been swelling with the knowledge of her own importance & with the Desire of making it known, could not remain long silent on the Subject after we were seated, & soon addressing herself to Kitty said,

'Dont you think it will be necessary to have all the Jewels new set?'

'Necessary for what?'

'For What! Why for my appearance.'*

'I beg your pardon but I really do not understand you. What Jewels do you speak of, and where is your appearance to be made?'

'At the next Ball to be sure after I am married.'

You may imagine their Surprise. They were at first incredulous, but on our joining in the Story they at last beleived it. 'And who is it to' was of course the first Question. Mary pretended Bashfulness, & answered in Confusion her Eyes cast down 'to Mr Watts'. This also required Confirmation from us, for that anyone who had the Beauty & fortune (tho' small yet a provision)* of Mary would willingly marry Mr Watts, could by them scarcely be credited. The subject being now fairly introduced and she found herself the object of every one's attention in company, she lost all her confusion & became perfectly unreserved & communicative.

'I wonder you should never have heard of it before for in general things of this Nature are very well known in the Neighbourhood.'

'I assure you said Jemima* I never had the least suspicion of such an affair. Has it been in agitation long?'

'Oh! yes, ever since Wednesday.'

They all smiled particularly Mr Brudenell.

'You must know Mr Watts is very much in love with me, so that it is quite a match of Affection on his side.'

'Not on his only, I suppose' said Kitty.

'Oh! when there is so much Love on one side there is no occasion for it on the other. However I do not much dislike him tho' he is very plain to be sure.'

Mr Brudenell stared, the Miss Duttons laughed & Sophy & I were heartily ashamed of our Sister. She went on.

'We are to have a new Postchaise and very likely may set up our Phaeton.'

This we knew to be false but the poor Girl was pleased at the idea of persuading the company that such a thing was to be & I would not deprive her of so harmless an Enjoyment. She continued.

'Mr Watts is to present me with the family Jewels which I fancy are very considerable.' I could not help whispering Sophy 'I fancy not'.

'These Jewels are what I suppose must be new set before they can be worn. I shall not wear them till the first Ball I go to after my Marriage. If Mrs Dutton should not go to it, I hope you will let me chaprone you; I shall certainly take Sophy & Georgiana.'

'You are very good (said Kitty) & since you are inclined to under-take the Care of young Ladies, I should advise you to prevail on Mrs Edgecumbe to let you chaprone her six Daughters which with your two Sisters and ourselves will make your Entrée* very respectable.'

Kitty made us all smile except Mary who did not understand her Meaning & coolly said that she should not like to chaprone so many.

Sophy & I now endeavoured to change the conversation but suc-ceeded only for a few Minutes, for Mary took care to bring back their attention to her & her approaching Wedding. I was sorry for my Sister's sake to see that Mr Brudenell seemed to take pleasure in listening to her account of it, & even encouraged her by his Questions & Remarks, for it was evident that his only Aim was to laugh at her. I am afraid he found her very ridiculous. He kept his Countenance extremely well, yet it was easy to see that it was with difficulty he kept it. At length however he seemed fatigued & Disgusted with her ridiculous Conversation, as he turned from her to us, & spoke but little to her for about half an hour before we left Stoneham. As soon as we were out of the House we all joined in praising the Person & Manners of Mr Brudenell.

We found Mr Watts at home.

'So, Miss Stanhope (said he) you see I am come a courting in a true Lover like Manner.'

'Well you need not have *told* me that. I knew why you came very well.'

Sophy & I then left the room, imagining of course that we must be in the way, if a Scene of Courtship were to begin. We were surprised at being followed almost immediately by Mary.

'And is your Courting so soon over?' said Sophy.

'Courting! (replied Mary) we have been quarrelling. Watts is such a Fool! I hope I shall never see him again.'

'I am afraid you will, (said I) as he dines here to day. But what has been your dispute?'

'Why only because I told him that I had seen a Man much handsomer than he was this Morning, he flew into a great Passion & called me a Vixen,* so I only stayed to tell him I thought him a Blackguard* & came away.'

'Short and sweet; (said Sophy.) but pray Mary how will this be made up?'

'He ought to ask my pardon; but if he did, I would not forgive him.'

'His Submission then would not be very useful.'

When we were dressed* we returned to the Parlour where Mama & Mr Watts were in close Conversation. It seems that he had been complaining to her of her Daughter's behaviour, & she had persuaded him to think no more of it. He therefore met Mary with all his accustomed Civility, & except one touch at the Phaeton and another at the Greenhouse, the Evening went off with great Harmony & Cordiality. Watts is going to Town to hasten the preparations for the Wedding.

I am your affec.^{te} Freind G. S.

[Detached peices]

My Dear Neice

Though you are at this period not many degrees removed from Infancy, Yet trusting that you will in time be older,* and that through the care of your excellent Parent* You will one day or another be able to read written hand, I dedicate to You the following Miscellanious Morsels, convinced that if you seriously attend to them, You will derive from them very important Instructions, with regard to your Conduct in Life.—If such my hopes should hereafter be realized, never shall I regret the Days and Nights that have been spent in composing these Treatises for your Benefit—.* I am my dear Neice

Your very Affectionate
Aunt.

June 2ᵈ   The Author

1793—

[A fragment—written to inculcate the practise of Virtue]*

A beautiful description* of the different effects of
Sensibility* on different Minds

═════════

I am but just returned from Melissa's* Bedside, & in my Life tho' it has been a pretty long one, & I have during the course of it been at many Bedsides, I never saw so affecting an object as she exhibits. She lies wrapped in a book muslin* bedgown, a chambray gauze shift,* & a french net nightcap.* Sir William is constantly at her bedside. The only repose he takes is on the Sopha in the Drawing room, where for five minutes every fortnight he remains in an imperfect Slumber, starting up every Moment & exclaiming 'Oh! Melissa, Ah! Melissa,' then sinking down again, raises his left arm and scratches his head. Poor Mrs Burnaby is beyond measure afflicted. She sighs every now and then, that is about once a week; while the melancholy Charles says every moment, 'Melissa how are you?' The lovely Sisters are much to be pitied. Julia is ever lamenting the situation of her friend, while lying behind her pillow & supporting her head—Maria more mild in her greif talks of going to Town next week, and Anna is always recurring to the pleasures we once enjoyed when Melissa was well.— I am usually at the fire cooking some little delicacy for the unhappy invalid—Perhaps hashing up the remains of an old Duck,* toasting some cheese* or making a Curry* which are the favourite dishes of our poor friend.—In these situations we were this morning surprized by receiving a visit from Dr Dowkins; 'I am come to see Melissa,' said he. 'How is She?' 'Very weak indeed,' said the fainting Melissa—'Very weak, replied the punning Doctor, aye indeed it is more than a very *week* since you have taken to your bed—How is your appetite?' 'Bad, very bad, said Julia.' 'That *is* very bad—replied he. Are her spirits good, Madam?' 'So poorly Sir that we are obliged to strengthen her with cordials* every Minute.'—'Well then she receives *Spirits* from your being with her. Does she sleep?' 'Scarcely ever—.' 'And Ever Scarcely I suppose when she does. Poor thing! Does she think of die-ing?' 'She has not strength to *think* at all.' 'Nay then she cannot think to have Strength.'—

The generous Curate*—

a moral Tale,* setting forth the
Advantages of being Generous and a Curate.

═══════════

In a part little known of the County of Warwick, a very worthy Clergyman* lately resided. The income of his living which amounted to about two hundred pound,* & the interest of his Wife's fortune which was nothing at all, was entirely sufficient for the Wants & Wishes of a Family who neither wanted or wished for anything beyond what their income afforded them. Mr Williams had been in posses-sion of his living above twenty Years, when this history commences, & his Marriage which had taken place soon after his presentation to it, had made him the father of six very fine Children. The eldest had been placed at the Royal Academy for Seamen at Portsmouth* when about thirteen years old, and from thence had been discharged on board of one of the Vessels of a small fleet destined for Newfoundland,* where his promising & amiable disposition had procured him many friends among the Natives, & from whence he regularly sent home a large Newfoundland Dog* every Month* to his family. The second,

who was also a Son had been adopted by a neighbouring Clergyman*
with the intention of educating him at his own expence, which would
have been a very desirable Circumstance had the Gentleman's fortune been equal to his generosity, but as he had nothing to support
himself and a very large family but a Curacy of fifty pound a year,*
Young Williams knew nothing more at the age of 18 than what a twopenny Dame's School* in the village could teach him. His Character
however was perfectly amiable though his genius* might be cramped,
and he was addicted to no vice, or ever guilty of any fault beyond what
his age and situation rendered perfectly excusable. He had indeed
sometimes been detected in flinging Stones at a Duck or putting
brickbats* into his Benefactor's bed; but these innocent efforts of wit
were considered by that good Man rather as the effects of a lively
imagination, than of anything bad in his Nature, and if any punishment were decreed for the offence it was in general no greater than
that the Culprit should pick up the Stones or take the brickbats
away.—

Finis

To Miss Austen,* the following Ode to Pity* is dedicated, from a thorough knowledge of her pitiful* Nature, by her obed^t hum^le Servt

The Author

Ode to Pity

1

Ever musing I delight to tread
   The Paths of honour* and the Myrtle* Grove
Whilst the pale Moon her beams doth shed
   On disappointed Love.
While Philomel* on airy hawthorn Bush
   Sings sweet & Melancholy, And the thrush
Converses with the Dove.

2

Gently brawling down the turnpike road,
   Sweetly noisy falls the Silent Stream*—
The Moon emerges from behind a Cloud
   And darts upon the Myrtle Grove her beam.
Ah! then what Lovely Scenes appear,
   The hut, the Cot, the Grot,* & Chapel queer,
And eke* the Abbey too a mouldering heap,*
   Conceal'd by aged pines* her head doth rear
And quite invisible doth take a peep.

End of the first volume.

June 3^d 1793*

VOLUME THE SECOND

Ex dono mei Patris*

CONTENTS*

To Madame La Comtesse De Feuillide*

This Novel is inscribed
by
Her obliged Humble Servant

The Author

Love and Freindship*

a novel
in a series of Letters.*

'Deceived in Freindship & Betrayed in Love'*

===

Letter the First

From Isabel to Laura*

How often, in answer to my repeated intreaties that you would give my Daughter a regular detail of the Misfortunes and Adventures of your Life,* have you said 'No, my freind never will I comply with your request till I may be no longer in Danger of again experiencing such dreadful ones.'

Surely that time is now at hand. You are this Day 55. If a woman may ever be said to be in safety from the determined Perseverance of disagreable Lovers and the cruel Persecutions of obstinate Fathers,* surely it must be at such a time of Life.

Isabel.

Letter 2^d

Laura to Isabel

Altho' I cannot agree with you in supposing that I shall never again be exposed to Misfortunes as unmerited as those I have already experienced, yet to avoid the imputation of Obstinacy or ill-nature, I will gratify the curiosity of your Daughter; and may the fortitude with which I have suffered the many afflictions of my past Life, prove to her a useful Lesson for the support of those which may befall her in her own.

Laura

Letter 3ᵈ

Laura to Marianne*

As the Daughter of my most intimate freind I think you entitled to that knowledge of my unhappy Story, which your Mother has so often solicited me to give you.

My Father was a native of Ireland & an inhabitant of Wales; my Mother was the natural Daughter of a Scotch Peer by an italian Opera-girl*— I was born in Spain & received my Education at a Convent in France.*

When I had reached my eighteenth Year I was recalled by my Parents to my paternal roof in Wales. Our mansion was situated in one of the most romantic* parts of the Vale of Uske.* Tho' my Charms are now considerably softened and somewhat impaired by the Misfortunes I have undergone, I was once beautiful. But lovely as I was the Graces of my Person were the least of my Perfections. Of every accomplishment accustomary to my sex, I was Mistress.——When in the Convent, my progress had always exceeded my instructions, my Acquirements had been wonderfull for my age, and I had shortly surpassed my Masters.*

In my Mind, every Virtue that could adorn it was centered; it was the Rendez-vous* of every good Quality & of every noble sentiment.

A sensibility too tremblingly alive* to every affliction of my Freinds, my Acquaintance and particularly to every affliction of my own, was my only fault, if a fault it could be called.

Alas! how altered now! Tho' indeed my own misfortunes do not make less impression on me than they ever did, yet now I never feel for those of an other.——My accomplishments too, begin to fade— I can neither sing so well nor Dance so gracefully as I once did—and I have entirely forgot the *Minuet Dela Cour*—

Adeiu.
Laura

Letter 4ᵗʰ

Laura to Marianne

Our neighbourhood was small, for it consisted only of your Mother. She may probably have already told you that being left by her Parents in indigent Circumstances she had retired into Wales on eoconomical motives.* There it was our freindship first commenced—. Isabel was then one and twenty—Tho' pleasing both in her Person and Manners (between ourselves) she never possessed the hundredth part of my Beauty or Accomplishments. Isabel had seen the World. She had passed 2 Years at one of the first Boarding-schools in London;* had spent a fortnight in Bath & had supped one night in Southampton.*

'Beware my Laura (she would often say) Beware of the insipid Vanities and idle Dissipations of the Metropolis* of England; Beware of the unmeaning Luxuries of Bath & of the Stinking fish of Southampton.'

'Alas! (exclaimed I) how am I to avoid those evils I shall never be exposed to? What probability is there of my ever tasting the Dissipations of London, the Luxuries of Bath, or the stinking Fish of Southampton? I who am doomed to waste my Days of Youth & Beauty in an humble Cottage in the Vale of Uske.'

Ah! little did I then think I was ordained so soon to quit that humble Cottage for the Deceitfull Pleasures of the World.

adeiu
Laura—

Letter 5th

Laura to Marianne

One Evening in December as my Father, my Mother and myself, were arranged in social converse round our Fireside, we were on a sudden, greatly astonished, by hearing a violent knocking on the outward Door of our rustic Cot.*

My Father started—'What noise is that,' (said he.) 'It sounds like a loud rapping at the Door'—(replied my Mother.) 'it does indeed.' (cried I.) 'I am of your opinion; (said my Father) it certainly does appear to proceed from some uncommon violence exerted against our unoffending Door.'

'Yes (exclaimed I) I cannot help thinking it must be somebody who knocks for admittance.'

'That is another point (replied he;) We must not pretend to determine on what motive the person may knock—tho' that some one *does* rap at the Door, I am partly convinced.'*

Here, a 2^d tremendous rap interrupted my Father in his speech and somewhat alarmed my Mother and me.

'Had we not better go and see who it is,? (said she) the Servants are out.' 'I think we had.' (replied I.) 'Certainly, (added my Father) by all means.' 'Shall we go now?' (said my Mother.) 'The sooner the better.' (answered he.) 'Oh! let no time be lost.' (cried I.)

A third more violent Rap than ever again assaulted our ears. 'I am certain there is somebody knocking at the Door.' (said my Mother.) 'I think there must,' (replied my Father) 'I fancy the Servants are returned; (said I) I think I hear Mary going to the Door.' 'I'm glad of it (cried my Father) for I long to know who it is.'*

I was right in my Conjecture; for Mary instantly entering the Room, informed us that a young Gentleman & his Servant were at the Door, who had lossed their way, were very cold and begged leave to warm themselves by our fire.

'Wont you admit them?' (said I) 'You have no objection, my Dear?' (said my Father.) 'None in the World.' (replied my Mother.)

Mary, without waiting for any further commands immediately left the room and quickly returned introducing the most beauteous and amiable Youth, I had ever beheld. The servant, She kept to herself.

My natural Sensibility had already been greatly affected by the sufferings of the unfortunate Stranger and no sooner did I first behold him, than I felt that on him the happiness or Misery of my future Life must depend.—

adeiu

Laura

Letter 6th

Laura to Marianne

The noble Youth informed us that his name was Lindsay—. for particular reasons however I shall conceal it under that of Talbot.* He told us that he was the son of an English Baronet,* that his Mother had been many years no more and that he had a Sister of the middle size. 'My Father (he continued) is a mean and mercenary wretch— it is only to such particular freinds as this Dear Party that I would thus betray his failings—. Your Virtues my amiable Polydore (addressing himself to my father) yours Dear Claudia* and yours my Charming Laura call on me to repose in you my Confidence.' We bowed. 'My Father, seduced by the false glare of Fortune and the Deluding Pomp of Title, insisted on my giving my hand to Lady Dorothea.* No never exclaimed I. Lady Dorothea is lovely and Engaging; I prefer no woman to her; but Know Sir, that I scorn to marry her in compliance with your Wishes. No! Never shall it be said that I obliged my Father.'*

We all admired the noble Manliness of his reply. He continued.

'Sir Edward was surprized; he had perhaps little expected to meet with so spirited an opposition to his will. "Where Edward in the name of wonder (said he) did you pick up this unmeaning Gibberish?* You have been studying Novels I suspect."* I scorned to answer: it would have been beneath my Dignity. I mounted my Horse and followed by my faithful William set forwards for my Aunts.'

'My Father's house is situated in Bedfordshire, my Aunt's in Middlesex,* and tho' I flatter myself with being a tolerable proficient in Geography, I know not how it happened, but I found myself entering this beautifull Vale which I find is in South Wales, when I had expected to have reached my Aunts.'

'After having wandered some time on the Banks of the Uske without knowing which way to go, I began to lament my cruel Destiny in the bitterest and most pathetic Manner. It was now perfectly Dark, not a single Star was there to direct my steps, and I know not what might have befallen me had I not at length discerned thro' the solemn Gloom that surrounded me a distant Light, which as I approached it, I discovered to be the chearfull Blaze of your fire—Impelled by the combination of Misfortunes under which I laboured, namely Fear, Cold and Hunger I hesitated not to ask admittance which at length I have gained; and now my Adorable Laura (continued he taking my Hand) when may I hope to receive that reward of all the painfull sufferings I have undergone during the course of my Attachment to you, to which I have ever aspired? Oh! when will you reward me with Yourself?'

'This instant, Dear and Amiable Edward.' (replied I.). We were immediately united by my Father, who tho' he had never taken orders had been bred to the Church.*

adeiu
Laura.

Letter 7th

Laura to Marianne

We remained but a few Days after our Marriage, in the Vale of Uske—. After taking an affecting Farewell of my Father, my Mother and my Isabel, I accompanied Edward to his Aunt's in Middlesex. Philippa received us both with every expression of affectionate Love. My arrival was indeed a most agreable surprize to her as she had not only been totally ignorant of my Marriage with her Nephew, but had never even had the slightest idea of there being such a person in the World.

Augusta, the sister of Edward was on a visit to her when we arrived. I found her exactly what her Brother had described her to be—of the middle size. She received me with equal surprize though not with equal Cordiality, as Philippa. There was a Disagreable Coldness and Forbidding Reserve in her reception of me which was equally Distressing and Unexpected. None of that interesting Sensibility or amiable Simpathy in her Manners and Address to me when we first met which should have Distinguished our introduction to each other—. Her Language was neither warm, nor affectionate, her expressions of regard were neither animated nor cordial; her arms were not opened to receive me to her Heart, tho' my own were extended to press her to mine.

A short Conversation between Augusta and her Brother, which I accidentally overheard encreased my Dislike to her, and convinced me that her Heart was no more formed for the soft ties of Love than for the endearing intercourse of Freindship.

'But do you think that my Father will ever be reconciled to this imprudent connection?' (said Augusta.)

'Augusta (replied the noble Youth) I thought you had a better opinion of me, than to imagine I would so abjectly degrade myself as to consider my Father's Concurrence in any of my Affairs, either of Consequence or concern to me—. Tell me Augusta tell me with sincerity; did you ever know me consult his inclinations or follow his Advice in the least trifling Particular since the age of fifteen?'

'Edward (replied she) you are surely too diffident in your own praise—. Since you were fifteen only!—My Dear Brother since you were five years old, I entirely acquit you of ever having willingly contributed to the Satisfaction of your Father. But still I am not without apprehensions of your being shortly obliged to degrade yourself in your own eyes by seeking a Support for your Wife in the Generosity of Sir Edward.'

'Never, never Augusta will I so demean myself. (said Edward). Support! What support will Laura want which she can receive from him?'

'Only those very insignificant ones of Victuals and Drink.' (answered she.)

'Victuals and Drink! (replied my Husband in a most nobly contemptuous Manner) and dost thou then imagine that there is no other support for an exalted Mind (such as is my Laura's) than the mean and indelicate employment of Eating and Drinking?'

'None that I know of, so efficacious.' (returned Augusta)

'And did you then never feel the pleasing Pangs of Love, Augusta? (replied my Edward). Does it appear impossible to your vile and corrupted Palate, to exist on Love? Can you not conceive the Luxury of living in every Distress that Poverty can inflict, with the object of your tenderest affection?'

'You are too ridiculous (said Augusta) to argue with;* perhaps however you may in time be convinced that . . .'

Here I was prevented from hearing the remainder of her Speech, by the appearance of a very Handsome young Woman, who was ushured into the Room at the Door of which I had been listening. On hearing her announced by the Name of 'Lady Dorothea', I instantly quitted my Post and followed her into the Parlour, for I well remembered that she was the Lady, proposed as a Wife for my Edward by the Cruel and Unrelenting Baronet.

Altho' Lady Dorothea's visit was nominally to Philippa and Augusta, yet I have some reason to imagine that (acquainted with the Marriage and arrival of Edward) to see me was a principal motive to it.

I soon perceived that tho' Lovely and Elegant in her Person and tho' Easy and Polite in her Address, she was of that inferior order of Beings with regard to Delicate Feeling, tender Sentiments, and refined Sensibility, of which Augusta was one.

She staid but half an hour and neither in the Course of her Visit, confided to me any of her Secret thoughts, nor requested me to confide in her, any of Mine. You will easily imagine therefore my Dear Marianne that I could not feel any ardent Affection or very sincere Attachment for Lady Dorothea.

Adeiu

Laura.

Letter 8th

Laura to Marianne, in continuation

Lady Dorothea had not left us long before another visitor as unexpected a one as her Ladyship, was announced. It was Sir Edward, who informed by Augusta of her Brother's marriage, came doubtless to reproach him for having dared to unite himself to me without his Knowledge. But Edward foreseeing his Design, approached him with heroic fortitude as soon as he entered the Room, and addressed him in the following Manner.

'Sir Edward, I know the motive of your Journey here—You come with the base Design of reproaching me for having entered into an indissoluble engagement with my Laura without your Consent—But Sir, I glory in the Act—. It is my greatest boast that I have incurred the Displeasure of my Father!'

So saying, he took my hand and whilst Sir Edward, Philippa, and Augusta were doubtless reflecting with Admiration on his undaunted Bravery, led me from the Parlour to his Father's Carriage which yet remained at the Door and in which we were instantly conveyed from the pursuit of Sir Edward.

The Postilions had at first received orders only to take the London road; as soon as we had sufficiently reflected However, we ordered them to Drive to M—. the seat of Edward's most particular freind, which was but a few miles distant.

At M—. we arrived in a few hours; and on sending in our names were immediately admitted to Sophia,* the Wife of Edward's freind. After having been deprived during the course of 3 weeks of a real freind (for such I term your Mother) imagine my transports at beholding one, most truly worthy of the Name. Sophia was rather above the middle size; most elegantly formed. A soft Languor spread over her lovely features, but increased their Beauty—. It was the Charectarestic of her Mind—. She was all Sensibility and Feeling. We flew into each others arms & after having exchanged vows of mutual Freindship for the rest of our Lives, instantly unfolded to each other the most inward secrets of our Hearts—. We were interrupted in this Delightfull Employment by the entrance of Augustus, (Edward's freind) who was just returned from a solitary ramble.

Never did I see such an affecting Scene as was the meeting of Edward & Augustus.

'My Life! my Soul!' (exclaimed the former) 'My Adorable Angel!' (replied the latter) as they flew into each other's arms.—It was too pathetic* for the feelings of Sophia and myself—We fainted Alternately on a Sofa.*

adeiu
Laura.

Letter the 9th

From the Same to the Same

Towards the close of the Day we received the following Letter from Philippa.

'Sir Edward is greatly incensed by your abrupt departure; he has taken back Augusta with him to Bedfordshire. Much as I wish to enjoy again your charming Society, I cannot determine to snatch you from that, of such dear & deserving Freinds—When your Visit to them is terminated, I trust you will return to the arms of your'

'Philippa'

We returned a suitable answer to this affectionate Note & after thanking her for her kind invitation assured her that we would certainly avail ourselves of it, whenever we might have no other place to go to. Tho' certainly nothing could to any reasonable Being, have appeared more satisfactory, than so gratefull a reply to her invitation, yet I know not how it was, but she was certainly capricious enough to be displeased with our behaviour and in a few weeks after, either to revenge our Conduct, or releive her own solitude, married a young and illiterate* Fortune-hunter. This imprudent Step (tho' we were sensible that it would probably deprive us of that fortune which Philippa had ever taught us to expect) could not on our own accounts, excite from our exalted Minds a single sigh; yet fearfull lest it might prove a source of endless misery to the deluded Bride, our trembling Sensibility was greatly affected when we were first informed of the Event. The affectionate Entreaties of Augustus and Sophia that we would for ever consider their House as our Home, easily prevailed on us to determine

never more to leave them—. In the Society of my Edward & this
Amiable Pair, I passed the happiest moments of my Life; Our time
was most delightfully spent, in mutual Protestations of Freindship, &
in vows of unalterable Love, in which we were secure from being
interrupted, by intruding & disagreable Visitors, as Augustus &
Sophia had on their first Entrance in the Neighbourhood, taken due
care to inform the surrounding Families, that as their Happiness centered wholly in themselves, they wished for no other society. But alas!
my Dear Marianne such Happiness as I then enjoyed was too perfect
to be lasting. A most severe & unexpected Blow at once destroyed
every Sensation of Pleasure. Convinced as you must be from what
I have already told you concerning Augustus & Sophia, that there
never were a happier Couple, I need not I imagine inform you that
their union had been contrary to the inclinations of their Cruel &
Mercenery Parents; who had vainly endeavoured with obstinate
Perseverance to force them into a Marriage with those whom they had
ever abhorred; but with an Heroic Fortitude worthy to be related &
Admired, they had both, constantly refused to submit to such despotic
Power.

After having so nobly disentangled themselves from the Shackles
of Parental Authority, by a Clandestine Marriage,* they were determined never to forfeit the good opinion they had gained in the World,
in so doing, by accepting any proposals of reconciliation that might be
offered them by their Fathers—to this farther tryal of their noble
independance however they never were exposed.

They had been married but a few months when our visit to them
commenced during which time they had been amply supported by
a considerable sum of Money which Augustus had gracefully purloined from his Unworthy father's Escritoire,* a few days before his
union with Sophia.

By our arrival their Expences were considerably encreased tho' their
means for supplying them were then nearly exhausted. But they, Exalted
Creatures!, scorned to reflect a moment on their pecuniary Distresses &
would have blushed at the idea of paying their Debts.*— Alas! what
was their Reward for such disinterested Behaviour! The beautifull
Augustus was arrested and we were all undone. Such perfidious
Treachery in the merciless perpetrators of the Deed will shock your
gentle nature Dearest Marianne as much as it then affected the
Delicate Sensibility of Edward, Sophia, your Laura, & of Augustus

himself. To compleat such unparalelled Barbarity we were informed
that an Execution in the House* would shortly take place. Ah! what
could we do but what we did! We sighed & fainted on the Sofa.

Adeiu
Laura

Letter 10th

Laura in continuation

When we were some what recovered from the overpowering Effusions
of our Greif, Edward desired that we would consider what was the
most prudent step to be taken in our unhappy situation while he
repaired to his imprisoned freind to lament over his misfortunes. We
promised that we would, & he set forwards on his Journey to Town.
During his Absence we faithfully complied with his Desire & after the
most mature Deliberation, at length agreed that the best thing we
could do was to leave the House; of which we every moment expected
the Officers of Justice* to take possession. We waited therefore with
the greatest impatience, for the return of Edward in order to impart
to him the result of our Deliberations—. But no Edward appeared—.
In vain did we count the tedious Moments of his Absence—in vain
did we weep—in vain even did we sigh—no Edward returned—.
This was too cruel, too unexpected a Blow to our Gentle Sensibility.—.
we could not support it—we could only faint—. At length collecting
all the Resolution I was Mistress of, I arose & after packing up some
necessary Apparel for Sophia & myself, I dragged her to a Carriage
I had ordered & we instantly set out for London. As the Habitation of
Augustus was within twelve miles of Town, it was not long e'er we
arrived there, & no sooner had we entered Holbourn* than letting
down one of the Front Glasses* I enquired of every decent-looking
Person that we passed 'If they had seen my Edward'?

But as we drove too rapidly to allow them to answer my repeated
Enquiries, I gained little, or indeed, no information concerning him.
'Where am I to Drive?' said the Postilion. 'To Newgate* Gentle Youth
(replied I), to see Augustus.' 'Oh! no, no, (exclaimed Sophia) I cannot
go to Newgate; I shall not be able to support the sight of my Augustus
in so cruel a confinement—my feelings are sufficiently shocked by the
recital, of his Distress, but to behold it will overpower my Sensibility.'

As I perfectly agreed with her in the Justice of her Sentiments the Postilion was instantly directed to return into the Country. You may perhaps have been somewhat surprized my Dearest Marianne, that in the Distress I then endured, destitute of any Support, & unprovided with any Habitation, I should never once have remembered my Father & Mother or my paternal Cottage in the Vale of Uske. To account for this seeming forgetfullness I must inform you of a trifling Circumstance concerning them which I have as yet never mentioned—. The death of my Parents a few weeks after my Departure, is the circumstance I allude to. By their decease I became the lawfull Inheritress of their House & Fortune. But alas! the House had never been their own & their Fortune had only been an Annuity* on their own Lives.—Such is the Depravity of the World! To your Mother I should have returned with Pleasure, should have been happy to have introduced to her, my Charming Sophia & should with Chearfullness have passed the remainder of my Life in their dear Society in the Vale of Uske, had not one obstacle to the execution of so agreable a Scheme, intervened; which was the Marriage & Removal of your Mother to a Distant part of Ireland.

Adeiu.

Laura.

Letter 11th

Laura in continuation

'I have a Relation in Scotland (said Sophia to me as we left London) who I am certain would not hesitate in receiving me.' 'Shall I order the Boy to drive there?' said I—but instantly recollecting myself, exclaimed, 'Alas I fear it will be too long a Journey for the Horses.' Unwilling however to act only from my own inadequate Knowledge of the Strength & Abilities of Horses, I consulted the Postilion, who was entirely of my Opinion concerning the Affair. We therefore determined to change Horses at the next Town & to travel Post* the remainder of the Journey.—. When we arrived at the last Inn we were to stop at, which was but a few miles from the House of Sophia's Relation, unwilling to intrude our Society on him unexpected & unthought of, we wrote a very elegant & well-penned Note to him containing an Account of our Destitute & melancholy Situation, and of our intention to spend some months with him in Scotland. As soon as we had dispatched this Letter, we immediately prepared to follow it in person & were stepping into the Carriage for that Purpose when our Attention was attracted by the Entrance of a coroneted Coach & 4* into the Inn-yard. A Gentleman considerably advanced in years, descended from it—. At his first Appearance my Sensibility was wonderfully affected & e'er I had gazed at him a 2ᵈ time, an instinctive Sympathy whispered to my Heart, that he was my Grandfather.

Convinced that I could not be mistaken in my conjecture I instantly sprang from the Carriage I had just entered, & following the Venerable Stranger into the Room he had been shewn to, I threw myself on my knees before him & besought him to acknowledge me as his Grand-Child.—He started, & after having attentively examined my features, raised me from the Ground & throwing his Grand-fatherly arms around my Neck, exclaimed, 'Acknowledge thee! Yes dear resemblance of my Laurina & my Laurina's Daughter, sweet image of my Claudia & my Claudia's Mother, I do acknowledge thee as the Daughter of the one & the Grandaughter of the other.' While he was thus tenderly embracing me, Sophia astonished at my precipitate Departure, entered the Room in search of me—. No sooner had she caught the eye of the venerable Peer, than he exclaimed with every mark of Astonishment— 'Another Grandaughter! Yes, yes, I see you are the Daughter of my Laurina's eldest Girl; Your resemblance to the beauteous Matilda sufficiently proclaims it.' 'Oh! replied Sophia, when I first beheld you the instinct of Nature whispered me that we were in some degree related—But whether Grandfathers, or Grandmothers, I could not pretend to determine.' He folded her in his arms, and whilst they were tenderly embracing, the Door of the Apartment opened and a most beautifull Young Man appeared. On perceiving him Lord St. Clair started & retreating back a few paces, with uplifted Hands, said, 'Another Grand-child! What an unexpected Happiness is this! to discover in the space of 3 minutes, as many of my Descendants! This, I am certain is Philander the son of my Laurina's 3ᵈ Girl the amiable Bertha; there wants now but the presence of Gustavus to compleat the Union of my Laurina's Grand-Children.'

'And here he is; (said a Gracefull Youth who that instant entered the room) here is the Gustavus you desire to see. I am the son of Agatha your Laurina's 4ᵗʰ & Youngest Daughter.' 'I see you are indeed; replied Lord St. Clair—But tell me (continued he looking fearfully towards

the Door) tell me, have I any other Grand-Children in the House?'*
'None my Lord.' 'Then I will provide for you all without further
delay—Here are 4 Banknotes of 50£ each—Take them & remember
I have done the Duty of a Grandfather—.' He instantly left the Room &
immediately afterwards the House.

Adeiu.

Laura.

Letter the 12th

Laura in continuation

You may imagine how greatly we were surprized by the sudden
departure of Lord St. Clair—. 'Ignoble Grand-sire!' exclaimed Sophia.
'Unworthy Grand-father!' said I, & instantly fainted in each other's
arms. How long we remained in this situation I know not; but when
we recovered we found ourselves alone, without either Gustavus,
Philander, or the Bank-notes. As we were deploring our unhappy fate,
the Door of the Apartment opened & 'Macdonald' was announced.
He was Sophia's cousin. The haste with which he came to our releif
so soon after the receipt of our Note, spoke so greatly in his favour
that I hesitated not to pronounce him at first sight, a tender & simpathetic Freind. Alas! he little deserved the name—for though he told
us that he was much concerned at our Misfortunes, yet by his own
account it appeared that the perusal of them, had neither drawn from
him a single sigh, nor induced him to bestow one curse on our vindic-
tive Stars.—. He told Sophia that his Daughter depended on her
returning with him to Macdonald-Hall; & that as his Cousin's freind
he should be happy to see me there also. To Macdonald-Hall, therefore we went, and were received with great kindness by Janetta* the
daughter of Macdonald, & the Mistress of the Mansion. Janetta was
then only fifteen; naturally well disposed, endowed with a susceptible
Heart, and a simpathetic Disposition, she might, had these amiable
Qualities been properly encouraged, have been an ornament to human
Nature; but unfortunately her Father possessed not a soul sufficiently
exalted to admire so promising a Disposition, and had endeavoured
by every means in his power to prevent its encreasing with her Years.
He had actually so far extinguished the natural noble Sensibility of
her Heart, as to prevail on her to accept an offer from a young Man of

his Recommendation. They were to be married in a few Months, and Graham, was in the House when we arrived. *We* soon saw through his Character—. He was just such a Man as one might have expected to be the choice of Macdonald. They said he was Sensible, well-informed, and Agreable; we did not pretend to Judge of such trifles, but as we were convinced he had no soul, that he had never read the Sorrows of Werter,* & that his Hair bore not the slightest resemblance to auburn,* we were certain that Janetta could feel no affection for him, or at least that she ought to feel none. The very circumstance of his being her father's choice too, was so much in his disfavour, that had he been deserving her, in every other respect yet *that* of itself ought to have been a sufficient reason in the Eyes of Janetta for rejecting him. These considerations we were determined to represent to her in their proper light & doubted not of meeting with the desired Success from one naturally so well disposed, whose errors in the affair had only arisen from a want of proper confidence in her own opinion, & a suitable contempt of her father's. We found her indeed all that our warmest wishes could have hoped for; we had no difficulty to convince her that it was impossible she could love Graham, or that it was her Duty to disobey her Father; the only thing at which she rather seemed to hesitate was our assertion that she must be attached to some other Person. For some time, she persevered in declaring that she knew no other young Man for whom she had the smallest Affection; but upon explaining the impossibility of such a thing she said that she beleived she *did like* Captain M'Kenzie better than any one she knew besides. This confession satisfied us and after having enumerated the good Qualities of M'Kenzie & assured her that she was violently in love with him, we desired to know whether he had ever in any wise declared his Affection to her.

'So far from having ever declared it, I have no reason to imagine that he has ever felt any for me.' said Janetta. 'That he certainly adores you (replied Sophia) there can be no doubt—. The Attachment must be reciprocal—. Did he never gaze on you with Admiration—tenderly press your hand—drop an involantary tear—& leave the room abruptly?' 'Never (replied She) that I remember—he has always left the room indeed when his visit has been ended, but has never gone away particularly abruptly or without making a bow.'

'Indeed my Love (said I) you must be mistaken—. for it is absolutely impossible that he should ever have left you but with Confusion,

Despair, & Precipitation—. Consider but for a moment Janetta, & you must be convinced how absurd it is to suppose that he could ever make a Bow, or behave like any other Person.' Having settled this Point to our satisfaction, the next we took into consideration was, to determine in what manner we should inform M'Kenzie of the favourable Opinion Janetta entertained of him.—. We at length agreed to acquaint him with it by an anonymous Letter which Sophia drew up in the following Manner.

'Oh! happy Lover of the beautifull Janetta, oh! enviable Possessor of *her* Heart whose hand is destined to another, why do you thus delay a confession of your Attachment to the amiable Object of it? Oh! consider that a few weeks will at once put an end to every flattering Hope that you may now entertain, by uniting the unfortunate Victim of her father's Cruelty to the execrable & detested Graham.'

'Alas! why do you thus so cruelly connive at the projected Misery of her & of yourself by delaying to communicate that scheme which has doubtless long possessed your imagination? A secret Union will at once secure the felicity of both.'

The amiable M'Kenzie, whose modesty as he afterwards assured us had been the only reason of his having so long concealed the violence of his affection for Janetta, on receiving this Billet* flew on the wings of Love to Macdonald-Hall, and so powerfully pleaded his Attachment to her who inspired it, that after a few more private interveiws, Sophia & I experienced the Satisfaction of seeing them depart for Gretna-Green,* which they chose for the celebration of their Nuptials, in preference to any other place although it was at a considerable distance from Macdonald-Hall.

Adeiu—

Laura—

Letter the 13th

Laura in Continuation

They had been gone nearly a couple of Hours, before either Macdonald or Graham had entertained any suspicion of the affair—. And they might not even then have suspected it, but for the following little Accident. Sophia happening one Day to open a private Drawer in Macdonald's Library with one of her own keys, discovered that it was the Place where he kept his Papers of consequence & amongst them some bank-notes of considerable amount. This discovery she imparted to me; and having agreed together that it would be a proper treatment of so vile a Wretch as Macdonald to deprive him of Money, perhaps dishonestly gained, it was determined that the next time we should either of us happen to go that way, we would take one or more of the Bank notes from the drawer. This well-meant Plan we had often successfully put in Execution; but alas! on the very day of Janetta's Escape, as Sophia was majestically removing the 5th Bank-note from the Drawer to her own purse, she was suddenly most impertinently interrupted in her employment by the entrance of Macdonald himself, in a most abrupt & precipitate Manner. Sophia (who though naturally all winning sweetness could when occasions demanded it call forth the Dignity of her Sex) instantly put on a most forbiding look, & darting an angry frown on the undaunted Culprit, demanded in a haughty tone of voice 'Wherefore her retirement was thus insolently broken in on?' The unblushing Macdonald, without even endeavouring to exculpate himself from the crime he was charged with, meanly endeavoured to reproach Sophia with ignobly defrauding him of his Money.—. The dignity of Sophia was wounded; 'Wretch (exclaimed she, hastily replacing the Bank-note in the Drawer) how darest thou to accuse me of an Act, of which the bare idea makes me blush?' The base wretch was still unconvinced & continued to upbraid the justly-offended Sophia in such opprobious Language, that at length he so greatly provoked the gentle sweetness of her Nature, as to induce her to revenge herself on him by informing him of Janetta's Elopement, and of the active Part we had both taken in the Affair. At this period of their Quarrel I entered the Library and was as you may imagine equally offended as Sophia at the ill-grounded Accusations of the malevolent and contemptible Macdonald. 'Base Miscreant! (cried I) how canst thou thus undauntedly endeavour to sully the spotless reputation of such bright Excellence? Why dost thou not suspect *my* innocence as soon?'

'Be satisfied Madam (replied he) I *do* suspect it, & therefore must desire that you will both leave this House in less than half an hour.'

'We shall go willingly; (answered Sophia) our hearts have long detested thee, & nothing but our freindship for thy Daughter could have induced us to remain so long beneath thy roof.'

'Your Freindship for my Daughter has indeed been most powerfully exerted by throwing her into the arms of an unprincipled Fortune-hunter.' (replied he)

'Yes, (exclaimed I) amidst every misfortune, it will afford us some consolation to reflect that by this one act of Freindship to Janetta, we have amply discharged every obligation that we have received from her father.'

'It must indeed be a most gratefull reflection, to your exalted minds.' (said he.)

As soon as we had packed up our wardrobe & valuables, we left Macdonald Hall, & after having walked about a mile & a half we sate down by the side of a clear limpid stream* to refresh our exhausted limbs. The place was suited to meditation—. A Grove of full-grown Elms sheltered us from the East—. A Bed of full-grown Nettles from the West—. Before us ran the murmuring brook & behind us ran the turn-pike road.* We were in a mood for contemplation & in a Disposition to enjoy so beautifull a spot. A mutual Silence which had for some time reigned between us, was at length broke by my exclaiming— 'What a lovely Scene! Alas why are not Edward & Augustus here to enjoy its Beauties with us?'

'Ah! my beloved Laura (cried Sophia) for pity's sake forbear recalling to my remembrance the unhappy situation of my imprisoned Husband. Alas, what would I not give to learn the fate of my Augustus!—to know if he is still in Newgate, or if he is yet hung.—But never shall I be able so far to conquer my tender sensibility as to enquire after him. Oh! do not I beseech you ever let me again hear you repeat his beloved Name—. It affects me too deeply—. I cannot bear to hear him mentioned—it wounds my feelings.'

'Excuse me my Sophia for having thus unwillingly offended you—' replied I—and then changing the conversation, desired her to admire the Noble Grandeur of the Elms which Sheltered us from the Eastern Zephyr.* 'Alas! my Laura (returned she) avoid so melancholy a subject, I intreat you—Do not again wound my Sensibility by Observations on those elms—. They remind me of Augustus—. He was like them, tall, magestic—. he possessed that noble grandeur which you admire in them.'

I was silent, fearfull lest I might any more unwillingly distress her by fixing on any other subject of conversation which might again remind her of Augustus.

'Why do you not speak my Laura? (said she after a short pause)

I cannot support this silence—you must not leave me to my own reflections; they ever recur to Augustus.'

'What a beautifull Sky! (said I) How charmingly is the azure varied by those delicate streaks of white!'

'Oh! my Laura (replied she hastily withdrawing her Eyes from a momentary glance at the sky) do not thus distress me by calling my Attention to an object which so cruelly reminds me of my Augustus's blue sattin Waistcoat striped with white!* In pity to your unhappy freind avoid a subject so distressing.' What could I do? The feelings of Sophia were at that time so exquisite, & the tenderness she felt for Augustus so poignant that I had not the power to start any other topic, justly fearing that it might in some unforseen manner again awaken all her sensibility by directing her thoughts to her Husband.—Yet to be silent would be cruel; She had intreated me to talk.

From this Dilemma I was most fortunately releived by an accident truly apropos;* it was the lucky overturning of a Gentleman's Phaeton, on the road which ran murmuring behind us. It was a most fortunate Accident as it diverted the attention of Sophia from the melancholy reflections which she had been before indulging.

We instantly quitted our seats & ran to the rescue of those who but a few moments before had been in so elevated a situation as a fashionably high Phaeton,* but who were now laid low and sprawling in the Dust—. 'What an ample subject for reflection on the uncertain Enjoyments of this World, would not that Phaeton & the Life of Cardinal Wolsey* afford a thinking Mind!' said I to Sophia as we were hastening to the field of Action.

She had not time to answer me, for every thought was now engaged by the horrid Spectacle before us. Two Gentlemen most elegantly attired but weltering in their blood was what first struck our Eyes—we approached—they were Edward & Augustus—Yes dearest Marianne they were our Husbands. Sophia shreiked & fainted on the Ground— I screamed & instantly ran mad—. We remained thus mutually deprived of our Senses, some minutes, & on regaining them were deprived of them again—. For an Hour & a Quarter did we continue in this unfortunate Situation—Sophia fainting every moment & I running Mad as often—. At length a Groan from the hapless Edward (who alone retained any share of Life) restored us to ourselves—. Had we indeed before imagined that either of them lived, we should have been more sparing of our Greif—but as we had supposed when we first beheld them that they were no more, we knew that nothing could remain to be done but what we were about—. No sooner therefore did we hear my Edward's groan than postponing our Lamentations for the present, we hastily ran to the Dear Youth and kneeling on each side of him implored him not to die—. 'Laura (said He fixing his now languid Eyes on me) I fear I have been overturned.'

I was overjoyed to find him yet sensible*—.

'Oh! tell me Edward (said I) tell me I beseech you before you die, what has befallen you since that unhappy Day in which Augustus was arrested & we were separated—'

'I will' (said he) and instantly fetching a Deep sigh, Expired—. Sophia immediately sunk again into a swoon—. *My* Greif was more audible My Voice faltered, My Eyes assumed a vacant Stare, My face became as pale as Death, and my Senses were considerably impaired—.

'Talk not to me of Phaetons (said I, raving in a frantic, incoherent manner)—Give me a violin—. I'll play to him & sooth him in his melancholy Hours—Beware ye gentle Nymphs of Cupid's Thunderbolts, avoid the piercing Shafts of Jupiter*—Look at that Grove of Firs— I see a Leg of Mutton—They told me Edward was not Dead; but they deceived me—they took him for a Cucumber*—' Thus I continued wildly exclaiming on my Edward's Death—. For two Hours did I rave thus madly and should not then have left off, as I was not in the least fatigued, had not Sophia who was just recovered from her swoon, intreated me to consider that Night was now approaching and that the Damps began to fall. 'And whither shall we go (said I) to shelter us from either?' 'To that white Cottage.' (replied she pointing to a neat Building which rose up amidst the Grove of Elms & which I had not before observed—) I agreed & we instantly walked to it—we knocked at the door—it was opened by an old Woman; on being requested to afford us a Night's Lodging, she informed us that her House was but small, that she had only two Bed-rooms, but that However we should be wellcome to one of them. We were satisfied & followed the good Woman into the House where we were greatly cheered by the sight of a comfortable fire—. She was a Widow & had only one Daughter, who was then just Seventeen—One of the best of ages; but alas! she was very plain & her name was Bridget*. . . . Nothing therefore could be expected from her———she could not be supposed to possess either exalted Ideas, Delicate Feelings or refined

Sensibilities—She was nothing more than a mere good-tempered, civil & obliging Young Woman; as such we could scarcely dislike her—she was only an Object of Contempt—.

Adeiu

Laura—

Letter the 14th

Laura in continuation

Arm yourself my amiable Young Freind with all the philosophy you are Mistress of; summon up all the fortitude you possess, for Alas! in the perusal of the following Pages your sensibility will be most severely tried. Ah! what were the Misfortunes I had before experienced & which I have already related to you, to the one I am now going to inform you of. The Death of my Father my Mother, and my Husband though almost more than my gentle Nature could support, were trifles in comparison to the misfortune I am now proceeding to relate. The morning after our arrival at the Cottage, Sophia complained of a violent pain in her delicate limbs, accompanied with a disagreable Head-ake. She attributed it to a cold caught by her continual faintings in the open Air as the Dew was falling the Evening before. This I feared was but too probably the case; since how could it be otherwise accounted for that I should have escaped the same indisposition, but by supposing that the bodily Exertions I had undergone in my repeated fits of frenzy had so effectually circulated & warmed my Blood as to make me proof against the chilling Damps of Night, whereas, Sophia lying totally inactive on the Ground must have been exposed to all their Severity. I was most seriously alarmed by her illness which trifling as it may appear to you, a certain instinctive Sensibility whispered me, would in the End be fatal to her.

Alas! my fears were but too fully justified; she grew gradually worse—& I daily became more alarmed for her.—At length she was obliged to confine herself solely to the Bed allotted us by our worthy Landlady—. Her disorder turned to a galloping Consumption* & in a few Days carried her off. Amidst all my Lamentations for her (& violent you may suppose they were) I yet received some consolation in the reflection of my having paid every Attention to her, that could be offered, in her illness. I had wept over her every Day—had bathed her sweet face with my tears & had pressed her fair Hands continually in mine—. 'My beloved Laura (said she to me a few Hours before she died) take warning from my unhappy End & avoid the imprudent conduct which has occasioned it . . . Beware of fainting-fits. . . . Though at the time they may be refreshing & Agreable yet beleive me they will in the end, if too often repeated & at improper seasons, prove destructive to your Constitution . . . My fate will teach you this . . . I die a Martyr to my greif for the loss of Augustus . . . One fatal swoon has cost me my Life . . . Beware of swoons Dear Laura. . . . A frenzy fit is not one quarter so pernicious; it is an exercise to the Body & if not too violent, is I dare say conducive to Health in its consequences—Run mad as often as you chuse; but do not faint—'.

These were the last words she ever addressed to me . . . It was her dieing Advice to her afflicted Laura, who has ever most faithfully adhered to it.

After having attended my lamented freind to her Early Grave, I immediately (tho' late at night) left the detested Village in which she died, & near which had expired my Husband & Augustus. I had not walked many yards from it before I was overtaken by a Stage-Coach, in which I instantly took a place, determined to proceed in it to Edinburgh, where I hoped to find some kind some pitying Freind who would receive & comfort me in my Afflictions.

It was so dark when I entered the Coach that I could not distinguish the Number of my Fellow-travellers; I could only perceive that they were Many. Regardless however of any thing concerning them, I gave myself up to my own sad Reflections. A general Silence prevailed—A Silence, which was by nothing interrupted but by the loud & repeated Snores of one of the Party.

'What an illiterate villain must that Man be! (thought I to myself) What a total Want of delicate refinement must he have, who can thus shock our senses by such a brutal Noise! He must I am certain be capable of every bad Action! There is no crime too black for such a Character!' Thus reasoned I within myself, & doubtless such were the reflections of my fellow travellers.

At length, returning Day enabled me to behold the unprincipled Scoundrel who had so violently disturbed my feelings. It was Sir Edward the father of my Deceased Husband. By his side, sate Augusta, & on the same seat with me were your Mother & Lady Dorothea. Imagine my Surprize at finding myself thus seated amongst my old

Acquaintance. Great as was my astonishment, it was yet increased, when on looking out of Windows, I beheld the Husband of Philippa, with Philippa by his side, on the Coach-box,* & when on looking behind I beheld, Philander & Gustavus in the Basket.* 'Oh! Heavens, (exclaimed I) is it possible that I should so unexpectedly be sur-rounded by my nearest Relations and Connections?' These words rouzed the rest of the Party, and every eye was directed to the corner in which I sat. 'Oh! my Isabel (continued I throwing myself, across Lady Dorothea into her arms) receive once more to your Bosom the unfortunate Laura. Alas! when we last parted in the Vale of Usk, I was happy in being united to the best of Edwards; I had then a Father & a Mother, & had never known misfortunes—But now deprived of every freind but you——'

'What! (interrupted Augusta) is my Brother dead then? Tell us I intreat you what is become of him?'

'Yes, cold & insensible Nymph, (replied I) that luckless Swain your Brother, is no more, & you may now glory in being the Heiress of Sir Edward's fortune.'

Although I had always despised her from the Day I had overheard her conversation with my Edward, yet in civility I complied with hers & Sir Edward's intreaties that I would inform them of the whole mel-ancholy Affair. They were greatly shocked—Even the obdurate Heart of Sir Edward & the insensible one of Augusta, were touched with Sorrow, by the unhappy tale. At the request of your Mother I related to them every other misfortune which had befallen me since we parted. Of the imprisonment of Augustus & the Absence of Edward—of our arrival in Scotland—of our unexpected Meeting with our Grand-father & our cousins—of our visit to Macdonald-Hall—of the singular Service we there performed towards Janetta—of her Fathers ingrati-tude for it. . . . of his inhuman Behaviour, unaccountable suspicions, & barbarous treatment of us, in obliging us to leave the House. . . . of our Lamentations on the loss of Edward & Augustus & finally of the melancholy Death of my beloved Companion.

Pity & Surprise were strongly depictured in your Mother's Counte-nance, during the whole of my narration, but I am sorry to say, that to the eternal reproach of her Sensibility, the latter infinitely predomi-nated. Nay, faultless as my Conduct had certainly been during the whole Course of my late Misfortunes & Adventures, she pretended to find fault with my Behaviour in many of the situations in which I had been placed. As I was sensible myself, that I had always behaved in a manner which reflected Honour on my Feelings & Refinement, I paid little attention to what she said, & desired her to satisfy my Curiosity by informing me how she came there, instead of wounding my spotless reputation with unjustifiable Reproaches. As soon as she had complyed with my wishes in this particular & had given me an accurate detail of every thing that had befallen her since our separation (the particulars of which if you are not already acquainted with, your Mother will give you) I applied to Augusta for the same information respecting herself, Sir Edward & Lady Dorothea.

She told me that having a considerable taste for the Beauties of Nature, her curiosity to behold the delightful scenes it exhibited in that part of the World had been so much raised by Gilpin's Tour to the Highlands,* that she had prevailed on her Father to undertake a Tour to Scotland & had persuaded Lady Dorothea to accompany them. That they had arrived at Edinburgh a few Days before & from thence had made daily Excursions into the Country around in the Stage Coach* they were then in, from one of which Excursions they were at that time returning. My next enquiries were concerning Philippa & her Husband, the latter of whom I learned having spent all her fortune, had recourse for subsistance to the talent in which, he had always most excelled, namely, Driving, & that having sold every thing which belonged to them except their Coach, had converted it into a Stage* & in order to be removed from any of his former Acquaintance, had driven it to Edinburgh from whence he went to Sterling* every other Day; That Philippa still retaining her affection for her ungratefull Husband, had followed him to Scotland & generally accompanied him in his little Excursions to Sterling. 'It has only been to throw a little money into their Pockets (continued Augusta) that my Father has always travelled in their Coach to veiw the beauties of the Country since our arrival in Scotland—for it would certainly have been much more agreable to us, to visit the Highlands in a Postchaise* than merely to travel from Edinburgh to Sterling & from Sterling to Edinburgh every other Day in a crouded & uncomfortable Stage.' I perfectly agreed with her in her sentiments on the Affair, & secretly blamed Sir Edward for thus sacrificing his Daughter's Pleasure for the sake of a ridiculous old Woman whose folly in marrying so young a Man ought to be punished. His Behaviour however was entirely of a peice with his general Character; for what could be expected from a Man who possessed not the smallest atom of Sensibility, who scarcely knew the meaning of Simpathy, & who actually snored—.

Adeiu
Laura.

Letter the 15th

Laura in continuation.

When we arrived at the town where we were to Breakfast, I was determined to speak with Philander & Gustavus, & to that purpose as soon as I left the Carriage, I went to the Basket & tenderly enquired after their Health, expressing my fears of the uneasiness of their situation. At first they seemed rather confused at my Appearance dreading no doubt that I might call them to account for the money which our Grandfather had left me & which they had unjustly deprived me of, but finding that I mentioned nothing of the Matter, they desired me to step into the Basket as we might there converse with greater ease. Accordingly I entered & whilst the rest of the party were devouring Green tea & buttered toast, we feasted ourselves in a more refined & sentimental* Manner by a confidential Conversation. I informed them of every thing which had befallen me during the course of my Life, & at my request they related to me every incident of theirs.

'We are the sons as you already know, of the two youngest Daughters which Lord St. Clair had by Laurina an italian Opera-girl. Our mothers could neither of them exactly ascertain who were our Fathers; though it is generally beleived that Philander, is the son of one Philip Jones a Bricklayer and that my Father was Gregory Staves a Staymaker* of Edinburgh. This is however of little consequence, for as our Mothers were certainly never married to either of them, it reflects no Dishonour on our Blood, which is of a most ancient & unpolluted kind. Bertha (the Mother of Philander) & Agatha (my own Mother) always lived together. They were neither of them very rich; their united fortunes had originally amounted to nine thousand Pounds, but as they had always lived upon the principal of it,* when we were fifteen it was diminished to nine Hundred. This nine Hundred, they always kept in a Drawer in one of the Tables which stood in our common sitting Parlour,* for the Convenience of having it always at Hand. Whether it was from this circumstance, of its being easily taken, or from a wish of being independant, or from an excess of Sensibility (for which we were always remarkable) I cannot now determine, but certain it is that when we had reached our 15th year, we took the Nine Hundred Pounds & ran away. Having obtained this prize we were determined to manage it with eoconomy & not to spend it either with folly or Extravagance. To this purpose we therefore divided it into nine parcels, one of which we devoted to Victuals, the 2^d to Drink, the 3^d to Housekeeping, the 4th to Carriages, the 5th to Horses, the 6th to Servants, the 7th to Amusements the 8th to Cloathes & the 9th to Silver Buckles.* Having thus arranged our Expences for two Months (for we expected to make the nine Hundred Pounds last as long) we hastened to London & had the good luck to spend it in 7 weeks & a Day which was 6 Days sooner than we had intended. As soon as we had thus happily disencumbered ourselves from the weight of so much Money, we began to think of returning to our Mothers, but accidentally hearing that they were both starved to Death, we gave over the design & determined to engage ourselves to some strolling Company of Players,* as we had always a turn for the Stage. Accordingly we offered our Services to one & were accepted; our Company was indeed rather small, as it consisted only of the Manager his Wife & ourselves, but there were fewer to pay and the only inconvenience attending it was the Scarcity of Plays which for want of People to fill the Characters, we could perform.—. We did not mind trifles however—. One of our most admired Performances was *Macbeth*, in which we were truly great. The Manager always played *Banquo* himself, his Wife my *Lady Macbeth*, I did the *Three Witches* & Philander acted *all the rest*. To say the truth this tragedy was not only the Best, but the only Play we ever performed; & after having acted it all over England, and Wales, we came to Scotland to exhibit it over the remainder of Great Britain. We happened to be quartered in that very Town, where you came and met your Grandfather—. We were in the Inn-yard when his Carriage entered & perceiving by the Arms to whom it belonged, & knowing that Lord St. Clair was our Grandfather, we agreed to endeavour to get something from him by discovering the Relationship—. You know how well it succeeded—. Having obtained the two Hundred Pounds, we instantly left the Town leaving our Manager & his wife to act *Macbeth* by themselves, & took the road to Sterling, where we spent our little fortune with great *eclat*.* We are now returning to Edinburgh in order to get some preferment* in the Acting way; & such my Dear Cousin is our History.'

I thanked the amiable Youth for his entertaining Narration, & after expressing my Wishes for their Welfare & Happiness, left them in their little Habitation & returned to my other Freinds who impatiently expected me.

My Adventures are now drawing to a close my dearest Marianne; at least for the present.

When we arrived at Edinburgh Sir Edward told me that as the Widow of his Son, he desired I would accept from his Hands of four Hundred a year. I graciously promised that I would, but could not help observing that the unsimpathetic Baronet offered it more on account of my being the Widow of Edward than in being the refined & amiable Laura.

I took up my Residence in a romantic Village in the Highlands of Scotland, where I have ever since continued, & where I can uninterrupted by unmeaning Visits, indulge in a melancholy solitude, my unceasing Lamentations for the Death of my Father, my Mother, my Husband & my Freind.

Augusta has been for several years united to Graham the Man of all others most suited to her; she became acquainted with him during her stay in Scotland.

Sir Edward in hopes of gaining an Heir to his Title & Estate, at the same time married Lady Dorothea—. His wishes have been answered.

Philander & Gustavus, after having raised their reputation by their Performances in the Theatrical Line at Edinburgh, removed to Covent Garden, where they still Exhibit under the assumed names of *Lewis* & *Quick*.*

Philippa has long paid the Debt of Nature,* Her Husband however still continues to drive the Stage-Coach from Edinburgh to Sterling:—

Adeiu my Dearest Marianne—.

Laura—

Finis

June 13th 1790*

To Henry Thomas Austen Esqre.*

Sir

I am now availing myself of the Liberty you have frequently honoured me with of dedicating one of my Novels to you.* That it is unfinished, I greive; yet fear that from me, it will always remain so; that as far as it is carried, it Should be so trifling and so unworthy of you, is

another concern to your obliged humble
Servant
The Author

Messrs Demand & Co*—please to pay Jane Austen Spinster the sum of one hundred guineas on account of your Hum^{bl}. Servant.

H T Austen.

£105: 0. 0

Lesley Castle*

an unfinished Novel in Letters.

Letter the first is from

Miss Margaret Lesley to Miss Charlotte Lutterell.

Lesley-Castle Jan^{ry} 3^d—1792.

My Brother has just left us. 'Matilda* (said he at parting) you and Margaret will I am certain take all the care of my dear little one, that she might have received from an indulgent, an affectionate an amiable Mother.' Tears rolled down his Cheeks as he spoke these words—the remembrance of her, who had so wantonly disgraced the Maternal character and so openly violated the conjugal Duties, prevented his adding anything farther; he embraced his sweet Child and after saluting Matilda & Me hastily broke from us—and seating himself in his Chaise, pursued the road to Aberdeen. Never was there a better young Man! Ah! how little did he deserve the misfortunes he has experienced in the Marriage state. So good a Husband to so bad a Wife!; for you know my dear Charlotte that the worthless Louisa* left him, her Child & reputation a few weeks ago in company with Danvers & †dishonour. Never was there a sweeter face, a finer form, or a less amiable Heart than Louisa owned! Her child already possesses the personal Charms of her unhappy Mother! May she inherit from her Father all his mental ones! Lesley is at present but five and twenty, and has already given himself up to melancholy and Despair; what a difference between him and his Father!; Sir George is 57 and still remains the Beau, the flighty stripling,* the gay Lad, and sprightly Youngster, that his Son was really about five years back, and that *he* has affected to appear ever since my remembrance. While our father is fluttering about the Streets of London, gay, dissipated, and Thoughtless at the age of 57, Matilda and I continue secluded from Mankind in our old and Mouldering Castle, which is situated two miles from Perth* on a bold projecting Rock,* and commands an extensive veiw of the Town and its delightful Environs. But tho' retired from almost all the World,* (for we visit no one but the M'Leods, The M'Kenzies, the M'Phersons, the M'Cartneys, the M'donalds, The M'kinnons, the M'lellans, the M'kays, the Macbeths and the Macduffs)* we are neither dull nor unhappy; on the contrary there never were two more lively, more agreable or more witty Girls, than we are; not an hour in the Day hangs heavy on our hands. We read, we work,* we walk, and when fatigued with these Employments releive our spirits, either by a lively song, a graceful Dance, or by some smart bon-mot,* and witty repartée.* We are handsome my dear Charlotte, very handsome and the greatest of our Perfections is, that we are entirely insensible of them ourselves. But why do I thus dwell on myself?* Let me rather repeat the praise of our dear little Neice the innocent Louisa, who is at present sweetly smiling in a gentle Nap, as she reposes on the Sofa. The dear Creature is just turned of two years old; as handsome as tho' 2 & 20, as sensible as tho' 2 & 30, and as prudent as tho' 2 & 40. To convince you of this, I must inform you that she has a very fine complexion and very pretty features, that she already knows the two first Letters in the Alphabet, and that she never tears her frocks—. If I have not now convinced you of her Beauty, Sense & Prudence, I have nothing more to urge in support of my assertion, and you will therefore have no way

---

† Rakehelly* Dishonor Esqre.

of deciding the Affair but by coming to Lesley-castle, and by a personal acquaintance with Louisa, determine for yourself. Ah! my dear Freind, how happy should I be to see you within these venerable Walls!* It is now four years since my removal from School has separated me from you; that two such tender Hearts, so closely linked together by the ties of simpathy and Freindship, should be so widely removed from each other, is vastly moving. I live in Perthshire, You in Sussex.* We might meet in London, were my Father disposed to carry me there, and were your Mother to be there at the same time. We might meet at Bath, at Tunbridge,* or any where else indeed, could we but be at the same place together. We have only to hope that such a period may arrive. My Father does not return to us till Autumn; my Brother will leave Scotland in a few Days; he is impatient to travel. Mistaken Youth! He vainly flatters himself that change of Air will heal the Wounds of a broken Heart! You will join with me I am certain my dear Charlotte, in prayers for the recovery of the unhappy Lesley's peace of Mind, which must ever be essential to that of your sincere freind

M. Lesley.

Letter the second

From Miss C. Lutterell to Miss M. Lesley in answer

Glenford Feb.^ry 12

I have a thousand excuses to beg for having so long delayed thanking you my dear Peggy* for your agreable Letter, which beleive me I should not have deferred doing, had not every moment of my time during the last five weeks been so fully employed in the necessary arrangements for my sisters Wedding, as to allow me no time to devote either to you or myself. And now what provokes me more than any thing else is that the Match is broke off, and all my Labour thrown away: Imagine how great the Dissapointment must be to me, when you consider that after having laboured both by Night and by Day, in order to get the Wedding dinner ready by the time appointed, after having roasted Beef, Broiled Mutton, and Stewed Soup* enough to last the new-married Couple through the Honey-moon, I had the mortification of finding that I had been Roasting, Broiling and Stewing both the Meat and Myself to no purpose. Indeed my dear Freind,

I never remember suffering any vexation equal to what I experienced on last Monday when my Sister came running to me in the Store-room with her face as White as a Whipt syllabub,* and told me that Hervey had been thrown from his Horse, had fractured his Scull and was pronounced by his Surgeon to be in the most emminent Danger.

'Good God! (said I) you dont say so? why what in the name of Heaven will become of all the Victuals! We shall never be able to eat it while it is good. However, we'll call in the Surgeon to help us—. I shall be able to manage the Sir-loin myself; my Mother will eat the soup, and You and the Doctor must finish the rest.' Here I was interrupted, by seeing my poor Sister fall down to appearance Lifeless upon one of the Chests, where we keep our Table linen. I immediately called my Mother and the Maids, and at last we brought her to herself again; as soon as ever she was sensible, she expressed a determination of going instantly to Henry, and was so wildly bent on this Scheme, that we had the greatest Difficulty in the World to prevent her putting it in execution; at last however more by Force than Entreaty we prevailed on her to go into her room; we laid her upon the Bed, and she continued for some Hours in the most dreadful Convulsions. My Mother and I continued in the room with her, and when any intervals of tolerable Composure in Eloisa* would allow us, we joined in heartfelt lamentations on the dreadful Waste in our provisions which this Event must occasion, and in concerting some plan for getting rid of them. We agreed that the best thing we could do was to begin eating them immediately, and accordingly we ordered up the cold Ham and Fowls, and instantly began our Devouring Plan on them with great Alacrity. We would have persuaded Eloisa to have taken a Wing of a Chicken, but she would not be persuaded. She was however much quieter than she had been; the Convulsions she had before suffered having given way to an almost perfect Insensibility. We endeavoured to rouse her by every means in our power, but to no purpose. I talked to her of Henry.

'Dear Eloisa (said I) there's no occasion for your crying so much about such a trifle. (for I was willing to make light of it in order to comfort her) I beg you would not mind it—. You see it does not vex me in the least; though perhaps *I* may suffer most from it after all; for I shall not only be obliged to eat up all the Victuals I have dressed* already, but must if Hervey should recover (which however is not very likely) dress as much for you again; or should he die (as I suppose he will) I shall still have to prepare a Dinner for you whenever you marry any one else. So you see that tho' perhaps for the present it may afflict you to think of Henry's sufferings, Yet I dare say he'll die soon, and then his pain will be over and you will be easy, whereas my Trouble will last much longer for work as hard as I may, I am certain that the pantry cannot be cleared in less than a fortnight.' Thus I did all in my power to console her, but without any effect, and at last as I saw that she did not seem to listen to me, I said no more, but leaving her with my Mother I took down the remains of The Ham & Chicken, and sent William to ask how Hervey did. He was not expected to live many Hours; he died the same day. We took all possible Care to break the Melancholy Event to Eloisa in the tenderest manner; yet in spite of every precaution, her Sufferings on hearing it were too violent for her reason, and she continued for many hours in a high Delirium. She is still extremely ill, and her Physicians are greatly afraid of her going into a Decline.* We are therefore preparing for Bristol,* where we mean to be in the course of the next week. And now my dear Margaret let me talk a little of your affairs; and in the first place I must inform you that it is confidently reported, your Father is going to be married; I am very unwilling to beleive so unpleasing a report, and at the same time cannot wholly discredit it. I have written to my freind Susan Fitzgerald, for information concerning it, which as she is at present in Town, she will be very able to give me. I know not who is the Lady. I think your Brother is extremely right in the resolution he has taken of travelling, as it will perhaps contribute to obliterate from his remembrance, those disagreable Events, which have lately so much afflicted him—I am happy to find that tho' secluded from all the World, neither You nor Matilda are dull or unhappy—that you may never know what it is to be either is the wish of your sincerely Affectionate

C.L.

P.S. I have this instant received an answer from my freind Susan, which I enclose to you, and on which you will make your own reflections.

The enclosed Letter

My dear Charlotte

You could not have applied for information concerning the report of Sir George Lesleys Marriage, to any one better able to give it you than I am. Sir George is certainly married; I was myself present at the Ceremony, which you will not be surprised at when I subscribe myself your

Affectionate Susan Lesley

Letter the third

From Miss Margaret Lesley to Miss C. Lutterell

Lesley Castle February the 16th

I *have* made my own reflections on the letter you enclosed to me, my Dear Charlotte and I will now tell you what those reflections were. I reflected that if by this second Marriage Sir George should have a second family, our fortunes must be considerably diminushed—that if his Wife should be of an extravagant turn, she would encourage him to persevere in that Gay & Dissipated way of Life to which little encouragement would be necessary, and which has I fear already proved but too detrimental to his health and fortune—that she would now become Mistress of those Jewels which once adorned our Mother, and which Sir George had always promised us*—that if they did not come into Perthshire I should not be able to gratify my curiosity of beholding my Mother-in-law,* and that if they did, Matilda would no longer sit at the head of her Father's table—.* These my dear Charlotte were the melancholy reflections which crouded into my imagination after perusing Susan's letter to you, and which instantly occurred to Matilda when she had perused it likewise. The same ideas, the same fears, immediately occupied her Mind, and I know not which reflection distressed her most, whether the probable Dim-inution of our Fortunes, or her own Consequence. We both wish very much to know whether Lady Lesley is handsome & what is your opin-ion of her; as you honour her with the appellation of your freind, we flatter ourselves that she must be amiable. My Brother is already in Paris. He intends to quit it in a few Days, and to begin his route to Italy. He writes in a most chearfull Manner, says that the air of France has greatly recovered both his Health and Spirits; that he has now entirely ceased to think of Louisa with any degree either of Pity or Affection, that he even feels himself obliged to her for her Elopement, as he thinks it very good fun to be single again. By this, you may per-ceive that he has entirely regained that chearful Gaiety, and sprightly

Wit, for which he was once so remarkable. When he first became acquainted with Louisa which was little more than three years ago, he was one of the most lively, the most agreable young Men of the age—. I beleive you never yet heard the particulars of his first acquaintance with her. It commenced at our cousin Colonel Drummond's; at whose house in Cumberland he spent the Christmas, in which he attained the age of two and twenty. Louisa Burton was the Daughter of a distant Relation of Mrs Drummond, who dieing a few Months before in extreme poverty, left his only Child then about eighteen to the protection of any of his Relations who would protect her. Mrs Drummond was the only one who found herself so disposed—Louisa was therefore removed from a miserable Cottage in Yorkshire to an elegant Mansion in Cumberland, and from every pecuniary Distress that Poverty could inflict, to every elegant Enjoyment that Money could purchase—. Louisa was naturally ill-tempered and Cunning; but she had been taught to disguise her real Disposition, under the appearance of insinuating Sweetness, by a father who but too well knew, that to be married, would be the only chance she would have of not being starved, and who flattered himself that with such an extroidinary share of personal beauty, joined to a gentleness of Manners, and an engaging address, she might stand a good chance of pleasing some young Man who might afford to marry a Girl without a Shilling. Louisa perfectly entered into her father's schemes and was determined to forward them with all her care & attention. By dint of Perseverance and Application, she had at length so thoroughly disguised her natural disposition under the mask of Innocence, and Softness, as to impose upon every one who had not by a long and constant intimacy with her discovered her real Character. Such was Louisa when the hapless Lesley first beheld her at Drummond-house. His heart which (to use your favourite comparison) was as delicate as sweet and as tender as a Whipt-syllabub, could not resist her attractions. In a very few Days, he was falling in love, shortly after actually fell, and before he had known her a Month, he had married her. My Father was at first highly displeased at so hasty and imprudent a connection; but when he found that they did not mind it, he soon became perfectly reconciled to the match. The Estate near Aberdeen which my brother possesses by the bounty of his great Uncle independant of Sir George, was entirely sufficient to support him and my Sister in Elegance & Ease. For the first twelvemonth, no one could be happier than Lesley, and no one more amiable to appearance than Louisa, and so plausibly did she act and so cautiously behave that tho' Matilda and I often spent several weeks together with them, yet we neither of us had any suspicion of her real Disposition. After the birth of Louisa however, which one would have thought would have strengthened her regard for Lesley, the mask she had so long supported was by degrees thrown aside, and as probably she then thought herself secure in the affection of her Husband (which did indeed appear if possible augmented by the birth of his Child) She seemed to take no pains to prevent that affection from ever diminushing. Our visits therefore to Dunbeath,* were now less frequent and by far less agreable than they used to be. Our absence was however never either mentioned or lamented by Louisa who in the society of young Danvers with whom she became acquainted at Aberdeen (he was at one of the Universities there,)* felt infinitely happier than in that of Matilda and your freind, tho' there certainly never were pleasanter Girls than we are. You know the sad end of all Lesleys connubial happiness; I will not repeat it—. Adeiu my dear Charlotte; although I have not yet mentioned any thing of the matter, I hope you will do me the justice to believe that I *think* and *feel*, a great deal* for your Sisters affliction. I do not doubt but that the healthy air of the Bristol-downs,* will intirely remove it, by erasing from her Mind the remembrance of Henry. I am my dear Charlotte y^rs ever

ML—

Letter the fourth

From Miss C. Lutterell to Miss M. Lesley

Bristol February 27th

My dear Peggy

I have but just received your letter, which being directed to Sussex while I was at Bristol was obliged to be forwarded to me here, & from some unaccountable Delay, has but this instant reached me—. I return you many thanks for the account it contains of Lesley's acquaintance, Love & Marriage with Louisa, which has not the less entertained me for having often been repeated to me before.

I have the satisfaction of informing you that we have every reason to imagine our pantry is by this time nearly cleared, as we left particular orders with the Servants to eat as hard as they possibly could, and to call in a couple of Chairwomen* to assist them. We brought a cold Pigeon-pye, a cold turkey, a cold tongue, and half a dozen Jellies* with us, which we were lucky enough with the help of our Landlady, her husband, and their three children, to get rid of, in less than two days after our arrival. Poor Eloisa is still so very indifferent both in Health & Spirits, that I very much fear, the air of the Bristol-downs, healthy as it is, has not been able to drive poor Henry from her remembrance—.

You ask me whether your new Mother in law is handsome & amiable—I will now give you an exact description of her bodily and Mental charms. She is short, and extremely well-made; is naturally pale, but rouges a good deal;* has fine eyes, and fine teeth, as she will take care to let you know as soon as she sees you, and is altogether very pretty. She is remarkably good-tempered when she has her own way, and very lively when she is not out of humour. She is naturally extravagant and not very affected; she never reads any thing but the letters she receives from me, and never writes any thing but her answers to them. She plays, sings & Dances, but has no taste for either, and excells in none, tho' she says she is passionately fond of all. Perhaps you may flatter me so far as to be surprised that one of whom I speak with so little affection should be my particular freind; but to tell you the truth, our freindship arose rather from Caprice on her side, than Esteem on mine. We spent two or three days together with a Lady in Berkshire with whom we both happened to be connected—. During our visit, the Weather being remarkably bad, and our party particularly stupid, she was so good as to conceive a violent partiality for me, which very soon settled in a downright Freindship, and ended in an established correspondence. She is probably by this time as tired of me, as I am of her; but as she is too polite and I am too civil to say so, our letters are still as frequent and affectionate as ever, and our Attachment as firm and sincere as when it first commenced.—As she had a great taste for the pleasures of London, and of Brighthelmstone,* she will I dare say find some difficulty in prevailing on herself even to satisfy the curiosity I dare say she feels of beholding you, at the expence of quitting those favourite haunts of Dissipation, for the melancholy tho' venerable gloom of the castle you inhabit. Perhaps however if she finds her health impaired by too much amusement, she may acquire fortitude sufficient to undertake a Journey to Scotland in

the hope of its proving at least beneficial to her health, if not conducive to her happiness. Your fears I am sorry to say, concerning your
father's extravagance, your own fortunes, your Mothers Jewels and
your Sister's consequence, I should suppose are but too well founded.
My freind herself has four thousand pounds,* and will probably
spend nearly as much every year in Dress and Public places, if she can
get it—she will certainly not endeavour to reclaim Sir George from
the manner of living to which he has been so long accustomed, and
there is therefore some reason to fear that you will be very well off, if
you get any fortune at all. The Jewels I should imagine too will
undoubtedly be hers, & there is too much reason to think that she will
preside at her Husbands table in preference to his Daughter. But as so
melancholy a subject must necessarily extremely distress you, I will
no longer dwell on it—.

Eloisa's indisposition has brought us to Bristol at so unfashionable
a season of the year, that we have actually seen but one genteel family
since we came. Mr & Mrs Marlowe are very agreable people; the ill
health of their little boy occasioned their arrival here; you may imagine that being the only family with whom we can converse, we are of
course on a footing of intimacy with them; we see them indeed almost
every day, and dined with them yesterday. We spent a very pleasant
Day, and had a very good Dinner, tho' to be sure the Veal was terribly
underdone, and the Curry* had no seasoning. I could not help wishing all dinner-time that I had been at the dressing it—. A brother of
Mrs Marlowe, Mr Cleveland* is with them at present; he is a good-
looking young Man, and seems to have a good deal to say for himself.
I tell Eloisa that she should set her cap at him,* but she does not at all
seem to relish the proposal. I should like to see the girl married and
Cleveland has a very good estate. Perhaps you may wonder that I do
not consider *myself* as well as my Sister in my matrimonial Projects;
but to tell you the truth I never wish to act a more principal part at
a Wedding than the superintending and directing the Dinner, and
therefore while I can get any of my acquaintance to marry for me,
I shall never think of doing it myself, as I very much suspect that
I should not have so much time for dressing my own Wedding-dinner,
as for dressing that of my freinds. Y^rs sincerely

CL.

Letter the fifth

Miss Margaret Lesley to Miss Charlotte Luttrell

Lesley-Castle March 18th

On the same day that I received your last kind letter, Matilda received one from Sir George which was dated from Edinburgh, and informed us that he should do himself the pleasure of introducing Lady Lesley to us on the following evening. This as you may suppose considerably surprised us, particularly as your account of her Ladyship had given us reason to imagine there was little chance of her visiting Scotland at a time that London must be so gay. As it was our business however to be delighted at such a mark of condescension as a visit from Sir George and Lady Lesley, we prepared to return them an answer expressive of the happiness we enjoyed in expectation of such a Blessing, when luckily recollecting that as they were to reach the Castle the next Evening, it would be impossible for my father to receive it before he left Edinburgh, We contented ourselves with leaving them to suppose that we were as happy as we ought to be. At nine in the Evening on the following day, they came, accompanied by one of Lady Lesleys brothers. Her Ladyship perfectly answers the description you sent me of her, except that I do not think her so pretty as you seem to consider her. She has not a bad face, but there is something so extremely unmajestic in her little diminutive figure, as to render her in comparison with the elegant height of Matilda and Myself, an insignificant Dwarf. Her curiosity to see us (which must have been great to bring her more than four hundred miles) being now perfectly gratified, she already begins to mention their return to town, and has desired us to accompany her—. We cannot refuse her request since it is seconded by the commands of our Father, and thirded by the entreaties of Mr Fitzgerald who is certainly one of the most pleasing young Men, I ever beheld. It is not yet determined when we are to go, but when ever we do we shall certainly take our little Louisa with us. Adeiu my dear Charlotte; Matilda unites in best Wishes to You & Eloisa, with yours ever

M L

Letter the sixth

Lady Lesley to Miss Charlotte Luttrell

Lesley-Castle March 20th

We arrived here my sweet Freind about a fortnight ago, and I already heartily repent that I ever left our charming House in Portman-Square* for such a dismal old weather-beaten Castle* as this. You can form no idea sufficiently hideous, of its dungeon-like form. It is actually perched upon a Rock to appearance so totally inaccessible, that I expected to have been pulled up by a rope; and sincerely repented having gratified my curiosity to behold my Daughters at the expence of being obliged to enter their prison in so dangerous & ridiculous a Manner. But as soon as I once found myself safely arrived in the inside of this tremendous building, I comforted myself with the hope of having my spirits revived, by the sight of two beautifull Girls, such as the Miss Lesleys had been represented to me, at Edinburgh. But here again, I met with nothing but Dissapointment and Surprise. Matilda and Margaret Lesley are two great, tall, out of the way, over-grown, Girls, just of a proper size to inhabit a Castle almost as Large in comparison as themselves. I wish my dear Charlotte that you could but behold these scotch Giants; I am sure they would frighten you out of your wits. They will do very well as foils to myself, so I have invited them to accompany me to London where I hope to be in the course of a fortnight. Besides these two fair Damsels, I found a little humoured Brat here who I beleive is some relation to them; they told me who she was, and gave me a long rigmerole Story* of her father and a Miss *Somebody* which I have entirely forgot. I hate Scandal and detest Children—. I have been plagued ever since I came here with tiresome visits from a parcel of Scotch wretches, with terrible hard-names; they were so civil, gave me so many invitations, and talked of coming again so soon, that I could not help affronting them. I suppose I shall not see them any more, and yet as a family party we are so stupid, that I do not know what to do with myself. These girls have no Music, but Scotch Airs, no Drawings but Scotch Mountains, and no Books but Scotch Poems—And I hate every thing Scotch.* In general I can spend half the Day at my toilett* with a great deal of pleasure, but why should I dress here, since there is not a creature in the House whom I have any wish to please.—. I have just had a conversation with my Brother in which he has greatly offended me, and which as I have nothing more entertaining to send you I will give you the particulars of. You must know that I have for these 4 or 5 Days past strongly suspected William of entertaining a partiality for my eldest Daughter. I own indeed that had *I* been inclined to fall in love with any woman, I should not have made choice of Matilda Lesley for the object of my passion; for there is nothing I hate so much as a tall Woman: but however there is no accounting for some men's taste and as William is himself nearly six feet high, it is not wonderful that he should be partial to that height. Now as I have a very great Affection for my Brother and should be extremely sorry to see him unhappy, which I suppose he means to be if he cannot marry Matilda, as moreover I know that his Circumstances will not allow him to marry any one with out a fortune, and that Matilda's is entirely dependant on her Father, who will neither have his own inclination nor my permission to give her any thing at present, I thought it would be doing a good-natured action by my Brother to let him know as much, in order that he might choose for himself, whether to conquer his passion, or Love and Despair. Accordingly finding myself this Morning alone with him in one of the horrid old rooms of this Castle, I opened the cause to him in the following Manner.

'Well my dear William what do you think of these girls? for my part, I do not find them so plain as I expected: but perhaps you may think me partial to the Daughters of my Husband and perhaps you are right—They are indeed So very like Sir George that it is natural to think' . . .

'My Dear Susan (cried he in a tone of the greatest amazement) You do not really think they bear the least resemblance to their Father! He is so very plain!—but I beg your pardon—I had entirely forgotten to whom I was speaking—'

'Oh! pray dont mind me; (replied I) every one knows Sir George is horribly ugly, and I assure you I always thought him a fright.'

'You surprise me extremely (answered William) by what you say both with respect to Sir George and his Daughters. You cannot think your Husband so deficient in personal Charms as you speak of, nor can you surely see any resemblance between him and the Miss Lesleys who are in my opinion perfectly unlike him & perfectly Handsome.'

'If that is your opinion with regard to the Girls it certainly is no proof of their Fathers beauty, for if they are perfectly unlike him and very handsome at the same time, it is natural to suppose that he is very plain.'

'By no means, (said he) for what may be pretty in a Woman, may be very unpleasing in a Man.'

'But you yourself (replied I) but a few Minutes ago allowed him to be very plain.'

'Men are no Judges of Beauty in their own Sex.' (said he)

'Neither Men nor Women can think Sir George tolerable.'

'Well, well, (said he) we will not dispute about *his* Beauty, but your opinion of his *Daughters* is surely very singular, for if I understood you right, you said you did not find them so plain as you expected to do.'!

'Why, do *you* find them plainer then?' (said I)

'I can scarcely beleive you to be serious (returned he) when you speak of their persons in so extroidinary a Manner. Do not you think the Miss Lesleys are two very handsome young Women?'

'Lord! No! (cried I) I think them terribly plain!'

'Plain! (replied He) My dear Susan, you cannot really think so! Why what single Feature in the face of either of them, can you possibly find fault with?'

'Oh! trust me for that; (replied I)—Come I will begin with the eldest—with Matilda. Shall I, William?' (I looked as cunning as I could when I said it, in order to shame him.)

'They are so much alike (said he) that I should suppose the faults of one, would be the faults of both.'

'Well, then, in the first place, they are both so horribly tall!'

'They are *taller* than you are indeed.' (said he with a saucy smile.)

'Nay, (said I); I know nothing of that.'

'Well, but (he continued) tho' they may be above the common size, their figures are perfectly elegant; and as to their faces, their Eyes are beautifull—.'

'I never can think such tremendous, knock-me-down figures in the least degree elegant, and as for their eyes, they are so tall that I never could strain my neck enough to look at them.'

'Nay, (replied he), I know not whether you may not be in the right in not attempting it, for perhaps they might dazzle you with their Lustre.'

'Oh! Certainly.' (said I, with the greatest Complacency, for I assure you my dearest Charlotte I was not in the least offended tho' by what followed, one would suppose that William was conscious of having given me just cause to be so, for coming up to me and taking my hand, he said) 'You must not look so grave Susan; you will make me fear I have offended you!'

'Offended me! Dear Brother, how came such a thought in your head! (returned I) No really! I assure you that I am not in the least surprised at your being so warm an advocate for the Beauty of these Girls—'

'Well, but (interrupted William) remember that we have not yet concluded our dispute concerning them. What fault do you find with their complexion?'

'They are so horridly pale.'

'They have always a little colour, & after any exercise it is considerably heightened.'

'Yes, but if there should ever happen to be any rain in this part of the world, they will never be able to raise more than their common stock—except indeed they amuse themselves with running up & Down these horrid old Galleries and Antichambers—'*

'Well, (replied my Brother in a tone of vexation, & glancing an impertinent Look at me) if they *have* but little colour, at least, it is all their own.'

This was too much my dear Charlotte, for I am certain that he had the impudence by that look, of pretending to suspect the reality of mine. But you I am sure will vindicate my character whenever you may hear it so cruelly aspersed, for you can witness how often I have protested against wearing Rouge, and how much I always told you I disliked it. And I assure you that my opinions are still the same.—. Well, not bearing to be so suspected by my Brother, I left the room immediately, and have been ever since in my own Dressing-room writing to you. What a long Letter have I made of it! But you must not expect to receive such from me when I get to Town; for it is only at Lesley-castle, that one has time to write even to a Charlotte Luttrell.—. I was so much vexed by William's Glance, that I could not summon Patience enough, to stay & give him that Advice respecting his Attachment to Matilda which had first induced me from pure Love to him to begin the conversation; and I am now so thoroughly convinced by it, of his violent passion for her, that I am certain he would never hear reason on the Subject, and I shall therefore give myself no more trouble either about him or his favourite. Adeiu my dear Girl—

Y^{rs} Affectionately Susan L.

Letter the seventh

From Miss C. Luttrell to Miss M. Lesley

Bristol the 27th of March.

I have received Letters from You & your Mother-in-Law within this week which have greatly entertained me, as I find by them that you are both downright jealous of each others Beauty. It is very odd that two pretty Women tho' actually Mother & Daughter cannot be in the same House without falling out about their faces. Do be convinced that you are both perfectly handsome and say no more of the Matter. I suppose this Letter must be directed to Portman Square where probably (great as is your affection for Lesley Castle) you will not be sorry to find yourself. In spite of all that People may say about Green fields and the Country I was always of opinion that London and its Amusements must be very agreable for a while, and should be very happy could my Mother's income allow her to jockey us into its Public-places,* during Winter. I always longed particularly to go to Vaux-hall,* to see whether the cold Beef there is cut so thin* as it is reported, for I have a sly suspicion that few people understand the art of cutting a slice of cold Beef so well as I do: nay it would be hard if I did not know something of the Matter, for it was a part of my Education that I took by far the most pains with. Mama always found me *her* best Scholar, tho' when Papa was alive Eloisa was *his*. Never to be sure were there two more different Dispositions in the World. We both loved Reading. *She* preferred Histories, & *I* Receipts.* She loved drawing Pictures, and I drawing Pullets.* No one could sing a better Song than She, and no one make a better Pye than I.—And so it has always continued since we have been no longer Children. The only difference is that all disputes on the superior excellence of our Employments *then* so frequent are now no more. We have for many years entered into an agreement always to admire each other's works; I never fail listening to *her* Music, & she is as constant in eating *my* pies. Such at least was the case till Henry Hervey made his appearance in Sussex. Before the arrival of his Aunt in our neighbourhood where she establish'd herself you know about a twelvemonth ago, his visits to her had been at stated times, and of equal & settled Duration; but on her removal to the Hall which is within a walk from our House,

they became both more frequent & longer. This as you may suppose
could not be pleasing to Mrs Diana who is a professed Enemy to every
thing which is not directed by Decorum and Formality, or which bears
the least resemblance to Ease and Good-breeding. Nay so great was
her aversion to her Nephews behaviour that I have often heard her
give such hints of it before his face that had not Henry at such times
been engaged in conversation with Eloisa, they must have caught his
Attention and have very much distressed him. The alteration in my
Sisters behaviour which I have before hinted at, now took place. The
Agreement we had entered into of admiring each others productions
she no longer seemed to regard, & tho' I constantly applauded even
every Country-dance,* She play'd, yet not even a pidgeon-pye* of my
making could obtain from her a single word of Approbation. This was
certainly enough to put any one in a Passion; however, I was as cool as
a Cream-cheese and having formed my plan & concerted a scheme of
Revenge, I was determined to let her have her own way & not even to
make her a single reproach. My Scheme was to treat her as she treated
me, and tho' she might even draw my own Picture or play Malbrook*
(which is the only tune I ever really liked) not to say so much as 'Thank
you Eloisa;' tho' I had for many years constantly hollowed whenever
she played, *Bravo, Bravissimo, Encora, Da capo, allegretto, con espressioné*, and *Poco presto** with many other such outlandish words, all of
them as Eloisa told me expressive of my Admiration; and so indeed
I suppose they are, as I see some of them in every Page of every
Music-book, being the Sentiments I imagine of the Composer.

I executed my Plan with great Punctuality, I can not say success,
for Alas! my silence while she played seemed not in the least to dis-
please her; on the contrary she actually said to me one day 'Well
Charlotte, I am very glad to find that you have at last left off that
ridiculous custom of applauding my Execution* on the Harpsichord*
till you made *my* head ake, & yourself hoarse. I feel very much obliged
to you for keeping your Admiration to yourself.' I never shall forget
the very witty answer I made to this speech.

'Eloisa (said I) I beg you would be quite at your Ease with respect
to all such fears in future, for be assured that I shall always keep my
Admiration to myself & my own pursuits & never extend it to yours.'
This was the only very severe thing I ever said in my Life; not but that
I have often felt myself extremely satirical* but it was the only time
I ever made my feelings public.

I suppose there never were two young people who had a greater affection for each other than Henry & Eloisa; no, the Love of your Brother for Miss Burton could not be so strong tho' it might be more violent. You may imagine therefore how provoked my Sister must have been to have him play her such a trick. Poor girl! she still laments his Death with undiminished Constancy, notwithstanding he has been dead more than six weeks; but some people mind such things more than others. The ill state of Health into which his Loss has thrown her makes her so weak, & so unable to support the least exertion, that she has been in tears all this Morning merely from having taken Leave of Mrs Marlowe who with her Husband, Brother and Child are to leave Bristol this Morning. I am sorry to have them go because they are the only family with whom we have here any acquaintance, but I never thought of crying; to be sure Eloisa & Mrs Marlowe have always been more together than with me, and have therefore contracted a kind of affection for each other, which does not make Tears so inexcusable in them as they would be in me. The Marlowes are going to Town; Cleveland accompanies them; as neither Eloisa nor I could catch him I hope You or Matilda may have better Luck. I know not when we shall leave Bristol, Eloisa's Spirits are so low that she is very averse to moving, and yet is certainly by no means mended by her residence here. A week or two will I hope determine our Measures—in the mean time beleive me

&c—&c—Charlotte Luttrell

Letter the eighth

Miss Luttrell to Mrs Marlowe.

Bristol April 4th

I feel myself greatly obliged to you my dear Emma for such a mark of your affection as I flatter myself was conveyed in the proposal you made me of our Corresponding; I assure you that it will be a great releif to me to write to you and as long as my Health & Spirits will allow me, you will find me a very constant Correspondent; I will not say an entertaining one, for you know my situation sufficiently not to be ignorant that in me Mirth would be improper & I know my own Heart too well not to be sensible that it would be unnatural. You must not expect News for we see no one with whom we are in the least acquainted, or in whose proceedings we have any Interest. You must not expect Scandal for by the same rule we are equally debarred either from hearing or inventing it.—You must expect from me nothing but the melancholy effusions of a broken Heart which is ever reverting to the Happiness it once enjoyed and which ill supports its present Wretchedness. The Possibility of being able to write, to speak, to you of my losst Henry will be a Luxury to me, & your Goodness will not I know refuse to read what it will so much releive my Heart to write. I once thought that to have what is in general called a Freind (I mean one of my own Sex to whom I might speak with less reserve than to any other person) independant of my Sister would never be an object of my wishes, but how much was I mistaken! Charlotte is too much engrossed by two confidential Correspondents of that sort, to supply the place of one to me, & I hope you will not think me girlishly romantic, when I say that to have some kind and compassionate Freind who might listen to my Sorrows without endeavoring to console me was what I had for some time wished for, when our acquaintance with you, the intimacy which followed it & the particular affectionate Attention you paid me almost from the first, caused me to entertain the flattering Idea of those attentions being improved on a closer acquaintance into a Freindship which if you were what my wishes formed you would be the greatest Happiness I could be capable of enjoying. To find that such Hopes are realized is a satisfaction indeed, a satisfaction which is now almost the only one I can ever experience.—I feel myself so languid that I am sure were you with me you would oblige me to leave off writing, & I can not give you a greater proof of my Affection for you than by acting, as I know you would wish me to do, whether Absent or Present. I am my dear Emmas sincere

freind E.L.

Letter the ninth

Mrs Marlowe to Miss Luttrell

Grosvenor Street,* April 10th*

Need I say my dear Eloisa how wellcome your Letter was to me? I cannot give a greater proof of the pleasure I received from it, or of the Desire I feel that our Correspondence may be regular & frequent than by setting you so good an example as I now do in answering it before the end of the week—. But do not imagine that I claim any merit in being so punctual; on the contrary I assure you, that it is a far greater Gratification to me to write to you, than to spend the Evening either at a Concert or a Ball. Mr Marlowe is so desirous of my appearing at some of the Public places every evening that I do not like to refuse him, but at the same time so much wish to remain at Home, that independant of the Pleasure I experience in devoting any portion of my Time to my Dear Eloisa, yet the Liberty I claim from having a Letter to write of spending an Evening at home with my little Boy, You know me well enough to be sensible, will of itself be a sufficient Inducement (if one is necessary) to my maintaining with Pleasure a Correspondence with you. As to the Subjects of your Letters to me, whether Grave or Merry, if they concern you they must be equally interesting to me; Not but that I think the Melancholy Indulgence of your own Sorrows by repeating them & dwelling on them to me, will only encourage and increase them, and that it will be more prudent in you to avoid so sad a subject; but yet knowing as I do what a soothing & Melancholy Pleasure it must afford you, I cannot prevail on myself to deny you so great an Indulgence, and will only insist on your not expecting me to encourage you in it, by my own Letters; on the contrary I intend to fill them with such lively Wit and enlivening Humour as shall even provoke a Smile in the sweet but sorrowfull Countenance of my Eloisa.

In the first place you are to learn that I have met your Sisters three freinds Lady Lesley and her Daughters, twice in Public since I have been here. I know you will be impatient to hear my opinion, of the Beauty of three Ladies of whom You have heard so much. Now, as you are too ill & too unhappy to be vain, I think I may venture to inform you that I like none of their faces so well as I do your own. Yet they are all handsome—Lady Lesley indeed I have seen before; her Daughters I beleive would in general be said to have a finer face than her Ladyship, and Yet what with the charms of a Blooming Complexion, a little Affectation and a great deal of Small-talk, (in each of which She is superior to the Young Ladies) she will I dare say gain herself as many admirers as the more regular features of Matilda, & Margaret. I am sure you will agree with me in saying that they can none of them be of a proper size for real Beauty,* when you know that two of them are taller & the other shorter than ourselves. In spite of this Defect (or rather by reason of it) there is something very noble & majectic in the figures of the Miss Lesleys, and something agreably Lively in the Appearance of their pretty little Mother-in-law. But tho' one may be majectic & the other Lively, yet the faces of neither possess that Bewitching Sweetness of my Eloisas, which her present Languor is so far from diminishing. What would my Husband and Brother say of us, if they knew all the fine things I have been saying to you in this Letter. It is very hard that a pretty Woman is never to be told she is so by any one of her own Sex, without that person's being suspected to be either her determined Enemy, or her professed Toad-eater.* How much more amiable are women in that particular! one Man may say forty civil things to another without our supposing that he is ever paid for it, and provided he does his Duty by our Sex, we care not how Polite he is to his own.

Mrs Luttrell will be so good as to accept my Compliments, Charlotte, my Love, and Eloisa the best wishes for the recovery of her Health & Spirits that can be offered by her Affectionate Freind

E. Marlowe.

I am afraid this Letter will be but a poor Specimen of my Powers in the Witty Way; and your opinion of them will not be greatly increased when I assure you that I have been as entertaining as I possibly could—.

Letter the tenth

From Miss Margaret Lesley to Miss Charlotte Luttrell.

Portman Square April 13th

My dear Charlotte

We left Lesley-Castle on the 28th of last Month, and arrived safely in London after a Journey of seven Days; I had the pleasure of finding your Letter here waiting my Arrival, for which you have my grateful Thanks. Ah! my dear Freind I every day more regret the serene & tranquil Pleasures of the Castle we have left, in exchange for the uncertain & unequal Amusements of this vaunted City. Not that I will pretend to assert that these uncertain and unequal Amusements are in the least Degree unpleasing to me; on the contrary I enjoy them extremely and should enjoy them even more, were I not certain that every appearance I make in Public but rivetts the Chains of those unhappy Beings whose Passion it is impossible not to pity, tho' it is out of my power to return. In short my Dear Charlotte it is my sensibility for the sufferings of so many amiable Young Men, my Dislike of the extreme Admiration I meet with, and my Aversion to being so celebrated both in Public, in Private, in Papers, & in Printshops,* that are the reasons why I cannot more fully enjoy, the Amusements so various and pleasing of London. How often have I wished that I possessed as little personal Beauty as you do; that my figure were as inelegant; my face as unlovely; and my Appearance as unpleasing as yours! But Ah! what little chance is there of so desirable an Event; I have had the Small-pox,* and must therefore submit to my unhappy fate.

I am now going to intrust you my dear Charlotte with a secret which has long disturbed the tranquility of my days, and which is of a kind to require the most inviolable Secrecy from you. Last Monday se'night* Matilda & I accompanied Lady Lesley to a Rout* at the Honourable Mrs Kickabout's;* we were escorted by Mr Fitzgerald who is a very amiable Young Man in the main, tho' perhaps a little singular in his Taste—He is in love with Matilda—.We had scarcely paid our Compliments to the Lady of the House and curtseyed to half a Score different people when my Attention was attracted by the appearance of a Young Man the most lovely of his Sex, who at that Moment entered the Room with another Gentleman & Lady. From the first moment I beheld him, I was certain that on him depended the future Happiness of my Life.* Imagine my surprise when he was introduced to me by the name of Cleveland—I instantly recognized him as the Brother of Mrs Marlowe, and the acquaintance of my Charlotte at Bristol. Mr and Mrs M. were the Gentleman & Lady who accompanied him. (You do not think Mrs Marlowe handsome?) The elegant address of Mr Cleveland, his polished Manners and Delightful Bow, at once confirmed my attachment. He did not speak; but I can imagine every thing he would have said, had he opened his Mouth. I can picture to myself the cultivated Understanding, the Noble Sentiments, & elegant Language which would have shone so conspicuous in the conversation of Mr Cleveland. The approach of Sir James Gower (one of my too numerous Admirers) prevented the Discovery of any such Powers, by putting an end to a Conversation we had never commenced, and by attracting my attention to himself. But Oh! how inferior are the accomplishments of Sir James to those of his so greatly envied Rival! Sir James is one of the most frequent of our Visitors, & is almost always of our Parties. We have since often met Mr & Mrs Marlowe but no Cleveland—he is always engaged some where else. Mrs Marlowe fatigues me to Death every time I see her by her tiresome Conversations about You & Eloisa. She is so Stupid! I live in the hope of seeing her irrisistable Brother to night, as we are going to Lady Flambeau's,* who is I know intimate with the Marlowes. Our party will be Lady Lesley, Matilda, Fitzgerald, Sir James Gower, & myself. We see little of Sir George, who is almost always at the Gaming-table. Ah! my poor Fortune where art thou by this time? We see more of Lady L. who always makes her appearance (highly rouged) at Dinner-time. Alas! what Delightful Jewels will she be decked in this evening at Lady Flambeau's!; Yet I wonder how she can herself delight in wearing them; surely she must be sensible of the ridiculous impropriety of loading her little diminutive figure with such superfluous ornaments; is it possible that she can not know how greatly superior an elegant simplicity is to the most studied apparel? Would she but present them to Matilda & me, how greatly should we be obliged to her. How becoming would Diamonds be on our fine majestic figures! and how surprising it is that such an Idea should never have occurred to *her*: I am sure if I have reflected in this Manner once, I have fifty times. Whenever I see Lady Lesley dressed in them such reflections immediately come across me. My own Mother's Jewels too! But I will say no more on so melancholy a Subject—Let me entertain you with something more pleasing—Matilda had a letter this Morning from Lesley, by which we have the pleasure of finding that he is at Naples has turned Roman-catholic, obtained one of the Pope's Bulls* for annulling his 1st Marriage and has since actually married a Neapolitan Lady of great Rank & Fortune. He tells us moreover that much the same sort of affair has befallen his first wife the worthless Louisa who is likewise at Naples has turned Roman-catholic, and is soon to be married to a Neapolitan Nobleman of great & Distinguished Merit. He says, that they are at present very good Freinds, have quite forgiven all past errors and intend in future to be very good Neighbours. He invites Matilda & me to pay him a visit in Italy and to bring him his little Louisa whom both her Mother, Step-Mother, and himself are equally desirous of beholding. As to our accepting his invitation, it is at present very uncertain; Lady Lesley advises us to go without loss of time; Fitzgerald offers to escort us there, but Matilda has some doubts of the Propriety of such a Scheme—She owns it would be very agreable. I am certain she likes the Fellow. My Father desires us not to be in a hurry, as perhaps if we wait a few months both he & Lady

Lesley will do themselves the pleasure of attending us. Lady Lesley says no, that nothing will ever tempt her to forego the Amusements of Brighthelmstone for a Journey to Italy merely to see our Brother. 'No (says the disagreable Woman) I have once in my Life been fool enough to travel I dont know how many hundred Miles to see two of the Family, and I found it did not answer, so Deuce take me, if ever I am so foolish again.' So says her Ladyship, but Sir George still perseveres in saying that perhaps in a Month or two, they may accompany us.

Adeiu my Dear Charlotte—

Y^r faithful Margaret Lesley

The History of England

from the reign of
Henry the 4th
to the death of
Charles the 1st.*

By a partial, prejudiced, & ignorant Historian.*

To Miss Austen* eldest daughter of the Revd George Austen, this
Work is inscribed with all due respect by

The Author

N.B. There will be very few Dates in this History.*

Henry the 4th*

Henry the 4th ascended the throne of England much to his own satisfaction in the year 1399, after having prevailed on his cousin & predecissor Richard the 2^d, to resign it to him, & to retire for the rest of his Life to Pomfret Castle,* where he happened to be murdered.* It is to be supposed that Henry was married, since he had certainly four sons, but it is not in my power to inform the Reader who was his Wife.* Be this as it may, he did not live for ever, but falling ill, his son the Prince of Wales came and took away the crown; whereupon the King made a long speech, for which I must refer the Reader to Shakespear's Plays, & the Prince made a still longer.* Things being thus settled between them the King died, & was succeeded by his son Henry who had previously beat Sir William Gascoigne.*

Henry the 5th*

This Prince after he succeeded to the throne grew quite reformed & Amiable, forsaking all his dissipated Companions,* & never thrashing Sir William again. During his reign, Lord Cobham was burnt alive,* but I forget what for. His Magesty then turned his thoughts to France,* where he went & fought the famous Battle of Azincourt.* He afterwards married the King's daughter Catherine, a very agreable Woman by Shakespear's account.* Inspite of all this however he died, and was succeeded by his son Henry.

Henry the 6th

I cannot say much for this Monarch's Sense*—Nor would I if I could, for he was a Lancastrian. I suppose you know all about the Wars between him & the Duke of York who was of the right side;* if you do not, you had better read some other History, for I shall not be very diffuse in this, meaning by it only to vent my Spleen* *against*, & shew my Hatred *to* all those people whose parties or principles do not suit with mine, & not to give information. This King married Margaret of Anjou, a Woman whose distresses & Misfortunes were so great as almost to make me who hate her, pity her.* It was in this reign that Joan of Arc lived & made such a *row** among the English. They should not have burnt her—but they did. There were several Battles between the Yorkists & Lancastrians, in which the former (as they ought) usually conquered. At length they were entirely over come; The King was murdered—The Queen was sent home*—& Edward the 4th Ascended the Throne.

Edward the 4th

This Monarch was famous only for his Beauty & his Courage, of which the Picture we have here given of him,* & his undaunted Behaviour in marrying one Woman while he was engaged to another,* are sufficient proofs. His Wife was Elizabeth Woodville, a Widow who poor Woman!, was afterwards confined in a Convent by that Monster of Iniquity & Avarice Henry the 7th.* One of Edward's Mistresses was Jane Shore, who has had a play written about her,* but it is a tragedy &

therefore not worth reading. Having performed all these noble actions, his Majesty died, & was succeeded by his Son.

Edward the 5th

This unfortunate Prince lived so little a while that no body had time to draw his picture.* He was murdered by his Uncle's Contrivance, whose name was Richard the 3^d.

Richard the 3^d

The Character of this Prince has been in general very severely treated by Historians, but as he was a *York*, I am rather inclined to suppose him a very respectable Man.* It has indeed been confidently asserted that he killed his two Nephews & his Wife, but it has also been declared that he did *not* kill his two Nephews,* which I am inclined to beleive true;* & if this is the case, it may also be affirmed that he did not kill his Wife,* for if Perkin Warbeck was really the Duke of York,* why might not Lambert Simnel be the Widow of Richard.* Whether innocent or guilty, he did not reign long in peace, for Henry Tudor E. of Richmond as great a Villain as ever lived, made a great fuss about getting the Crown* & having killed the King at the battle of Bosworth,* he suceeded to it.

Henry the 7ᵗʰ

This Monarch soon after his accession married the Princess Elizabeth of York,* by which alliance he plainly proved that he thought his own right inferior to hers, tho' he pretended to the contrary. By this Marriage he had two sons & two daughters, the elder of which Daughters was married to the King of Scotland & had the happiness of being grand-mother* to one of the first Characters in the World. But of *her*, I shall have occasion to speak more at large in future. The Youngest, Mary, married first the King of France & secondly the D. of Suffolk,* by whom she had one daughter, afterwards the Mother of Lady Jane Grey, who tho' inferior to her lovely Cousin the Queen of Scots, was yet an amiable young Woman & famous for reading Greek while other people were hunting.* It was in the reign of Henry the 7ᵗʰ that Perkin Warbeck & Lambert Simnel before mentioned made their appearance, the former of whom was set in the Stocks, took shelter in Beaulieu Abbey, & was beheaded with the Earl of Warwick, & the latter was taken into the Kings kitchen.* His Majesty died & was succeeded by his son Henry whose only merit was his not being *quite* so bad as his daughter Elizabeth.

Henry the 8th*—

It would be an affront to my Readers were I to suppose that they were not as well acquainted with the particulars of this King's reign as I am myself. It will therefore be saving *them* the task of reading again what they have read before, & *myself* the trouble of writing what I do not perfectly recollect, by giving only a slight sketch of the principal Events* which marked his reign. Among these may be ranked Cardinal Wolsey's telling the father Abbott of Leicester Abbey that 'he was come to lay his bones among them,'* the reformation in Religion, & the King's riding through the streets of London with Anna Bullen. It is however but Justice, & my Duty to declare that this amiable Woman was entirely innocent of the Crimes with which she was accused,* of which her Beauty, her Elegance, & her Sprightliness were sufficient proofs, not to mention her solemn protestations of Innocence, the weakness of the Charges against her, & the king's Character; all of which add some confirmation, tho' perhaps but slight ones when in comparison with those before alledged in her favour. Tho' I do not profess giving many dates, yet as I think it proper to give some & shall of course make choice of those which it is most necessary for the Reader to know, I think it right to inform him that her letter to the King was dated on the 6th of May.* The Crimes & Cruelties of this Prince,* were too numerous to be mentioned, (as this history I trust has fully shewn;) & nothing can be said in his vindication, but that his abolishing Religious Houses* & leaving them to the ruinous depredations of time has been of infinite use to the landscape of England in general,* which probably was a principal motive for his doing it, since otherwise why should a Man who was of no Religion himself be at so much trouble to abolish one which had for Ages been established in the Kingdom. His Majesty's 5ᵗʰ Wife was the Duke of Norfolk's Neice who, tho' universally acquitted of the crimes for which she was beheaded, has been by many people supposed to have led an abandoned Life before her Marriage*—Of this however I have many doubts, since she was a relation of that noble Duke of Norfolk* who was so warm in the Queen of Scotland's cause, & who at last fell a victim to it. The kings last wife* contrived to survive him, but with difficulty effected it. He was succeeded by his only son Edward.

Edward the 6ᵗʰ

As this prince was only nine years old at the time of his Father's death, he was considered by many people as too young to govern, & the late King happening to be of the same opinion, his mother's Brother the Duke of Somerset was chosen Protector of the realm during his minority.* This Man was on the whole of a very amiable Character, & is somewhat of a favourite with me, tho' I would by no means pretend to affirm that he was equal to those first of Men Robert Earl of Essex, Delamere, or Gilpin.* He was beheaded, of which he might with reason have been proud, had he known that such was the death of Mary Queen of Scotland; but as it was impossible that he should be conscious of what had never happened, it does not appear that he felt particularly delighted with the manner of it.* After his decease the Duke of Northumberland* had the care of the King & the Kingdom, & performed his trust of both so well that the King died & the Kingdom was left to his daughter in law the Lady Jane Grey, who has been already mentioned as reading Greek. Whether she really understood that language or whether such a Study proceeded only from an excess of vanity* for which I beleive she was always rather remarkable, is uncertain. Whatever might be the cause, she preserved the same appearance of knowledge, & contempt of what was generally esteemed pleasure, during the whole of her Life, for she declared herself displeased with being appointed Queen, and while conducting to the Scaffold, she wrote a Sentence in latin & another in Greek on seeing the dead Body of her Husband accidentally passing that way.*

Mary*

This woman had the good luck of being advanced to the throne of England, inspite of the superior pretensions, Merit, & *Beauty* of her Cousins Mary Queen of Scotland & Jane Grey. Nor can I pity the Kingdom for the misfortunes they experienced during her Reign, since they fully deserved them, for having allowed her to succeed her Brother—which was a double peice of folly, since they might have foreseen that as she died without Children, she would be succeeded by that disgrace to humanity, that pest of society, Elizabeth. Many were the people who fell Martyrs to the protestant Religion during her reign; I suppose not fewer than a dozen.* She married Philip King of Spain who in her Sister's reign was famous for building Armadas.* She died without issue, & then the dreadful moment came in which the destroyer of all comfort, the deceitful Betrayer of trust reposed in her, & the Murderess of her Cousin succeeded to the Throne.—

Elizabeth*—

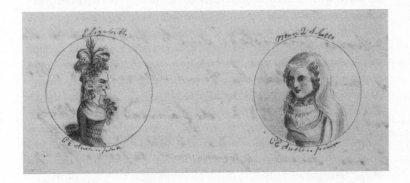

It was the peculiar Misfortune of this Woman to have bad Ministers*— Since wicked as she herself was, she could not have committed such extensive Mischeif, had not these vile & abandoned Men connived at, & encouraged her in her Crimes. I know that it has by many people been asserted & beleived that Lord Burleigh, Sir Francis Walsingham,* & the rest of those who filled the cheif Offices of State were deserving, experienced, & able Ministers. But Oh! how blinded such Writers & such Readers must be to true Merit, to Merit despised, neglected & defamed, if they can persist in such opinions when they reflect that these Men, these boasted Men were such Scandals to their Country & their Sex as to allow & assist their Queen in confining for the Space of nineteen Years, a *Woman* who if the claims of Relationship & Merit were of no avail, yet as a Queen & as one who condescended to place confidence in her, had every reason to expect Assistance & protection; and at length in allowing Elizabeth to bring this amiable Woman to an untimely, unmerited, and scandalous Death. Can any one if he reflects but for a moment on this blot, this everlasting blot upon their

Understanding & their Character, allow any praise to Lord Burleigh
or Sir Francis Walsingham? Oh! what must this bewitching Princess
whose only freind was then the Duke of Norfolk, and whose only ones
are now Mr Whitaker, Mrs Lefroy, Mrs Knight* & myself, who was
abandoned by her son,* confined by her Cousin, Abused, reproached &
vilified by all, what must not her most noble Mind have suffered when
informed that Elizabeth had given orders for her Death! Yet she bore
it with a most unshaken fortitude; firm in her Mind; Constant in her
Religion; & prepared herself to meet the cruel fate to which she was
doomed, with a magnanimity that could alone proceed from conscious Innocence. And Yet could you Reader have beleived it possible
that some hardened & zealous Protestants have even abused her for
that Steadfastness in the Catholic Religion which reflected on her
so much credit? But this is a striking proof of *their* narrow Souls
& prejudiced Judgements who accuse her. She was executed in the
Great Hall at Fotheringay Castle (sacred Place!) on Wednesday the 8th
of February—1586*—to the everlasting Reproach of Elizabeth, her
Ministers, and of England in general. It may not be unnecessary
before I entirely conclude my account of this ill-fated Queen, to
observe that she had been accused of several crimes during the time
of her reigning in Scotland, of which I now most seriously do assure
my Reader that she was entirely innocent; having never been guilty of
anything more than Imprudencies into which she was betrayed by the
openness of her Heart, her Youth, & her Education. Having I trust by
this assurance entirely done away every Suspicion & every doubt which
might have arisen in the Reader's mind, from what other Historians
have written of her, I shall proceed to mention the remaining Events,
that marked Elizabeth's reign. It was about this time that Sir Francis
Drake the first English Navigator who sailed round the World, lived,
to be the ornament of his Country & his profession. Yet great as he
was, & justly celebrated as a Sailor, I cannot help foreseeing that he
will be equalled in this or the next Century by one who tho' now but
young,* already promises to answer all the ardent & sanguine expectations of his Relations & Freinds, amongst whom I may Class the amiable Lady to whom this work is dedicated, & my no less amiable Self.

Though of a different profession, and shining in a different Sphere of
Life, yet equally conspicuous in the Character of an *Earl*, as Drake was
in that of a *Sailor*, was Robert Devereux Lord Essex. This unfortunate
young Man was not únlike in Character to that equally unfortunate one

Frederic Delamere. The simile may be carried still farther, & Elizabeth the torment of Essex may be compared to the Emmeline of Delamere.* It would be endless to recount the misfortunes of this noble & gallant Earl. It is sufficient to say that he was beheaded on the 25th of Feb.ry,* after having been Lord Leuitenant of Ireland, after having clapped his hand on his Sword,* and after performing many other services to his Country. Elizabeth did not long survive his loss, & died *so* miserable* that were it not an injury to the memory of Mary I should pity her.

James the 1st*

Though this King had some faults, among which & as the most principal, was his allowing his Mother's death,* yet considered on the whole I cannot help liking him. He married Anne of Denmark,* and had several Children; fortunately for him his eldest son Prince Henry died before his father or he might have experienced the evils which befell his unfortunate Brother.*

As I am myself partial to the roman catholic religion,* it is with infinite regret that I am obliged to blame the Behaviour of any Member of it; yet Truth being I think very excusable in an Historian, I am necessitated to say that in this reign the roman Catholics of England did not behave like Gentlemen to the protestants. Their Behaviour indeed to the Royal Family & both Houses of Parliament might justly be considered by them as very uncivil,* and even Sir Henry Percy tho' certainly the best bred Man of the party, had none of that general politeness which is so universally pleasing, as his Attentions were entirely Confined to Lord Mounteagle.*

Sir Walter Raleigh* flourished in this & the preceding reign, & is by many people held in great veneration & respect—But as he was an enemy of the noble Essex, I have nothing to say in praise of him, & must refer all those who may wish to be acquainted with the particulars of his Life, to Mr Sheridan's play of the Critic,* where they will find many interesting Anecdotes as well of him as of his freind Sir Christopher Hatton.—His Majesty was of that amiable disposition which inclines to Freindships, & in such points was possessed of a keener penetration in Discovering Merit* than many other people. I once heard an excellent Sharade* on a Carpet, of which the subject I am now on reminds me, and as I think it may afford my Readers some Amusement to *find it out*, I shall here take the liberty of presenting it to them.

Sharade

My first is what my second was to King James the 1st, and you tread on my whole.*

The principal favourites of his Magesty were Car, who was afterwards created Earl of Somerset and whose name perhaps may have some share in the above-mentioned Sharade, & George Villiers afterwards Duke of Buckingham.* On his Majesty's death he was succeeded by his son Charles.

Charles the 1st

This amiable Monarch seems born to have suffered Misfortunes equal to those of his lovely Grandmother;* Misfortunes which he could not deserve since he was her descendent. Never certainly were there before so many detestable Characters at one time in England as in this period of its History; Never were amiable Men so scarce. The number of them throughout the whole Kingdom amounting only to *five*, besides the inhabitants of Oxford who were always loyal to their King & faithful to his interests. The names of this noble five who never forgot the duty of the Subject, or swerved from their attachment to his Majesty, were as follows—The King himself, ever stedfast in his own support—Archbishop Laud, Earl of Strafford, Viscount Faulkland & Duke of Ormond,* who were scarcely less strenuous or zealous in the cause. While the *Villains* of the time would make too long a list to be written or read; I shall therefore content myself with mentioning the leaders of the Gang. Cromwell, Fairfax, Hampden, & Pym* may be considered as the original Causers of all the disturbances Distresses, & Civil Wars in which England for many years was embroiled. In this reign as well as in that of Elizabeth, I am obliged in spite of my Attachment to the Scotch, to consider them as equally guilty with the generality of the English, since they dared to think differently from their Sovereign, to forget the Adoration which as *Stuarts* it was their Duty to pay them, to rebel against, dethrone & imprison the unfortunate Mary; to oppose, to deceive, and to sell the no less unfortunate Charles. The Events of this Monarch's reign are too numerous for my pen, and indeed the recital of any Events (except what I make myself) is uninteresting to me; my principal reason for undertaking the History of England being to prove the innocence of the Queen of Scotland, which I flatter myself with having effectually done, and to abuse Elizabeth, tho' I am rather fearful of having fallen short in the latter part of my Scheme.—. As therefore it is not my intention to give any particular account of the distresses into which this King was involved through the misconduct & Cruelty of his Parliament, I shall satisfy myself with vindicating him from the Reproach of Arbitrary & tyrannical Government with which he has often been Charged. This, I feel, is not difficult to be done, for with one argument I am certain of satisfying every sensible & well disposed person whose opinions have been properly guided by a good Education—& this Argument is that he was a **Stuart**.

Finis

Saturday Nov. 26th. 1791

[Collection of Letters]*

To Miss Cooper*—

Cousin

Conscious of the Charming Character which in every Country, &
every Clime* in Christendom is Cried, Concerning you, with Caution &
Care I Commend to your Charitable Criticism this Clever Collection
of Curious* Comments, which have been Carefully Culled, Collected
& Classed by your Comical Cousin

The Author.

A Collection of Letters—

Letter the first

From a Mother to her freind.

My Children begin now to claim all my attention in a different Manner
from that in which they have been used to receive it, as they are now
arrived at that age when it is necessary for them in some measure to
become conversant with the World.* My Augusta is 17 & her Sister
scarcely a twelvemonth younger. I flatter myself that their education
has been such as will not disgrace their appearance in the World, &
that *they* will not disgrace their Education I have every reason to beleive.
Indeed they are sweet Girls—. Sensible yet unaffected—Accomplished
yet Easy—. Lively yet Gentle—. As their progress in every thing they
have learnt has been always the same, I am willing to forget the difference of age, and to introduce them together into Public. This very
Evening is fixed on as their first entrée into Life,* as we are to drink
tea* with Mrs Cope & her Daughter. I am glad that we are to meet no
one for my Girls sake, as it would be awkward for them to enter too
wide a Circle on the very first day. But we shall proceed by degrees—.
Tomorrow Mr Stanly's family will drink tea with us, and perhaps the
Miss Phillips's will meet them. On Tuesday we shall pay Morning-
Visits*—On Wednesday We are to dine at Westbrook. On Thursday
we have Company at home. On Friday we are to be at a private Concert
at Sir John Wynne's—& on Saturday we expect Miss Dawson to call

in the Morning,—which will complete my Daughters Introduction into Life. How they will bear so much dissipation I cannot imagine; of their Spirits I have no fear, I only dread their health.

———

This mighty affair is now happily over, & my Girls *are out*. As the moment approached for our departure, you can have no idea how the sweet Creatures trembled with fear & expectation. Before the Carriage drove to the door, I called them into my dressing-room, & as soon as they were seated thus addressed them. 'My dear Girls the moment is now arrived when I am to reap the rewards of all my Anxieties and Labours towards you during your Education. You are this Evening to enter a World in which you will meet with many wonderfull Things; Yet let me warn you against suffering yourselves to be meanly swayed by the Follies & Vices of others, for beleive me my beloved Children that if you do———I shall be very sorry for it.' They both assured me that they would ever remember my Advice with Gratitude, & follow it with Attention; That they were prepared to find a World full of things to amaze & to shock them: but that they trusted their behaviour would never give me reason to repent the Watchful Care with which I had presided over their infancy* & formed their Minds—'With such expect-ations & such intentions (cried I) I can have nothing to fear from you—& can chearfully conduct you to Mrs Cope's without a fear of your being seduced by her Example, or contaminated by her Follies. Come, then my Children (added I) the Carriage is driving to the door, & I will not a moment delay the happiness you are so impatient to enjoy.' When we arrived at Warleigh, poor Augusta could scarcely breathe, while Margaret was all Life & Rapture. 'The long-expected Moment is now arrived (said she) and we shall soon be in the World.'—In a few Moments we were in Mrs Cope's parlour—, where with her daughter she sate ready to receive us. I observed with delight the impression my Children made on them—. They were indeed two sweet, elegant-looking Girls, & tho' somewhat abashed from the peculiarity of their Situation, Yet there was an ease in their Manners & Address which could not fail of pleasing—. Imagine my dear Madam how delighted I must have been in beholding as I did, how attentively they observed every object they saw, how disgusted with some Things, how enchanted with others, how astonished at all! On the whole however they returned in raptures with the World, its Inhabitants, & Manners.

Y^rs Ever—A—F—.

Letter the second

From a Young lady crossed in Love to her freind—

———

Why should this last disappointment hang so heavily on my Spirits? Why should I feel it more, why should it wound me deeper than those I have experienced before? Can it be that I have a greater affection for Willoughby than I had for his amiable predecessors—? Or is it that our feelings become more acute from being often wounded? I must suppose my dear Belle that this is the Case, since I am not conscious of being more sincerely attached to Willoughby than I was to Neville, Fitzowen, or either of the Crawfords,* for all of whom I once felt the most lasting affection that ever warmed a Woman's heart. Tell me then dear Belle why I still sigh when I think of the faithless Edward, or why I weep when I behold his Bride, for too surely this is the case—. My Freinds are all alarmed for me; They fear my declining health; they lament my want of Spirits; they dread the effects of both. In hopes of releiving my Melancholy,* by directing my thoughts to other objects, they have invited several of their freinds to spend the Christmas with us. Lady Bridget Dashwood* & her Sister-in-Law Miss Jane are expected on Friday; & Colonel Seaton's family will be with us next week. This is all most kindly meant by my Uncle & Cousins; but what can the presence of a dozen indifferent people do to me, but weary & distress me—. I will not finish my Letter till some of our Visitors are arrived.

———

Friday Evening—

Lady Bridget came this Morning, and with her, her sweet Sister* Miss Jane—. Although I have been acquainted with this charming Woman above fifteen Years, Yet I never before observed how lovely she is. She is now about 35, & in spite of sickness, Sorrow and Time is more blooming than I ever saw a Girl of 17. I was delighted with her, the moment she entered the house, & she appeared equally pleased with me, attaching herself to me during the remainder of the day. There is something so sweet, so mild in her Countenance, that she seems more than Mortal. Her Conversation is as bewitching as her appearance—; I could not help telling her how much she engaged my Admiration—. 'Oh! Miss Jane (said I)—and stopped from an inability at the moment

of expressing myself as I could wish—'Oh! Miss Jane (I repeated)—
I could not think of words to suit my feelings—. She seemed waiting
for my Speech—. I was confused—distressed— My thoughts were
bewildered—and I could only add— 'How do you do?' She saw & felt
for my Embarrassment & with admirable presence of mind releived me
from it by saying—'My dear Sophia be not uneasy at having exposed
Yourself—I will turn the Conversation without appearing to notice it.'
Oh! how I loved her for her kindness! 'Do you ride as much as you used
to do?' said she—. 'I am advised to ride by my Physician,* We have
delightful Rides round us, I have a Charming horse, am uncommonly
fond of the Amusement, replied I quite recovered from my Confusion,
& in short I ride a great deal.' 'You are in the right my Love,' said She,
Then repeating the following Line which was an extempore & equally
adapted to recommend both Riding & Candour—
'Ride where you may, Be Candid where You can,'*
She added, '*I* rode once, but it is many years ago'—She spoke this in
so low & tremulous a Voice, that I was silent—Struck with her Manner
of Speaking I could make no reply. 'I have not ridden, continued she
fixing her Eyes on my face, since I was married.' I was never so surprised— 'Married, Ma'am!' I repeated. 'You may well wear that look
of astonishment, said she, since what I have said must appear improbable to you—Yet nothing is more true than that I once was married.'
   'Then why are you called Miss Jane?'
'I married, my Sophia without the consent or knowledge of my father
the late Admiral Annesley. It was therefore necessary to keep the
secret from him & from every one, till some fortunate opportunity
might offer of revealing it—. Such an opportunity alas! was but too
soon given in the death of my dear Capt. Dashwood—Pardon these
tears, continued Miss Jane wiping her Eyes, I owe them to my
Husband's Memory. He fell my Sophia, while fighting for his Country
in America* after a most happy Union of seven years—. My Children,
two sweet Boys & a Girl, who had constantly resided with my Father &
me, passing with him & with every one as the Children of a Brother
(tho' I had ever been an only Child) had as yet been the Comforts of
my Life. But no sooner had I lossed my Henry, than these sweet
Creatures fell sick & died—. Conceive dear Sophia what my feelings
must have been when as an Aunt I attended my Children to their early
Grave—. My Father did not survive them many weeks—He died,
poor Good old Man, happily ignorant to his last hour of my Marriage.'

'But did not you own it, & assume his name at your husband's death?'

'No; I could not bring myself to do it; more especially when in my Children I lost all inducement for doing it. Lady Bridget, and yourself are the only persons who are in the knowledge of my having ever been either Wife or Mother. As I could not prevail on myself to take the name of Dashwood (a name which after my Henry's death I could never hear without emotion) and as I was conscious of having no right to that of Annesley,* I dropt all thoughts of either, & have made it a point of bearing only my Christian one since my Father's death.' She paused. 'Oh! my dear Miss Jane (said I) how infinitely am I obliged to you for so entertaining a Story! You cannot think how it has diverted me! But have you quite done?'

'I have only to add my dear Sophia, that my Henry's elder Brother dieing about the same time, Lady Bridget became a Widow like myself, and as we had always loved each other in idea from the high Character in which we had ever been spoken of, though we had never met, we determined to live together. We wrote to one another on the same subject by the same post, so exactly did our feelings & our Actions coincide! We both eagerly embraced the proposals we gave & received of becoming one family, & have from that time lived together in the greatest affection.'

'And is this all? said I, I hope you have not done.'

'Indeed I have; and did you ever hear a Story more pathetic?'

'I never did—and it is for that reason it pleases me so much, for when one is unhappy nothing is so delightful to one's sensations as to hear of equal Misery.'

'Ah! but my Sophia why *are you* unhappy?'

'Have you not heard Madam of Willoughby's Marriage?' 'But my Love why lament *his* perfidy, when you bore so well that of many young Men before?' 'Ah! Madam. I was used to it then, but when Willoughby broke his Engagements I had not been dissapointed for half a year.' 'Poor Girl!' said Miss Jane.

Letter the third

From A young Lady in distress'd Circumstances to her freind.

————

A few days ago I was at a private Ball given by Mr Ashburnham. As my Mother never goes out she entrusted me to the care of Lady

Greville who did me the honour of calling for me in her way & of allowing me to sit forwards,* which is a favour about which I am very indifferent especially as I know it is considered as confering a great obligation on me. 'So Miss Maria (said her Ladyship as she saw me advancing to the door of the Carriage) you seem very smart tonight—*My* poor Girls will appear quite to disadvantage by *you*—I only hope your Mother may not have distressed herself to set *you* off. Have you got a new Gown on?'

'Yes Ma'am,' replied I with as much indifference as I could assume.

'Aye, and a fine one too I think—(feeling it, as by her permission I seated myself by her) I dare say it is all very smart—But I must own, for you know I always speak my mind, that I think it was quite a need-less peice of expence—Why could not you have worn your old striped one?* It is not my way to find fault with people because they are poor, for I always think that they are more to be despised & pitied than blamed for it, especially if they cannot help it, but at the same time I must say that in my opinion your old striped Gown would have been quite fine enough for its wearer—for to tell you the truth (I always speak my mind) I am very much afraid that one half of the people in the room will not know whether you have a Gown on or not—But I suppose you intend to make your fortune tonight—: Well, the sooner the better; & I wish you success.'

'Indeed Ma'am I have no such intention—'

'Who ever heard a Young Lady own that she was a Fortune-hunter?' Miss Greville laughed, but I am sure Ellen felt for me.

'Was your Mother gone to bed before you left her?' said her Ladyship—

'Dear Ma'am, said Ellen it is but nine o'clock.'

'True Ellen, but Candles cost money, and Mrs Williams is too wise to be extravagant.'*

'She was just sitting down to supper Ma'am—'

'And what had she got for Supper?' 'I did not observe.' 'Bread & Cheese I suppose.' 'I should never wish for a better supper.' said Ellen. 'You have never any reason replied her Mother, as a better is always provided for you.' Miss Greville laughed excessively, as she constantly does at her Mother's wit.

Such is the humiliating Situation in which I am forced to appear while riding in her Ladyship's Coach—I dare not be impertinent, as my Mother is always admonishing me to be humble & patient if

I wish to make my way in the world. She insists on my accepting every invitation of Lady Greville, or you may be certain that I would never enter either her House, or her Coach with the disagreable certainty I always have of being abused for my Poverty while I am in them.— When we arrived at Ashburnham, it was nearly ten o'clock, which was an hour and a half later than we were desired to be there; but Lady Greville is too fashionable (or fancies herself to be so) to be punctual. The Dancing however was not begun as they waited for Miss Greville. I had not been long in the room before I was engaged to dance by Mr Bernard, but just as we were going to stand up, he recollected that his Servant had got his white Gloves,* & immediately ran out to fetch them. In the mean time the Dancing began & Lady Greville in passing to another room went exactly before me—She saw me and instantly stopping, said to me though there were several people close to us,

'Hey day, Miss Maria! What cannot you get a partner? Poor Young Lady! I am afraid your new Gown was put on for nothing. But do not despair; perhaps you may get a hop* before the Evening is over.' So saying, she passed on without hearing my repeated assurance of being engaged, & leaving me very much provoked at being so exposed before every one—Mr Bernard however soon returned & by coming to me the moment he entered the room, and leading me to the Dancers my Character I hope was cleared from the imputation Lady Greville had thrown on it, in the eyes of all the old Ladies who had heard her speech. I soon forgot all my vexations in the pleasure of dancing and of having the most agreable partner in the room. As he is moreover heir to a very large Estate I could see that Lady Greville did not look very well pleased when she found who had been his Choice—She was determined to mortify me, and accordingly when we were sitting down between the dances, she came to me with *more* than her usual insulting importance attended by Miss Mason and said loud enough to be heard by half the people in the room, 'Pray Miss Maria in what way of business was your Grandfather? for Miss Mason & I cannot agree whether he was a Grocer or a Bookbinder.'* I saw that she wanted to mortify me, and was resolved if I possibly could to prevent her seeing that her scheme succeeded. 'Neither Madam; he was a Wine Merchant.' 'Aye, I knew he was in some such low way—He broke* did not he?' 'I beleive not Ma'am.' 'Did not he abscond?' 'I never heard that he did.' 'At least he died insolvent?' 'I was never told so before.' 'Why, was not your *Father* as poor as a Rat?'* 'I fancy not;' 'Was not he in the Kings Bench* once?' 'I never saw him there.' *She* gave me *such* a look, & turned away in a great passion; while I was half delighted with myself for my impertinence, & half afraid of being thought too saucy.* As Lady Greville was extremely angry with me, she took no further notice of me all the Evening, and indeed had I been in favour I should have been equally neglected, as she was got into a party of great folks & she never speaks to me when she can to any one else. Miss Greville was with her Mother's party at Supper, but Ellen preferred staying with the Bernards & me. We had a very pleasant Dance & as Lady G— slept all the way home, I had a very comfortable ride.

The next day while we were at dinner Lady Greville's Coach stopped at the door, for that is the time of day she generally contrives it should. She sent in a message by the Servant to say that 'she should not get out but that Miss Maria must come to the Coach-door, as she wanted to speak to her, and that she must make haste & come immediately—' 'What an impertinent Message Mama!' said I—'Go Maria—' replied She—Accordingly I went & was obliged to stand there at her Lady-ships pleasure though the Wind was extremely high and very cold.

'Why I think Miss Maria you are not quite so smart as you were last night—But I did not come to examine your dress, but to tell you that you may dine with us the day after tomorrow—Not tomorrow, remember, do not come tomorrow, for we expect Lord and Lady Clermont & Sir Thomas Stanley's family—There will be no occasion for your being very fine for I shant send the Carriage—If it rains you may take an umbrella*—' I could hardly help laughing at hearing her give me leave to keep myself dry—'And pray remember to be in time, for I shant wait—I hate my Victuals over-done—But you need not come *before* the time—How does your Mother do—? She is at dinner is not she?' 'Yes Ma'am we were in the middle of dinner when your Ladyship came.' 'I am afraid you find it very cold Maria.' said Ellen. 'Yes, it is an horrible East wind—said her Mother—I assure you I can hardly bear the window down—But you are used to be blown about by the wind Miss Maria & that is what has made your Complexion so ruddy & coarse. You young Ladies who cannot often ride in a Carriage never mind what weather you trudge in, or how the wind shews your legs.* I would not have *my* Girls stand out of doors as you do in such a day as this. But some sort of people have no feelings either of cold or Delicacy—Well, remember that we shall expect you on Thursday at 5 o'clock—You must tell your Maid to come for you at night—There

will be no Moon—and you will have an horrid walk home—My
Compts to your Mother—I am afraid your dinner will be cold—Drive
on—' And away she went, leaving me in a great passion with her as
she always does.

Maria Williams

Letter the fourth

From a young Lady rather impertinent to her freind.

———

We dined yesterday with Mr Evelyn where we were introduced to
a very agreable looking Girl his Cousin. I was extremely pleased with
her appearance, for added to the charms of an engaging face, her manner & voice had something peculiarly interesting in them. So much
so, that they inspired me with a great curiosity to know the history of
her Life, who were her Parents, where she came from, and what had
befallen her,* for it was then only known that she was a relation of Mr
Evelyn, and that her name was Grenville.* In the evening a favourable
opportunity offered to me of attempting at least to know what I wished
to know, for every one played at Cards but Mrs Evelyn, My Mother,
Dr Drayton, Miss Grenville and myself, and as the two former were
engaged in a whispering Conversation,* & the Doctor fell asleep, we
were of necessity obliged to entertain each other. This was what I wished
and being determined not to remain in ignorance for want of asking,
I began the Conversation in the following Manner.
'Have you been long in Essex Ma'am?'
'I arrived on Tuesday.'
'You came from Derbyshire?'
'No Ma'am—! appearing surprised at my question, from Suffolk.'*
You will think this a good dash* of mine my dear Mary, but you know
that I am not wanting for Impudence when I have any end in veiw.
'Are you pleased with the Country Miss Grenville? Do you find it
equal to the one you have left?'
'Much superior Ma'am in point of Beauty.' She sighed. I longed to
know for why.
'But the face of any Country however beautiful said I, can be but
a poor consolation for the loss of one's dearest Freinds.' She shook
her head, as if she felt the truth of what I said. My Curiosity was so
much raised, that I was resolved at any rate to satisfy it.

'You regret having left Suffolk then Miss Grenville?' 'Indeed I do.'
'You were born there I suppose?' 'Yes Ma'am I was & passed many
happy years there—'

'That is a great comfort—said I—I hope Ma'am that you never
spent any *un*happy one's there.'

'Perfect Felicity is not the property of Mortals, & no one has a right
to expect uninterrupted Happiness*—*Some* Misfortunes I have certainly met with—'

'*What* Misfortunes dear Ma'am?' replied I, burning with impatience
to know every thing. '*None* Ma'am I hope that have been the effect of
any wilfull fault in me.' 'I dare say not Ma'am; & have no doubt but
that any sufferings you may have experienced could arise only from the
cruelties of Relations or the Errors of Freinds.' She sighed—'You seem
unhappy, my dear Miss Grenville—Is it in my power to soften your
Misfortunes.' '*Your* power Ma'am replied she extremely surprised; it is
in *no ones* power to make me happy.' She pronounced these words in
so mournfull & solemn an accent, that for some time I had not courage
to reply. I was actually silenced. I recovered myself however in a few
moments & looking at her with all the affection I could, 'My dear Miss
Grenville said I, you appear extremely young—& may probably stand in
need of some one's advice whose regard for you, joined to superior Age,
perhaps superior Judgement might authorise her to give it—. I am that
person, & I now challenge you to accept the offer I make you of my Confidence and Freindship, in return to which I shall only ask for yours—'

'You are extremely obliging Ma'am—said She—& I am highly
flattered by your attention to me—. But I am in no difficulty, no
doubt, no uncertainty of situation in which any Advice can be wanted.
Whenever I am however continued she brightening into a complaisant
smile, I shall know where to apply.'

I bowed, but felt a good deal mortified by such a repulse; Still
however I had not given up my point. I found that by the appearance
of Sentiment & Freindship nothing was to be gained & determined
therefore to renew my Attacks by Questions & Suppositions.

'Do you intend staying long in this part of England Miss Grenville?'
'Yes Ma'am, some time I beleive.'

'But how will Mr & Mrs Grenville bear your Absence?'

'They are neither of them alive Ma'am.'

This was an answer I did not expect—I was quite silenced, & never
felt so awkward in my Life—.

Letter the fifth

From a Young Lady very much in love to her Freind.

————

My Uncle gets more stingy, my Aunt more particular, & I more in love every day. What shall we all be at this rate by the end of the year! I had this morning the happiness of receiving the following Letter from my dear Musgrove.*

Sackville St.* Jan.ʳʸ 7ᵗʰ

It is a month to day since I first beheld my lovely Henrietta, & the sacred anniversary must & shall be kept in a manner becoming the day—by writing to her. Never shall I forget the moment when her Beauties first broke on my sight—No time as you well know can erase it from my Memory. It was at Lady Scudamores. Happy Lady Scudamore to live within a mile of the divine Henrietta! When the lovely Creature first entered the room, Oh! what were my sensations? The sight of you was like the sight of a wonderful fine Thing. I started—I gazed at her with Admiration—She appeared every moment more Charming, and the unfortunate Musgrove became a Captive to your Charms before I had time to look about me. Yes Madam, I had the happiness of adoring you, an happiness for which I cannot be too grateful. 'What said he to himself is Musgrove allowed to die for Henrietta,? Enviable Mortal,! and may he pine for her who is the object of universal Admiration, who is adored by a Colonel, & toasted* by a Baronet!—' Adorable Henrietta how beautiful you are! I declare you are quite divine! You are more than Mortal. You are an Angel. You are Venus herself.* Inshort Madam you are the prettiest Girl I ever saw in my Life—& her Beauty is encreased in her Musgrove's Eyes, by permitting him to love her & allowing me to hope. And Ah! Angelic Miss Henrietta Heaven is my Witness how ardently I do hope for the death of your villanous Uncle & his Abandoned* Wife, Since my fair one, will not consent to be mine till their decease has placed her in affluence above what my fortune can procure—. Though it is an improvable Estate*—. Cruel Henrietta to persist in such a resolution! I am at present with my Sister where I mean to continue till my own house which tho' an excellent one is at present somewhat out of repair, is ready to receive me. Amiable princess of my Heart farewell—Of that Heart which trembles while it signs itself your most ardent Admirer

> & devoted humble Serv.ᵗ
>
> T. Musgrove

There is a pattern for a Love-letter* Matilda! Did you ever read such a masterpeice of Writing? Such Sense, Such Sentiment, Such purity of Thought, Such flow of Language & such unfeigned Love in one Sheet?* No, never I can answer for it, since a Musgrove is not to be met with by every Girl. Oh! how I long to be with him! I intend to send him the following in answer to his Letter tomorrow.

My dearest Musgrove———. Words cannot express how happy your Letter made me; I thought I should have cried for Joy, for I love you better than any body in the World. I think you the most amiable, & the handsomest Man in England, & so to be sure you are. I never read so sweet a Letter in my Life. Do write me another just like it, & tell me you are in love with me in every other line. I quite die to see you. How shall we manage to see one another—? for we are so much in love that we cannot live asunder. Oh! my dear Musgrove you cannot think how impatiently I wait for the death of my Uncle and Aunt—If they will not die soon, I beleive I shall run mad,* for I get more in love with you every day of my Life. How happy your Sister is to enjoy the pleasure of your Company in her house, and how happy every body in London must be because you are there. I hope you will be so kind as to write to me again soon, for I never read such sweet Letters as yours. I am my dearest Musgrove most truly & faithfully Yours for ever & ever*

> Henrietta Halton———

I hope he will like my answer; it is as good a one as I can write, though nothing to his; Indeed I had always heard what a dab* he was at a Love-letter. I saw him you know for the first time at Lady Scudamore's—And when I saw her Ladyship afterwards she asked me how I liked her Cousin Musgrove?

'Why upon my word said I, I think he is a very handsome young Man.'

'I am glad you think so replied she, for he is distractedly in love with you.'

'Law! Lady Scudamore said I, how can you talk so ridiculously?'

'Nay, t'is very true answered She, I assure you, for he was in love with you from the first moment he beheld you.'

'I wish it may be true said I, for that is the only kind of love I would give a farthing for*—There is some Sense in being in love at first sight.'

'Well, I give you Joy of your conquest, replied Lady Scudamore, and I beleive it to have been a very complete one; I am sure it is not a contemptible one, for my Cousin is a charming young fellow, has seen a great deal of the World, & writes the best Love-letters I ever read.'

This made me very happy, and I was excessively pleased with my conquest. However I thought it was proper to give myself a few Airs—So I said to her—

'This is all very pretty Lady Scudamore, but you know that we young Ladies who are Heiresses must not throw ourselves away upon Men who have no fortune at all.'

'My dear Miss Halton said She, I am as much convinced of that as you can be, and I do assure you that I should be the last person to encourage your marrying any one who had not some pretensions to expect a fortune with you. Mr Musgrove is so far from being poor that he has an estate of Several hundreds an year* which is capable of great Improvement, and an excellent House, though at present it is not quite in repair.'

'If that is the case replied I, I have nothing more to say against him, and if as you say he is an informed young Man and can write good Love-letters, I am sure I have no reason to find fault with him for admiring me, tho' perhaps I may not marry him for all that Lady Scudamore.'

'You are certainly under no obligation to marry him answered her Ladyship, except that which love himself will dictate to you, for if I am not greatly mistaken you are at this very moment unknown to yourself, cherishing a most tender affection for him.'

'Law, Lady Scudamore replied I blushing how can you think of such a thing?'

'Because every look, every word betrays it, answered She; Come my dear Henrietta, consider me as a freind, and be sincere with me— Do not you prefer Mr Musgrove to any man of your acquaintance?'

'Pray do not ask me such questions Lady Scudamore, said I turning away my head, for it is not fit for me to answer them.'

'Nay my Love replied she, now you confirm my suspicions. But why Henrietta should you be ashamed to own a well-placed Love, or why refuse to confide in me?'

'I am not ashamed to own it; said I taking Courage. I do not refuse to confide in you or blush to say that I do love your cousin Mr Musgrove, that I am sincerely attached to him, for it is no disgrace to love a handsome Man. If he were plain indeed I might have had reason to be ashamed of a passion which must have been mean since the Object would have been unworthy. But with such a figure & face, & such beautiful hair as your Cousin has, why should I blush to own that such Superior Merit has made an impression on me.'

'My sweet Girl (said Lady Scudamore embracing me with great Affection) what a delicate way of thinking you have in these Matters, and what a quick discernment for one of your years! Oh! how I honour you for such Noble Sentiments!'

'Do you Ma'am,? said I; you are vastly obliging. But pray Lady Scudamore did your Cousin himself tell you of his Affection for me? I shall like him the better if he did, for what is a Lover without a Confidante?'

'Oh! my Love replied She, you were born for each other. Every word you say more deeply convinces me that your Minds are actuated by the invisible power of simpathy, for your opinions and Sentiments so exactly coincide. Nay, the colour of your Hair is not very different. Yes my dear Girl, the poor despairing Musgrove did reveal to me the story of his Love——. Nor was I surprised at it——I know not how it was, but I had a kind of presentiment that he *would* be in love with you.'

'Well, but how did he break it to you?'

'It was not till after Supper. We were sitting round the fire together talking on indifferent subjects, though to say the truth the Conversation was cheifly on my side for he was thoughtful and silent, when on a sudden he interrupted me in the midst of something I was saying, by exclaiming in a most Theatrical tone—

Yes I'm in love I feel it now

And Henrietta Halton has undone me*—'

'Oh! What a sweet Way replied I, of declaring his Passion! To make such a couple of charming Lines about me! What a pity it is that they are not in rhime!'

'I am very glad you like it answered She; To be sure there was a great deal of Taste in it. And are you in love with her, Cousin?, said I, I am very sorry for it, for unexceptionable as you are in every respect, with a pretty Estate capable of Great improvements, and an excellent House tho' somewhat out of repair, Yet who can hope to aspire with success to the adorable Henrietta who has had an offer from a Colonel & been toasted by a Baronet'—'*That* I have—' cried I. Lady Scudamore continued. 'Ah dear Cousin replied he, I am so well convinced of the little Chance I can have of winning her who is adored by thousands, that I need no assurances of yours to make me more thoroughly so. Yet surely neither you or the fair Henrietta herself will deny me the exquisite Gratification of dieing for her, of falling a victim to her Charms. And when I am dead'—continued he—

'Oh Lady Scudamore, said I wiping my eyes, that such a sweet Creature should talk of dieing!'

'It is an affecting Circumstance indeed,' replied Lady Scudamore. 'When I am dead said he, Let me be carried & lain at her feet, & perhaps She may not disdain to drop a pitying tear on my poor remains.'

'Dear Lady Scudamore interrupted I, say no more on this affecting Subject. I cannot bear it.'

'Oh! how I admire the sweet Sensibility of your Soul, and as I would not for Worlds wound it too deeply, I will be silent.'

'Pray go on.' said I. She did so.

'And then added he, Ah! Cousin imagine what my transports will be when I feel the dear precious drops trickle o'er my face! Who would not die to taste such extacy! And when I am interred, may the divine Henrietta bless some happier Youth with her affection, May he be as tenderly attached to her as the hapless Musgrove & while *he* crumbles to dust, May they live an example of Felicity in the Conjugal state!'

Did you ever hear any thing so pathetic? What a charming wish, to be lain at my feet when he was dead! Oh! what an exalted mind he must have to be capable of Such a wish! Lady Scudamore went on.

'Ah! my dear Cousin replied I to him, such noble behaviour as this, must melt the heart of any Woman however obdurate it may naturally be; and could the divine Henrietta but hear your generous wishes for her happiness, all gentle as is her Mind, I have not a doubt but that she would pity your affection & endeavour to return it.' 'Oh! Cousin answered he, do not endeavour to raise my hopes by such flattering Assurances. No, I cannot hope to please this angel of a Woman, and the only thing which remains for me to do, is to die.' 'True Love is ever desponding replied I, but *I* my dear Tom will give you even greater hopes of conquering this fair one's heart, than I have yet given you, by assuring you that I watched her with the strictest attention during the whole day, and could plainly discover that she cherishes in her bosom though unknown to herself, a most tender affection for you.'

'Dear Lady Scudamore cried I, This is more than I ever knew!'

'Did not I say that it was unknown to yourself? I did not, continued I to him, encourage you by saying this at first, that Surprise might render the pleasure Still Greater.' 'No Cousin replied he in a languid voice, nothing will convince me that *I* can have touched the heart of Henrietta Halton, and if you are deceived yourself, do not attempt deceiving me.' 'Inshort my Love it was the work of some hours for me to persuade the poor despairing Youth that you had really a preference for him; but when at last he could no longer deny the force of my arguments, or discredit what I told him, his transports, his Raptures, his Extacies are beyond my power to describe.'

'Oh! the dear Creature, cried I, how passionately he loves me! But dear Lady Scudamore did you tell him that I was totally dependant on my Uncle & Aunt?'

'Yes, I told him every thing.'

'And what did he say.'

'He exclaimed with virulence against Uncles & Aunts; Accused the Laws of England for allowing them to possess their Estates when wanted by their Nephews or Neices, and wished *he* were in the House of Commons, that he might reform the Legislature, & rectify all its abuses.'

'Oh! the sweet Man! What a spirit he has!' said I.

'He could not flatter himself he added, that the adorable Henrietta would condescend for his Sake to resign those Luxuries & that Splendor to which She had been used, and accept only in exchange the Comforts and Elegancies which his limitted Income could afford her, even supposing that his house were in Readiness to receive her. I told him that it could not be expected that she would; it would be doing her an injustice to suppose her capable of giving up the power she now possesses & so nobly uses of doing such extensive Good to the poorer part of her fellow Creatures, merely for the gratification of you and herself.'

'To be sure said I, I *am* very Charitable every now and then. And what did Mr Musgrove say to this?'

'He replied that he was under a melancholy Necessity of owning the truth of what I said, and that therefore if he should be the happy Creature destined to be the Husband of the Beautiful Henrietta he must bring himself to wait, however impatiently, for the fortunate day, when she might be freed from the power of worthless Relations and able to bestow herself on him.'

What a noble Creature he is! Oh! Matilda what a fortunate one *I am*, who am to be his Wife! My Aunt is calling to me to come & make the pies.* So adeiu my dear freind.

                                 & beleive me your &c.—H. Halton.

———

Finis

———

[Scraps]

To Miss Fanny Catherine Austen*

My dear Neice

As I am prevented by the great distance between Rowling & Steventon* from superintending Your Education Myself, the care of which will probably on that account devolve on your Father & Mother, I think it is my particular Duty to prevent your feeling as much as possible the want of my personal instructions, by addressing to You on paper my Opinions & Admonitions on the conduct of Young Women,* which you will find expressed in the following pages.—I am my dear Neice

Your affectionate Aunt
The Author.

The female philosopher*—.

a Letter.

My dear Louisa

Your friend Mr Millar called upon us yesterday in his way to Bath, whither he is going for his health; two of his daughters were with him, but the eldest & the three Boys are with their Mother in Sussex. Though you have often told me that Miss Millar was remarkably handsome, You never mentioned anything of her Sisters' beauty; yet they are certainly extremely pretty. I'll give you their description.— Julia is eighteen; with a countenance in which Modesty, Sense & Dignity are happily blended, she has a form which at once presents you with Grace, Elegance & Symmetry. Charlotte who is just sixteen is shorter than her Sister, and though her figure cannot boast the easy dignity of Julia's, yet it has a pleasing plumpness which is in a different way as estimable. She is fair & her face is expressive sometimes of softness the most bewitching, and at others of Vivacity the most striking. She appears to have infinite Wit and a good humour unalterable; her conversation during the half hour they set with us, was replete with humorous Sallies, Bonmots & repartées;* while the sensible, the amiable Julia uttered Sentiments of Morality* worthy of a heart like her own.

Mr Millar appeared to answer the character I had always received of him. My Father met him with that look of Love, that social Shake, & cordial kiss* which marked his gladness at beholding an old & valued friend from whom thro' various circumstances he had been separated nearly twenty Years. Mr Millar observed (and very justly too) that many events had befallen each during that interval of time, which gave occasion to the lovely Julia for making most sensible reflections on the many changes in their situation which so long a period had occasioned, on the advantages of some, & the disadvantages of others. From this subject she made a short digression to the instability of human pleasures & the uncertainty of their duration, which led her to observe that all earthly Joys must be imperfect. She was proceeding to illustrate this doctrine by examples from the Lives of great Men* when the Carriage came to the Door and the amiable Moralist* with her Father & Sister was obliged to depart; but not without a promise of spending five or six months with us* on their return. We of course mentioned you, and I assure you that ample Justice was done to your Merits by all. 'Louisa Clarke (said I) is in general a very pleasant Girl, yet sometimes her good humour is clouded by Peevishness, Envy & Spite. She neither wants Understanding or is without some pretensions to Beauty, but these are so very trifling, that the value she sets on her personal charms, & the adoration she expects them to be offered are at once a striking example of her vanity, her pride, & her folly.' So said I, & to my opinion every one added weight by the concurrence of their own.

your affec.ᵗᵉ Arabella* Smythe

The first Act of a Comedy—

Characters

Popgun*	Maria
Charles	Pistoletta*
Postilion*	Hostess
Chorus of ploughboys*	Cook
&	and
Strephon*	Chloe

Scene—an Inn—

Enter Hostess, Charles, Maria, & Cook.

Host.ˢˢ to Maria) If the gentry in the Lion* should want beds, shew them number 9.—

Maria) Yes Mistress.—   exit Maria—

Host.ˢˢ to Cook) If their Honours in the Moon ask for the bill of fare,* give it them.

Cook)—I wull, I wull—   exit Cook.

Host.ˢˢ to Charles) If their Ladyships in the Sun ring their Bell—answer it.

Charles) Yes, Ma'am.—   Exeunt Severally—

Scene changes to the Moon, & discovers
Popgun & Pistoletta.

Pistol.ᵗᵗᵃ) Pray papa how far is it to London?

Popgun) My Girl, my Darling, my favourite of all my Children, who art the picture of thy poor Mother who died two months ago, with whom I am going to Town to marry to Strephon,* and to whom I mean to bequeath my whole Estate, it wants seven Miles.*

Scene changes to the Sun—
Enter Chloe & a chorus of ploughboys.

Chloe) Where am I? At Hounslow.*—Where go I? To London—. What to do? To be married—. Unto whom? Unto Strephon. Who is he? A Youth.—Then I will sing a Song.

Song—

I go to Town
And when I come down,
I shall be married to Stree-phon
And that to me will be fun.*

Chorus)   Be fun, be fun, be fun,
And that to me will be fun.

Enter Cook—

Cook) Here is the bill of fare.

Chloe reads) 2 Ducks, a leg of beef, a stinking partridge,* & a tart.—
I will have the leg of beef and the Partridge.   exit Cook.
And now I will sing another song.

Song—

I am going to have my dinner,
After which I shan't be thinner,
I wish I had here Strephon
For he would carve the partridge if it should
    be a tough one.

Chorus)   Tough one, tough one, tough one,
For he would carve the partridge if it
    Should be a tough one.

Exit Chloe and Chorus—.

Scene changes to the inside of the Lion.
Enter Strephon & Postilion

Streph.) You drove me from Staines* to this place, from whence
I mean to go to Town to marry Chloe. How much is your due?

Post.) Eighteen pence.

Streph.) Alas, my friend, I have but a bad guinea* with which I mean
to support myself in Town. But I will pawn to you an undirected
Letter* that I received from Chloe.

Post.) Sir, I accept your offer.

End of the first Act.—

A Letter from a Young Lady, whose feelings
being too strong for her Judgement led her into
the commission of Errors which her
Heart disapproved.*—

———

Many have been the cares & vicissitudes of my past life, my beloved
Ellinor,* & the only consolation I feel for their bitterness is that on
a close examination of my conduct, I am convinced that I have strictly
deserved them. I murdered my father at a very early period of my Life,
I have since murdered my Mother, & I am now going to murder my
Sister. I have changed my religion so often that at present I have not
an idea of any left. I have been a perjured witness in every public tryal
for these last twelve Years;* and I have forged my own Will. In short
there is scarcely a crime that I have not committed—But I am now
going to reform. Colonel Martin of the Horseguards* has paid his
Addresses to me, & we are to be married in a few days. As there is
something singular in our Courtship, I will give you an account of it.
Col. Martin is the second Son of the late Sir John Martin who died
immensely rich, but bequeathing only one hundred thousand pound
apeice to his three younger Children, left the bulk of his fortune, about
eight Million to the present Sir Thomas. Upon his small pittance the
Colonel lived tolerably contented for nearly four months when he took
it into his head to determine on getting the whole of his eldest Brother's
Estate. A new will was forged & the Colonel produced it in Court—but
nobody would swear to it's being the right Will except himself, & he
had sworn so much that Nobody beleived him. At that moment I happened to be passing by the door of the Court, and was beckoned in by
the Judge who told the Colonel that I was a Lady ready to witness anything for the cause of Justice, & advised him to apply to me. In short
the Affair was soon adjusted. The Colonel & I swore to its' being the
right will, & Sir Thomas has been obliged to resign all his illgotten
Wealth. The Colonel in gratitude waited on me the next day with an
offer of his hand—. I am now going to murder my Sister. Yᵣˢ Ever,
                                                    Anna Parker.*

══════

A Tour through Wales*—

in a Letter from a young Lady—

My dear Clara

I have been so long on the ramble* that I have not till now had it in my power to thank you for your Letter—. We left our dear home on last Monday Month;* and proceeded on our tour through Wales, which is a principality contiguous to England and gives the title to the Prince of Wales. We travelled on horseback by preference. My Mother rode upon our little poney & Fanny & I walked by her side or rather ran, for my Mother is so fond of riding fast that She galloped all the way. You may be sure that we were in a fine perspiration* when we came to our place of resting. Fanny has taken a great Many Drawings of the Country, which are very beautiful, tho' perhaps not such exact resemblances as might be wished, from their being taken as she ran along. It would astonish you to see all the Shoes we wore out in our Tour. We determined to take a good Stock with us & therefore each took a pair of our own besides those we set off in. However we were obliged to have them both capped & heelpeiced* at Carmarthen,* & at last when they were quite gone, Mama was so kind as to lend us a pair of blue Sattin Slippers,* of which we each took one and hopped home from Hereford* delightfully—

I am your ever affectionate
Elizabeth Johnson.*

A Tale.

A Gentleman whose family name I shall conceal,* bought a small Cottage in Pembrokeshire* about two Years ago. This daring Action was suggested to him by his elder Brother who promised to furnish two rooms & a Closet* for him, provided he would take a small house near the borders of an extensive Forest, and about three Miles from the Sea. Wilhelminus* gladly accepted the Offer and continued for some time searching after such a retreat when he was one morning agreably releived from his Suspence by reading this advertisement in a Newspaper.

To be Lett

A Neat Cottage on the borders of an extensive forest & about three Miles from the Sea. It is ready furnished except two rooms & a Closet.

The delighted Wilhelminus posted away immediately to his brother, & shewed him the advertisement. Robertus congratulated him & sent him in his Carriage to take possession of the Cottage. After travelling for three days & six Nights without Stopping, they arrived at the Forest & following a track which led by it's side down a steep Hill over which ten Rivulets meandered, they reached the Cottage in half an hour. Wilhelminus alighted, and after knocking for some time without receiving any answer or hearing anyone stir within, he opened the door which was fastened only by a wooden latch & entered a small room, which he immediately perceived to be one of the two that were unfurnished—From thence he proceeded into a Closet equally bare. A pair of Stairs that went out of it led him into a room above, no less destitute, & these apartments he found composed the whole of the House. He was by no means displeased with this discovery, as he had the comfort of reflecting that he should not be obliged to lay out any thing on furniture himself—. He returned immediately to his Brother, who took him next day to every Shop in Town, & bought what ever was requisite to furnish the two rooms & the Closet. In a few days every thing was completed, and Wilhelminus returned to take possession of his Cottage. Robertus accompanied him, with his Lady the amiable Cecilia & her two lovely Sisters Arabella and Marina to whom Wilhelminus was tenderly attached, and a large number of Attendants—An ordinary Genius* might probably have been embarrassed in endeavouring to accomodate so large a party, but Wilhelminus with admirable presence of mind gave order for the immediate erection of two noble Tents in an open Spot in the Forest adjoining to the house. Their Construction was both simple & elegant—A Couple of old blankets, each supported by four sticks, gave a striking proof of that taste for Architecture & that happy ease in overcoming difficulties which were some of Wilhelminus's most striking Virtues.

Finis

End of the Second Volume

VOLUME THE THIRD

Jane Austen—May 6ᵗʰ 1792.*

CONTENTS*

To Miss Mary Lloyd,*

The following Novel is by permission
Dedicated,
by her Obed.ʳ humble Serv.ᵗ

The Author

Evelyn*

In a retired part of the County of Sussex there is a village (for what I know to the Contrary) called Evelyn, perhaps one of the most beautiful Spots in the south of England. A Gentleman passing through it on horseback about twenty years ago, was so entirely of my opinion in this respect, that he put up at the little Alehouse in it & enquired with great earnestness whether there were any house to be lett* in the Parish. The Landlady, who as well as every one else in Evelyn was remarkably amiable, shook her head at this question, but seemed unwilling to give him any answer. He could not bear this uncertainty—yet knew not how to obtain the information he desired. To repeat a question which had already appear'd to make the good woman uneasy was impossible—. He turned from her in visible agitation. 'What a situation am I in!' said he to himself as he walked to the window and threw up the sash.* He found himself revived by the Air, which he felt to a much greater degree when he had opened the window than he had done before. Yet it was but for a moment—. The agonizing pain of Doubt & Suspence again weighed down his Spirits. The good woman who had watched in eager silence every turn of his Countenance with that benevolence which characterizes the inhabitants of Evelyn, intreated him to tell her the cause of his uneasiness. 'Is there anything Sir in my power to do that may releive your Greifs—Tell me in what manner I can sooth them, & beleive me that the freindly balm of Comfort and Assistance shall not be wanting; for indeed Sir I have a simpathetic Soul.'

'Amiable Woman (said Mr Gower, affected almost to tears by this generous offer) This Greatness of mind in one to whom I am almost a Stranger, serves but to make me the more warmly wish for a house in this sweet village—. What would I not give to be your Neighbour, to be blessed with your Acquaintance, and with the farther knowledge of your virtues! Oh! with what pleasure would I form myself by such an example!* Tell me then, best of Women,* is there no possibility?— I cannot speak—you know my Meaning——.'

'Alas! Sir, replied Mrs Willis, there *is none*. Every house in this village, from the sweetness of the Situation, & the purity of the Air, in which neither Misery, Illhealth, or Vice are ever wafted, is inhabited. And yet, (after a short pause) there is a Family, who tho' warmly attached to the spot, yet from a peculiar Generosity of Disposition would perhaps be willing to oblige you with their house.'* He eagerly caught at this idea, and having gained a direction to the place, he set off immediately on his walk to it. As he approached the House, he was delighted with its situation. It was in the exact center of a small circular paddock,* which was enclosed by a regular paling,* & bordered with a plantation of Lombardy poplars,* & Spruce firs alternatively placed in three rows.* A gravel walk ran through this beautiful Shrubbery,* and as the remainder of the paddock was unincumbered with any other Timber, the surface of it perfectly even & smooth, and grazed by four white Cows which were disposed at equal distances* from each other, the whole appearance, of the place as Mr Gower entered the Paddock was uncommonly striking. A beautifully-rounded, gravel road without any turn or interruption* led immediately to the house. Mr Gower rang—the Door was soon opened. 'Are Mr & Mrs Webb at home?' 'My Good Sir they are'—replied the Servant; And leading the way, conducted Mr Gower up stairs into a very elegant Dressing room,* where a Lady rising from her seat, welcomed him with all the Generosity which Mrs Willis had attributed to the Family.

'Welcome best of Men—Welcome to this House, & to every thing it contains. William, tell your Master of the happiness I enjoy—invite him to partake of it—. Bring up some Chocolate* immediately; Spread a Cloth in the dining Parlour, and carry in the venison pasty*—. In the mean time let the Gentleman have some sandwiches, and bring in a Basket of Fruit—Send up some Ices and a bason of Soup, and do not forget some Jellies and Cakes.' Then turning to Mr Gower, & taking out her purse, 'Accept this my good Sir,—. Beleive me you are welcome to everything that is in my power to bestow.—I wish my purse were weightier, but Mr Webb must make up my deficiences—. I know he has cash in the house to the amount of an hundred pounds, which he shall bring you immediately.' Mr Gower felt overpowered by her generosity as he put the purse in his pocket, and from the excess of his Gratitude, could scarcely express himself intelligibly when he accepted her offer of the hundred pounds. Mr Webb soon entered the room, and repeated every protestation of Freindship & Cordiality which his Lady had already made.—The Chocolate, The Sandwiches, the Jellies, the Cakes, the Ice, and the Soup soon made their appearance, and Mr Gower having tasted something of all, and pocketted the rest, was conducted into the dining parlour, where he eat a most excellent Dinner & partook of the most exquisite Wines, while Mr and Mrs Webb stood by him still pressing him to eat and drink a little more. 'And now my good Sir, said Mr Webb, when Mr Gower's repast was concluded, what else can we do to contribute to your happiness and express the Affection we bear you. Tell us what you wish more to receive; and depend upon our gratitude for the communication of your wishes.' 'Give me then your house & Grounds; I ask for nothing else.' 'It is yours, exclaimed both at once; from this moment it is yours.' This Agreement concluded on and the present accepted by Mr Gower, Mr Webb rang to have the Carriage ordered, telling William at the same time to call the young Ladies.

'Best of Men, said Mrs Webb, we will not long intrude upon your Time.'

'Make no Apologies dear Madam, replied Mr Gower, You are welcome to stay this half hour if you like it.'

They both burst forth into raptures of Admiration at his politeness, which they agreed served only to make their Conduct appear more inexcusable in trespassing on his time.

The young Ladies soon entered the room. The eldest of them was about seventeen, the other, several years younger. Mr Gower had no sooner fixed his Eyes on Miss Webb than he felt that something more was necessary to his happiness than the house he had just received— Mrs Webb introduced him to her daughter. 'Our dear freind Mr Gower my Love—He has been so good as to accept of this house, small as it is, & to promise to keep it for ever.' 'Give me leave to assure you Sir, said Miss Webb, that I am highly sensible of your kindness in this respect, which from the shortness of my Father's & Mother's acquaintance with you, is more than usually flattering.' Mr Gower bowed—'You are too obliging Ma'am—I assure you that I like the house extremely—and if they would complete their generosity by giving me their eldest daughter in Marriage with a handsome portion,* I should have nothing more to wish for.' This compliment brought a blush into the cheeks of the lovely Miss Webb, who seemed however to refer herself to her father & Mother. *They* looked delighted at each other—At length Mrs Webb breaking silence, said—'We bend under a weight of obligations to you which we can never repay. Take our girl, take our Maria, and on her must the difficult task fall, of endeavouring to make some return to so much Beneficence.' Mr Webb added, 'Her fortune is but ten thousand pounds,* which is almost too small a sum to be offered.' This objection however being instantly removed by the generosity of Mr Gower, who declared himself satisfied with the sum mentioned, Mr & Mrs Webb, with their youngest daughter took their leave, and on the next day, the nuptials of their eldest with Mr Gower were celebrated.*—This amiable Man now found himself perfectly happy; united to a very lovely and deserving young woman, with an handsome fortune, an elegant house, settled in the village of Evelyn, & by that means enabled to cultivate his acquaintance with Mrs Willis, could he have a wish ungratified?—For some months he found that he could *not*, till one day as he was walking in the Shrubbery with Maria leaning on his arm, they observed a rose full-blown lyeing on the gravel; it had fallen from a rose tree which with three others had been planted by Mr Webb to give a pleasing variety* to the walk. These four Rose trees served also to mark the quarters of the Shrubbery, by which means the Travellor might always know how far in his progress round the Paddock he was got—. Maria stooped to pick up the beautiful flower, and with all her Family Generosity presented it to her Husband. 'My dear Frederic, said she, pray take this charming rose.' 'Rose! exclaimed Mr Gower—. Oh! Maria, of what does not that remind me! Alas my poor Sister, how have I neglected you!' The truth was that Mr Gower was the only son of a very large Family, of which Miss Rose Gower was the thirteenth daughter. This young Lady whose merits deserved a better fate than she met with, was the darling of her relations—From the clearness of her skin & the Brilliancy of her Eyes, she was fully entitled to all their partial affection. Another circumstance contributed to the general Love they bore her, and that was one of the finest heads of hair in the world. A few Months before her Brother's marriage, her heart had been engaged by the attentions and charms of a young Man whose high rank and expectations seemed to foretell objections from his Family to a match which would be highly desirable to theirs. Proposals were made on the young Man's part, and proper objections on his Father's—He was desired to return from Carlisle where he was with his beloved Rose, to the family seat in Sussex.* He was obliged to comply, and the angry father then finding from his Conversation how determined he was to marry no other woman, sent him for a fortnight to the Isle of Wight* under the care of the Family Chaplain,* with the hope of overcoming his Constancy by Time and Absence in a foreign Country. They accordingly prepared to bid a long adeiu to England—The young Nobleman was not allowed to see his Rosa. They set sail—A storm arose which baffled the arts of the Seamen. The Vessel was wrecked on the coast of Calshot* and every Soul on board perished. This sad Event soon reached Carlisle, and the beautiful Rose was affected by it, beyond the power of Expression. It was to soften her affliction by obtaining a picture of her unfortunate Lover that her brother undertook a Journey into Sussex, where he hoped that his petition would not be rejected, by the severe yet afflicted Father. When he reached Evelyn he was not many miles from——Castle, but the pleasing events which befell him in that place had for a while made him totally forget the object of his Journey & his unhappy Sister. The little incident of the rose however brought everything concerning her to his recollection again, & he bitterly repented his neglect. He returned to the house immediately and agitated by Greif, Apprehension and Shame wrote the following Letter to Rosa.

July 14th—. Evelyn

My dearest Sister

As it is now four months since I left Carlisle, during which period I have not once written to you, You will perhaps unjustly accuse me of Neglect and Forgetfulness. Alas! I blush when I own the truth of your Accusation.—Yet if you are still alive, do not think too harshly of me, or suppose that I could for a moment forget the situation of my Rose. Beleive me I will forget you no longer, but will hasten as soon as possible to——Castle if I find by your answer that you are still alive. Maria joins me in every dutiful and affectionate wish, & I am yours sincerely

F. Gower.

He waited in the most anxious expectation for an answer to his Letter, which arrived as soon as the great distance from Carlisle would admit of.—But alas, it came not from Rosa.

Carlisle July 17th—

Dear Brother

My Mother has taken the liberty of opening your Letter to poor Rose, as she has been dead these six weeks. Your long absence and continued Silence gave us all great uneasiness and hastened her to the Grave.

Your Journey to——Castle therefore may be spared. You do not tell
us where you have been since the time of your quitting Carlisle, nor in
any way account for your tedious absence, which gives us some surprise.
We all unite in Compts to Maria, & beg to know who she is—.

Y^r affect.^{te} Sister

M. Gower.

    This Letter, by which Mr Gower was obliged to attribute to his own
conduct, his Sister's death, was so violent a shock to his feelings, that
in spite of his living at Evelyn where Illness was scarcely ever heard
of, he was attacked by a fit of the gout,* which confining him to his
own room afforded an opportunity to Maria of shining in that favourite
character of Sir Charles Grandison's, a nurse.* No woman could ever
appear more amiable than Maria did under such circumstances, and
at last by her unremitting attentions had the pleasure of seeing him
gradually recover the use of his feet. It was a blessing by no means lost
on him, for he was no sooner in a condition to leave the house, than
he mounted his horse, and rode to——Castle, wishing to find whether
his Lordship softened by his Son's death, might have been brought to
consent to the match, had both *he* and Rosa been alive. His amiable
Maria followed him with her Eyes till she could see him no longer,
and then sinking into her chair overwhelmed with Greif, found that
in his absence she could enjoy no comfort.

    Mr Gower arrived late in the evening at the castle, which was situ-
ated on a woody Eminence commanding a beautiful prospect of the
Sea. Mr Gower did not dislike the Situation, tho' it was certainly
greatly inferior to that of his own house. There was an irregularity in
the fall of the ground, and a profusion of old Timber which appeared
to him illsuited to the stile of the Castle, for it being a building of
a very ancient date, he thought it required the Paddock of Evelyn
lodge to form a Contrast, and enliven the structure.* The gloomy
appearance of the old Castle frowning on him as he followed it's
winding approach, struck him with terror.* Nor did he think himself
safe, till he was introduced into the Drawing room where the Family
were assembled to tea. Mr Gower was a perfect Stranger to every one
in the Circle but tho' he was always timid in the Dark and easily terrified when alone, he did not want that more necessary & more noble
courage which enabled him without a Blush to enter a large party of
superior Rank, whom he had never seen before, & to take his Seat

amongst them with perfect Indifference. The name of Gower was not unknown to Lord———. He felt distressed & astonished; Yet rose and received him with all the politeness of a well-bred Man. Lady——— who felt a deeper Sorrow at the loss of her Son, than his Lordships harder heart was capable of, could hardly keep her Seat when she found that he was the Brother of her lamented Henry's Rosa. 'My Lord said Mr Gower as soon as he was seated, You are perhaps surprised at receiving a visit from a Man whom you could not have the least expectation of seeing here. But my Sister my unfortunate Sister is the real cause of my thus troubling you: That luckless Girl is now no more—and tho' *she* can receive no pleasure from the intelligence, yet for the satisfaction of her Family I wish to know whether the Death of this unhappy Pair has made an impression on your heart sufficiently strong to obtain that consent to their Marriage which in happier circumstances you would not be persuaded to give supposing that they now were both alive.' His Lordship seemed lossed in astonishment. Lady——— could not support the mention of her Son, and left the room in tears; the rest of the Family remained attentively listening, almost persuaded that Mr Gower was distracted. 'Mr Gower, replied his Lordship This is a very odd question—It appears to me that you are supposing an impossibility—No one can more sincerely regret the death of my Son than I have always done, and it gives me great concern to know that Miss Gower's was hastened by his—. Yet to suppose them alive is destroying at once the Motive for a change in my sentiments concerning the affair.' 'My Lord, replied Mr Gower in anger, I see that you are a most inflexible Man, and that not even the death of your Son can make you wish his future Life happy. I will no longer detain your Lordship. I see, I plainly see that you are a very vile Man—And now I have the honour of wishing all your Lordships, and Ladyships a good Night.' He immediately left the room, forgetting in the heat of his Anger the lateness of the hour, which at any other time would have made him tremble, & leaving the whole Company unanimous in their opinion of his being mad. When however he had mounted his horse and the great Gates of the Castle had shut him out, he felt an universal tremor through out his whole frame. If we consider his Situation indeed, alone, on horseback, as late in the year as August, and in the day, as nine o'clock, with no light to direct him but that of the Moon almost full, and the Stars which alarmed him by their twinkling, who can refrain from pitying him?—No house within a quarter of a mile, and a Gloomy Castle blackened by the deep shade of Walnuts and Pines, behind him.—He felt indeed almost distracted with his fears, and shutting his Eyes till he arrived at the Village to prevent his seeing either Gipsies or Ghosts,* he rode on a full gallop all the way.*

To Miss Austen*

Madam

Encouraged by your warm patronage of The beautiful Cassandra, and The History of England, which through your generous support, have obtained a place in every library in the Kingdom,* and run through threescore Editions,* I take the liberty of begging the same Exertions in favour of the following Novel, which I humbly flatter myself, possesses Merit beyond any already published, or any that will ever in future appear, except such as may proceed from the pen of Your Most Grateful Humble Serv.ᵗ

The Author

Steventon August 1792—

Kitty,* or the Bower

Kitty had the misfortune, as many heroines have had before her, of losing her Parents when she was very young,* and of being brought up under the care of a Maiden Aunt, who while she tenderly loved her, watched over her conduct with so scrutinizing a severity, as to make it very doubtful to many people, and to Kitty amongst the rest, whether she loved her or not. She had frequently been deprived of a real pleasure through this jealous Caution, had been sometimes obliged to relinquish a Ball because an Officer was to be there, or to dance with a Partner of her Aunt's introduction in preference to one of her own Choice. But her Spirits were naturally good, and not easily depressed, and she possessed such a fund of vivacity and good humour as could only be damped by some very serious vexation.—Besides these antidotes against every disappointment, and consolations under them, she had another, which afforded her constant releif in all her misfortunes, and that was a fine shady Bower,* the work of her own infantine* Labours assisted by those of two young Companions who had resided in the same village—. To this Bower, which terminated a very pleasant and retired walk in her Aunt's Garden, she always wandered whenever anything disturbed her, and it possessed such a charm

over her senses, as constantly to tranquillize her mind & quiet her
spirits—Solitude & reflection might perhaps have had the same effect
in her Bed Chamber, yet Habit had so strengthened the idea which
Fancy had first suggested, that such a thought never occurred to
Kitty who was firmly persuaded that her Bower alone could restore
her to herself. Her imagination was warm, and in her Freindships, as
well as in the whole tenure* of her Mind, she was enthousiastic.* This
beloved Bower had been the united work of herself and two amiable
Girls, for whom since her earliest years, she had felt the tenderest regard.
They were the daughters of the Clergyman of the Parish with whose
Family, while it had continued there, her Aunt had been on the most
intimate terms, and the little Girls tho' separated for the greatest part
of the year by the different Modes of their Education, were constantly
together during the holidays of the Miss Wynnes. In those days of
happy Childhood, now so often regretted by Kitty this arbour had
been formed, and separated perhaps for ever from these dear freinds,
it encouraged more than any other place the tender and Melancholly
recollections of hours rendered pleasant by *them*, at once so sorrowful, yet so soothing! It was now two years since the death of Mr Wynne,
and the consequent dispersion of his Family who had been left by it
in great distress. They had been reduced to a state of absolute depend-
ance on some relations, who though very opulent, and very nearly connected with them, had with difficulty been prevailed on to contribute
anything towards their Support. Mrs Wynne was fortunately spared
the knowledge & participation of their distress, by her release from
a painful illness a few months before the death of her husband.—.
The eldest daughter had been obliged to accept the offer of one of her
cousins to equip her for the East Indies,* and tho' infinitely against
her inclinations had been necessitated to embrace the only possibility
that was offered to her, of a Maintenance;* Yet it was *one*, so opposite
to all her ideas of Propriety, so contrary to her Wishes, so repugnant
to her feelings, that she would almost have preferred Servitude to it,
had Choice been allowed her—. Her personal Attractions had gained
her a husband as soon as she had arrived at Bengal,* and she had now
been married nearly a twelvemonth. Splendidly, yet unhappily married. United to a Man of double her own age, whose disposition was not
amiable, and whose Manners were unpleasing, though his Character
was respectable. Kitty had heard twice from her freind since her marriage, but her Letters were always unsatisfactory, and though she did

not openly avow her feelings, yet every line proved her to be Unhappy. She spoke with pleasure of nothing, but of those Amusements which they had shared together and which could return no more, and seemed to have no happiness in veiw but that of returning to England again. Her sister had been taken by another relation the Dowager* Lady Halifax as a companion* to her Daughters, and had accompanied her family into Scotland about the same time of Cecilia's leaving England. From Mary therefore Kitty had the power of hearing more frequently, but her Letters were scarcely more comfortable—. There was not indeed that hopelessness of sorrow in her situation as in her sisters; she was not married, and could yet look forward to a change in her circumstances; but situated for the present without any immediate hope of it, in a family where, tho' all were her relations she had no freind, she wrote usually in depressed Spirits, which her separation from her Sister and her Sister's Marriage had greatly contributed to make so.—Divided thus from the two she loved best on Earth, while Cecilia & Mary were still more endeared to her by their loss, everything that brought a remembrance of them was doubly cherished, & the Shrubs they had planted, & the keepsakes they had given were rendered sacred—. The living of Chetwynde* was now in the possession of a Mr Dudley, whose Family unlike the Wynnes were productive only of vexation & trouble to Mrs Peterson,* and her Neice. Mr Dudley, who was the younger Son of a very noble Family,* of a Family more famed for their Pride than their opulence, tenacious of his Dignity, and jealous of his rights, was forever quarrelling, if not with Mrs Peterson herself, with her Steward and Tenants concerning tythes,* and with the principal Neighbours themselves concerning the respect & parade,* he exacted. His Wife, an ill-educated, untaught Woman of ancient family, was proud of that family almost without knowing why, and like him too was haughty and quarrelsome, without considering for what. Their only daughter, who inherited the ignorance, the insolence, & pride of her parents, was from that Beauty of which she was unreasonably vain, considered by them as an irresistable Creature, and looked up to as the future restorer, by a Splendid Marriage, of the dignity which their reduced Situation and Mr Dudley's being obliged to take orders for a Country Living had so much lessened. They at once despised the Petersons as people of mean family, and envied them as people of fortune. They were jealous of their being more respected than themselves and while they affected to consider them as of no

Consequence, were continually seeking to lessen them in the opinion of the Neighbourhood by Scandalous & Malicious reports. Such a family as this, was ill calculated to console Kitty for the loss of the Wynnes, or to fill up by their Society, those occasionally irksome hours which in so retired a Situation would sometimes occur for want of a Companion. Her aunt was most excessively fond of her, and miserable if she saw her for a moment out of spirits; Yet she lived in such constant apprehension of her marrying imprudently if she were allowed the opportunity of Choosing, and was so dissatisfied with her behaviour when she saw her with Young Men, for it was, from her natural disposition remarkably open and unreserved, that though she frequently wished for her Neice's sake, that the Neighbourhood were larger, and that She had used herself to mix more with it, yet the recollection of there being young Men in almost every Family in it, always conquered the Wish. The same fears that prevented Mrs Peterson's joining much in the Society of her Neighbours, led her equally to avoid inviting her relations to spend any time in her House—She had therefore constantly repelled the Annual attempt of a distant relation to visit her at Chetwynde, as there was a young Man in the Family of whom she had heard many traits that alarmed her. This Son was however now on his travels, and the repeated solicitations of Kitty, joined to a consciousness of having declined with too little Ceremony the frequent overtures of her Freinds to be admitted, and a real wish to see them herself, easily prevailed on her to press with great Earnestness the pleasure of a visit from them during the Summer. Mr & Mrs Stanley* were accordingly to come, and Kitty, in having an object to look forward to, a something to expect that must inevitably releive the dullness of a constant tete a tete with her Aunt, was so delighted, and her spirits so elevated, that for the three or four days immediately preceding their Arrival, she could scarcely fix herself to any employment. In this point Mrs Peterson always thought her defective, and frequently complained of a want of Steadiness & perseverance in her occupations, which were by no means congenial to the eagerness of Kitty's Disposition, and perhaps not often met with in any young person. The tediousness too of her Aunt's conversation and the want of agreable Companions greatly encreased this desire of Change in her Employments, for Kitty found herself much sooner tired of Reading, Working,* or Drawing, in Mrs Peterson's parlour than in her own Arbour, where Mrs Peterson for fear of its being damp never accompanied her.

As her Aunt prided herself on the exact propriety and Neatness with which every thing in her Family was conducted, and had no higher Satisfaction than that of knowing her house to be always in complete order, as her fortune was good, and her Establishment* Ample, few were the preparations necessary for the reception of her Visitors. The day of their arrival so long expected, at length came, and the Noise of the Coach & 4 as it drove round the sweep,* was to Catherine a more interesting sound, than the Music of an Italian Opera, which to most Heroines is the hight of Enjoyment.* Mr and Mrs Stanley were people of Large Fortune & high Fashion. He was a Member of the house of Commons, and they were therefore most agreably necessitated to reside half the year in Town;* where Miss Stanley had been attended by the most capital Masters from the time of her being six years old to the last Spring, which comprehending a period of twelve Years had been dedicated to the acquirement of Accomplishments which were now to be displayed and in a few Years entirely neglected. She was elegant in her appearance, rather handsome, and naturally not deficient in Abilities; but those Years which ought to have been spent in the attainment of useful knowledge and Mental Improvement, had been all bestowed in learning Drawing, Italian and Music, more especially the latter, and she now united to these Accomplishments, an Understanding unimproved by reading and a Mind totally devoid either of Taste or Judgement. Her temper was by nature good, but unassisted by reflection, she had neither patience under Disappointment, nor could sacrifice her own inclinations to promote the happiness of others. All her Ideas were towards the Elegance of her appearance, the fashion of her dress, and the Admiration she wished them to excite. She professed a love of Books without Reading, was Lively without Wit, and generally good humoured without Merit. Such was Camilla Stanley; and Catherine, who was prejudiced by her appearance, and who from her solitary Situation was ready to like anyone, tho' her Understanding and Judgement would not otherwise have been easily satisfied, felt almost convinced when she saw her, that Miss Stanley would be the very companion She wanted, and in some degree make amends for the loss of Cecilia & Mary Wynne. She therefore attached herself to Camilla from the first day of her arrival, and from being the only young People in the house, they were by inclination constant Companions. Kitty was herself a great reader, tho' perhaps not a very deep one, and felt therefore highly delighted to find that Miss Stanley was

equally fond of it. Eager to know that their sentiments as to Books
were similar, she very soon began questioning her new Acquaintance
on the subject; but though she was well read in Modern history* herself, she chose rather to speak first of Books of a lighter kind, of Books
universally read and Admired.

'You have read Mrs Smith's Novels,* I suppose?' said she to her
Companion—. 'Oh! Yes, replied the other, and I am quite delighted
with them—They are the sweetest things in the world—' 'And which do
you prefer of them?' 'Oh! dear, I think there is no comparison between
them—Emmeline* is *so much* better than any of the others—'

'Many people think so, I know; but there does not appear so great
a disproportion in their Merits to *me;* do you think it is better written?'

'Oh! I do not know anything about *that*—but it is better in *everything*—Besides, Ethelinde is so long*—' 'That is a very common
Objection I beleive, said Kitty, but for my own part, if a book is well
written, I always find it too short.'

'So do I, only I get tired of it before it is finished.' 'But did not you
find the story of Ethelinde very interesting? And the Descriptions of
Grasmere, are not they Beautiful?' 'Oh! I missed them all, because
I was in such a hurry to know the end of it—Then from an easy transition she added, We are going to the Lakes* this Autumn, and I am
quite Mad with Joy; Sir Henry Devereux* has promised to go with us,
and that will make it so pleasant, you know—'

'I dare say it will; but I think it is a pity that Sir Henry's powers of
pleasing were not reserved for an occasion where they might be more
wanted.—However I quite envy you the pleasure of such a Scheme.'
'Oh! I am quite delighted with the thoughts of it; I can think of nothing else. I assure you I have done nothing for this last Month but plan
what Cloathes I should take with me, and I have at last determined to
take very few indeed besides my travelling Dress,* and so I advise you
to do, when ever you go; for I intend in case we should fall in with any
races, or stop at Matlock or Scarborough,* to have some Things made
for the occasion.'

'You intend then to go into Yorkshire?'

'I beleive not—indeed I know nothing of the Route, for I never
trouble myself about such things—. I only know that we are to go
from Derbyshire to Matlock and Scarborough, but to which of them
first, I neither know nor care—I am in hopes of meeting some particular freinds of mine at Scarborough—Augusta told me in her last

Letter that Sir Peter talked of going; but then you know that is so uncertain. I cannot bear Sir Peter, he is such a horrid Creature*—'

'He *is*, is he?' said Kitty, not knowing what else to say. 'Oh! he is quite Shocking.' Here the Conversation was interrupted, and Kitty was left in a painful Uncertainty, as to the particulars of Sir Peter's Character; She knew only that he was Horrid and Shocking, but why, and in what, yet remained to be discovered. She could scarcely resolve what to think of her new Acquaintance; She appeared to be shamefully ignorant as to the Geography of England, if she had understood her right, and equally devoid of Taste and Information. Kitty was however unwilling to decide hastily; she was at once desirous of doing Miss Stanley justice, and of having her own Wishes in her answered; she determined therefore to suspend all Judgement for some time. After Supper, the Conversation turning on the state of Affairs in the political World, Mrs Peterson, who was firmly of opinion that the whole race of Mankind were degenerating,* said that for her part, Every thing she beleived was going to rack and ruin, all order was destroyed over the face of the World,* The house of Commons she heard did not break up sometimes till five in the Morning, and Depravity never was so general before; concluding with a wish that she might live to see the Manners of the People in Queen Elizabeth's reign, restored again. 'Well Ma'am, said her Neice,* but I hope you do not mean with the times to restore Queen Eliz.^th herself.'

'Queen Eliz.^th, said Mrs Stanley who never hazarded a remark on History that was not well founded, lived to a good old age, and was a very Clever Woman.' 'True Ma'am, said Kitty; but I do not consider either of those Circumstances as meritorious in herself, and they are very far from making me wish her return, for if she were to come again with the same Abilities and the same good Constitution She might do as much Mischeif and last as long as she did before*—then turning to Camilla who had been sitting very silent for some time, she added, What do *you* think of Elizabeth Miss Stanley? I hope you will not defend her.'

'Oh! dear, said Miss Stanley, I know nothing of Politics, and cannot bear to hear them mentioned.' Kitty started at this repulse, but made no answer; that Miss Stanley must be ignorant of what she could not distinguish from Politics she felt perfectly convinced.—She retired to her own room, perplexed in her opinion about her new Acquaintance, and fearful of her being very unlike Cecilia and Mary. She arose the next morning to experience a fuller conviction of this, and every future day encreased it—. She found no variety in her conversation; She received no information from her but in fashions, and no Amusement but in her performance on the Harpsichord;* and after repeated endeavours to find her what she wished, she was obliged to give up the attempt and to consider it as fruitless. There had occasionally appeared a something like humour in Camilla which had inspired her with hopes, that she might at least have a natural Genius, tho' not an improved one, but these Sparklings of Wit happened so seldom, and were so ill-supported that she was at last convinced of their being merely accidental. All her stock of knowledge was exhausted in a very few Days, and when Kitty had learnt from her, how large their house in Town was, when the fashionable Amusements began, who were the celebrated Beauties and who the best Millener, Camilla had nothing further to teach, except the Characters of any of her Acquaintance as they occurred in Conversation, which was done with equal Ease and Brevity, by saying that the person was either the sweetest Creature in the world,* and one of whom she was doatingly fond, or horrid, Shocking and not fit to be seen.

As Catherine was very desirous of gaining every possible information as to the Characters of the Halifax Family, and concluded that Miss Stanley must be acquainted with them, as she seemed to be so with every one of any Consequence, she took an opportunity as Camilla was one day enumerating all the people of rank that her Mother visited, of asking her whether Lady Halifax were among the number.

'Oh! Thank you for reminding me of her; She is the sweetest Woman in the world, and one of our most intimate Acquaintance; I do not suppose there is a day passes during the six Months that we are in Town, but what we see each other in the course of it—. And I correspond with all the Girls.'

'They *are* then a very pleasant Family? said Kitty. They ought to be so indeed, to allow of such frequent Meetings, or all Conversation must be at end.'

'Oh! dear, not at all, said Miss Stanley, for sometimes we do not speak to each other for a month together. We meet perhaps only in Public,* and then you know we are often not able to get near enough; but in that case we always nod & smile.'

'Which does just as well—. But I was going to ask you whether you have ever seen a Miss Wynne with them?'

'I know who you mean perfectly—she wears a blue hat—. I have frequently seen her in Brook Street,* when I have been at Lady Halifax's Balls—She gives one every Month during the Winter—. But only think how good it is in her to take care of Miss Wynne, for she is a very distant relation, and so poor that, as Miss Halifax told me, her Mother was obliged to find her in Cloathes.* Is not it shameful?'

'That she should be so poor?; it is indeed, with such wealthy connexions as the Family have.'

'Oh! no; I mean, was not it shameful in Mr Wynne to leave his Children so distressed, when he had actually the Living of Chetwynde and two or three Curacies,* and only four Children to provide for—. What would he have done if he had had ten, as many people have?'

'He would have given them all a good Education and have left them all equally poor.'

'Well I do think there never was so lucky a Family. Sir George Fitzgibbon you know sent the eldest Girl to India entirely at his own Expence, where they say she is most nobly married and the happiest Creature in the World—Lady Halifax you see has taken care of the youngest and treats her as if she were her Daughter; She does not go out into Public with her to be sure; but then she is always present when her Ladyship gives her Balls, and nothing can be kinder to her than Lady Halifax is; she would have taken her to Cheltenham* last year, if there had been room enough at the Lodgings, and therefore I do not think that *she* can have anything to complain of. Then there are the two Sons; one of them the Bishop of M——has sent to Sea;* as a Leiutenant I suppose; and the other is extremely well off I know, for I have a notion that somebody puts him to School somewhere in Wales.* Perhaps you knew them when they lived here?'

'Very well, We met as often as your Family and the Halifaxes do in Town, but as we seldom had any difficulty in getting near enough to speak, we seldom parted with merely a Nod & a Smile. They were indeed a most charming Family, and I beleive have scarcely their Equals in the World; The Neighbours we now have at the Parsonage, appear to more disadvantage in coming after them.'

'Oh! horrid Wretches! I wonder you can endure them.'

'Why, what would you have one do?'

'Oh! Lord, If I were in your place, I should abuse them all day long.'

'So I do, but it does no good.'

'Well, I declare it is quite a pity that they should be suffered to live. I wish my Father would propose knocking all their Brains out, some day or other when he is in the House. So abominably proud of their Family! And I dare say after all, that there is nothing particular in it.'

'Why Yes, I beleive thay *have* reason to value themselves on it, if any body has; for you know he is Lord Amyatt's Brother.'

'Oh! I know all that very well, but it is no reason for their being so horrid. I remember I met Miss Dudley last Spring with Lady Amyatt at Ranelagh,* and she had such a frightful Cap on, that I have never been able to bear any of them since.—And so you used to think the Wynnes very pleasant?'

'You speak as if their being so were doubtful! Pleasant! Oh! they were every thing that could interest and Attach. It is not in my power to do Justice to their Merits, tho' not to feel them, I think must be impossible. They have unfitted me for any Society but their own!'

'Well, That is just what I think of the Miss Halifaxes; by the bye, I must write to Caroline tomorrow, and I do not know what to say to her. The Barkers too are just such other sweet Girls; but I wish Augusta's hair was not so dark. I cannot bear Sir Peter—Horrid Wretch! He is *always* laid up with the Gout, which is exceedingly disagreable to the Family.'

'And perhaps not very pleasant to *himself*—.But as to the Wynnes; do you really think them very fortunate?'

'Do I? Why, does not every body? Miss Halifax & Caroline & Maria all say that they are the luckiest Creatures in the World. So does Sir George Fitzgibbon and so do Every body.'

'That is, Every body who have themselves conferred an obligation on them. But do you call it lucky, for a Girl of Genius & Feeling to be sent in quest of a Husband to Bengal, to be married there to a Man of whose Disposition she has no opportunity of judging till her Judgement is of no use to her, who may be a Tyrant, or a Fool or both for what she knows to the Contrary. Do you call *that* fortunate?'

'I know nothing of all that; I only know that it was extremely good in Sir George to fit her out and pay her Passage, and that she would not have found Many who would have done the same.'

'I wish she had not found *one*, said Kitty with great Eagerness, she might then have remained in England and been happy.'

'Well, I cannot conceive the hardship of going out in a very agreable Manner with two or three sweet Girls for Companions, having a delightful voyage to Bengal or Barbadoes* or wherever it is, and being married soon after one's arrival to a very charming Man immensely rich—. I see no hardship in all that.'

'Your representation of the Affair, said Kitty laughing, certainly gives a very different idea of it from Mine. But supposing all this to be true, still, as it was by no means certain that she would be so fortunate either in her voyage, her Companions, or her husband; in being obliged to run the risk of their proving very different, she undoubtedly experienced a great hardships—. Besides, to a Girl of any Delicacy, the voyage in itself, since the object of it is so universally known, is a punishment that needs no other to make it very severe.'

'I do not see that at all. She is not the first Girl who has gone to the East Indies for a Husband, and I declare I should think it very good fun if I were as poor.'

'I beleive you would think very differently *then*. But at least you will not defend her Sister's situation? Dependant even for her Cloathes on the bounty of others, who of course do not pity her, as by your own account, they consider her as very fortunate.'

'You are extremely nice* upon my word; Lady Halifax is a delightful woman, and one of the sweetest tempered Creatures in the World; I am sure I have every reason to speak well of her, for we are under most amazing Obligations to her. She has frequently chaproned me when my Mother has been indisposed, and last Spring she lent me her own horse three times, which was a prodigious favour, for it is the most beautiful Creature that ever was seen, and I am the only person she ever lent it to. And then, continued she, the Miss Halifaxes are quite delightful—. Maria is one of the cleverest Girls that ever were known—Draws in Oils,* and plays anything by sight. She promised me one of her Drawings before I left Town, but I entirely forgot to ask her for it. I would give anything to have one.'

'But was not it very odd, said Kitty, that the Bishop should send Charles Wynne to sea, when he must have had a much better chance of providing for him in the Church, which was the profession that Charles liked best, and the one for which his Father had intended him? The Bishop I know had often promised Mr Wynne a living, and as he never gave him one, I think it was incumbant on him to transfer the promise to his Son.'

'I beleive you think he ought to have resigned his Bishopric to him; you seem determined to be dissatisfied with every thing that has been done for them.'

'Well, said Kitty, this is a subject on which we shall never agree, and therefore it will be useless to continue it farther, or to mention it again—'

She then left the room, and running out of the House was soon in her dear Bower where she could indulge in peace all her affectionate Anger against the relations of the Wynnes, which was greatly heightened by finding from Camilla that they were in general considered as having acted particularly well by them—. She amused herself for some time in Abusing, and Hating them all, with great spirit, and when this tribute to her regard for the Wynnes, was paid, and the Bower began to have its usual influence over her Spirits, she contributed towards settling them, by taking out a book, for she had always one about her, and reading—. She had been so employed for nearly an hour, when Camilla came running towards her with great Eagerness, and apparently great Pleasure—. 'Oh! my Dear Catherine, said she, half out of Breath—I have such delightful News for You—But you shall guess what it is—We are all the happiest Creatures in the World; would you beleive it, the Dudleys have sent us an invitation to a Ball at their own House—. What Charming People they are! I had no idea of there being so much sense in the whole Family—I declare I quite doat upon them—. And it happens so fortunately too, for I expect a new Cap from Town tomorrow which will just do for a Ball—Gold Net.* It will be a most angelic thing—Every Body will be longing for the pattern—'. The expectation of a Ball was indeed very agreable intelligence to Kitty, who fond of Dancing and seldom able to enjoy it, had reason to feel even greater pleasure in it than her Freind; for to *her*, it was now no novelty—. Camilla's delight however was by no means inferior to Kitty's, and she rather expressed the most of the two. The Cap came and every other preparation was soon completed; while these were in agitation the Days passed gaily away, but when Directions were no longer necessary, Taste could no longer be displayed, and Difficulties no longer overcome, the short period that intervened before the day of the Ball hung heavily on their hands, and every hour was too long. The very few Times that Kitty had ever enjoyed the Amusement of Dancing was an excuse for *her* impatience, and an apology for the Idleness it occasioned to a Mind naturally very Active; but her Freind without such a plea was infinitely worse than herself. She could do nothing but wander from the house to the Garden, and from the Garden to the avenue, wondering when Thursday would come, which she might easily have ascertained, and counting the hours as they passed which served only to lengthen them.—. They retired to their rooms in high Spirits on Wednesday night, but Kitty awoke the next Morning with a violent Toothake. It was in vain that she endeavoured at first to deceive herself; her feelings were witnesses too acute of it's reality; with as little success did she try to sleep it off, for the pain she suffered prevented her closing her Eyes—. She then summoned her Maid and with the Assistance of the Housekeeper, every remedy that the receipt book* or the head of the latter contained, was tried, but ineffectually; for though for a short time relieved by them, the pain still returned. She was now obliged to give up the endeavour, and to reconcile herself not only to the pain of a Toothake, but to the loss of a Ball; and though she had with so much eagerness looked forward to the day of its arrival, had received such pleasure in the necessary preparations, and promised herself so much delight in it, Yet she was not so totally void of philosophy as many Girls of her age, might have been in her situation. She considered that there were Misfortunes of a much greater magnitude than the loss of a Ball, experienced every day by somepart of Mortality,* and that the time might come when She would herself look back with Wonder and perhaps with Envy on her having known no greater vexation. By such reflections as these, she soon reasoned herself into as much Resignation & Patience as the pain she suffered, would allow of, which after all was the greatest Misfortune of the two, and told the Sad Story when she entered the Breakfast room, with tolerable Composure. Mrs Peterson more greived for her toothake than her Disappointment, as she feared that it would not be possible to prevent her Dancing with a *Man* if she went, was eager to try everything that had already been applied to alleviate the pain, while at the same time She declared it was impossible for her to leave the House. Miss Stanley who joined to her concern for her Freind, felt a mixture of Dread lest her Mother's proposal that they should all remain at home, might be accepted, was very violent in her sorrow on the occasion, and though her apprehensions on the subject were soon quieted by Kitty's protesting that sooner than allow any one to stay with her, she would herself go, she continued to lament it with such unceasing vehemence as at last drove Kitty to her own room. Her Fears for herself being now entirely dissipated left her more than ever at leisure to pity and persecute her Freind who tho' safe when in her own room, was frequently removing from it to some other in hopes of being more free from pain, and then had no opportunity of escaping her—.

'To be sure, there never was anything so shocking, said Camilla; To come on such a day too! For one would not have minded it you know

had it been at *any other* time. But it always is so. I never was at a Ball
in my Life, but what something happened to prevent somebody from
going! I wish there were no such things as Teeth in the World; they are
nothing but plagues to one, and I dare say that People might easily invent
something to eat with instead of them; Poor Thing! what pain you are
in! I declare it is quite Shocking to look at you. But you won't have it
out, will you? For Heaven's sake don't; for there is nothing I dread
so much. I declare I had rather undergo the greatest Tortures in the
World than have a tooth drawn.* Well! how patiently you do bear it!
how can you be so quiet? Lord, if I were in your place I should make
such a fuss, there would be no bearing me. I should torment you to
Death.'

'So you do, as it is.' thought Kitty.

'For my own part, Catherine said Mrs Peterson I have not a doubt
but that you caught this toothake by sitting so much in that Arbour,
for it is always damp. I know it has ruined your Constitution entirely;
and indeed I do not beleive it has been of much service to mine; I sate
down in it last May to rest myself, and I have never been quite well
since—. I shall order John to pull it all down I assure you.'

'I know you will not do that Ma'am, said Kitty, as you must be convinced how unhappy it would make me.'

'You talk very ridiculously Child; it is all whim & Nonsense. Why
cannot you fancy this room an Arbour?'

'Had this room been built by Cecilia & Mary, I should have valued
it equally Ma'am, for it is not merely the name of an Arbour, which
charms me.'

'Why indeed Mrs Peterson, said Mrs Stanley, I must think that
Catherine's affection for her Bower is the effect of a Sensibility that
does her Credit. I love to see a Freindship between young Ladies and
always consider it as a sure mark of their being disposed to like one
another. I have from Camilla's infancy taught her to think the same,
and have taken great pains to introduce her to young people of her
own age who were likely to be worthy of her regard. There is something mighty pretty I think in young Ladies corresponding with each
other, and nothing forms the taste more than sensible & Elegant
Letters—. Lady Halifax thinks just like me—. Camilla corresponds
with her Daughters, and I beleive I may venture to say that they are
none of them *the worse* for it.'

These ideas were too modern to suit Mrs Peterson who considered a correspondence between Girls as productive of no good, and as the frequent origin of imprudence & Error by the effect of pernicious advice and bad Example. She could not therefore refrain from saying that for her part, she had lived fifty Years in the world without having ever had a correspondent, and did not find herself at all the less respectable for it—. Mrs Stanley could say nothing in answer to this, but her Daughter who was less governed by Propriety, said in her thoughtless way, 'But who knows what you might have been Ma'am, if you *had* had a Correspondent; perhaps it would have made you quite a different Creature. I declare I would not be without those I have for all the World. It is the greatest delight of my Life, and you cannot think how much their Letters have formed my taste as Mama says, for I hear from them generally every week.'

'You received a Letter from Augusta to day, did not you my Love? said her Mother—. She writes remarkably well I know.'

'Oh! Yes Ma'am, the most delightful Letter you ever heard of. She sends me a long account of the new Pierrot* Lady Susan has given her, and it is so beautiful that I am quite dieing with envy for it.'

'Well, I am prodigiously happy to hear such pleasing news of my young freind; I have a high regard for Augusta, and most sincerely partake in the general Joy on the occasion. But does she say nothing else? it seemed to be a long Letter—Are they to be at Scarborough?'

'Oh! Lord, she never once mentions it, now I recollect it; and I entirely forgot to ask her when I wrote last. She says nothing indeed except about the Pierrot.'

'She *must* write well thought Kitty, to make a long Letter upon a Jacket and petticoat.'* She then left the room tired of listening to a conversation which tho' it might have diverted her had she been well, served only to fatigue and depress her, while in pain. Happy was it for *her*, when the hour of dressing came, for Camilla satisfied with being surrounded by her Mother and half the Maids in the House did not want her assistance, and was too agreably employed to want her Society. She remained therefore alone in the parlour, till joined by Mr Stanley & her Aunt, who however after a few enquiries, allowed her to continue undisturbed and began their usual conversation on Politics. This was a subject on which they could never agree, for Mr Stanley who considered himself as perfectly qualified by his Seat in the House, to decide on it without hesitation, resolutely maintained that the Kingdom had not for ages been in so flourishing & prosperous

a state,* and Mrs Peterson with equal warmth, tho' perhaps less argument, as vehemently asserted that the whole Nation would speedily
be ruined, and every thing as she expressed herself be at sixes &
sevens.* It was not however unamusing to Kitty to listen to the Dispute,
especially as she began then to be more free from pain, and without
taking any share in it herself, she found it very entertaining to observe
the eagerness with which they both defended their opinions, and
could not help thinking that Mr Stanley would not feel more disappointed if her Aunt's expectations were fulfilled, than her Aunt would
be mortified by their failure. After waiting a considerable time Mrs
Stanley & her daughter appeared, and Camilla in high Spirits, & perfect good humour with her own looks, was more violent than ever in
her lamentations over her Freind as she practised her scotch Steps*
about the room——. At length they departed, & Kitty better able to
amuse herself than she had been the whole Day before, wrote a long
account of her Misfortunes to Mary Wynne. When her Letter was
concluded she had an opportunity of witnessing the truth of that
assertion which says that Sorrows are lightened by Communication,
for her toothake was then so much releived that she began to entertain
an idea of following her Freinds to Mr Dudley's. They had been gone
but half an hour, and as every thing relative to her Dress was in complete readiness, She considered that in an hour & a half since there
was so little a way to go, She might be there——. They were gone in Mr
Stanley's Carriage and therefore She might follow in her Aunt's. As
the plan seemed so very easy to be executed, and promising so much
pleasure, it was after a few Minutes deliberation finally adopted, and
running up stairs, She rang in great haste for her Maid. The Bustle &
Hurry which then ensued for nearly an hour was at last happily concluded by her finding herself very well-dressed and in high Beauty.
Nanny* was then dispatched in the same haste to order the Carriage,
while her Mistress was putting on her gloves, arranging the folds
of her dress, and providing herself with Lavender water.* In a few
Minutes she heard the Carriage drive up to the Door, and tho' at first
surprised at the expedition with which it had been got ready, she concluded after a little reflection that the Men had received some hint
of her intentions beforehand, and was hastening out of the room,
when Nanny came running into it in the greatest hurry and agitation,
exclaiming 'Lord Ma'am! Here's a Gentleman in a Chaise and four*
come, and I cannot for my Life conceive who it is! I happened to

be crossing the hall when the Carriage drove up, and I knew nobody would be in the way to let him in but Tom, and he looks so awkward you know Ma'am, now his hair is just done up,* that I was not willing the gentleman should see him, and so I went to the door myself. And he is one of the handsomest young Men you would wish to see; I was almost ashamed of being seen because you know Ma'am I am all over powder, but however he is vastly handsome and did not seem to mind it at all.—And he asked me whether the Family were at home; and so I said every body was gone out but you Ma'am, for I would not deny you because I was sure you would like to see him. And then he asked me whether Mr and Mrs Stanley were not here, and so I said Yes, and then—'

'Good Heavens! said Kitty, what can all this mean! And who can it possibly be! Did you never see him before? And Did not he tell you his Name?'

'No Ma'am, he never said anything about it—So then I asked him to walk into the parlour, and he was prodigious agreable, and—'

'Whoever he is, said her Mistress, he has made a great impression upon you Nanny—But where did he come from? and what does he want here?'

'Oh! Ma'am, I was going to tell you, that I fancy his business is with you; for he asked me whether you were at leisure to see anybody, and desired I would give his Compliments to you, & say he should be very happy to wait on you—However I thought he had better not come up into your Dressing room, especially as everything is in such a litter, so I told him if he would be so obliging as to stay in the parlour, I would run up stairs and tell you he was come, and I dared to say that you would wait upon *him*. Lord Ma'am, I'd lay anything that he is come to ask you to dance with him tonight, & has got his Chaise ready to take you to Mr Dudley's.'

Kitty could not help laughing at this idea, & only wished it might be true, as it was very likely that she would be too late for any other partner—'But what in the name of wonder, can he have to say to me? Perhaps he is come to rob the house—. he comes in stile at least; and it will be some consolation for our losses to be robbed by a Gentleman in a chaise & 4—. What Livery* has his Servants?'

'Why that is the most wonderful thing about him Ma'am, for he has not a single servant with him, and came with hack horses;* But he is as handsome as a Prince for all that, and has quite the look of one—.

Do dear Ma'am, go down, for I am sure you will be delighted with
him—'

'Well, I beleive I must go; but it is very odd! What can he have to
say to me.' Then giving one look at herself in the Glass, she walked
with great impatience, tho' trembling all the while from not knowing
what to expect, down Stairs, and after pausing a moment at the door
to gather Courage for opening it, she resolutely entered the room.

The Stranger, whose appearance did not disgrace the account she
had received of it from her Maid, rose up on her entrance, and laying
aside the Newspaper he had been reading, advanced towards her with
an air of the most perfect Ease & Vivacity, and said to her, 'It is certainly a very awkward circumstance to be thus obliged to introduce
myself, but I trust that the necessity of the case will plead my Excuse,
and prevent your being prejudiced by it against me—. *Your* name,
I need not ask Ma'am—. Miss Peterson is too well known to me by
description to need any information of that.' Kitty, who had been
expecting him to tell his own name, instead of hers, and who from
having been little in company, and never before in such a situation,
felt herself unable to ask it, tho' she had been planning her speech all
the way down stairs, was so confused & distressed by this unexpected
address that she could only return a slight curtesy to it, and accepted
the chair he reached her, without knowing what she did. The gentleman then continued. 'You are, I dare say, surprised to see me returned
from France so soon, and nothing indeed but business could have
brought me to England; a very melancholy affair has now occasioned
it, and I was unwilling to leave it without paying my respects to the
Family in Devonshire whom I have so long wished to be acquainted
with—.' Kitty, who felt much more surprised at his supposing her
to be so, than at seeing a person in England, whose having ever left it
was perfectly unknown to her, still continued silent from Wonder &
Perplexity, and her visitor still continued to talk. 'You will suppose
Madam that I was not the *less* desirous of waiting on you, from your
having Mr & Mrs Stanley with you—. I hope they are well? And Mrs
Peterson, how does *she* do?' Then without waiting for an answer he
gaily added, 'But my dear Miss Peterson you are going out I am sure;
and I am detaining you from your appointment. How can I ever
expect to be forgiven for such injustice! Yet how can I, so circum-
stanced, forbear to offend! You seem dressed for a Ball? But this is the
Land of gaiety I know; I have for many years been desirous of visiting

it. You have Dances I suppose at least every week—But where are the rest of your party gone, and what kind Angel in compassion to me, has excluded *you* from it?'

'Perhaps Sir, said Kitty extremely confused by his manner of speaking to her, and highly displeased with the freedom of his Conversation towards one who had never seen him before and did not *now* know his name, perhaps Sir, you are acquainted with Mr & Mrs Stanley; and your business may be with *them?*'

'You do me too much honour Ma'am, replied he laughing, in supposing me to be acquainted with Mr & Mrs Stanley; I merely know them by sight; very distant relations; only my Father & Mother; Nothing more I assure you.'

'Gracious Heaven! said Kitty, are *you* Mr Stanley then?—I beg a thousand pardons—Though really upon recollection I do not know for what—for you never told me your name—'

'I beg your pardon—I made a very fine speech when you entered the room, all about introducing myself; I assure you it was very great for *me.*'

'The speech had certainly great Merit, said Kitty smiling; I thought so at the time; but since you never mentioned your name in it, as an *introductory one* it might have been better.'

There was such an air of good humour and Gaiety in Stanley, that Kitty, tho' perhaps not authorized to address him with so much familiarity on so short an acquaintance, could not forbear indulging the natural Unreserve & Vivacity of her own Disposition, in speaking to him, as he spoke to her. She was intimately acquainted too with his Family who were her relations, and she chose to consider herself entitled by the connexion to forget how little a while they had known each other. 'Mr & Mrs Stanley & your Sister are extremely well, said She, and will I dare say be very much surprised to see you—But I am sorry to hear that your return to England has been occasioned by any unpleasant circumstance.'

'Oh! Don't talk of it, said he, it is a most confounded shocking affair, & makes me miserable to think of it; But where are my Father & Mother, & your Aunt gone? Oh! Do you know that I met the prettiest little waiting maid in the world, when I came here; she let me into the house; I took her for you at first.'

'You did me a great deal of honour, and give me more credit for good nature than I deserve, for I *never* go to the door when any one comes.'*

'Nay do not be angry; I mean no offence. But tell me, where are you going to so smart? Your carriage is just coming round.'

'I am going to a Dance at a Neighbour's, where your Family and my Aunt are already gone.'

'Gone, without you! what's the meaning of *that?* But I suppose you are like myself, rather long in dressing.'

'I must have been so indeed, if that were the case for they have been gone nearly these two hours; The reason however was not what you suppose—I was prevented going by a pain—'

'By a pain! interrupted Stanley, Oh! heavens, that is dreadful indeed! No Matter where the pain was. But my dear Miss Peterson, what do you say to my accompanying you? And suppose you were to dance with me too? *I* think it would be very pleasant.'

'I can have no objection to either I am sure, said Kitty laughing to find how near the truth her Maid's congecture had been; on the contrary I shall be highly honoured by both, and I can answer for your being extremely welcome to the Family who give the Ball.'

'Oh! hang them; who cares for that; they cannot turn me out of the house. But I am afraid I shall cut a sad figure among all your Devonshire Beaux in this dusty, travelling apparel,* and I have not wherewithal to change it. You can lend me some powder perhaps, and I must get a pair of Shoes from one of the Men, for I was in such a devil of a hurry to leave Lyons that I had not time to pack up any-thing but some linen.'* Kitty very readily undertook to procure for him every thing he wanted, and telling the footman to shew him into Mr Stanley's dressing room, gave Nanny orders to send in some pow-der & pomatum,* which orders Nanny chose to execute in person. As Stanley's preparations in dressing were confined to such very trifling articles, Kitty of course expected him in about ten minutes; but she found that it had not been merely a boast of vanity in saying that he was dilatory in that respect, as he kept her waiting for him above half an hour, so that the Clock had struck ten before he entered the room and the rest of the party had gone by eight.

'Well, said he as he came in, have not I been very quick? I never hurried so much in my Life before.'

'In that case you certainly have, replied Kitty, for all Merit you know is comparative.'

'Oh! I knew you would be delighted with me for making so much haste—. But come, the Carriage is ready; so, do not keep me waiting.'

And so saying he took her by the hand, & led her out of the room. 'Why, my dear Cousin, said he when they were seated, this will be a most agreable surprize to every body to see you enter the room with such a smart young Fellow as I am—I hope your Aunt won't be alarmed.'

'To tell you the truth, replied Kitty, I think the best way to prevent it, will be to send for her, or your Mother before we go into the room, especially as you are a perfect stranger, & must of course be introduced to Mr & Mrs Dudley—'

'Oh! Nonsense, said he; I did not expect *you* to stand upon such Ceremony; Our acquaintance with each other renders all such Prudery, ridiculous; Besides, if we go in together, we shall be the whole talk of the Country—'

'To *me* replied Kitty, that would certainly be a most powerful inducement; but I scarcely know whether my Aunt would consider it as such—. Women at her time of life, have odd ideas of propriety you know.'

'Which is the very thing that you ought to break them of; and why should you object to entering a room with me where all our relations are, when you have done me the honour to admit me without any chaprone into your Carriage? Do not you think your Aunt will be as much offended with you for one, as for the other of these mighty crimes?'

'Why really said Catherine, I do not know but that she may; however, it is no reason that I should offend against Decorum a second time, because I have already done it once.'

'On the contrary, that is the very reason which makes it impossible for you to prevent it, since you cannot offend for the *first time* again.'

'You are very ridiculous, said she laughing, but I am afraid your arguments divert me too much to convince me.'

'At least they will convince you that I am very agreable, which after all, is the happiest conviction for me, and as to the affair of Propriety we will let that rest till we arrive at our Journey's end—. This is a monthly Ball* I suppose. Nothing but Dancing here—.'

'I thought I had told you that it was given by a Mr Dudley—'

'Oh! aye so you did; but why should not Mr Dudley give one every month? By the bye who *is that* Man? Every body gives Balls now I think; I beleive I must give one myself soon—. Well, but how do you like my Father & Mother? And poor little Camilla too, has not she plagued you to death with the Halifaxes?' Here the Carriage fortunately

stopped at Mr Dudley's, and Stanley was too much engaged in hand-
ing her out of it, to wait for an answer, or to remember that what he
had said required one. They entered the small vestibule which
Mr Dudley had raised to the Dignity of a Hall, & Kitty immediately
desired the footman who was leading the way upstairs, to inform either
Mrs Peterson, or Mrs Stanley of her arrival, & beg them to come to
her, but Stanley unused to any contradiction & impatient to be amongst
them, would neither allow her to wait, or listen to what she said, &
forcibly seizing her arm within his, overpowered her voice with the
rapidity of his own, & Kitty half angry, & half laughing was obliged to
go with him up stairs, and could even with difficulty prevail on him to
relinquish her hand before they entered the room. Mrs Peterson was
at that very moment engaged in conversation with a Lady at the upper
end of the room, to whom she had been giving a long account of her
Neice's unlucky disappointment, & the dreadful pain that she had
with so much fortitude, endured the whole Day— 'I left her however,
said She, thank heaven!, a little better, and I hope she has been able to
amuse herself with a book, poor thing! for she must otherwise be very
dull. She is probably in bed by this time, which while she is so poorly,
is the best place for her you know Ma'am.' The Lady was going to
give her assent to this opinion, when the Noise of voices on the stairs,
and the footman's opening the door as if for the entrance of Company,
attracted the attention of every body in the room; and as it was in one
of those Intervals between the Dances when every one seemed glad to
sit down, Mrs Peterson had a most unfortunate opportunity of seeing
her Neice whom she had supposed in bed, or amusing herself as the
height of gaity with a book, enter the room most elegantly dressed,
with a smile on her Countenance, and a glow of mingled Chearfulness
& Confusion on her Cheeks, attended by a young Man uncommonly
handsome, and who without any of her Confusion, appeared to have
all her vivacity. Mrs Peterson colouring with anger & Astonishment,
rose from her Seat, & Kitty walked eagerly towards her, impatient
to account for what she saw appeared wonderful to every body, and
extremely offensive to *her*, while Camilla on seeing her Brother ran
instantly towards him, and very soon explained who he was by her
words & her actions. Mr Stanley, who so fondly doated on his son,
that the pleasure of seeing him again after an absence of three Months
prevented his feeling for the time any anger against him for returning
to England without his knowledge, received him with equal surprise

& delight; and soon comprehending the cause of his Journey, forbore any farther conversation with him, as he was eager to see his Mother, & it was necessary that he should be introduced to Mr Dudley's family. This introduction to any one but Stanley would have been highly unpleasant, for they considered their dignity injured by his coming uninvited to their house, & received him with more than their usual haughtiness: But Stanley who with a vivacity of temper seldom subdued, & a contempt of censure not to be overcome, possessed an opinion of his own Consequence, & a perseverance in his own schemes which were not to be damped by the conduct of others, appeared not to perceive it. The Civilities therefore which they coldly offered, he received with a gaiety & ease peculiar to himself, and then attended by his Father & Sister walked into another room where his Mother was playing at Cards, to experience another Meeting, and undergo a repetition of pleasure, surprise, & Explanations. While these were passing, Camilla eager to communicate all she felt to some one who would attend to her, returned to Catherine, & seating herself by her, immediately began—'Well, did you ever know anything so delightful as this? But it always is so; I never go to a Ball in my Life but what something or other happens unexpectedly that is quite charming!'

'A Ball replied Kitty, seems to be a most eventful thing to you—'

'Oh! Lord, it is indeed—But only think of my brother's returning so suddenly—and how shocking a thing it is that has brought him over! I never heard any thing so dreadful—!'

'What is it pray that has occasioned his leaving France? I am sorry to find that it is a melancholy event.'

'Oh! it is beyond any thing you can conceive! His favourite Hunter* who was turned out in the park on his going abroad, somehow or other fell ill—No, I beleive it was an accident, but however it was something or other, or else it was something else, and so they sent an Express* immediately to Lyons where my Brother was, for they knew that he valued this Mare more than any thing else in the World besides; and so my Brother set off directly for England, and without packing up another Coat; I am quite angry with him about it; it was so shocking you know to come away without a change of Cloathes—'

'Why indeed said Kitty, it seems to have been a very shocking affair from beginning to end.'

'Oh! it is beyond anything you can conceive! I would rather have had *anything* happen than that he should have lossed that mare.'

'Except his coming away without an other coat.'

'Oh! yes, that has vexed me more than you can imagine—. Well, & so Edward got to Brampton* just as the poor Thing was dead,—but as he could not bear to remain there *then*, he came off directly to Chetwynde on purpose to see us—. I hope he may not go abroad again.'

'Do you think he will not?'

'Oh! dear, to be sure he must, but I wish he may not with all my heart—. You cannot think how fond I am of him! By the bye are not you in love with him yourself?'

'To be sure I am replied Kitty laughing, I am in love with every handsome Man I see.'

'That is just like me—*I* am always in love with every handsome Man in the World.'

'There you outdo me replied Catherine for I am only in love with those I *do* see.' Mrs Peterson who was sitting on the other side of her, & who began now to distinguish the words, *Love* & *handsome Man*, turned hastily towards them, & said 'What are you talking of Catherine?' To which Catherine immediately answered with the simple artifice of a Child, 'Nothing Ma'am.' She had already received a very severe lecture from her Aunt on the imprudence of her behaviour during the whole evening; She blamed her for coming to the Ball, for coming in the same Carriage with Edward Stanley, and still more for entering the room with him. For the last-mentioned offence Catherine knew not what apology to give, and tho' she longed in answer to the second to say that she had not thought it would be civil to make Mr Stanley *walk*, she dared not so to trifle with her aunt, who would have been but the more offended by it. The first accusation however she considered as very unreasonable, as she thought herself perfectly justified in coming. This conversation continued till Edward Stanley entering the room came instantly towards her, and telling her that every one waited for *her* to begin the next Dance led her to the top of the room,* for Kitty impatient to escape from so unpleasant a Companion, without the least hesitation, or one civil scruple at being so distinguished, immediately gave him her hand, & joyfully left her seat. This Conduct however was highly resented by several young Ladies present, and among the rest by Miss Stanley whose regard for her brother tho' *excessive*, & whose affection for Kitty tho' *prodigious*, were not proof against such an injury to her importance and her peace. Edward had however only consulted his own inclinations in desiring Miss Peterson to begin the Dance, nor had he any reason to know that it was either wished or expected by anyone else in the Party. As an heiress she was certainly of consequence, but her Birth gave her no other claim to it, for her Father had been a Merchant. It was this very circumstance which rendered this unfortunate affair so offensive to Camilla, for tho' she would sometimes boast in the pride of her heart, & her eagerness to be admired that she did not know who her grandfather had been,* and was as ignorant of every thing relative to Genealogy as to Astronomy, (and she might have added, Geography) yet she was really proud of her family & Connexions, and easily offended if they were treated with Neglect. 'I should not have minded it, said she to her Mother, if she had been *anybody* else's daughter; but to see her pretend to be above *me*, when her Father was only a tradesman,* is too bad! It is such an affront to our whole Family! I declare I think Papa ought to interfere in it, but he never cares about anything but Politics. If I were Mr Pitt or the Lord Chancellor,* he would take care I should not be insulted, but he never thinks about *me*; And it is so provoking that *Edward* should let her stand there. I wish with all my heart that he had never come to England! I hope she may fall down & break her neck, or sprain her Ancle.' Mrs Stanley perfectly agreed with her daughter concerning the affair, & tho' with less violence, expressed almost equal resentment at the indignity. Kitty in the meantime remained insensible of having given any one Offence, and therefore unable either to offer an apology, or make a reparation; her whole attention was occupied by the happiness she enjoyed in dancing with the most elegant young Man in the room, and every one else was equally unregarded. The Evening indeed to *her*, passed off delightfully; he was her partner during the greatest part of it,* and the united attractions that he possessed of Person, Address* & vivacity, had easily gained that preference from Kitty which they seldom fail of obtaining from every one. She was too happy to care either for her Aunt's illhumour which she could not help remarking, or for the Alteration in Camilla's behaviour which forced itself at last on her observation. Her Spirits were elevated above the influence of Displeasure in any one, and she was equally indifferent as to the cause of Camilla's, or the continuance of her Aunt's. Though Mr Stanley could never be really offended by any imprudence or folly in his Son that had given him the pleasure of seeing him, he was yet perfectly convinced that Edward ought not to remain in England, and was resolved to hasten his leaving it as soon as possible; but when he talked to Edward about it, he found him much less disposed towards returning to France, than to accompany them in their projected tour, which he assured his Father would be infinitely more pleasant to him, and that as to the affair of travelling he considered it of no importance, and what might be pursued at any little odd time, when he had nothing better to do. He advanced these objections in a manner which plainly shewed that he had scarcely a doubt of their being complied with, and appeared to consider his father's arguments in opposition to them, as merely given with a veiw to keep up his authority, & such as he should find little difficulty in combating. He concluded at last by saying, as the chaise in which they returned together from Mr Dudley's reached Mrs Petersons, 'Well Sir, we will settle this point some other time, and fortunately it is of so little consequence, that an immediate discussion of it is unnecessary.' He then got out of the chaise & entered the house without waiting for his Father's reply. It was not till their return that Kitty could account for that coldness in Camilla's behaviour to her, which had been so pointed as to render it impossible to be entirely unnoticed. When however they were seated in the Coach with the two other Ladies, Miss Stanley's indignation was no longer to be suppressed from breaking out into words, & found the following vent.

'Well, I must say *this*, that I never was at a stupider Ball in my Life! But it always is so; I am always disappointed in them for some reason or other. I wish there were no such things.'

'I am sorry Miss Stanley, said Mrs Peterson drawing herself up, that you have not been amused; every thing was meant for the best I am sure, and it is a poor encouragement for your Mama to take you to another if you are so hard to be satisfied.'

'I do not know what you mean Ma'am about Mama's *taking* me to another. You know I am come out.'*

'Oh! dear Mrs Peterson said Mrs Stanly, you must not beleive every thing that my lively Camilla says, for her spirits are prodigiously high sometimes, and she frequently speaks without thinking. I am sure it is impossible for *any one* to have been at a more elegant or agreable dance, and so she wishes to express herself I am certain.'

'To be sure I do, said Camilla very sulkily, only I must say that it is not very pleasant to have any body behave so rude to one as to be quite shocking! I am sure I am not at all offended, and should not care if all the World were to stand above me, but still it is extremely abominable, & what I cannot put up with. It is not that I mind it in the least, for

I had just as soon stand at the bottom as at the top all night long, if it was not so very disagreable—. But to have a person come in the middle of the Evening & take every body's place is what I am not used to, and tho' I do not care a pin about it myself, I assure you I shall not easily forgive or forget it.'

This speech which perfectly explained the whole affair to Kitty, was shortly followed on her side by a very submissive apology, for she had too much good Sense to be proud of her family, and too much good Nature to live at variance with any one. The Excuses she made, were delivered with so much real concern for the Offence, and such unaffected Sweetness, that it was almost impossible for Camilla to retain that anger which had occasioned them; She felt indeed most highly gratified to find that no insult had been intended and that Catherine was very far from forgetting the difference in their birth for which she could *now* only pity her, and her good humour being restored with the same Ease in which it had been affected, she spoke with the highest delight of the Evening, & declared that she had never before been at so pleasant a Ball. The same endeavours that had procured the forgiveness of Miss Stanly ensured to her the cordiality of her Mother, and nothing was wanting but Mrs Peterson's good humour to render the happiness of the others complete; but She, offended with Camilla for her affected Superiority, Still more so with her brother for coming to Chetwynde, & dissatisfied with the whole Evening, continued silent & Gloomy and was a restraint on the vivacity of her Companions. She eagerly seized the very first opportunity which the next Morning offered to her, of speaking to Mr Stanley on the subject of his son's return, and after having expressed her opinion of its being a very silly affair that he came at all, concluded with desiring him to inform Mr Edward Stanley that it was a rule with her never to admit a young Man into her house as a visitor for any length of time.

'I do not speak Sir, she continued, out of any disrespect to You; but I could not answer it to myself to allow of his stay; there is no knowing what might be the consequence of it, if he were to continue here, for girls nowadays will always give a handsome young Man the preference before any other, tho' for why, I never could discover, for what after all is Youth and Beauty? Why in fact, it is nothing more than being Young & Handsome—and that is but a poor substitute for real worth & Merit; Beleive me Cousin that, what ever people may say to the contrary, there is certainly nothing like Virtue for making us what

we ought to be, and as to a young Man's, being young & handsome & having an agreable person, it is nothing at all to the purpose for he had much better be respectable. I always *did* think so, and I always *shall*, and therefore you will oblige me very much by desiring your son to leave Chetwynde, or I cannot be answerable for what may happen between him and my Neice. You will be surprised to hear *me* say it, she continued, lowering her voice, but truth will out, and I must own that Kitty is one of the most impudent* Girls that ever existed. I assure you Sir, that I have seen her sit and laugh and whisper with a young Man whom she has not seen above half a dozen times. Her behaviour indeed is scandalous, and therefore I beg you will send your Son away immediately, or everything will be at sixes & sevens.'
Mr Stanley who from one part of her Speech had scarcely known to what length her insinuations of Kitty's impudence were meant to extend, now endeavoured to quiet her fears on the occasion, by assuring her, that on every account he meant to allow only of his son's continuing that day with them, and that she might depend on his being more earnest in the affair from a wish of obliging her. He added also that he knew Edward to be very desirous himself of returning to France, as he wisely considered all time lost that did not forward the plans in which he was at present engaged, tho' he was but too well convinced of the contrary himself. His assurances in some degree quieted Mrs Peterson, & left her tolerably relieved of her Cares & Alarms, & better disposed to behave with civility towards his Son during the short remainder of his stay at Chetwynde. Mr Stanley went immediately to Edward, to whom he repeated the Conversation that had passed between Mrs Peterson & himself, & strongly pointed out the necessity of his leaving Chetwynde the next day, since his word was already engaged for it. His son however appeared struck only by the ridiculous apprehensions of Mrs Peterson; and highly delighted at having occasioned them himself, seemed engrossed alone in thinking how he might encrease them, without attending to any other part of his Father's Conversation. Mr Stanley could get no determinate Answer from him, and tho' he still hoped for the best, they parted almost in anger on his side. His Son though by no means disposed to marry, or any otherwise attached to Miss Peterson than as a good natured lively Girl who seemed pleased with him, took infinite pleasure in alarming the jealous fears of her aunt by his attentions to her, without considering what effect they might have on the Lady herself. He would always

sit by her when she was in the room, appear dissatisfied if she left it, and was the first to enquire whether she meant soon to return. He was delighted with her Drawings, and enchanted with her performance on the Harpsichord; Everything that she said, appeared to interest him; his Conversation was addressed to her alone, and she seemed to be the sole object of his attention. That such efforts should succeed with one so tremblingly alive* to every alarm of the kind as Mrs Peterson, is by no means unnatural, and that they should have equal influence with her Neice whose imagination was lively, and whose Disposition romantic, who was already extremely pleased with him, and of course desirous that he might be so with her, is as little to be wondered at. Every moment as it added to the conviction of his liking her, made him still more pleasing, and strengthened in her Mind a wish of knowing him better. As for Mrs Peterson, she was in tortures the whole Day; Nothing that she had ever felt before on a similar occasion was to be compared to the sensations which then distracted her; her fears had never been so strongly, or indeed so reasonably excited.—Her dislike of Stanly, her anger at her Neice, her impatience to have them separated conquered every idea of propriety & Goodbreeding, and though he had never mentioned any intention of leaving them the next day, she could not help asking him after Dinner, in her eagerness to have him gone, at what time he meant to set out.

'Oh! Ma'am, replied he, if I am off by twelve at night, you may think yourself lucky; and if I am not, you can only blame yourself for having left so much as the *hour* of my departure to my own disposal.' Mrs Peterson coloured very highly at this speech, and without addressing herself to any one in particular, immediately began a long harangue on the shocking behaviour of modern young Men, & the wonderful Alteration that had taken place in them, since her time, which she illustrated with many instructive anecdotes of the Decorum & Modesty which had marked the Characters of those whom she had known, when she had been young. This however did not prevent his walking in the Garden with her Neice, without any other companion for nearly an hour in the course of the Evening. They had left the room for that purpose with Camilla at a time when Mrs Peterson had been out of it, nor was it for some time after her return to it, that she could discover where they were. Camilla had taken two or three turns with them in the walk which led to the Arbour, but soon growing tired of listening to a Conversation in which she was seldom invited to join, & from its turning occasionally on Books, very little able to do it, she left them together in the arbour, to wander alone to some other part of the Garden, to eat the fruit, & examine Mrs Peterson's Greenhouse. Her absence was so far from being regretted, that it was scarcely noticed by them, & they continued conversing together on almost every subject, for Stanley seldom dwellt long on any, and had something to say on all, till they were interrupted by her Aunt.

Kitty was by this time perfectly convinced that both in Natural Abilities, & acquired information, Edward Stanley was infinitely superior to his Sister. Her desire of knowing that he was so, had induced her to take every opportunity of turning the Conversation on History and they were very soon engaged in an historical dispute, for which no one was more calculated than Stanley who was so far from being really of any party, that he had scarcely a fixed opinion on the Subject. He could therefore always take either side, & always argue with temper.* In his indifference on all such topics he was very unlike his Companion, whose judgement being guided by her feelings which were eager & warm, was easily decided, and though it was not always infallible, she defended it with a Spirit & Enthouisasm which marked her own reliance on it. They had continued therefore for sometime conversing in this manner on the character of Richard the 3^{d}*, which he was warmly defending when he suddenly seized hold of her hand, and exclaiming with great emotion, 'Upon my honour you are entirely mistaken,' pressed it passionately to his lips, & ran out of the arbour. Astonished at this behaviour, for which she was wholly unable to account, she continued for a few Moments motionless on the seat where he had left her, and was then on the point of following him up the narrow walk through which he had passed, when on looking up the one that lay immediately before the arbour, she saw her Aunt walking towards her with more than her usual quickness. This explained at once the reason of his leaving her, but his leaving her in such Manner was rendered still more inexplicable by it. She felt a considerable degree of confusion at having been seen by her in such a place with Edward, and at having that part of his conduct, for which she could not herself account, witnessed by one to whom all gallantry was odious. She remained therefore confused distressed & irresolute, and suffered her Aunt to approach her, without leaving the Arbour. Mrs Peterson's looks were by no means calculated to animate the spirits of her Neice, who in silence awaited her accusation, and in silence meditated her Defence. After a few Moments suspence, for Mrs Peterson was too much fatigued to speak immediately, she began with great Anger and Asperity, the following harangue. 'Well; *this* is beyond anything I could have supposed. *Profligate** as I *knew* you to be, I was not prepared for such a sight. This is beyond any thing you ever did *before*; beyond any thing I ever heard of in my Life! Such Impudence, I never witnessed before in such a girl! And this is the reward for all the cares I have taken in your Education; for all my troubles & Anxieties; and Heaven knows how many they have been! All I wished for, was to breed you up virtuously; I never wanted you to play upon the Harpsichord, or draw better than any one else; but I had hoped to see you respectable and good; to see you able & willing to give an example of Modesty and Virtue to the Young people here abouts. I bought you Blair's Sermons,* and Seccar's explanation of the Catechism,* I gave you the key to my own Library,* and borrowed a great many good books of my Neighbours for you, all to this purpose. But I might have spared myself the trouble——Oh! Catherine, you are an abandoned Creature, and I do not know what will become of you. I am glad however, she continued softening into some degree of Mildness, to see that you have some shame for what you have done, and if you are really sorry for it, and your future life is a life of penitence and reformation perhaps you may be forgiven. But I plainly see that every thing is going to sixes & sevens and all order will soon be at an end throughout the Kingdom.'

'Not however Ma'am the sooner, I hope, from any conduct of mine, said Catherine in a tone of great humility, for upon my honour I have done nothing this evening that can contribute to overthrow the establishment of the kingdom.'*

'You are Mistaken Child, replied she; the welfare of every Nation depends upon the virtue of it's individuals, and any one who offends in so gross a manner against decorum & propriety, is certainly hastening it's ruin. You have been giving a bad example to the World, and the World is but too well disposed to receive such.'

'Pardon me Madam, said her Neice; 'but I *can* have given an Example only to *you*, for you alone have seen the offence. Upon my word however there is no danger to fear from what I have done; Mr Stanley's behaviour has given me as much surprise, as it has done to you, and I can only suppose that it was the effect of his high spirits, authorized in his opinion by our relationship. But do you consider Madam that it is growing very late? Indeed you had better return to the house.'

This speech as she well knew, would be unanswerable with her Aunt, who instantly rose, and hurried away under so many apprehensions for her own health, as banished for the time all anxiety about her Neice, who walked quietly by her side, revolving within her own Mind the occurrence that had given her Aunt so much alarm. 'I am astonished at my own imprudence, said Mrs Peterson; How could I be so forgetful as to sit down out of doors at such a time of night? I shall certainly have a return of my rheumatism after it—I begin to feel very chill already. I must have caught a dreadful cold by this time—I am sure of being lain-up all the winter after it—' Then reckoning with her fingers, 'Let me see; This is July; the cold Weather will soon be coming in—August—September—October—November,—December—January—February—March—April—Very likely I may not be tolerable again before May. I must and will have that arbour pulled down—it will be the death of me; who knows *now*, but what I may never recover—Such things *have* happened—My particular freind Miss Sarah Hutchinson's death was occasioned by nothing more—She staid out late one Evening in April, and got wet through for it rained very hard, and never changed her Cloathes when she came home—It is unknown how many people have died in consequence of catching Cold! I do not beleive there is a disorder in the World except the Small pox which does not spring from it.' It was in vain that Kitty endeavoured to convince her that her fears on the occasion were groundless; that it was not yet late enough to catch cold, and that even if it were, she might hope to escape any other complaint, and to recover in less than ten Months. Mrs Peterson only replied that she hoped she knew more of Ill health than to be convinced in such a point by a Girl who had always been perfectly well, and hurried up stairs leaving Kitty to make her apologies to Mr & Mrs Stanley for going to bed—. Tho' Mrs Peterson seemed perfecdy satisfied with the goodness of the Apology herself, yet Kitty felt somewhat embarrassed to find that the only one she could offer to their Visitors was that her Aunt had *perhaps* caught cold, for Mrs Peterson charged her to make light of it, for fear of alarming them. Mr & Mrs Stanley however who well knew that their Cousin was easily terrified on that Score, received the account of it with very little surprise, and all proper concern. Edward & his Sister soon came in, & Kitty had no difficulty in gaining an explanation of his Conduct from him, for he was too warm on the subject himself, and too eager to learn its success, to refrain from making immediate Enquiries about it; & she could

not help feeling both surprised & offended at the ease & Indifference
with which he owned that all his intentions had been to frighten her
Aunt by pretending an affection for *her*; a design so very incompatible
with that partiality which she had at one time been almost convinced
of his feeling for her. It is true that she had not yet seen enough of him
to be actually in love with him, yet she felt greatly disappointed that
so handsome, so elegant, so lively a young Man should be so perfectly
free from any such Sentiment as to make it his principal sport. There
was a Novelty in his character which to *her* was extremely pleasing;
his person was uncommonly fine, his Spirits & Vivacity suited to her
own, and his Manners at once so animated & insinuating, that she
thought it must be impossible for him to be otherwise than amiable,
and was ready to give him Credit for being perfectly so. He knew the
powers of them himself; to them he had often been endebted for his
father's forgiveness of faults which had he been awkward & inelegant
would have appeared very serious; to them, even more than to his
person or his fortune, he owed the regard which almost every one was
disposed to feel for him, and which young Women in particular were
inclined to entertain. Their influence was acknowledged on the present
occasion by Kitty, whose Anger they entirely dispelled, and whose
Chearfulness they had power not only to restore, but to raise—. The
Evening passed off as agreably as the one that had preceded it; they
continued talking to each other, during the cheif part of it, And such
was the power of his Address, & the Brilliancy of his Eyes, that when
they parted for the Night, tho' Catherine had but a few hours before
totally given up the idea, yet she felt almost convinced again that he
was really in love with her. She reflected on their past Conversation,
and tho' it had been on various & indifferent subjects, and she could
not exactly recollect any speech on his side expressive of such a partiality, she was still however nearly certain of it's being so; But fearful
of being vain enough to suppose such a thing without sufficient reason, she resolved to suspend her final determination on it, till the next
day, and more especially till their parting which she thought would
infallibly explain his regard if any he had—. The more she had seen
of him, the more inclined was she to like him, & the more desirous
that he should like *her*. She was convinced of his being naturally very
clever and very well disposed, and that his thoughtlessness & negligence, which tho' they appeared to *her* as very becoming in *him*, she was
aware would by many people be considered as defects in his Character,

merely proceeded from a vivacity always pleasing in Young Men, & were far from testifying a weak or vacant Understanding. Having settled this point within herself, and being perfectly convinced by her own arguments of it's truth, she went to bed in high spirits, determined to study his Character, and watch his Behaviour still more the next day. She got up with the same good resolutions and would probably have put them in execution, had not Nanny informed her as soon as she entered the room that Mr Edward Stanley was already gone. At first she refused to credit the information, but when her Maid assured her that he had ordered a Carriage the evening before to be there at seven o'clock in the Morning and that she herself had actually seen him depart in it a little after eight, she could no longer deny her beleif to it. 'And this, thought she to herself blushing with anger at her own folly, this is the affection for me of which I was so certain. Oh! what a silly Thing is Woman! How vain, how unreasonable!* To suppose that a young Man would be seriously attached in the course of four & twenty hours, to a Girl who has nothing to recommend her but a good pair of eyes! And he is really gone! Gone perhaps without bestowing a thought on me! Oh! why was not I up by eight o'clock? But it is a proper punishment for my Lazyness & Folly, and I am heartily glad of it. I deserve it all, & ten times more for such insufferable vanity. It will at least be of service to me in that respect; it will teach me in future *not* to think Every Body is in love with me. Yet I *should* like to have seen him before he went, for perhaps it may be many Years before we meet again. By his Manner of leaving us however, he seems to have been perfectly indifferent about it. How very odd, that he should go without giving us Notice of it, or taking leave of any one! But it is just like a young Man, governed by the whim of the moment, or actuated merely by the love of doing anything oddly! Unaccountable Beings indeed! And Young Women are equally ridiculous! I shall soon begin to think like my Aunt that everything is going to sixes & Sevens, and that the whole race of Mankind are degenerating.' She was just dressed, and on the point of leaving her room to make her personal enquiries after Mrs Peterson, when Miss Stanley knocked at her door, & on her being admitted began in her Usual Strain a long harangue upon her Father's being so shocking as to make Edward go at all, and upon Edward's being so horrid as to leave them at such an hour in the Morning. 'You have no idea, said she, how surprised I was, when he came into my Room to bid me good bye—'

'Have you seen him then, this Morning?' said Kitty.

'Oh Yes! And I was so sleepy that I could not open my eyes. And so he said, Camilla, goodbye to you for I am going away—. I have not time to take leave of any body else, and I dare not trust myself to see Kitty, for then you know I should never get away—'

'Nonsense, said Kitty; he did not say that, or he was in joke if he did.'

'Oh! no I assure you he was as much in earnest as he ever was in his life; he was too much out of spirits to joke *then*. And he desired me when we all met at Breakfast to give his Compts to your Aunt, and his Love to you, for you was a nice* Girl he said, and he only wished it were in his power to be more with you. You were just the Girl to suit him, because you were so lively and good-natured, and he wished with all his heart that you might not be married before he came back, for there was nothing he liked better than being here. Oh! You have no idea what fine things he said about you, till at last I fell asleep and he went away. But he certainly is in love with you—I am sure he is—I have thought so a great while I assure you.'

'How can you be so ridiculous? said Kitty smiling with pleasure; I do not beleive him to be so easily affected. But he *did* desire his Love to me then? And wished I might not be married before his return? And said I was a nice Girl, did he?'

'Oh! dear, yes, and I assure you it is the greatest praise in his opinion, that he can bestow on any body; I can hardly ever persuade him to call *me* one, tho' I beg him sometimes for an hour together.'

'And do you really think that he was sorry to go?'

Oh! you can have no idea how wretched it made him. He would not have gone this Month, if my Father had not insisted on it; Edward told me so himself yesterday. He said that he wished with all his heart he had never promised to go abroad, for that he repented it more and more every day; that it interfered with all his other schemes, and that since Papa had spoke to him about it, he was more unwilling to leave Chetwynde than ever.'

'Did he really say all this? And why would your father insist upon his going? "His leaving England interfered with all his other plans, and his Conversation with Mr Stanley had made him still more averse to it." What can this Mean?'

'Why that he is excessively in love with you to be sure; what other plans can he have? And I suppose my father said that if he had not been going abroad, he should have wished him to marry you immediately.—But I must go and see your Aunt's plants—There is one of them that I quite doat on—and two or three more besides—'.

'Can Camilla's explanation be true? said Catherine to herself, when her freind had left the room. And after all my doubts and Uncertainties, can Stanley really be averse to leaving England for *my sake* only? "His plans interrupted." And what indeed can his plans be, but towards Marriage? Yet *so soon* to be in love with me!—But it is the effect perhaps only of a warmth of heart which to *me* is the highest recommendation in any one. A Heart disposed to love—And such under the appearance of so much Gaity and Inattention, is Stanly's! Oh! how much does it endear him to me! But he is gone—Gone perhaps for years—Obliged to tear himself from what he most loves, his happiness is sacrificed to the vanity of his Father! In what anguish he must have left the house! Unable to see me, or to bid me adeiu, while I, senseless wretch, was daring to sleep. This, then explains his leaving us at such a time of day—. He could not trust himself to see me—. Charming Young Man! How much must you have suffered! I *knew* that it was impossible for one so elegant, and so well bred, to leave any Family in such a Manner, but for a Motive like this unanswerable.' Satisfied, beyond the power of Change, of this, she went in high spirits to her Aunt's apartment, without giving a Moment's recollection on the vanity of Young Women, or the unaccountable conduct of Young Men.——

[Family Continuations to VOLUME THE THIRD]

[Continuation of Evelyn, by James Edward Austen]*

On his return home, he rang the housebell, but no one appeared, a second time he rang, but the door was not opened, a third & a fourth with as little success,* when observing the dining parlour window open he leapt in,* & persued his way through the house till he reached Maria's Dressingroom, where he found all the servants assembled at tea.* Surprized at so very unusual a sight, he fainted, on his recovery he found himself on the Sofa, with his wife's maid kneeling by him, chafing his temples with Hungary water*—. From her he learned that his beloved Maria had been so much grieved at his departure that she died of a broken heart about 3 hours after his departure.

He then became sufficiently composed to give necessary orders for her funeral which took place the Monday following this being the Saturday—When Mr Gower had settled the order of the procession* he set out himself to Carlisle, to give vent to his sorrow in the bosom of his family*—He arrived there in high health & Spirits, after a delightful journey of 3 days & a ½—What was his surprize on entering the Breakfast parlour to see Rosa his beloved Rosa seated on a Sofa; at the sight of him she fainted & would have fallen had not a Gentleman sitting with his back to the door, started up & saved her from sinking to the ground*—She very soon came to herself & then introduced this gentleman to her Brother as her Husband a Mr Davenport—

But my dearest Rosa said the astonished Gower, I thought you were dead & buried. Why my dr Frederick replied Rosa I wished you to think so, hoping that you would spread the report about the country & it would thus by some means reach——Castle*—By this I hoped some how or other to touch the hearts of its inhabitants. It was not till the day before yesterday that I heard of the death of my beloved Henry which I learned from Mr D——who concluded by offering me his hand. I accepted it with transport, & was married yesterday*— Mr Gower, embraced his sister & shook hands with Mr Davenport, he then took a stroll into the town—As he passed by a public house he called for a pot of beer,* which was brought him immediately by his old friend Mrs Willis—

Great was his astonishment at seeing Mrs Willis in Carlisle. But not forgetful of the respect he owed her, he dropped on one knee, & received the frothy cup from her, more grateful to *him* than Nectar*— He instantly made her an offer of his hand & heart, which she graciously condescended to accept,* telling him that she was only on a visit to her cousin, who kept the *Anchor** & should be ready to return to Evelyn, whenever he chose—The next morning they were married & immediately proceeded to Evelyn—When he reached home, he recollected that he had never written to Mr & Mrs Webb to inform them of the death of their daughter, which he rightly supposed they knew nothing of, as they never took in any newspapers—He immediately dispatched the following Letter—

Evelyn—Augst 19th 1809—

Dearest Madam,

How can words express the poignancy of my feelings! Our Maria, our beloved Maria is no more, she breathed her last, on Saturday the 12th of Augst I see you now in an agony of grief lamenting not your own, but my loss—Rest satisfied I am happy, possessed of my lovely Sarah what more can I wish for?—

I remain
respectfully Yours
F. Gower—

Westgate Buil^{gs}* Augst 2^d

Generous, best of Men

how truly we rejoice to hear of your present welfare & happiness ! & how truly grateful are we for your unexampled generosity in writing to condole with us on the late unlucky accident which befel our Maria—I have enclosed a draught on our banker for 50 pounds, which Mr Webb joins with me in entreating you & the aimiable Sarah to accept—

Your most grateful
Anne Augusta Webb

Mr & Mrs Gower resided many years at Evelyn enjoying perfect happiness the just reward of their virtues. The only alteration which took place at Evelyn was that Mr & Mrs Davenport settled there in Mrs Willis's former abode & were for many years the proprietors of the White horse Inn*——

[Continuation of Evelyn, by Anna Lefroy]

On re entering his circular domain, his round-Robin of perpetual peace;* where enjoyment had no End, and calamity no commence-ment,* his spirits became wonderfully composed, and a delicious calm extended itself through every nerve—With his pocket hanker-chief (once hemmed by the genius of the too susceptible Rosa) he wiped the morbid moisture from his brow;—then flew to the Boudoir of his Maria—And, did *she* not fly to meet her Frederick? Did she not dart from the couch on which she had so gracefully reclined, and, bounding like an agile Fawn over the intervening Foot stool, precipi-tate herself into his arms?* Does she not, though fainting between every syllable, breathe forth as it were by installments* her Frederick's adored name? Who is there of perception so obtuse as not to realize the touching scene? Who, of ear so dull as not to catch the soft mur-mur of Maria's voice? Ah! Who? The heart of every sympathetic reader repeats, Ah, Who? Vain Echo! vain sympathy!* There is no meeting—no Murmur—No Maria—It is not in the power of lan-guage however potent; nor in that of style, however diffuse to render justice to the astonishment of Mr Gower—Arming him self with a mahogany ruler,* which some fatality had placed on Maria's writing table, and calling repeatedly on her beloved Name, he rushed forward to examine the adjacent apartments—In the Dressing room of his lost one he had the melancholy satisfaction of picking up a curl paper,* and a gust of wind, as he re entered the Boudoir, swept from the table, & placed at his feet, a skein of black sewing silk*—These were the only traces of Maria!! Carefully locking the doors of these now desolate rooms, burying the key deep in his Waistcoat pocket, & the mystery of Maria's disappearance yet deeper in his heart of hearts, Mr Gower left his once happy home, and sought a supper, and a Bed, at the house of the hospitable Mrs Willis——There was an oppres-sion on his chest which made him extremely uncomfortable; he regretted that instead of the skein of silk carefully wrapped up in the curl paper & placed beneath his pillow, he had not rather swallowed

Laudanum*—It would have been, in all probability, more efficacious—
At last, Mr Gower slept a troubled sleep, and in due course of time he
dreamt, a troubled dream—He dreamed of Maria, as how could he
less? She stood by his Bed side, in her Dressing gown—one hand held
an open book, with the forefinger of the other she pointed to this omin-
ous passage—'Tantôt c'est un vide; qui nous Ennuie; tantôt c'est un
poids qui nous oppresse'*—The unfortunate Frederick uttered a deep
groan—& as the vision closed the volume he observed these characters strangely imprinted on the Cover—Rolandi—Berners Street.*
Who was this dangerous Rolandi? Doubtless a Bravo or a Monk*—
possibly both—and what was he to Maria? Vainly he would have dared
the worst, and put the fatal question—the semblance of Maria raised
her monitory finger, and interdicted speech*—Yet, some words she
spoke, or seemed to speak her self; Mr Gower could distinguish only
these—Search—Cupboard—Top shelf*—Once more he essayed to
speak, but it was all bewilderment—He heard strange Demon-like
Sounds; hissing and spitting—he smelt an unearthly smell the agony
became unbearable, and he awoke—Maria had vanished; the Rush light
was expiring in the Socket;* and the benevolent Mrs Willis entering
his room, threw open the shutters, and in accordance with her own
warmth of heart admitted the full blaze of a Summer morning's
sun—JAEL

[Continuation of Kitty, or the Bower, by James Edward Austen]

Kitty continued in this state of satisfaction during the remainder of
the Stanley's visit—Who took their leave with many pressing invitations to visit them in London, when as Camilla said, she might have
an opportunity of becoming acquainted with that sweet girl Augusta
Hallifax—Or Rather (thought Kitty,) of seeing my d^r Mary Wynn
again—Mrs Percival in answer to Mrs Stanley's invitation replied—
That she looked upon London as the hot house of Vice where virtue
had long been banished from Society & wickedness of every description was daily gaining ground*—that Kitty was of herself sufficiently
inclined to give way to, & indulge in vicious inclinations*—& therefore
was the last girl in the world to be trusted in London, as she would be
totally unable to withstand temptation——

After the departure of the Stanleys Kitty returned to her usual occupations, but alas! they had lost their power of pleasing. Her bower alone retained its interest in her feelings, & perhaps that was oweing to the particular remembrance it brought to her mind of Ed^wd Stanley.

The Summer passed away unmarked by any incident worth narrating, or any pleasure to Catharine save one, which arose from the reciept of a letter from her friend Cecilia now Mrs Lascelles,* announcing the speedy return of herself & Husband to England. A correspondence productive indeed of little pleasure to either party had been established between Camilla & Catharine. The latter had now lost the only satisfaction she had ever received from the letters of Miss Stanley, as that young Lady having informed her Friend of the departure of her Brother to Lyons* now never mentioned his name—Her letters seldom contained any Intelligence except a description of some new Article of Dress, an enumeration of various engagements, a panegirge* on Augusta Halifax & perhaps a little abuse of the unfortunate Sir Peter—

The Grove, for so was the Mansion of Mrs Percival at Chetwynde denominated was situated w^hin five miles from Exeter, but though that Lady possessed a carriage & horses of her own, it was seldom that Catharine could prevail on her to visit that town for the purpose of shopping, on account of the many Officers perpetually Quartered there & who infested the principal Streets*—A company of strolling players in their way from some Neighbouring Races* having opened a temporary Theatre there, Mrs Percival was prevailed on by her Niece to indulge her by attending the performance once during their stay—Mrs Percival insisted on paying Miss Dudley the compliment of inviting her to join the party, when a new difficulty arose, from the necessity of having some Gentleman to attend them*——

APPENDIX

LETTER OF SOPHIA SENTIMENT FROM
THE LOITERER, 28 MARCH 1789

THE text of Sophia Sentiment's letter is reproduced below from the ninth issue of *The Loiterer*, a humorous weekly paper launched on Saturday 31 January 1789 by Jane Austen's eldest brother, James, at the time a Fellow of St John's College, Oxford.[1] The paper's articles were largely written by James himself, with help from his younger brother Henry and various undergraduate friends.[2] In his first editorial James proposed to supply the reader with 'a regular succession of moral lectures, critical remarks, and elegant humour'. *The Loiterer* ran for sixty issues to 20 March 1790, when James left Oxford, and was issued commercially, though its circulation was small, through booksellers in Oxford, Birmingham, Bath, Reading, and London. Its model was Joseph Addison and Richard Steele's *Spectator*, whose first series ran daily from March 1711 to December 1712. Later examples of its enduring format—a partly simulated and partly genuine interaction between readers and writers, a kind of conversation in print—can be found in two popular periodicals conducted by Henry Mackenzie, *The Mirror* (1779–80) and *The Lounger* (1785–7). More immediate precedents were the hugely successful Eton journal *The Microcosm* (1786–7), written by schoolboy George Canning and friends, and the forty-eight numbers of the *Olla Podrida*, edited by Thomas Monro of Magdalen College, Oxford, and published in book form in 1788. Mentioned in Sophia Sentiment's letter as among 'the entertaining papers of our most celebrated periodical writers', they represented a fashion for teenage (schoolboy and undergraduate) journals in the late 1780s and early 1790s.

It has been suggested that Sophia Sentiment's letter is Jane Austen's first published piece. In it the writer complains to the editor of the absence of stories to interest women, 'about love and honour, and all that', from *The Loiterer*'s first eight numbers. Jane Austen was at the

[1] The text is taken from the first collected edition, issued in 2 vols. (Oxford, 1790).
[2] Contributions are unsigned, but James Austen provided a key to their authorship in the final issue, no. 60.

time 13 years old. But the attribution remains uncertain, with critical opinion divided. There is no extant family tradition of her authorship of the letter, and its style is not entirely consonant with that of her other teenage writings. As Claire Tomalin astutely observes:

The trouble with attributing this to her is that the letter is not an encouragement to *The Loiterer* to address women readers so much as a mockery of women's poor taste in literature. 'Sophia Sentiment' is more likely to have been a transvestite, Henry or James.[3]

That view is supported by the conventions under which these periodicals operated. Like the make-believe of the letters themselves (often the work of the editor writing in various guises), gender masquerades were a regular feature, as far back as Jenny Distaff, half-sister of Steele's fictional alias, Isaac Bickerstaff, in *The Tatler* (1709–11). In the pages of George Coleman's weekly *Connoisseur* (1755–6), for example, such correspondents are to be met with as Dilly Dimple ('a Pretty Miss in breeches'), Harriot Hare-Brain ('a Blood in petticoats'), and Arabella Whimsey.[4] Sophia Sentiment may well belong to this ambiguous company.[5]

What is certain is that, regardless of Sophia Sentiment's true identity (male or female, Jane or Henry or James Austen or their sister Cassandra or cousin Eliza de Feuillide or any other female acquaintance who shared in their literary and dramatic enterprises), *The Loiterer* belongs to the period when Jane Austen was beginning to test her skill as a writer. Individual issues would have been prepared and discussed at Steventon in a sociably scribbling circle of family and friends. The reader easily discovers a conversation between the paper and Jane Austen's developing teenage voice: their shared use of pseudo-Johnsonian prose and of the epistolary form, their playful engagement with conventional

[3] Claire Tomalin, *Jane Austen: A Life* (London: Viking, 1997), 63.

[4] George Coleman, *The Connoisseur*, 2 vols. (London: R. Baldwin, 1755–6), i, no. 52, 307–12; no. 56, 336.

[5] For a range of views for and against Jane Austen's authorship of the letter, see A. Walton Litz, '*The Loiterer*: A Reflection of Jane Austen's Early Environment', *Review of English Studies*, new series, 12 (1961), 251–61; Sir Zachary Cope, 'Who Was Sophia Sentiment? Was She Jane Austen?', *Book Collector*, 15 (1966), 143–51; John Gore, 'Sophia Sentiment: Jane Austen?', *Jane Austen Society Reports*, 2 (1966–75), 9–12. For a reassessment of the influence of the young James and Henry Austen's journalism on their sister's early literary experiments, see Li-Ping Geng, '*The Loiterer* and Jane Austen's Literary Identity', *Eighteenth-Century Fiction*, 13 (2001), 579–92; and *The Loiterer*, ed. Robert L. Mack (Lampeter: Edward Mellen Press, 2006).

views of education and morality, and with the excesses of sensibility. Who can say precisely whether Jane's opinions are openly expressed or ventriloquized in *The Loiterer*'s pages? For this reason, Sophia Sentiment's letter merits consideration alongside Jane Austen's three notebooks.

As Deirdre Le Faye first showed, Sophia Sentiment's literary credentials are easier to trace than her precise biographical origins. The name derives from a character in William Hayley's rhyming comedy *The Mausoleum* (1785).[6] We know that Jane Austen acquired a set of Hayley's works in 1791, but she could have read the play earlier. Perhaps, too, the later warnings of the dying Sophia in 'Love and Friendship' ('Run mad as often as you chuse; but do not faint—', p. 90) proceed from Sophia Sentiment's recipe for literary titillation, voiced in *The Loiterer*: 'as for his mistress, she will of course go mad; or if you will, you may kill the lady, and let the lover run mad'. Appropriately, the ninth number of the paper, in which Sophia Sentiment's letter appears, was the first to include on its title page booksellers in Reading, not far from Jane's home in north Hampshire, as among those stocking the periodical. Robin Vick sees the advertisement for issue 9 in the local newspaper, the *Reading Mercury* (on 6 Apr. 1789), as further support for Jane's authorship, arguing that it may even have been placed not by the bookseller announcing his new wares but by James Austen himself, seeking to enhance his little sister's pleasure 'on seeing her first words in print'. It is a nice story, but pure speculation.[7] Whether or not she wrote it, what is certain is that the letter grows out of and is reabsorbed into the same world of reading, writing, and literary fun as that of Jane Austen's teenage fiction. Local sales of issue 9 emphasize the strength and versatility of these family ties.

[6] Deirdre Le Faye, 'Jane Austen and William Hayley', *Notes and Queries*, 232 (1987), 25–6.
[7] Robin Vick, 'More on "Sophia Sentiment"', *Jane Austen Society Reports*, 5 (1996–2000), 218–20.

No. IX.
OF THE
LOITERER.

SATURDAY, *March* 28, 1789.

Non venit ante suum nostra querela diem.
Ovid.*

THE following letter was brought us the last week, while we were deliberating on a proper subject for the Loiterer; and as it is the first favour of the kind we have ever received from the fair sex (I mean in our capacity of authors)* we take the earliest opportunity of laying it before our readers, and hope the fair writer of it will consider our present eagerness to comply with her commands as some expiation for our past neglect, and will no longer condemn our paper as a pedantic performance, or set its authors down for old bachelors.

To the AUTHOR of the LOITERER.

Sir,

I write this to inform you that you are very much out of my good graces, and that, if you do not mend your manners, I shall soon drop your acquaintance. You must know, Sir, I am a great reader, and not to mention some hundred volumes of Novels and Plays, have, in the two last summers, actually got through all the entertaining papers of our most celebrated periodical writers, from the Tatler and Spectator to the Microcosm and the Olla Podrida.* Indeed I love a periodical work beyond any thing, especially those in which one meets with a great many stories, and where the papers are not too long.* I assure you my heart beat with joy when I first heard of your publication, which I immediately sent for, and have taken in ever since.

I am sorry, however, to say it, but really, Sir, I think it the stupidest work of the kind I ever saw: not but that some of the papers are well written; but then your subjects are so badly chosen, that they never interest one.—Only conceive, in eight papers, not one sentimental story about love and honour, and all that.—Not one Eastern Tale full of Bashas and Hermits, Pyramids and Mosques—no, not even an allegory or dream have yet made their appearance in the Loiterer.* Why, my dear Sir—what do you think we care about the way in which Oxford men spend their time and money—we, who have enough to do to spend our own. For my part, I never, but once, was at Oxford in my life, and I am sure I never wish to go there again—They dragged me through so many dismal chapels, dusty libraries, and greasy halls, that it gave me the vapours for two days afterwards.* As for your last paper, indeed, the story was good enough, but there was no love, and no lady in it, at least no young lady; and I wonder how you could be guilty of such an omission, especially when it could have been so easily avoided. Instead of retiring to Yorkshire, he might have fled into France, and there, you know, you might have made him fall in love with a French *Paysanne*, who might have turned out to be some great person.* Or you might have let him set fire to a convent, and carry off a nun, whom he might afterwards have converted, or any thing of that kind, just to have created a little bustle, and made the story more interesting.*

In short, you have never yet dedicated any one number to the amusement of our sex, and have taken no more notice of us, than if you thought, like the Turks, we had no souls.* From all which I do conclude, that you are neither more nor less than some old Fellow of a College, who never saw any thing of the world beyond the limits of the University, and never conversed with a female, except your bed-maker and laundress.* I therefore give you this advice, which you will follow as you value our favour, or your own reputation.—Let us hear no more of your Oxford Journals, your Homelys and Cockney:* but send them about their business, and get a new set of correspondents, from among the young of both sexes, but particularly ours; and let us see some nice affecting stories, relating the misfortunes of two lovers, who died suddenly, just as they were going to church.* Let the lover be killed in a duel, or lost at sea, or you may make him shoot himself, just as you please; and as for his mistress, she will of course go mad; or if you will, you may kill the lady, and let the lover run mad; only remember, whatever you do, that your hero and heroine must possess a great deal of feeling, and have very pretty names.* If you think fit to comply with this my injunction, you may expect to hear from me again, and perhaps I may even give you a little assistance;—but, if not—may your work be condemned to the pastry-cook's shop, and may you always continue a bachelor, and be plagued with a maiden sister to keep house for you.*

Your's, as you behave,

SOPHIA SENTIMENT.*

ABBREVIATIONS

JA	Jane Austen
JEA	James Edward Austen
E	*Emma*
MP	*Mansfield Park*
NA	*Northanger Abbey*
P	*Persuasion*
P&P	*Pride and Prejudice*
S&S	*Sense and Sensibility*

Catharine and Other Writings	Jane Austen, *Catharine and Other Writings*, ed. Margaret Anne Doody and Douglas Murray, Oxford World's Classics (Oxford: Oxford University Press, 1993; repr. 2009)
Classical Dictionary	Francis Grose, *A Classical Dictionary of the Vulgar Tongue* (London, [1785])
Family Record	Deirdre le Faye, *Jane Austen: A Family Record*, 2nd edn (Cambridge: Cambridge University Press, 2004)
History of England	Oliver Goldsmith, *The History of England, from the Earliest Times to the Death of George II*, 4 vols. (London, 1771)
Hume's *History of England*	David Hume, *The History of England from the Invasion of Julius Caesar to the Revolution in 1688*, 6 vols. (London, 1754–62)
Johnson's *Dictionary*	Samuel Johnson, *A Dictionary of the English Language* (London, 1755)
Journal of a Tour	James Boswell, *The Journal of a Tour to the Hebrides* (London, 1785)
Juvenilia	*Juvenilia*, ed. Peter Sabor, *The Cambridge Edition of the Works of Jane Austen* (Cambridge: Cambridge University Press, 2006)
Letters	*Jane Austen's Letters*, ed. Deirdre Le Faye, 4th edn (Oxford: Oxford University Press, 2011)
Life of Johnson	James Boswell, *The Life of Samuel Johnson, LL.D.*, 2 vols. (London, 1791)
Love and Freindship	Jane Austen, *Love and Freindship and Other Youthful Writings*, ed. Christine Alexander (London: Penguin, 2014)

Memoir	*A Memoir of Jane Austen and Other Family Recollections*, ed. Kathryn Sutherland, Oxford World's Classics (Oxford: Oxford University Press, 2002)
Minor Works	Jane Austen, *Minor Works*, ed. R. W. Chapman (1954); rev. B. C. Southam (Oxford: Oxford University Press, 1969)
OED	*The Oxford English Dictionary*, 2nd edn, 20 vols. (Oxford: Oxford University Press, 1989), with revisions in the online edition up to 2016

TEXTUAL NOTES

In correcting and revising her text, Jane Austen worked in much the same way as anyone writing by hand, then or now: she deleted words by striking through and by erasure (scrubbing out); she wrote alongside, above, and across old material, and, on occasion, she refashioned one word into another without the added clarity of either deletion or erasure; she inserted new text between the lines of old and, where corrections or revisions occurred immediately to her during the process of first writing down, new text emerged directly out of revised material. To capture this range of evidence, different symbols, brackets, and type styles are used, as shown in the following examples, where all forms of strikethrough and erasure are represented by a single strikeout line:

10.18–19	Characters ^of the party^ introduced	
		[*addition made above or between the lines of text*]
116.23	arrived safe^ly^ in London	[*'ly' added as an inline insertion*]
11.15	the concourse ~~of masks~~	[*deletion*]
25.11	Mr Willmot was ~~a younger~~ the representative	[*running deletion*]
4.1	enamelled ~~by~~ ^with^	[*deletion and substitution inline*]
11.32	~~by his side~~ ^in their hand^	
		[*deletion and substitution above or between the lines of text of one or more whole words*]
55.16	mos~~t~~^re^ strictly	
		[*deletion and substitution above the line of part of a word*]
30.1	able to ~~scarce(?)~~ ^save^	
		[*deletion of an uncertain word and substitution above the line*]
22.25	my Lucy be united ~~be united~~	[*deletion of a phrase repeated in error*]
14.19	I'll [tell] you why	
		[*square brackets to indicate missing text that has been editorially supplied*]
16.32	to > for one of my sex	
		[*one word refashioned as another—in this case 'to' refashioned as 'for'*]
14.13	interrupt~~ing~~ > interrupted	
		[*a word altered by partial erasure and refashioning*]
5.22	tender years of the ~~party~~ > young	
		[*one word erased and overwritten by another*]
6.21	~~at~~ <a loss> > ignorant of	
		[*'at' erased and replaced by 'ignorant'; angle brackets around 'a loss' to indicate a conjectural completion of the first version, editorially supplied*]

29.8–9   & E̶l̶<iza> > Cecil having declared her > his first
                    [*'El' erased and overwritten by 'Cecil'; 'iza' conjectural
                    completion of the first version of the name; 'her'
                    refashioned as 'his' without erasure*]

All editorial comments within the Textual Notes appear in italics.

VOLUME THE FIRST

2.4	my ^muslin Cloak
3.4	M̶o̶t̶h̶e̶r̶ ^Father
3.8	politenness
3.10	attachment, ^either to the object beloved, or to
3.11	exceee > exceed[ingly]
4.1	enamelled b̶y̶ ^with^
4.23	rightly imagined ^them to be
5.22	tender years of the p̶a̶r̶t̶y̶ > young couple
5.24	good deal l̶o̶n̶g̶e̶r̶(?) > older
5.33	R̶o̶u̶g̶e̶ ^Patches
5.34	endeavoured > endeavouring
6.14	With h̶e̶a̶v̶y̶ h̶ > a heavy heart *JA anticipated 'heavy', omitting 'a'*
6.16	she little thought o̶f̶ in
6.17	she w̶o̶u̶l̶d̶ ^should return
6.21	a̶t̶ <a loss> > ignorant of
6.26	accordingly ^did &
7.1	blue coat, &̶ entered &
7.23	Thro > Threw her sweet Body
7.30	J̶o̶h̶n̶s̶o̶n̶ > Roger
8.2	m̶u̶s̶t̶ ^first *from ink and hand the alteration appears to have been made on an occasion distinct from the general copying of this piece*
8.13	persuation > persuasion
9.12	But the Happiness f̶ she had expected from *'f' anticipated 'from'*
10.4	Magesty's *cf. 37.18 'magestic'; see also Note on Spelling*
10.8	once ^upon a time
10.8	twelvemonth̶s̶
10.18–19	Characters ^of the party introduced
10.20	were ^both rather tall
10.28	a̶g̶r̶e̶a̶b̶l̶e̶ ^pleasing
11.4	S̶u̶c̶h̶ w̶a̶s̶ The Johnsons *'Such was' anticipated the following paragraph*
11.15	the i̶n̶ c̶o̶n̶v̶e̶n̶i̶e̶n̶c̶e̶ ^feirceness of his beams
11.15	the concourse o̶f̶ m̶a̶s̶k̶s̶
11.25	attidude > attitude
11.32	b̶y̶ h̶i̶s̶ s̶i̶d̶e̶ ^in their hand
12.21	so much her i̶n̶f̶e̶r̶i̶o̶r̶ ^Junior
13.6	p̶e̶r̶c̶e̶i̶v̶e̶d̶ > discovered *by partial deletion (p̶e̶r̶ ^dis) and partial erasure and overwriting (ceived > covered), perhaps because 'perceive' follows three lines below*

13.6	the ^unreturned affection

13.6   the ^unreturned affection

13.9   *the sustained use of running marginal speech marks begins here; see*
        Note on the Text

14.1   & ~~had not~~ might perhaps by this time . . . had not

14.7   the following ~~Xmas~~ ^Year

14.9   & fortune; ~~but~~ > she

14.13   interrupt~~ing~~ > interrupted

14.17   too ~~much colour~~ ^red a look

14.19   I'll [tell] you why

14.25   his > her eyes

14.31   my ideas of the case ~~are~~ ^is these > this

15.4   so hot ~~that~~, on the part of Alice that

15.5   'From Words ~~they~~ ^she . . . '

15.6–7 forced ^her away ~~his Daughter~~

15.16   ~~her ladyship~~ ^Lady Williams

15.22   roused from ~~a~~ ^the reflection

15.34   for what they may do~~; a woman in such a situation is particularly off~~
        ~~her guard because her head is not strong enough to support intoxi-~~
        ~~cation.'>~~ .'

16.3   at the time, ^because

16.16   not to attract their notice   *JA wrote 'attrack' here in error for*
        'attract'; see Note on Spelling

16.27   a sister . . . who ~~was~~ ^is

16.29   I ^have lived

16.30–1 during which time ~~some~~ she provided me with some   *anticipation*

16.32   to > for one of my sex

17.14   if they > there were any chance

17.33   of his modesty than any ~~other reason~~ ^thing else,

17.34   any ~~of~~ more of my Letters

17.37   I should ~~soon~~ ^shortly

18.6   gentleman's > gentlemen's

18.9   ~~or~~ ^since we might ^otherwise perhaps

18.11   as you ^may easily imagine

19.2   of Lucy ~~on~~ ^her thoughts on the subject & ~~when~~ ^as soon as

19.10   I fancy ~~tho'~~ not one

19.13–14 ~~yesterday~~ ^the other Evening!

19.18–19 tho' ^I am very partial to her . . . her real defects ~~I may be partial; indeed I beleive~~
         ~~I am; yes I am very partial to her~~   *heavily deleted and rewritten passage*

19.32   this > these Ladies

19.34   ~~I'll~~ hope you'll   *anticipation*

20.8   she was to go. & The Miss Simpsons

20.30   expected to appear   *JA wrote 'expected to appeared'; corrected by*
        modern editors

20.30   pleased ^at & gratefull for

20.31   offer you have made ^me

21.2   of yourself & ^of her

21.13	obliged to ~~him~~ ^Mr Adams
21.21	conquering every Heart *JA wrote 'ever Heart'; corrected by most modern editors*
21.25	what she determined; ^to do;
21.29	of her ^having accomplished
21.35	pracure > procure *see Note on Spelling*
22.4	^That One should receive
22.5–6	instilled into me > my ^mind by my worthy aunt, is > in my early years
22.25	my Lucy be united ~~be united~~
22.27–8	'!;' *twice in these lines JA combined exclamation mark with semi-colon in a manner that defies print conventions of punctuation; the symbols are therefore presented serially*
22.30	admire ~~the~~ ^your noble sentiments
22.31–2	obligations, ~~but yet me beg you not to suffer their preventing you from~~ ^yet, let me beg that they may not prevent ~~them to prevent~~ your making me happy. *heavily deleted and rewritten passage; the uncharacteristic use of pothook strokes for the purpose of deletion has led to major transcription errors in previous editions*
22.36	~~&~~ ^or refuse
23.7	Thus fell ~~Lucy~~ > the amiable & lovely Lucy *probably anticipation*
23.8	stained by no ~~plot by~~>~~but~~ ^blemish but
23.11	the 2 ~~last~~ > first ~~having~~ ^of whom had
23.28	is ^at present the favourite Sultana
23.31	~~Mr & Mrs Jones~~ > The Lady's *correction suggests anticipation*
24.10	come at all ~~is~~ ^indeed, has been to me a wonder
24.22	unwholesome town, ~~&~~ > which
25.11	Mr Willmot was ~~a younger~~ the representative
25.14	Their Children were ^too numerous
25.18	stopped at ~~the~~ > Sir Godfrey's door
25.20	beholding ^a family
25.25	Emma began to ~~fear~~ ^tremble.
26.3	which ~~must~~ ^much against her will
26.4	injictions > injunctions
26.10	so ~~faultering a manner~~ ^faltering a voice
26.21	Our children are all extreamly > extremely well *see Note on Spelling*
28.6	amused herself ~~with~~ some hours, with *anticipation*
28.12–13	Mrs ~~Jones~~ ^Willson . . . ~~had~~ ^was no sooner *'Willson' here but later on this page (28.22) and elsewhere JA alters 'Jones' to 'Wilson'*
28.23–4	of obliging her & ~~of expressing the Love she bore her.~~ ^accordingly sate out immediately on the receipt of her letter *the continuation of the sentence after the revision shows that the alteration was made at the moment of transcription and not later*
29.4	Lady Hariet *later on this page JA spells the name 'Harriet'; see 29.7*
29.4	so much pleased ~~by~~ > with
29.5	as his > her Sister
29.7	being ~~engaged~~ > often with the family

29.8–9   & ~~El<iza>~~ > Cecil having declared her > his first   *a significant alteration: it seems that JA originally intended Eliza to make the first declaration*

29.10–11   effected, ^as the dutchess's chaplain being ~~likewise~~ very much in love with Eliza her>himself

29.21   Her Grace ~~after having read it,~~ ^as soon as she had read the letter

29.24   sent out ~~after~~ after them 300 £ armed Men

29.25   not to return with^out their Bodies

29.36   12,00£, ~~y~~ > '18,00£, a year   *JA originally wrote '12,00£, y<ear>' before overwriting '2' with '8' to make '18,00£' and erasing 'y' and overwriting with 'a'. This is a typical alteration whereby JA raises numbers to make them even more extravagant.*

30.1   able to ~~scarce(?)~~ ^save but a trifle

30.21   nor would it ^be possible

30.26   the > Her ^little boys

30.28   ~~el<oathses>~~ > wardrobe

30.30   relics > reliques .

30.35   biting off too > two of her fingers   *an occasional slip still found in JA's later writings*

31.7   this > these happy *Junkettings*

31.8   on the steps ~~of~~ ^at the door of

31.39   found ~~this~~ > her in the very Haycock

32.2   than you ~~do~~ ^had ,

32.4   which ~~never before struck me with~~ ^now strikes me as being

32.17   with which ^she entirely demolished

33.3   his Magestys Ship   *cf. 10.4 and 37.18 'magestic'; this preferred teenage spelling continues into* Volume the Second, *86.34, 122.5; see Note on Spelling*

33.11   travellors > travellers   *'travellors' is a preferred spelling in the teenage writings that continued into JA's later writings: cf.* Volume the Third *164.17; and see* The Watsons *booklet 9, p. 5, line 22, and* Sanditon, *booklet 1, p. 2, line 3 (www.janeausten.ac.uk)*

34.4   obadiant > obedient   *cf. 52.5; at 37.22 'obadiant' remains uncorrected*

34.22   enamoured ~~with~~ ^of

34.24   a Husband, ^whom she had

34.34   but ~~I(?) would~~ ^as he knew that he should have been . . . greived ~~at~~ ^by

35.4   at ~~a~~ ^the Village

35.16   a ~~a~~ charming

35.19   Lady Percival, ~~with~~ ^at which

36.3   ~~Permit~~ Your

36.32   a ~~violent~~ ^dangerous fever

37.18   manners, ^are

38.11   Mother's ^shop

39.10   grew ~~arrogant~~ ^peremptory

40.2   her freind ~~a~~ > the Widow

40.4   ~~Miss~~ > Cassandra curtseyed

42.16   that ~~we~~ > I did not stop

42.17–18   inform you of ^besides; but ~~the Con~~<clusion> > my Paper reminds me

44.8   'The s^chool for Jealousy'

44.10   in veiw when ~~they~~ ^it was

44.12   Dramatis Personae   *in the manuscript, characters' names appear in a single column*

44.13   Sir Author > Arthur   *and at 44.16; see Note on Spelling*

45.18   Authur > Arthur   *here and in all further instances in the play*

45.27   went ^any farther

45.29   he has ~~ever~~ ^always been

45.30   adherent to the Truth. ~~He never told a Lie but once, & that was merely to oblige me. Indeed I may truly say there never was such a Brother!~~

46.16   they > there are but 6

46.17   & Sophy, ^take my Brother

46.26   ~~St~~<anly> > Your Brother

47.15   but ~~however~~ Sophy

47.18   ~~a~~ ^a toast and nutmeg

47.19   warmed ale with a ^toast and^ nutmeg   *from spacing and darker ink, 'toast and' appear to have been inserted at a later stage than the general copying*

47.26   too savoury for ~~Children,~~ ^him

47.31   never eats ^suet pudding

48.2   take away the ^suet Pudding

49.1   The Mistery > Mystery

49.6   Patronage ~~of~~ ^to

49.7   compleat^e^

49.12   The Mistery > Mystery

49.14   Dramatis Personae   *in the manuscript, characters' names appear in a single column*

50.18   indeed? > indeed!

50.29   I'll go ~~and dress.~~ ^away.

52.5   obediant^ent   *cf. 34.4 and 37.22 above*

53.11   he hates dancing & ~~has a great idea of Women's~~ ^never ~~going from home~~ what he hates himself   *the continuation of the sentence after the deletion shows that the alteration was made at the moment of transcription and not later*

53.12–13   he ~~has a great idea~~ ^talks a great deal of Women's always staying at home

53.28   if I dont like ~~him.~~ ^it.

53.29   I am ^not going to force you

55.5   in case of a refusal from ~~refusal~~ > herself

55.6   he told her ~~should be the case,~~ ^he should do, for

55.13   wont have ^him

55.16   most^re strictly kept & than rationally formed

56.23   three thousand a year;?' ~~who keeps a post-chaise & pair, with silver Harness, a boot behind before & a window to look out at behind?'~~ 'Very true (she replied)

56.33   would not have done to ~~have made us really so.~~ ^ensure it in reality.

57.22   if he will be ~~so angry &~~(?) so cross

58.6–7 Diamonds such as never were seen! ~~Pearls as large as those of the Princess Badroulbadour in the 4th Volume of the Arabian Nights, and Rubies, Emeralds, Toppazes, Sapphires, Amythists, Turkey stones, Agate, Beads, Bugles & Garnets~~ ^and Pearls, Rubies, Emeralds, and Beads out of number   *the interlinear substitution 'and Pearls, Rubies, Emeralds, and Beads' (and presumably also the strikethrough) is not certainly in JA's hand, resembling more closely that of her nephew James Edward Austen, who made significant alterations and revisions to* Volume the Third

59.24   this > thise [for 'these'] three Years

60.3   could have ^with Mary

60.7–8 He is the son of Sir Henry Brudenell of Leicestershire. ~~Not related to the Family & even but distantly connected with it. His Sister is married to John Dutton's Wife's Brother. When you have puzzled over this account a little you will understand it.~~ Mr Brudenell is the handsomest Man I ever saw

60.28   the object of ~~greatest~~ ^every one's attention

61.27   & even encouraged her ~~in doing so~~ by his Questions

62.13   how will this be made up?   *JA wrote 'how will be this be made up?'; corrected by modern editors*

63.6   your excellent Parent~~s~~   *Anna Austen's mother died in May 1795; this is therefore a significant correction. Hand and date are unknown.*

~~A fragment—written to inculcate the practise of Virtue~~

~~We all know that many are unfortunate in their progress through the world, but we do not know all that are so. To seek them out to study their wants, & to leave them unsupplied is the duty, and ought to be the Business of Man. But few have time, fewer still have inclination, and no one has either the one or the other for such employments. Who amidst those that perspire away their Evenings in crouded assemblies can have leisure to bestow a thought on such as sweat under the fatigue of their daily Labour.~~   *after the dedication to Anna Austen, these lines follow, struck through*

64.5   favourite ~~wishes~~ > dishes

64.7   surprized ~~at~~ > by

64.17   cannot think ~~of~~ ^to

64.21   Warwickshire

64.35   ~~Year~~ > Month

VOLUME THE SECOND

67.4   Freindship > Friendship   *the disposition of the forms 'freind' and 'friend' across the teenage notebooks suggests this alteration may be late; see Note on Spelling*

69.11   ~~cruel~~ ^dreadful

69.14	~~reiterated~~ ^cruel
69.23	afflictions of ~~that~~ my
70.16–17	~~were~~ ^had been
70.17	I ^had shortly
70.18	that could ^adorn it
70.19	good Quality & ~~the place of appointment~~ of every noble sentiment
70.22	own > only
71.3	Sh(?) > Isabel
71.5	~~slept~~ ^supped
71.22	astonished, ~~considerably amazed and somewhat surprized,~~ by hearing
71.31–3	That is another point (replied he;) ~~I can not pretend to assert that any one knocks; tho' for my own part, I own I rather imagine it is a knock at the Door that somebody does. Yet as we have no ocular Demonstration. . . .~~ ^We must not pretend to determine on what motive the person may knock – tho' that some one *does* rap at the Door, I am partly convinced.
72.2	let ~~us go immediately.~~ ^no time be lost.
72.3	a > A third
72.15	introducing a > the most
72.19–20	I felt ~~myself instantaneously in Love with him.~~ ^that on him the happiness or Misery of my future Life must depend.
73.1	I > K[now]
73.1–2	~~if you wish I should.~~ ^in compliance with your Wishes.
73.4	had ^perhaps little expected to ~~have met~~ ^meet
73.6	these > this
73.19	befallen ^me had I not
74.5	had ~~not even the~~ ^never even had the
74.8	~~Her~~ I found her
74.33	acquit you of ^ever having willingly
74.38	so demean myself ^(said Edward). Support!
75.7	~~replied~~ ^returned Augusta
75.9–10	~~Did~~ ^Does it appear . . . ~~Vulgar~~ ^corrupted Palate
75.11	every Distress than > that
75.15	~~interrupted~~ ^prevented
75.27	P<olite> > E[asy]
75.28	Felling > Feeling
75.29	Augusta was one *JA wrote 'once'; corrected by modern editors*
76.6	dared ^to unite
76.22	most particular ^freind,
76.24	in ~~less than an hour;~~ ^a few hours;
76.30	Charectarestic *JA struggled with the spelling, changing 'Chareteristic' to 'Charecterestic' and finally to 'Charectarestic'*
77.11	~~When we were somewhat recovered from the overpowering effusions of ou~~ Towards the close of the Day *the deleted opening lines of Letter the 9ᵗʰ are later used to form the opening of Letter 10ᵗʰ*
77.15	charming Society, ~~yet~~ I cannot
77.25	with it > our behaviour

77.28	fortune ^which Philippa
77.31	~~needless~~ > endless
78.5	from being interrupted, & > by
78.9	as I ^there > then enjoyed
78.13	never ~~were~~ ^werewere *JA seems to have written 'were' in all three instances*
78.13	I imagine ^inform you
78.16	those ^whom they
78.18–19	submit to ~~their~~ ^such despotic ~~will~~ Power
78.22	the ^good opinion
78.23	~~by~~ ^in so doing
78.31	Expenses > Expences
78.39	Sensibility of ~~Augus~~<tus> Edward
79.12	promised that ~~he~~ ^we
79.21	too unexpected ~~to~~ a Blow to *anticipation*
79.26	within ~~six~~ ^twelve miles
79.27	no sooner hd > had we entered
79.27	~~Piccadilly~~ ^Holbourn
80.4	& ^unprovided with any
81.3	to follow ~~her~~ ^it
81.16	Laura > Laurina's Daughter
81.20	caught the ... (?) eye of *two or three uncertain characters struck through*
82.2	provide ~~with~~ > for you *anticipation*
82.35	natural ^noble Sensibility
83.10	circumstance of ~~her~~ > ~~his~~ his being *an example of the recurrent gender confusion that is a feature of the teenage manuscripts; after erasing 'her/his', JA began again with 'his' on a new line*
83.23	no other ~~person~~ >young
83.27	assured her ^thatshe was
83.31	to imagine ^that he
83.39	but with ~~with,~~ Confusion
84.3	like ~~other People~~ ^any other Person
84.26–7	although it was at ^a considerable distance from Macdonald-Hall. *JA makes three attempts to write this short passage, each taking the sense in a different direction: (i)* as it was a most agreable Drive from Macdonald-Hall *(ii)* ~~as it was a most agreable Drive~~ ^from its wonderful Celebrity, although it was at ^a^ considerable distance from Macdonald-Hall *(iii)* ^~~from its wonderful Celebrity,~~ although it was at ^a^ considerable distance from Macdonald-Hall
84.34	have suspected it, ~~had it not~~ but for
85.1	& ~~with~~ ^amongst them
85.4	deprive of > him *anticipation*
85.9	magestically > majestically *see Note on Spelling*
85.24	opprobious *for 'opprobrious'*
85.35	desire ^that you will
86.21	recalling to ~~y~~ my remembrance
86.34	magestic *see Note on Spelling*
87.14	would be ~~cruel;~~ ^cruel;

87.19   melancholy reflections ~~of Augustus~~

88.18   Beware ~~of~~ > ye

88.21   This > Thus I continued

88.22   on my ^Edward's Death

88.24   not in the least ~~tired~~ > fatigued

89.1   Sensibility > Sensibilities

89.31   allotted ~~her~~ us

90.1   her ~~fair~~ ^sweet

90.13   the last ^words she

90.17   Village ~~where~~ ^in which

90.26   A ~~mutual~~ ^general Silence prevailed ~~amongst us all~~

91.3   when ^on looking behind

91.23   Sir Edward ^& the insensible one

91.29   the singular ^Service we there performed

92.2   reflected ^Honour on my Feelings

92.5   ~~unmanly~~ ^unjustifiable Reproaches

92.7   every thing what > that

92.12   behold the ~~Beautifull~~ ^delightful scenes

92.15   & ~~she~~ > had persuaded

92.17   had ~~many~~ ^made daily Excursions

92.21   subsistence^ance

92.27–8 & ~~always~~ ^generally accompanied

93.10   fears ~~for~~ ^of

93.19   had befallen ~~them~~ ^me

93.29   Agatha (my own ^Mother)   *in the manuscript, a closing parenthesis*
        appears after 'own' and another after the superlinear insertion 'Mother'

94.4   & run > ran away

94.10   we ~~were determined~~ ^expected

94.16   ~~dead~~ ^starved to Death

94.28   England, ~~Ireland~~ and Wales

94.29   happened to ~~quit~~ be quartered

94.35   left the ~~room,~~ ^Town

94.37   little fortunes~~s~~

95.5   now ~~growing~~ > ~~drawing~~ ^drawing to a close

95.13   my ~~Lodging~~ Residence

95.18–19 united to ^Graham^ the Man of all others most suited to her;
        ~~Graham;~~   *JA shifted the position of 'Graham' after completing the*
        clause, adding the new instance as an end-of-line insertion

95.25   they still ~~continue to~~ Exhibit

95.32   ~~Sunday~~ June 13th 1790   *'Sunday' has been erased before 'June 13th*
        1790'; '90' may also be written over an illegible erasure. 13 June 1790
        fell on a Sunday.

96.5   will ^always remain so

96.6   it ^is carried

96.11–14 Messrs Demand . . . £105: 0. 0   *a mock note written in a hand other*
        than JA's, presumably that of her brother Henry Austen

96.30	Wife!; *exclamation mark combined with semi-colon is a characteristic device: cf. line 97.8 below, and 'Jack & Alice', Volume the First 22.27–8 above*
97.7	Desper<ation>(?) > Despair
97.11	~~for~~(?) ever since
97.14	a > two mile^s^ from
97.19	Macduf > Macbeths
97.22	we walk, ^and^ when *'and' appears to be an inline insertion*
97.30	2 & ~~4~~20 *as '2 & 40' appears in the following line, it may be that the erased '4' was an anticipation*
98.5	~~too~~ ^two^ such
98.10	or any where ^else^ indeed
98.11	~~We~~ > ~~I~~ ^We^ have only ^to^ hope
98.32	Broiled B>Mutton
98.33	Honey-moon, ~~to find that~~ ^I had the^ mortification of finding that
99.13	brought her~~se~~ to herself *anticipation*
99.15	going ^instantly^ to
99.15	was so ~~very~~ > wildly bent
99.18	into her room; ~~where~~ we laid
99.19	in ^the^ most
99.22	Waste ^in our provisions^ which this Event
99.23	concerting some ~~Scheme~~ > plan
99.24	the ~~only~~ > best
99.25	Fowles > Fowls
99.31	but ^to^ no purpose
99.35	suffer most ~~for~~ ^from^ it
100.2	afflict you to think~~s~~ of *'s' deleted from the end of 'think' in pencil*
100.5	all ~~m~~ > in my *anticipation*
100.7–8	~~I left~~ ^but leaving^ her with my Mother ~~and I taking~~ ^took^ down
100.11	Melancholy ~~Account~~ ^Event^
100.13	for her reason~~s~~
100.14–15	her Physician^s^ is>are . . . ~~being in~~ > going into *'s' is an inline insertion*
100.27	neither You ^n^or Matilda
101.9	reflections ~~are~~ > were
101.25	distressed ~~us~~ ^her^
101.28	as you~~r~~ honour her
101.31	a most ~~lively~~ ^chearfull^ Manner
101.34	fells > feels himself
101.36	Gai^e^ty
102.1	for which he d<id> > was
102.3	agreable young Man > Men
102.7	of a a>distant
102.9–10	protection~~s~~
102.12	removed ~~to an elegant~~ > from a miserable
102.20	s<weetness> > gentleness

102.22   who might ~~to~~ afford to   *anticipation*
102.32   actually ~~felled~~ ^fell
103.6   as probably ~~L~~<ouisa> > she
103.8   did indeed ~~if~~ >appear if   *anticipation*
103.9   seemed to take~~n~~
103.10   Our visits therefore to ~~the N~~<orth> > Dunbeath
103.15   there certainly ^never^ were
103.25   Miss C. Lutterell to Miss M. ~~Lutterell~~ > Lesley
104.4–5   ~~hus~~ > her husband   *anticipation*
104.15   remarkably good~~-humoured~~>tempered
104.21   of whom ~~of-~~> I speak
104.23   Caprice on ~~herself~~ ^her side,
104.27–8 violent ~~freindship~~ ^partiality . . . ~~turned into~~ > settled in
104.32   as when it ~~was~~ first commenced
104.33   and ~~the Amusements~~ of Brighthelmstone
104.35   satisfy the ~~certainty~~ ^curiosity
105.7   Sir George ~~what(?)~~ > from
105.33   of my ~~freinds~~ ^acquaintance
106.2   Miss Margaret Lesley ~~and~~ ^to Miss Charlotte Luttrell   *the latter*
          name is previously spelled 'Lutterell' and from this point 'Luttrell'
106.9   to imagine ~~that~~ there was
106.10   ~~giddy~~ > gay
106.16   We ~~therefore~~ contented
106.22   unmagestic > unmajestic   *see 85.9 and Note on Spelling*
106.23   in comparison ~~to~~ ^with
106.25   to ~~have brought us~~ ^bring her
107.7–8   dungeon-like ~~appearance~~ ^form . . . upon a Rock ^to appearance so totally
          inaccessible
107.14   beautifull Girls, ^such as
107.18   almost as ~~g~~<reat> > Large
107.32   to do ~~m~~>with myself   *anticipation*
108.7   theres is
108.14   to marry ~~if~~ any one with out a fortune
108.19   to conquer ~~her~~ ^his
108.23   plain as I ~~sus~~>expected:
108.36   resemblance ~~with~~ ^between
109.11   you said ~~that~~ you did not find
109.14   Do not you think ~~that~~
109.38   ~~that~~ I was not in the least
110.8   concerning them!   *exclamation mark partly erased, leaving full stop*
110.9   complexions~~s~~
110.11   ~~exercise(?)~~ exercise   *erased and reinscribed, perhaps because originally*
          misspelled; cf. 'Mr Clifford', Volume the First 36.33, 'Excercise'; see
          Note on Spelling
110.13   should ever be > happen to be
110.14   be able to raise   *JA wrote 'be able raise'; corrected by modern editors*

110.26	to be ^so suspected
110.28	you must not ~~sus~~>expect *see 108.23 above*
110.33	induced me to > from
110.36	give myself ~~little~~ > no more trouble
111.4	~~this~~ > within this *anticipation*
111.10	I suppose ~~that~~ this Letter
111.15–16	into ~~her~~ ^its Public-places
111.21	of my Education ~~I always took~~ ^that I took by far the most pains with
111.27	so it ^has always continued
111.35	of equal ~~of~~ ^& settled Duration
112.10	Agrea^e^ment
112.13	single word of ~~Praise~~ ^^Approbation
112.19	which ~~was~~ ^is the only tune
112.21	*expressioné > espressioné*
112.29	have at ~~least~~ > last
112.37	only very severe ~~speech~~ thing
113.15	contracted ~~an~~ ^a kind of affection
113.18	I hope ~~that~~ You or Matilda
113.33	ignorant that in me *JA wrote 'than'; corrected by modern editors*
113.34	my own Heart ~~well enough~~ ^too well not to
114.5	to write, ^to speak, to you
115.1	end of a > the week
115.3	to write ^to you
115.13	interesting to ~~you~~ > me
115.22	of my Eloisa. ~~I~~ *'I' erased and a new paragraph begun: 'In the first place . . .'*
115.35	I am sure ~~that~~ you
115.38	majectic *though 'c' and 's' can be difficult to distinguish in JA's hand, here and at 116.1 she does appear to write 'majectic; cf. 118.16 below, where 'c' is altered to 's'*
116.2	possess than > that
116.6	by any ^one of her own Sex
116.9	^one ~~Men~~ > Man
116.12	my ~~best~~ Compliments
116.13	of ~~his~~ > her Health
116.16	I am afraid ~~that~~ this Letter
116.18	I have ~~as~~ been as
116.23	arrived safe^ly^ in London
116.28	this ~~vauted~~ > vaunted city
117.4	the reasons ^why I cannot
117.11	tranquility *'ity' written over erased letters, possibly 'lity' ('tranquil\<lity>'), a spelling used in* Sanditon, *booklet 2, p. 17, lines 23–4 (www.janeausten.ac.uk)*
117.12	~~On~~ last > Last
117.13	Monday ~~sen'nit~~ ^se'night *in the manuscript, there is a further insertion 'ight' in pencil between the deletion and superlinear correction*

117.25 Gentlemen > Gentleman

117.35 a Conversation we had ^never commenced

117.36 how inferior ~~the~~ > are the   *anticipation*

117.37 one of the most ^frequent of our ~~most~~ Visitors

118.10 Lady Flambeau's!;   *exclamation mark combined with semi-colon;*
cf. 96.30 above

118.15 ~~Margaret~~ > Matilda

118.16 majectic > majestic   *cf. 115.38 above*

118.25 his ^1st Marriage

118.28–9 has ~~obtained another of the Pope's Bulls for annulling~~ ^turned Roman-
catholic, and is soon to be married

118.37 she owns ~~me to~~ it would be

120.6 pregudiced > prejudiced   *cf. 85.9 and 106.22, 'g' > 'j' in 'majestically' and 'unmajestic'; see Note on Spelling*

122.6 Azincourt   *JA wrote long 'z' not 'g', adopting the French spelling as in her model Oliver Goldsmith,* History of England *(1771), ii, 183*

122.7 dag>ughter   *'u' over erased 'g' in 'daughter'*

123.10 should not ^have burnt her

123.18 have ^here given

123.21 poor Woman!,   *exclamation mark combined with comma; cf. 96.30 above*

123.21 an > Convent   *'C' is written over and deletes 'n'*

124.6   *below 'Richard the 3ᵈ' the words 'Edward th' have been erased*

124.12 his ^two Nephews

124.16 did not reign ~~for ever~~ > long

125.15 former of ~~which~~ ^whom

125.18 his ~~Gran-~~daughter

126.2   ~~It would be an~~   *written and erased, to make room for the medallion portrait of 'Henry the 8ᵗʰ'; re-inscribed one line below*

126.6   giving ^only a slight sketch

126.12–13 Crimes ^with which she was accused ~~with~~ ^of

126.16 tho' perhaps but slight ones   *from the position of the word and the change of ink colour, 'perhaps' may be an inline insertion*

126.17 those ^before alledged

127.4   His Magesty's > Majesty's 4ᵗʰ > 5ᵗʰ Wife   *see Note on Spelling*

128.1   the manner of ~~his death~~ ^it

128.7   an excess of ~~Cockylorum~~ ^vanity

129.2   was famous for   *JA wrote 'for famous for'; corrected by modern editors*

129.12 Offices's > Offices of State

129.18 the ~~the~~ claims

129.19 condescend^ed^   *'ed' squeezed in at the end of the line*

130.8   in m>her Mind   *presumably anticipation*

130.15 The > She was executed

130.16 ~~in North~~<amptonshire> > on Wednesday

130.32 this or ^the next Century

130.32–3 tho' ^now but young

131.6   and h<aving> after performing

132.12   an ex<c>ellent Sharade   *JA wrote 'exellent' in error*

133.13   Wi>While the *Villains*

133.15   may be ~~all~~ considered

133.25   is ~~tedious~~ ^uninteresting

134.3   ~~Madam~~ > Cousin

134.4   every County > Country

134.6   Criticism   *JA struggled with the spelling: she first wrote 'Critisisim'; the second 'c' is written over 's', and 'm' over 'im'*

134.6   this ~~Short~~ > Clever Collection   *to enforce the multiple alliteration on the letter 'c'*

134.8   Classed by ~~her~~ > your

134.14   different Manner ~~to~~ ^from

134.26   my Girls sake   *in the manuscript, an apostrophe after Girls' has been erased; cf. 'my Daughters Introduction' (no apostrophe) at 135.1*

134.28   drink ^tea with us

135.6   ~~Apprehension~~ > expectation

135.16   follow it with ~~at~~ Attention

135.19   Minds—'   *JA provided closing speech marks in error (omitted in this edition), perhaps mistaking those at line 14 above (sorry for it.') as opening the reported speech from the daughters rather than closing their mother's direct speech begun at 'My dear Girls . . .*

135.22   ~~contaminated~~ ^seduced by her Example, or ^contaminated by her Follies   *an example of JA rewriting to emphasize stylistic balance and, through the inserted verbal discrimination, to reinforce the moral effect she parodied*

135.33–4   ~~have~~ > must have

136.3   hang so heavy > heavily

136.13   Bride,~~?~~

136.20   kindly meant ~~in~~ > by

136.29   she entered ~~she~~ > the

137.13   Then repeated >repeating the following Line

137.24   without the consent ~~of my~~ > or knowledge of my

137.29   wiping ~~my~~ ^her Eyes

138.8   & ^have made it

138.9   Christin > Christian

138.22   all?? said I

139.2   a favour ~~for~~ ^about which

139.7   distressed ~~your~~>herself

139.13   could not ^you have

139.15   poor, ~~because~~ ^for I always think

139.15–16   & pitied ~~& bl~~>than blamed   *'th' is written over '& bl', which appears to be partly erased*

139.25   ~~Fanny~~ > Ellen   *here and throughout; the substitution occurs four times within the next seven lines*

139.28   ~~Fanny~~ > Ellen

139.29   ~~Fanny~~ > Ellen

139.33   Bread & Chea>ese

139.33   ~~Fanny~~ ^Ellen

140.12   In the mean time ~~Lady Greville~~ > the Dancing

140.25   of ^having the most

140.39   ~~but your~~ > Why, was   *JA first wrote* 'I was never told so before, but your, *before erasing* , but your *and replacing it with.*' 'Why, was *and a change of speaker. This line and the next four lines, with their trial and deletion of the phrases* but your Ladyship knows best *and* Just as your Ladyship chooses, *suggest direct revision rather than copying from an earlier version.*

141.1   'I fancy not; ~~but your Ladyship knows best~~' 'Was not he in the Kings Bench once?' '~~Just as your Ladyship chooses—it is the same to me.~~' ^'I never saw him there.'

141.3–4   of ~~having~~ being thought too ~~much so~~ > saucy

141.8   ~~Fanny~~ > Ellen

141.19   as you ~~may~~ > were

141.27–8   need not come ~~for~~ > before

141.30   ~~Fanny~~ > Ellen

141.32   blown about ~~of~~ > by

141.34   so ruddy & ~~course~~ > coarse

141.35   shews your ~~Ancles~~ > legs

141.37   But ~~you sort~~ ^low ^cold > odd ^some sort of people   *there are four possible levels of revision here: (i)* you sort *changed to* you low sort*; (ii)* low *deleted and replaced by* cold *(*you cold sort*); (iii)* cold *subsequently altered to* odd*; (iv) the whole phrase deleted and replaced by* some sort

142.2   ~~Drive on~~ > I am afraid

142.20   we were on > of

143.5   *un*happy one's there?>.

143.7   uninterrupted ~~Felicity~~ ^Happiness

143.11   wifull> wilfull

143.12   arrise > arise

143.15   ans<wered> > replied

143.18   I was actually silenced. ~~Could you have beleived it Mary?~~ I recovered myself

143.36   bear your Absence ^?'^ ~~during a long stay in Essex?'~~

144.14   what ^were my sensations

144.30   my fair ^one,

144.34   tho' an excellent ~~House~~ ^one

145.1   ~~Of~~ >—Of   *'Of' erased and overwritten by a long dash, followed by 'Of'*

145.4   T. Musgrove

~~May I hope to receive an answer to this e'er many days have tortured me with Suspence! Any Letter (post paid) will be most welcome.~~   *after the signature, this postscript follows, struck through*

145.21   every day of my Life. ~~How fond we shall be of one another when we are married! oh! do not you long for the time?~~   *heavily deleted*

146.12   thought it was ~~best~~ > proper

146.25–6   can write ~~a~~ good Love-letters

147.13	have ~~on~~ > in these Matters
147.38	~~Indeed~~ ^To be sure
148.1	as you are ^in every
148.27–8	of ~~conjugal~~ > Felicity in the Conjugal state
149.1	my dear ~~Cousin~~ > Tom
149.6	than I ~~never~~ knew
149.23	for allowing him > them
149.38	every now and then. ~~I gave away two pence this Morning.~~
150.1	He ~~said~~ ^replied that he
150.3	destined ~~as~~ ^to be
151.27	as ~~pleasing~~ ^estimable
152.4	freind > friend
152.20	~~nor~~ ^is without
152.28	Characters *in the manuscript, characters' names appear in a single column*
153.17	to marry ~~you to~~ > to Strephon
154.3	a leg of ~~m<utton>~~ > beef
154.21	I have ~~not~~ > but a bad guinea
155.1	Young ~~Ladies~~>y
155.3	the commission of ~~several faults~~ ^Errors
155.12	these last twelve ~~months~~ > Years
155.13	I am ^now going to reform
155.19	to her > his three
155.26	I happened ~~to~~ to be passing *'to' erased before reinsertion, perhaps because at first written too high, above the line*
156.7	Wales, which is a principality *JA wrote 'with is a principality'; corrected by modern editors*
156.11	You way > may
157.8	led by ~~th(?)~~ it's side *two characters erased before 'it's'*
157.12	fastened only ^by a wooden latch
157.19	on furniture her^imself *the correction has been inserted in paler ink above the deleted 'er'*
157.24	amiable ~~Sisters~~ > Cecilia
157.27	accomodate *this is JA's spelling*

VOLUME THE THIRD

159.1	Volume the Third *there is an unattributed pencil inscription on the front inside cover of the notebook:*

'Effusions of Fancy
By a very Young Lady
Consisting of Tales
In a Style entirely new'

It has been suggested that the hand is that of JA's father, the Revd George Austen (Family Record, 78). But the letter shapes are also consistent with the hands of Cassandra Austen and JA herself.

159.2   Jane Austen – May 6ᵗʰ 1792.   *in ink in the hand of JA. The date pre-*
cedes that of the dedication to 'Kitty, or the Bower' (August 1792), the
second and longer item in the notebook. JA may have recorded her owner-
ship of the notebook several months before she filled in the Contents page,
or she may have signed and dated the volume at the same time as she began
the Contents page and transcribed the first item, 'Evelyn'. Above this
inscription are the words 'for James Edward Austen Leigh', written in pen-
cil, presumably in the hand of Cassandra Austen. James Edward Austen,
JA's nephew, took the name 'Leigh' in 1837. There are signs of re-inscription
of the name 'James Edward Austen' and it is not clear if 'Leigh' was part
of the original inscription or added at re-inscription. Cassandra, who
inherited the fiction manuscripts at JA's death in 1817, is known to have
apportioned them to surviving family members in 1843.

159.5   Kitty, or the Bower   *this is JA's title on the Contents page of her note-*
book. Although the work is known in most modern editions by the revised
title 'Catharine, or the Bower', the title on the Contents page was never
altered. Moreover, evidence of handwriting suggests that the major alter-
ations to the novella (including the name change of 'Kitty' to 'Catharine')
were the work not of JA but of her nephew James Edward Austen, revising
the story and adding a continuation some time between 1815 and 1817
when the notebook was again in use by JA, after more than twenty years,
as material for an informal composition class for her teenage nephew and
his older half-sister Anna Lefroy. Their continuations to the notebook's two
stories, 'Evelyn' and 'Kitty, or the Bower', are included here in a separate
section; see below, p. 205.

161.17   The agonizing ~~idea~~ ^pain

161.23   that ^the freindly balm

162.4   with ~~the remainder of their Lease.~~ ^their house.

162.5   a direction to the ~~House~~ ^place

162.11   unincumbered ~~by~~ with

162.13   Cows who > which

162.29   taking out a > her purse

162.30   everything that is m<y> > in my   *anticipation*

162.35   from the ~~effusions~~ ^excess

162.36   offer of an > the hundred

162.38   had ~~before expressed.~~ ^already made.—

163.7   we bear ~~for~~ you

163.27   & to ^promise to keep it

164.17   Travellor   *JA preferred the distinct spelling 'Travellor' to the commoner*
'Traveller' not only in the teenage writings but as late as Sanditon, *the*
manuscript left incomplete at her death; see note to 33.11 above

164.18   Maria stoopped > stooped

165.15   agitated ~~with~~ ^by

165.24   I ^will forget you

165.31   it came not ~~for~~   *'for' deleted and corrected below to 'from' in pencil,*
possibly in a hand other than JA's

166.9   his life > living at Evelyn

166.26   greatly ~~superior~~ ^inferior

166.29   of a very ~~old~~ ^ancient date

167.6   lamented ~~Charles~~ ^Henry's Rosa   *the heavily deleted 'Charles' may be written over a previous word, 'Rosa's'(?)*

169.13   Kitty, or the Bower | ~~Kitty~~ ^Catharine *(JEA) here and throughout altered in the hand of JEA. The original title 'Kitty, or the Bower' is retained on the Contents page, while 'Kitty', deleted three times on the story's opening page, stands elsewhere. JA's name for her heroine is 'Kitty' (used some eighty times), occasionally varied by the use of 'Catherine' (seventeen times). JEA revised the name to 'Catharine' (a spelling never used by JA in any of her fictions) on seven occasions. The text of 'Kitty, or the Bower' in this edition restores JA's original teenage text of 1792 for the first time in any printed edition. All JEA's considerable alterations to it have been removed and are recorded in the following notes. In the lists below, JA's original and now restored reading is given first and JEA's revision after a vertical bar.*

169.14   Kitty had the misfortune | ~~Kitty~~ ^Catharine had the misfortune *(JEA)*

169.18   Kitty amongst the rest | ~~Kitty~~ ^Catharine amongst the rest *(JEA)*

169.30   To this ~~Garden,~~ ^Bower

170.14   during the holidays of the Miss Wynnes;^.^ ~~they were companions in their walks, their Schemes & Amusements, and while the sweetness of their dispositions~~ ^had ~~prevented any serious Quarrels, the trifling disputes which it was impossible wholly to avoid, had been far from lessening their affection.~~   *the emphatic full stop following the semi-colon is presumably an inline insertion after the deletion of the second part of the sentence. It is possible that JEA deleted this section.*

170.18   at once so sorrowful   *JA wrote 'one' for 'once'; corrected by modern editors*

170.34   had gained her ^a husband

170.36   of double ~~of~~ her own age

171.22   Mrs Peterson, and her Neice | Mrs ~~Peterson~~ ^Percival and her Neice *(JEA) the revision is not consistently made: sometimes, only 'eterson' is deleted, leaving 'Mrs P.' or 'Mrs P', and sometimes 'Peterson' is refashioned as 'Percival', while elsewhere 'Peterson' is left unchanged; see the notes below*

171.26   Mrs Peterson herself | Mrs ~~Peterson~~ herself *(JEA)*

171.28   This > His Wife

171.32   pride of ^her parents

171.37   despised the Petersons | despised the ~~Petersons~~ ^Percivals *(JEA)*

171.37   people of ~~me<an>no~~ ^mean family   *'no' was written over partially erased 'me<an>', then 'no' was deleted and replaced by 'mean' above the line*

172.5   sometimes occur ^~~to her~~ for want of a Companion

172.8   apprehension~~s~~

172.9   and ^was so dissatisfied

172.23   frequent ~~endeavours~~ ^overtures

172.26 Kitty, in having an object | ~~Kitty,~~ ^Catharine in having an object (*JEA*)

172.31 Mrs Peterson always thought | Mrs Peterson > Percival always thought (*JEA*)

172.35 her aunt's > Aunt's;

173.6 at length ~~arrived,~~ ^came,

173.7 Catherine *JA began here to vary 'Kitty' with 'Catherine' as the name of her heroine*

173.8 than an > the Music of an

173.9 to most Heroines ^is the hight *JA's distinctive spelling of 'height'*

173.10–11 of the house ~~and~~ of Commons, and

173.16–17 She was ^not in ~~about Kitty's age,~~ elegant in her appearance *JA first wrote* She was about Kitty's age, elegant. *After the deletion of* about Kitty's age, not in *was inserted above the line, perhaps to begin the phrase 'not inelegant'—a characteristic Austenian double negative—before that too was deleted, leaving* elegant.

173.33 almost convinced ^when she saw her, that

174.1 sentiments as ^to Books *'to' inserted in pencil above the line, possibly in a hand other than JA's*

174.5 Admired,>. ~~and that have given rise perhaps to more frequent Arguments than any other of the same sort~~ *full stop inserted over comma after the deletion of the final part of the sentence. It is possible that JEA deleted this section.*

174.13–14 better ~~all together~~ > in *everything*

174.19 are not they Beautiful? *JA wrote 'the' for 'they'; corrected by modern editors*

174.26 ^However I quite envy you

174.28 I ~~shall~~ > assure you I have ^done nothing

174.28–9 plan what Cloths > what Cloathes *'what' has been written over erased 'what Cloths'*

174.35 I never trouble myself *'never' has been written over an earlier illegible word*

175.13 therefore ~~al<l>~~ > to suspend all *anticipation*

175.15 Mrs Peterson | Mrs ~~Peterson~~ (*JEA*)

175.22 said her Neice, ~~I beleive you have as good a chance of it as any one else,~~ but I hope *it is possible that JEA deleted this section*

175.22 do no^t^ mean

175.36 could not distinguish from ~~History,~~ ^Politics

176.12 fashionable Amusements again > began *'again' altered in pencil to 'began', possibly in a hand other than JA's*

176.35 we are ~~not always~~ ^often not able

176.38 you have ^ever seen

177.19 go out wit<h> > into Public with her *anticipation*

177.21 to Cheltenham ~~to C~~ > last year *JA began, in error, to recopy the previous phrase*

177.23 There > Then there are the two Sons

177.24   the Bishop of M— has sent to Sea; | ~~sent to Sea;~~ ^got into the Army
         (JEA)

177.26   I have ^a notion

177.28   ~~Slightly:~~ ^Very well,

178.8   been able to w<ear> > bear any of them

178.16   The Barkers too | The ~~Barkers~~ ^Barlows too *(JEA)*

178.34   she might ^then have remained

179.23   lent it to.' ~~'If so, Mary Wynne can receive very little advantage from~~
         ~~her having it.' 'And then,~~ ^continued she, the Miss Halifaxes *along with*
         the retort from Kitty, the speech marks closing and reopening Camilla's
         comments have been deleted and 'continued she,' has been added above
         the line since now there is no change of speaker

179.25   that ever were knows > known

179.27–8 I would give anything to have one.' ~~'Why indeed, if Maria will give~~
         ~~my Freind a drawing, she can have nothing to complain of, but as she~~
         ~~does not write in Spirits, I suppose she has not yet been fortunate~~
         ~~enough to be so distinguished.~~ 'But was not it very odd^, said Kitty, that
         the Bishop . . . *a second retort from Kitty is here deleted and instead*
         her reply continues in milder form at 'But was not it . . . JA rather than
         JEA probably struck through this and the preceding passage in an attempt
         to soften Kitty's open sarcasm towards Camilla. This seems likely because,
         *despite heavy local deletion, the detail that immediately follows—*the
         Bishop should send Charles Wynne to sea—*has not been changed in*
         line with the alteration made by JEA at 177.24.

180.7   tribute to ~~the~~ ^her regard

180.11   towards ^her with great Eagerness

180.19   will just do for a Ball—^Gold Net.

181.16   and ^that ~~then~~ time

181.22   Mrs Peterson | Mrs ~~Peterson~~ ^Percival *(JEA)*

182.4   dare say ^that People

182.14   Mrs Peterson | Mrs ~~Peterson~~ ^Percival *(JEA)*

182.27   Mrs Peterson | Mrs ~~Peterson~~ ^Percival *(JEA)*

182.29   young Ladies | young ~~Ladies~~ ^Persons *(JEA)*

182.30–1 a sure mark of their being disposed to like one another | a sure
         mark ~~of their being disposed to like one another~~ ^of an aimiable affectionate
         disposition *(JEA)   the spelling 'aimiable' (never used by JA) distin-*
         guishes JEA's continuation of 'Evelyn' (at 206.31) and is a further
         sign that he made this revision

182.33–5 worthy of her regard. There is something might pretty I think in
         young Ladies corresponding with each other, and nothing forms
         the taste | worthy of her regard. ~~There is something might pretty~~
         ~~I think in young Ladies corresponding with each other, and~~ nothing
         forms the taste *(JEA)*

182.39   Mrs Peterson | Mrs ~~Peterson~~ ^Percival *(JEA)*

183.14   a Letter from Augusta to day | a Letter from Augusta ^Barlow to day
         (JEA)

183.17   a long account of the new Pierrot Lady Susan has given her | a long account of the new ~~Pierrot~~ ^Regency walking dress^ Lady Susan has given her (*JEA*) *a fashion detail that brings the story from the 1790s into the 1810s. For the reading 'Pierrot' here and at 183.25 below, see Jenny McAuley, '"A Long Letter Upon a Jacket and a Petticoat": Reading Beneath some Deletions in the Manuscript of "Catharine, or The Bower"', Persuasions: The Jane Austen Journal, 31 (2009), 191–8. The reading has been conjectured by all previous editors as 'Bonnet(?)' or 'Parisol(?)' for 'Parasol(?)'.*

183.25   nothing indeed except about the Pierrot | nothing indeed except about the ~~Pierrot~~ ^Regency^ (*JEA*)

183.26–7   to make a long Letter upon a Jacket and petticoat | to make a long Letter upon a ~~Jacket and petticoat~~ ^Bonnet & Pelisse^ (*JEA*)

183.27   left ^the^ room

183.29   fatigue and depress ^her,^

183.35   to ~~remain~~ ^continue^

184.1   Mrs Peterson; Mrs ~~Peterson~~ ^Percival^ (*JEA*)

184.20–1   They had been gone but half an hour | They had been gone ~~but half~~ an hour (*JEA*)

184.21   and as every ^thing^

184.22   in an hour & a half | in ~~an hour & a half~~ ^another hour^ (*JEA*)

184.26   so much pleasure, ~~in itself~~

184.28   for ~~about~~ ^nearly^

184.30   Nanny was then dispatched | ~~Nanny~~ ^Anne^ was then dispatched (*JEA*)

184.31–2   arranging the folds of her dress, and providing herself with Lavender water. | ^&^ arranging the folds of her dress, ~~and providing herself with Lavender water.~~ (*JEA*)

184.37   Nanny came running | ~~Nanny~~ ^Anne^ came running (*JEA*)

185.1   and ~~as~~ I knew nobody

185.6–7   ashamed of being seen because you know Ma'am I am all over powder | ashamed of being seen ~~because you know Ma'am I am all over powder~~ ^in my Apron Ma'am^ (*JEA*)

186.15   Miss Peterson | ~~Miss Peterson~~ ^Miss Percival^ (*JEA*)

186.34   Mrs Peterson | Mrs ~~Peterson~~ ^Percival^ (*JEA*)

186.35   Miss Peterson | Miss ~~Peterson~~ercival^ (*JEA*)

186.39   Land of gai^e^ty *cf. the same insertion, this time above the line, at 187.21, and 191.12. The spelling remains 'gaity' at 190.27, and 204.11. The occasional nature of the correction may be a further sign of JEA's revising hand, though see 101.36 where a similar revision occurs in JA's hand.*

187.19   but ~~as~~ ^since^ you

187.21   good humour and Gai^e^ty *see 186.39 above*

188.2   just coming ~~to th~~<e door> > round

188.3   at a Neighbour's, ~~of ours,~~

188.11   Miss Peterson | Miss ~~Peterson~~ ^Percival^ (*JEA*)

188.15 congecture *it is unclear whether JA has altered 'g' to 'j' or 'j' to 'g'*
    here. JA shows similar early uncertainty in spelling 'prejudiced' and
    'majesty'; cf. Volume the Second *120.6 and 127.4.*

188.21 You can lend me some powder | You can ~~lend~~ ^procure me some pow-
    der *(JEA)*

188.23–4 I had not time to pack up anything | I had not time to ~~pack up any-~~
    ~~thing~~ ^have anything pack'd up *(JEA)*

188.33 gone ~~before~~ > by

188.38 so much haste *JA wrote 'must'; corrected by modern editors*

189.1 & led ^her out

189.12 if we go int<o> together

190.10 with the rapidity of ~~hers~~ > his

190.12 Mrs Peterson | Mrs ~~Peterson~~ ^Percival *(JEA)* *at 190.6 and 25*
    'Peterson' remains unchanged, the unsystematic attention to the form of
    the name supporting the view that these alterations are non-authorial

190.18 with a p<oor > book, poor thing! *anticipation*

190.31 Mrs Peterson | Mrs ~~Peterson~~ ^Percival *(JEA)*

191.7 who ~~joined to~~ ^with

191.12 gai^ety *see 186.39 above*

191.15 a repetition of pleasure *JA wrote 'repetitition', perhaps confused by*
    breaking the word across two lines: repeti/tition; corrected by modern
    editors

191.31 to Lyons ~~to my~~ > where

192.1 Except ~~your Brother's~~ ^his coming away

192.9 in love with him ~~wit~~<h> > yourself

192.15 Mrs Peterson | Mrs ~~Peterson~~ ^Percival *(JEA)*

193.1 nor had an<y> > he

193.27 The Evening indeed ~~with~~ > to

193.32 could not help ~~observing~~ ^remarking *a typical stylistic revision by JA to*
    remove the repetition with 'observation' immediately below

193.37 or folly ^in his Son . . . of seeing his>m ~~Son~~ *as in the revision at 193.32,*
    JA tightens the sense by rewriting: in this instance, she achieves greater
    clarity by removing 'his Son' and inserting it earlier in the sentence

194.1 about it, ^he found him much less disposing>ed

194.12 Mrs Petersons | Mrs ~~Petersons~~ ^Percivals *(JEA)*

194.24 Mrs Peterson | Mrs ~~Peterson~~ ^Percival *(JEA)*

194.26 it is a poor encouragement *JA repeated 'it' across a line break: 'it /*
    it is'; corrected by modern editors

194.30 Mrs Peterson | Mrs ~~Peterson~~ ^Percival *(JEA)*

194.30 Mrs Stanly *here and at 195.19, 197.17, and 204.11 JA varies the*
    spelling (usually 'Stanley'). She does this elsewhere, with other names:
    'Lutterell' and 'Luttrell' in Volume the Second *for example (see*
    106.2 above and Note on Spelling).

194.36 rude to one *some editors read this as 'rude to me'—in JA's hand the*
    words 'one' and 'me' are almost impossible to distinguish. In this instance,
    'one' suits better Camilla's slightly preposterous style of speaking.

195.2–3   come in the middle   *JA wrote* come in, the middle, *but given the
           further development of the sentence, the comma represents an error.
           She may have intended to write 'in' again (*come in, in the middle*)
           or she may have changed her mind as to how the sentence would con-
           tinue. Modern editors omit the comma.*

195.20   Mrs Peterson's | Mrs ~~Peterson's~~ *(JEA)*

195.25–6   which ~~offered~~ the next Morning ^offered to her,

195.35–7   for what after all is Youth and Beauty? Why in fact, it is nothing
           more than being Young & Handsome—and that is but a poor sub-
           stitute | for what after all is Youth and Beauty? ~~Why in fact, it is
           nothing more than being Young & Handsome—and that~~^It is but a
           poor substitute *(JEA?)*

196.1   a ~~handsome~~ young Man's, being young & handsome *(JA?)*

196.8–9   that ever existed. ~~Her intimacies with Young Men are abominable;
           and it is all the same to her, who it is, no one comes amiss to her—~~
           I assure you Sir *(JA?)*   *here and at 196.1 the deletion is less vigorous
           than those that signal JEA's entries into the text*

196.23   Mrs Peterson | Mrs ~~Peterson~~ *(JEA)*

196.27   Mrs Peterson | Mrs ~~Peterson~~ *(JEA)*

196.33–4   no determinate Answer ^from him,

196.36   Miss Peterson | Miss ~~Peterson~~ ^Percival *(JEA)*

197.7   Mrs Peterson | Mrs ~~Peterson~~ ^Percival *(JEA)*

197.14   As for Mrs Peterson | As for Mrs ~~Peterson~~^ercival   *'ercival' written
           in pencil (JEA)*

197.17   so reasonably excited. ~~before—~~

197.26   Mrs Peterson | Mrs ~~Peterson~~ ^Percival *(JEA)*

198.2   left them ^together in the arbour, to wander

198.5   conversing together on ~~allmost~~ > almost

198.13   Stanley who ^was so far from being

198.14   any party, than > that

198.19   Spirit & Enthouisasm   *JA's distinctive spelling*

198.37   Mrs Peterson's | Mrs ~~Peterson's~~ ^Percival's *(JEA)*

199.12   to give any example

199.13–14 and Seccar's explanation of the Catechism | and ~~Seccar's explanation
           of the Catechism~~ ^Coelebs in Search of a Wife *(JEA)*   *see Explanatory Notes*

200.6   Mrs Peterson | Mrs ~~Peterson~~ ^Percival *(JEA)*

200.25   Mrs Peterson | Mrs ~~Peterson~~ ^Peterson > Percival   *'Peterson' has been
           reinserted above the line and then overwritten by 'Percival' (JEA)*

200.26   Mrs Peterson ^only replied

200.29   Mrs Peterson | Mrs ~~Peterson~~ ^Percival   *'Percival' inserted in pencil
           (JEA)*

200.37   no difficulty ~~of~~ ^in gaining ^an explanation

201.3   compatible > incompatible

201.11   animated & ~~gentle~~ > insinuating

201.12   otherwise ^than amiable

201.13   ~~completely~~ ^perfectly so

201.19   were ~~disposed to feel.~~ ^inclined to entertain.^   *the small, subtle changes on*
         201 all appear to be in JA's hand

202.7   had not Nanny informed her | had not ~~Nanny~~ ^^Anne^^ informed her
         (JEA)

202.21   insufferable vanty > vanity

203.9   desired w<hen> > me   *anticipation*

203.14   might not ^be^ married

203.24   bestow on any one > body

203.35–7 "His leaving England . . . averse to it."   *JA uses a set of double*
         speech marks to denote Kitty's repetition, within her speech, of Edward
         Stanley's reported words

204.6–7 "His plans interrupted."   *as at 203.35–7, a reported speech is repre-*
         sented within Kitty's inner reflections, both set inside speech marks

FAMILY CONTINUATIONS TO VOLUME THE THIRD

CONTINUATION OF EVELYN, BY JAMES EDWARD AUSTEN

205.3–207.3   On his return home . . . the proprietors of the White horse
         Inn—   *written in a different hand, that of JEA. After breaking off*
         'Evelyn' at p. 21 of her notebook, JA left the next nine pages blank,
         beginning 'Kitty, or the Bower' at p. 30. Probably between 1815 and
         1817, the teenage JEA completed 'Evelyn' in a competent pastiche of
         his aunt's comic style.

205.3   stet   *'let it stand' (Latin), inserted in pencil at an unknown date, pos-*
         sibly in a hand other than JA's, restoring the deleted words '~~On his~~'. *These*
         words mark the beginning of the continuation of 'Evelyn' (pp. 21–7 in the
         original notebook <www.janeausten.ac.uk>) in the hand of JEA.

205.6   dining parlour window open~~ed~~

205.21   seated on a ~~chaise long~~ Sofa

205.30   inhab^itants^

206.4   of the respect~~ful~~ he owed her

206.27   wefare > welfare

206.29   acident > accident

207.2   proprieters > proprietors

CONTINUATION OF EVELYN, BY ANNA LEFROY

207.5–208.22   On re entering his circular domain . . . of a Summer morning's
         sun—JAEL   *four loose leaves inserted at the end of the notebook con-*
         tain a different, abandoned attempt to continue 'Evelyn' in a more
         melodramatic style. They are signed with the initials 'JAEL' (Jane
         Anna Elizabeth Lefroy), indicating that this continuation was not
         executed before November 1814 when its writer, JA's niece Anna
         Austen, aged 21, married Ben Lefroy.

207.20   ~~language~~ power of language

207.24   writing table he > and

207.36   curl paper ~~which~~ ^&^

208.6   ~~tantôt~~ qui

208.10   mysterious > dangerous ^dangerous   *the refashioning of 'mysterious' as*
         'dangerous' is poorly legible, so Anna Lefroy clarified the change by
         repeating 'dangerous'

208.22   JAEL   *Jane Anna Elizabeth Lefroy*

CONTINUATION OF KITTY, OR THE BOWER,
BY JAMES EDWARD AUSTEN

208.25–209.28   Kitty continued in this state . . . having some Gentleman to
         attend them—   *JA broke off 'Kitty, or the Bower' at p. 124 of her*
         notebook after the words the unaccountable conduct of Young Men.
         The story was continued from this point for a little more than three pages
         (pp. 124–7) in the hand of the teenage JEA, c.1815–17.

208.28–9 Augusta Hallifax   *a possible misreading of the earlier part of the story,*
         where 'Augusta' was a 'Barker' (later changed by JEA to 'Barlow')
         when she was introduced at p. 178; the 'Halifax' girls (p. 178) are
         'Miss Halifax', 'Caroline', and 'Maria'

208.29   Mary Wynn   *'Mary Wynne' in the earlier part of the story (pp. 170ff)*

208.30   Mrs ~~Peterson~~ ^Percival   *the deletion and replacement offer further*
         strong support for the view that the alteration to the name throughout is
         non-authorial and may have occurred at a late stage in JEA's revision
         of the piece, perhaps not before the section beginning at 209.5 was added

209.4   to the particular remembrance ^it brought to her mind of Ed^wd Stanley

209.6   incident worth narrating, ~~save one~~ > or any

209.6   Catharine   *the first occasion on which this appears as a first choice*
         spelling of the heroine's name, as opposed to a revision. Like the substi-
         tution of 'Percival' for 'Peterson', still occurring as late in JEA's con-
         tinuation as 208.30, it suggests that the superlinear alteration from 'Kitty'
         to 'Catharine' in the earlier parts of the manuscript may be a late revi-
         sion, after the paragraph beginning at 209.5 ('The Summer passed
         away') was added.

209.8   announcing ~~their~~ > the

209.8–9 correspondance > correspondence

209.14   except ~~the account~~ ^a description

209.15   panegirge(?)   *in error for 'panegyric'*

209.16   abuse of Sir > the

209.17   Mrs. Percival   *the first and only use of this name not introduced as a*
         substitution; as with the first primary use of 'Catharine' at 209.6 above,
         it suggests that the alteration (always superlinear) from 'Peterson' to
         'Percival' in earlier portions of the manuscript may have occurred only
         after the paragraph beginning at 'The Summer passed away' was added

209.18   five miles from ~~the town~~ Exeter

209.19   of her own   *JEA wrote 'of her her own'; corrected by the editors*

209.22   there & <who> infested

209.25   attending the performance ~~& an~~

209.28   some Gentleman ~~of their party~~ ^to attend them^

EXPLANATORY NOTES

We are indebted to the work of previous editors; in particular, to the explanatory annotations of Austen's early work compiled by R. W. Chapman, Brian Southam, Margaret Anne Doody, Peter Sabor, and Christine Alexander. The following notes have been written with the aim of expanding the reader's sense of what the young Austen might have been responding to. It is not always possible to identify the books that she read—she owned relatively few herself, but had access to a number of libraries and other collections. Her teenage writings often appear to be saturated in an idiom and atmosphere of popular fiction rather than to be alluding to a single or specific text. Nevertheless, the sources given below suggest a richer and fuller sense of her mental furniture and range of allusions than has been previously available.

Where we cannot establish which version of a text Austen herself might have read, first editions are cited. Reference is made by volume and chapter, letter, or page number (for novels), by act and scene number (for plays), and by canto, epistle, or book, and line number (for poems), these being the most stable locations for readers consulting a variety of scholarly, standard, and non-standard editions.

References to Austen's novels follow the practice of modern editions and therefore cite continuous chapter numbers, not volume and chapter number.

VOLUME THE FIRST

1 *CONTENTS*: JA inserted page numbers beside each of the listed items. 'Detached peices' covers a number of different items whose individual titles are not listed here, nor are those pieces referred to collectively as 'Detached peices' other than on the Contents page. The original page numbers are here suppressed and replaced with the correct pagination for this edition.

FREDERIC & ELFRIDA

2 *To Miss Lloyd*: Martha Lloyd (1765–1843), who with her mother and sisters Eliza and Mary (1771–1843) rented Deane parsonage from JA's father in spring 1789. Martha was 23 or 24 and Mary 18; Cassandra was 16 and JA 13. They became firm friends, as this dedication attests, and—as in 'Frederic & Elfrida'—'the intimacy between the Families . . . daily encreased' (p. 5). In 1797 Mary became the second wife of JA's brother James; in 1828 Martha became the second wife of JA's brother Francis. Martha was at that time 63, the age (or thereabouts) at which Captain Roger in this tale contemplates marriage to Rebecca (p. 5). 'Frederic & Elfrida' may date from as early as 1787, when JA was 11, but (as Brian Southam notes) the dedication was added some time after this tale was transcribed into *Volume the First* ('The Manuscript of Jane Austen's "Volume the First"', *The Library*, 5th series, 17 (1962), 231–7, 232, n. 4).

2 *my muslin Cloak*: cf. the later reference in this tale to 'Indian & English Muslins' (p. 5). Cloaks made of muslin, a finely woven cotton, were fashionable in the late 1780s and early 1790s. In Elizabeth Hervey's *Louisa. A Novel*, 3 vols. (1790), a beautiful, mysterious stranger partly conceals her figure in 'a long muslin cloak' (iii, 187). JA's interest in muslin is evident in *NA* (ch. 3) and in letters to Cassandra, e.g. that of 25 Jan. 1801 (*Jane Austen's Letters*, ed. Deirdre Le Faye, 4th edn (Oxford: Oxford University Press, 2011) (hereafter *Letters*), 81).

this little production: such phrasing may allude to the theatrical aspect of JA's teenage works, many of which (whether or not they are styled plays or playlets) seem designed to be read aloud or performed.

3 *Frederic & Elfrida / a novel*: the names of the title characters are elaborate near-anagrams of one another, echoing the tale's insistence on how impossible it is to tell them apart. 'Elfrida' is a highly unusual, romantic name not used elsewhere in JA's work; 'Frederic', however, she liked enough to give it to Captain Wentworth in *P*. Cf. *Elfrida; or Paternal Ambition. A Novel*, 2 vols. (1786); there is another 'Elfrida' in *Beatrice, or The Inconstant. A Tragic Novel*, 2 vols. (1788), and another in *Agatha; or, A Narrative of Recent Events. A Novel* (1796). The name gained currency in such works due to William Mason's popular historical tragedy *Elfrida, A Dramatic Poem* (1752), which is quoted in Frances Burney's *Cecilia; or, Memoirs of an Heiress* (1782), bk 4, ch. 5. Of JA's teenage works, 'Jack & Alice', 'Henry & Eliza', 'The beautifull Cassandra', 'The three Sisters', 'Love and Friendship', 'Lesley-Castle', and 'Evelyn' are described as novels. The books JA published in her lifetime are all subtitled *A Novel*.

the Father's side: Frederic and Elfrida therefore share a surname, 'Falknor', as Elfrida signs herself in her letter to Miss Drummond (p. 3). The Faulknors were a naval dynasty with Hampshire connections (see e.g. *The Naval Chronicle*, 16 (1806), 1). JA first wrote that Frederic's uncle was the 'Mother' of Elfrida before correcting it to 'Father', showing a trace of the same confusion of male and female that occurs at the level of plot (see Textual Notes, p. 220).

one school: an impossibility, since schools for children of the gentry and aristocracy were strictly divided according to gender.

something more than bare politeness: marriages between first cousins were not unusual in this period. JA's brother Henry married his widowed first cousin (on the paternal side) Eliza de Feuillide in 1797. In *P&P*, Lady Catherine de Bourgh plans for her daughter to marry her maternal first cousin, Mr Darcy, by 'the wishes of both sisters' and to 'unite the two estates' (ch. 16). In *MP*, Mrs Norris tells Sir Thomas Bertram that 'the only sure way of providing against' a marriage between one of his sons and their maternal first cousin, Fanny Price, is 'to breed her up with them' (ch. 1).

rules of Propriety: Frederic and Elfrida's restraint goes well beyond the strictest conventions. Even Arabella, the wildly unrealistic heroine of Charlotte

Lennox's *The Female Quixote; or, The Adventures of Arabella*, 2 vols. (1752), criticizes a romance heroine who 'thought all Expressions of Love were criminal' (bk 2, ch. 9). In any case, the 'rules of Propriety' traditionally confined only the female lover, who was supposed to conceal any preference for a man until he had indicated some feeling for her. Samuel Richardson's *Rambler*, no. 97 (1751) insists on this rule; his last novel, *The History of Sir Charles Grandison* (1753–4), one of JA's favourite works, dwells on the complications arising from superhuman efforts at self-control.

so much alike: the doubling plot or trope, whereby siblings or lovers appear to be identical, is common in romance and sentimental fiction and derives from Shakespearean comedy. Cf. 'Lesley-Castle', in which William declares of the Miss Lesleys that 'They are so much alike . . . that I should suppose the faults of one, would be the faults of both' (p. 109). The convention as applied to lovers is sent up in 'Frederic & Elfrida' and 'Collection of Letters', where Lady Scudamore tells Henrietta that she and Musgrove are 'born for each other . . . your opinions and Sentiments so exactly coincide. Nay, the colour of your Hair is not very different' (p. 147).

intimate freinds: sentimental and novelistic phrasing; cf. 'her most intimate freind' ('Henry & Eliza'); 'my most intimate freind' ('Love and Friendship', pp. 28, 70). In the opening paragraph of 'Kitty, or the Bower', JA expands on what such friendship might involve: 'the little Girls tho' separated for the greatest part of the year by the different Modes of their Education, were constantly together during the holidays of the Miss Wynnes. In those days of happy Childhood, now so often regretted by Kitty this arbour had been formed' (p. 170).

fashionable Bonnet, to suit the complexion: hats and bonnets were worn by men and women; the bonnet typically had a smaller brim, or no brim at all, and was tied under the chin with ribbons. Female complexions were meant to be pale, as Lady Williams reminds Alice: 'when a person has too great a degree of red in their Complexion, it gives their face in my opinion, too red a look' ('Jack & Alice', p. 14). Susan in 'Lesley-Castle' claims to find the complexions of the Lesley sisters 'so horridly pale' (p. 110).

Crankhumdunberry . . . sweet village: alluding to Oliver Goldsmith's poem 'The Deserted Village' (1770), which laments the lost charms of 'Sweet Auburn, loveliest village of the plain' (l. 1). Crankhumdunberry is a spoof Irish compound: 'Crank' means funny, deceitful, or odd; 'hum' is a hoax or imposition; the Gaelic 'dun' means 'a fortified place'; 'berry' presses home the comic use of 'sweet' (five times) in 'Frederic & Elfrida' (the word appears eleven times in 'The Deserted Village'). Cf. the mock-Irish 'Kilhoobery Park' in 'Sir William Mountague' and the mock-Welsh 'Pammydiddle' in 'Jack & Alice' (pp. 34, 10).

pressing her alternately to their Bosoms: cf. the comic use of 'alternately' in 'Edgar & Emma' (p. 25) and 'Love and Friendship': 'We fainted Alternately on a Sofa' (p. 77). The source for all three moments may be a stage direction in Richard Brinsley Sheridan's *The Critic: or, A Tragedy Rehearsed*

(1781): 'They faint alternately in each others arms'; Sheridan is parodying a scene in act 2 of John Home's *Douglas: A Tragedy* (1757). Symmetrical gestures and mirrored emotions, like doubleness and coincidence, are conventions of sentimental fiction; in 'Frederic & Elfrida', even Rebecca's and Roger's ages, 36 and 63 (or 'little more than 63'), are mirror images of each other (p. 5). In e.g. *The False Friends. A Novel. In a series of letters*, 2 vols. (1785), 'Now rage, then despair, alternately took place' (ii, 107).

3 *Grove of Poplars*: a staple ingredient of sentimental prose and verse of the late 18th century; see e.g. 'a beautiful grove of poplars' in John Langhorn, *The Effusions of Friendship and Fancy. In several letters to and from select friends*, 2 vols., 2nd edn (1766), i, 147–8.

4 *verdant Lawn . . . variety of variegated flowers*: stock pastoral and sentimental language; 'variety of variegated' is notably repetitive. A 'verdant lawn' appears in countless 18th-century poems and songs, including Mark Akenside's highly influential and popular *The Pleasures of the Imagination* (1744), bk 2, l. 364. *Elegant Extracts: or useful and entertaining passages in prose* (1784), a copy of which JA gave to her niece Anna in 1801, includes a tale about Arachne and Melissa, two friends 'alike in birth, fortune, education, and accomplishments'. But where Arachne sees only the dark side of life, Melissa finds 'numberless beauties' in 'the variegated flowers of weeds and poppies' (101–2).

purling Stream . . . Valley of Tempé: more hackneyed pastoral phrases, already being sent up in 1701 in John Philips's Miltonic parody *The Splendid Shilling* (1701): 'Or des'prate lady near a purling stream, | Or lover pendent on a willow tree' (ll. 104–5); 'purling' means eddying, swirling, or murmuring. The Vale or Valley of Tempe is a gorge in northern Thessaly, Greece, praised by Greek poets and their translators and imitators for its beauty, and as a favourite haunt of Apollo and the Muses. It features in Lennox's *Female Quixote* as 'the Valley of *Tempe*, so celebrated by all the Poets and Historians' (bk 7, ch. 3).

Damon . . . I was deceiv'd: Damon is the lovelorn swain and singer of Virgil's Eclogue 8; his name is given to pastoral lovers and shepherds in the poetry of Milton, Marvell, and others. JA's mock-melancholy song of seduction and betrayal may allude to that of Olivia in a scene of 'pleasing distress' in Goldsmith's *The Vicar of Wakefield: A Tale*, 2 vols. (1766): 'When lovely woman stoops to folly . . .' (ii, ch. 5).

elegant dressing room . . . festoons of artificial flowers: Humphry Repton, in his *Observations on the Theory and Practice of Landscape Gardening* (1803), refers to 'The present dressing-room . . . added to each modern bed-room' (178); dressing rooms were often treated as sitting rooms. *Female Stability: or, The History of Miss Belville*, 5 vols. (1780) features 'an elegant dressing room, where Miss Duncannon was reading on a sopha' (i, 106). The same novel includes an outdoor scene with 'festoons of lamps . . . ornamented in the most elegant manner' and 'wreaths of artificial flowers' (ii, 266); in an indoor setting, however, such 'artificial flowers' may be carved woodwork in the shape of wreaths or garlands. JA wrote to Cassandra on 1 Dec. 1798: 'We live entirely in the dressing-room now, which I like very much; I always feel so much more elegant in it than in the parlour' (*Letters*, 25).

Jezalinda: a nonce name that unites the Old Testament Jezebel (1 and 2 Kings)—whose dressing in finery and use of makeup led to the association of cosmetics with painted women or prostitutes—with the suffix 'linda', as in the name 'Ethelinda', which appears several times in *The False Friends*, i, 130. Depending on when 'Frederic & Elfrida' was composed, JA may have in mind the heroine of Charlotte Smith's novel *Ethelinde, or the Recluse of the Lake*, 5 vols. (1789).

the amiable Rebecca: 'amiable' and 'agreeable' are stock epithets attached to sentimental heroines and their intimate friends; 'amiable', as noted in Johnson's *Dictionary*, can mean both 'lovely' and 'pretending' or merely 'shewing' love. Cf. Knightley's comments on the double meaning of 'amiable' in *E* (ch. 18). (On 'agreeable', see also Note on Spelling, see p. xliv.) Rebecca is an Old Testament name, unusual in JA's time. She also gives it to the Prices' servant in *MP* (ch. 38).

5 *Lovely & too charming Fair one*: cant sentimental and novelistic language; cf. 'too lovely, and unfortunate Fair-one' in Lennox's *The Female Quixote* (bk 6, ch. 11).

your forbidding Squint . . . your swelling Back: the glaring, mock-instructive contrast of Jezalinda with Rebecca may parody a moment in Samuel Richardson's *The History of Sir Charles Grandison. In a Series of Letters Published from the Originals*, 6 vols. (1753–4) when Harriet Byron contrasts the pretty but 'visibly proud, affected, and conceited' Miss Cantillon with plain Miss Clements, 'of a fine understanding, improved by reading; and who having no personal advantages to be vain of, has, by the cultivation of her mind, obtained a preference in every one's opinion over the fair Cantillon' (i, letter 10).

profound Curtesy: that is, a very low curtsy, indicating extreme deference and respect.

kick one another . . . slightest provocation: such violence is common in Austen's early writings, and was evidently a family joke. In *The Loiterer*, a humorous weekly periodical launched on Saturday 31 Jan. 1789 by JA's eldest brother, James, and written largely by him and his younger brother Henry, men are on two occasions kicked downstairs (*The Loiterer*, no. 4 (21 Feb. 1789); no. 24 (11 July 1789)). The periodical ran for sixty issues, until Mar. 1790, and focused on university matters (see also Appendix 1). Cf. Mrs Kickabout in 'Lesley-Castle' and Sir William Gascoigne in 'The History of England'. In Samuel Richardson's *Pamela: or, Virtue Rewarded. In a series of familiar letters, from a beautiful young Damsel, to her parents*, 2 vols. (dated 1741 [pub. 1740]), Mr B threatens to throw Mrs Jervis out of the window; after her marriage, Pamela escapes her brutal sister-in-law via the window (i, letter 25; ii, '*TUESDAY Morning, Eleven O'Clock*').

5 *ran off with the Coachman*: Tristram Shandy's great aunt Dinah marries and has a child by her coachman (Laurence Sterne, *The Life and Opinions of Tristram Shandy, Gentleman*, 9 vols. (1759–67), i, ch. 21). Miss Dickins, in 'Jack & Alice', elopes with the butler (p. 14). Richardson's Mr B makes a comparably socially lopsided match when he marries his servant, Pamela, a union that is mocked in Henry Fielding's *An Apology for the Life of Mrs. Shamela Andrews* (1741). Fielding himself went on to marry his deceased first wife's maid, who was pregnant.

little more than 63: here, old age is presented as extreme youth; in 'The three Sisters', the joke is reversed: Mr Watts (aged 32) is 'quite an old Man' (p. 52). Colonel Brandon (aged 35) in *S&S* strikes Marianne as 'an old bachelor', while a woman of 27 'can never hope to feel or inspire affection again' (ch. 8).

parents of Frederic proposed . . . between them: in 18th-century fiction, parents typically impede the union of two lovers by withholding their consent; here, in proposing the marriage of Frederic and Elfrida, they are doing quite the opposite—without, however, ascertaining the wishes of the two parties themselves. Cf. 'Love and Friendship', pp. 72–3.

the naming of the Day: traditionally, it was the bride's prerogative to choose the date of the wedding.

Patches, Powder, Pomatum & Paint: an echo of the most celebrated list in 18th-century literature: 'Puffs, Powders, Patches, Bibles, Billet-doux' (*The Rape of the Lock*, canto 1, l. 138). 'Pomatum' is an ointment for the skin or hair. JA originally wrote 'Rouge, Powder, Pomatum & Paint'; by changing 'Rouge' to 'Patches' she heightens the comic alliteration and makes the allusion to Pope more overt.

6 *postilion*: 'A person who rides the (leading) nearside (left-hand side) horse drawing a coach or carriage, esp. when one pair only is used and there is no coachman. Also in extended use: an outrider for a carriage' (*OED*). Cf. the postilion in 'Henry & Eliza' and 'The first Act of a Comedy'.

Condescension: 'Voluntary submission to equality with inferiors' (Johnson's *Dictionary*). Here, the word appears in a benign sense, but JA's lifetime spans the period in which the negative sense is beginning to predominate: in *P&P*, Lady Catherine de Bourgh's condescension, as fawningly praised by Mr Collins, comes closer to the modern understanding of the word. Cf. also 'condescension' in 'Henry & Eliza' (p. 29) and 'Lesley-Castle' (p. 106).

Portland Place: a magnificent, unusually wide street in central London, laid out by Robert and James Adam for the Duke of Portland in the late 18th century; frequently a backdrop in fiction of the period (see e.g. Agnes Maria Bennett's *Anna: or Memoirs of a Welch Heiress*, 4 vols. (1785), ii, ch. 43). It originally ran north from the gardens of a detached mansion called Foley House. In the early 19th century, Portland Place was incorporated into the royal route from Carlton House to Regent's Park, developed for the Prince Regent by John Nash.

seated . . . in one chair: cf. 'The Visit' (act 2, scene 1), in which only six chairs are available for eight people, and two men sit in ladies' laps. JA is echoing a weird moment in *The Vicar of Wakefield*, in which 'We happened not to have chairs enough for the whole company; but Mr. Thornhill immediately proposed that every gentleman should sit in a lady's lap' (i, ch. 9). The Vicar, unsurprisingly, disapproves of the suggestion.

old pink Coat: in *MP*, the stiff and pompous Mr Rushworth plans to don a 'pink satin cloak' as Count Cassel in *Lovers' Vows* (ch. 15). JA possibly refers here to a hunting coat. Thomas Pink, an 18th-century tailor in Mayfair, designed the coat worn by Masters of Foxhounds, whippers-in, huntsmen and other hunt staff. The coat was made of red cloth but known as 'pink' after its originator.

a post-chaise [footnote]: JA's note; it tells us, succinctly, why Charlotte's carriage is 'lovely'. A 'post chaise' was the most expensive form of hired transport: 'A horse-drawn, usually four-wheeled carriage (in Britain usually having a closed body, the driver or postilion riding on one of the horses) used for carrying mail and passengers, esp. in the 18th and early 19th centuries' (*OED*). Elsewhere in the teenage writings, there is only one other authorial note—to 'Letter the first' in 'Lesley-Castle'.

7 *new blue coat*: a very fashionable item, partly thanks to the blue frock coat worn by the suicidal hero of Goethe's best-selling sentimental epistolary novel *Die Leiden des jungen Werthers* [*The Sorrows of Young Werther*] (1774). The naval hero of *Catharine; or, The Wood of Llewellyn*, 2 vols. (1788) is admired for 'the splendour of his blue coat, and milk white lapels', as contrasted unfavourably with the 'russet frocks' of the locals (i, p. 15). Bingley wears a blue coat in *P&P* (ch. 3) and Lydia Bennet wants Wickham to 'be married in his blue coat' (ch. 51). See also 'Love and Friendship', note to p. 87.

something in the appearance . . . account for it: as in the contrast of Jezalinda and Rebecca (p. 4), JA may be parodying a stock debate between the charms of the mind and those of the body—in *Sir Charles Grandison*, Harriet is said to be attracted primarily to Sir Charles's intellect rather than to his appearance (ii, letter 9). Cf. 'The three Sisters', in which Georgiana says of Mr Watts: 'He is rather plain to be sure, but then what is Beauty in a Man' (p. 55).

a young Leveret, a brace of Partridges, a leash of Pheasants: the list ascends in numerical order. A leveret is 'A young hare, strictly one in its first year'; a 'brace' is a pair; a 'leash' is a set of three (see *OED*). Cf. the extravagant consumption of food in 'Lesley-Castle' (especially pp. 103–4).

double engagement: a very serious breach of propriety; in *Sir Charles Grandison*, the hero narrowly avoids becoming engaged to two women, Clementina della Porretta and Harriet Byron, at the same time.

reflection of her past folly . . . guilty of a greater: possibly an echo of the scene in which Richardson's Pamela—imprisoned, despondent, and injured—contemplates suicide by drowning herself in a pond (*Pamela*:

or, Virtue Rewarded, i, ('THURSDAY, FRIDAY, SATURDAY, SUNDAY . . . *Days of my Distress*'). Perhaps also an echo of Olivia's song in *The Vicar of Wakefield*. 'When lovely woman stoops to folly', the song concludes, the only solution is death (ii, ch. 5).

7 *deep stream . . . Portland Place*: neither pleasure grounds nor a stream adorned the town-houses of Portland Place.

sweet lines, as pathetic as beautifull: cf. *The Loiterer*, no. 59: 'When an author describes a scene which he wishes to be affecting, let him boldly pronounce it so himself' (p. 9).

8 *seven days . . . expired, together with the lovely Charlotte*: for other instances of JA's syllepsis, or zeugma, whereby one verb governs two different, incongruous objects (here, 'days' and 'Charlotte'), see e.g. 'Jack & Alice': 'cruel Charles to wound the hearts & legs of all the fair' (p. 18). She probably learned the technique from Pope's *Rape of the Lock*, in which Queen Anne is famously said to 'take' both 'Counsel' and '*Tea*' (canto 3, l. 8).

smelling Bottle . . . dagger: a parody of the legendary choice between dagger and bowl. Eleanor of Aquitaine, wife of Henry II, was said to have given her rival, 'Fair Rosamund', the choice of killing herself by drinking poison from a bowl or of being stabbed. The tale is re-told in Joseph Addison's *Rosamond an Opera* (1707). Smelling bottles held perfume or smelling salts, used as a restorative in cases of fainting.

When Corydon . . . very fess: like Damon, Corydon is a stock name for a pastoral singer–swain; there is a shepherd with this name in Theocritus' *Idylls* and in Virgil's *Eclogues*. Cf. another Corydon in 'The Mystery', who appears in 'A Garden' and says only 'But Hush! I am interrupted' (the opening line of the play). 'Bess' is, contrastingly, an archetypally English rustic name, while 'fess' narrows the linguistic field still further; it is a dialect word from the south and south-west of England, meaning 'Lively, active, strong; gay "smart", clever' (*English Dialect Dictionary*, ed. Joseph Wright (1898–1905), ii, 338).

Stage Waggon: 'one of the wagons belonging to an organized system of conveyance for heavy goods and passengers by road' (*OED*): the cheapest, slowest, and most uncomfortable type of public transport.

9 *delicate frame of her mind . . . press her on the subject*: Elfrida's coy reluctance ever to name the day takes to its logical conclusion a comparable wish in countless heroines of 18th-century fiction, including Richardson's Pamela. Cf. JA's letter to Cassandra of 5 Sept. 1796, where she jokes about lovers being kept 'apart for five Volumes' (*Letters*, 9).

spluttered: to splutter is to speak hastily and indistinctly, quite possibly while spitting; Johnson considers 'splutter' a 'low word' (*Dictionary*).

fainting fits . . . fell into another: cf. 'Love and Friendship': 'For an Hour & a Quarter did we continue in this unfortunate Situation—Sophia fainting every moment & I running Mad as often' (p. 87). Sir Hargrave Pollexfen declares in the Austen family's dramatic skit 'Sir Charles Grandison' (after 1799): 'I wish Women were not quite so delicate, with all their faints and fits!' (act 2, scene 1).

bold as brass . . . soft as cotton: 'bold as brass' is a proverbial simile; 'soft as cotton' appears to be JA's invention.

JACK & ALICE

10 *Francis William Austen . . . Perseverance*: this dedication must have been written between Dec. 1789 and Nov. 1791, when JA's brother Francis (1774–1865) served as midshipman on the *Perseverance* in the East Indies (these dates cannot, however, assist us in establishing precisely when the tale itself was written; see Introduction, Chronology of the Teenage Writings, and 'Mr Harley', note to p. 33). 'Esq' (Esquire) is a courtesy title for gentlemen rather than teenagers, though Francis had by this stage left home; cf. the dedication of 'Sir William Mountague' to Charles Austen (p. 34). JA also dedicated 'Mr Harley' to Francis. In *MP*, Fanny Price's brother William is a midshipman, defined by William Falconer in *An Universal Dictionary of the Marine* (1769) as 'a sort of naval cadet, appointed by the captain of a ship of war, to second the orders of the superior officers, and assist in the necessary business of the vessel, either aboard or ashore'.

Mr Johnson: in 'Jane Austen and the Stuarts', Brigid Brophy suggests an allusion to the Revd Augustus Johnson, who in 1791 became rector of Hamstall-Ridware, Staffordshire, a living on which the Austen family had its eye (in B. C. Southam (ed.), *Critical Essays on Jane Austen* (London: Routledge & Kegan Paul, 1968), 21–38, at 23). However, the later reference in this chapter to 'Johnson Court' suggests that JA may (also) be thinking of Samuel Johnson, who once lived at Johnson or Johnson's Court. James Boswell's *Life of Johnson* was published on 16 May 1791; in it, Boswell recalled his own sensations on learning that Johnson had moved elsewhere: 'I felt a foolish regret that he had left a court which bore his name'. *Life of Johnson*, ii, 15 (15 Mar. 1776).

Masquerade: a masked ball, sometimes involving elaborate or fantastical disguises and hence associated with excess and disorder. Masquerades in 18th-century novels often end badly for the central characters (as in Henry Fielding's *The History of Tom Jones* (1749), bk 13, ch. 7). Sir Charles Grandison is against masquerades (i, letter 27); in the Austen family's 'Sir Charles Grandison', Harriet Byron calls them 'odious' (act 3, scene 1). Frances Burney's *Evelina, or A Young Lady's Entrance into the World*, 3 vols. (1778) and *Cecilia* include masquerade scenes; the name 'Cecilia' appears later in this chapter and nowhere else in JA's works.

55th year: in 'Love and Friendship' (p. 69), Laura is said to be 'this Day 55'.

tickets: Mr Johnson plans to invite just four families to a private party—for which printed tickets, of the kind typically issued for a large public ball, would be comically inappropriate ('tickets' here may mean calling cards with handwritten invitations). In Burney's *Cecilia*, the joke works in the other direction as Captain Aresby nonchalantly informs the heroine that 'our select masquerade at the Pantheon . . . shall have but 500 tickets' (bk 1, ch. 8).

10 *Pammydiddle*: a nonsense compound: 'pam' is a card game in which the knave of clubs is the highest trump (see *The Rape of the Lock*: 'The Rebel-*Knave*, that dares his Prince engage, | Proves the just Victim of his Royal Rage. | Ev'n mighty *Pam* that Kings and Queens o'erthrew', canto 3, ll. 59–61); 'diddle' means to cheat. There may also be an echo of Richardson's heroine, Pamela.

rather tall: JA refers to herself as 'a tall woman' on 25 Jan. 1801 (*Letters*, 81); cf. *Memoir*: 'her figure was rather tall' (70). The Lesley sisters are said to be 'two great, tall, out of the way, over-grown, Girls, just of a proper size to inhabit a Castle almost as Large in comparison as themselves' (p. 107).

passionate: 'Easily moved to anger' (Johnson's *Dictionary*). In the supporting quotation for this definition, 'passionate' is paired with 'haughty', suggesting the implications of wealth, status, and arrogance that often accompany tall male characters in 18th-century fiction. In *Harcourt: A Sentimental Novel*, 2 vols. (1780), a work attributed on the title page to Burney (but not in fact hers), the 'absolutely irresistible' hero, Edmond, is 'tall' and 'very thin'. As is the case with Charles Adams, no-one 'views his approach without transport, or his departure without regret' (i, 12–13).

Charles Adams: this irresistibly beautiful, dazzling character may be named with reference to Sir Charles Grandison, another impossibly perfect man; the youngest Austen brother was also called Charles—a Stuart name (see 'The History of England' for JA's overt, outrageous Stuart bias).

none but Eagles . . . Face: eagles are traditionally believed to be able to look at the sun; later in this chapter, Charles wears a 'Mask representing the Sun' (p. 11).

Sukey: a pet-form of Susan (itself a diminutive of Susannah), as in P. Gibbes's *The Niece; or, The History of Sukey Thornby. A Novel*, 3 vols. (1788). According to the *OED*, from at least 1823 'sukey' was a child's or slang name for a tea-kettle; given this tale's jokes about over-heating it may well have been current before then.

Jointure: property settled on a woman at marriage, to be used when her husband has died. Johnson's *Dictionary* suggests the welcome, indeed unique, independence afforded by this provision: 'Estate settled on a wife to be enjoyed after her husband's decease'. Mrs Jennings in *S&S* shows how enjoyable such wealth might be.

11 *Tho' Benevolent . . . Entertaining*: the syntax here imitates Johnsonian symmetry and parallelism; the passage comically lacks the expected contrasts between diametrically opposing qualities.

family of Love: originally the name of a 16th-century religious sect; by the 18th century, a phrase commonly deployed in novels and without religious implication. See e.g. *Tom Jones*, bk 14, ch. 6; Sarah Fielding, *The Adventures of David Simple* (1753), bk 6, ch. 7; *Sir Charles Grandison*, iii, letter 28; Charlotte Lennox, *Euphemia*, 4 vols. (1790), iv, 42. In *Edward. A Novel*, 2 vols. (1774), James Wharton declares: 'there is not so enchanting a society as that of a well-regulated family, a family of love' (ii, 82). But the phrase had a less reputable connotation that may also have been in JA's mind; in *Classical Dictionary*, 'FAMILY OF LOVE' is said to mean 'lewd women'.

the Bottle & the Dice: drinking and gambling, here referred to metonymically; cf. Mr Harrel's fatal attraction to both in *Cecilia* (bk 5, ch. 12).

Drawing Room: a room designed for the reception and entertainment of guests, but typically more intimate and less formal than other, more public rooms. See 'Edgar & Emma', note to p. 26.

Sultana: the wife, concubine, mistress, or female relative of a sultan; the Turkish dress of a sultana was a popular choice for women at masquerades.

female Masks: as in *Tom Jones* (bk 13, ch. 7), 'masks' here are, metonymically, the masqueraders themselves.

Mask representing the Sun: a parodic reference to Grandison, whose face is 'overspread with a manly sunniness' (i, letter 36). This is the only citation given in the *OED* to support a now obsolete sense of 'sunniness'— 'Sunburn, tan'; women sometimes wore masks to prevent burning, tanning, and freckles. Mythological characters such as Apollo and Flora were popular at masquerades; cf. *Cecilia*, bk 2, ch. 3.

plain green Coat: dark green was a fashionable choice for men's coats. In *The History of Sir William Harrington. Written some years since, and revised and corrected by the late Mr Richardson*, 4 vols. (1771), the ladies are warned to beware an injured stranger lying in the next room: 'he is such a handsome man, I am almost afraid for you'. This 'fine figure' is dressed in a green coat. Large draughts of strong drink and cordials feature in this episode, as do implausible preparations for emergency surgery (cf. Lady Williams, p. 18). *The History of Sir William Harrington* also features a housekeeper called 'Knightly' (i, 196–8), anticipating the hero's name in *E*.

2 Domino's: a domino is a unisex garment, 'A kind of loose cloak, app. of Venetian origin, chiefly worn at masquerades, with a small mask covering the upper part of the face, by persons not personating a character' (*OED*). Cf. *Cecilia*: 'Dominos of no character, and fancy-dresses of no meaning, made, as is usual at such meetings, the general herd of the company' (bk 2, ch. 3).

a beautifull Flora: 'In Latin mythology, the goddess of flowers; hence, in modern poetical language, the personification of nature's power in producing flowers' (*OED*).

a studied attitude: in other words, a contrived pose designed to attract attention. A 'rather handsome' male correspondent in the *Literary Fly*, no. 4 (1779), who writes for advice 'but dare not ask it of anyone without a mask', recalls an evening at the opera in which, 'Intoxicated with pleasure,

I displayed my glass, and, carelessly leaning on a bench, in an attitude studied for the purpose, and not very unbecoming, took a prospect of the gallery' (17, 18, 21).

11 *character of Virtue*: popular characters to impersonate at masquerades included abstract qualities such as Virtue, Hope, Temperance, and Liberty. Richardson's *Pamela* is subtitled *or Virtue Rewarded*, suggesting that the heroine, like Lady Williams, might be read as such a personification.

Entertainment: 'Treatment at the table' (Johnson's *Dictionary*); a formal or elegant meal or banquet.

12 *tout ensemble*: the overall or general effect (French).

so much her Junior: JA originally wrote 'so much her inferior' (see Textual Notes, p. 220); her revision changes the emphasis. Rather than feel constrained by the rule that a woman should not marry a man of lower rank, Lady Williams is made to respond to a different convention: that a woman should not marry a younger man. Both potential infractions apply to Lady Booby's wooing of her teenage footman in Henry Fielding's *The History of the Adventures of Joseph Andrews and of his Friend Mr. Abraham Adams* (1742), his second response to Richardson's *Pamela*.

polite to all but partial to none: an echo of Pope's description of Belinda in *The Rape of the Lock*: 'Favours to none, to all she Smiles extends' (canto 2, l. 11). Belinda has eyes like Charles, too: 'Bright as the Sun, her Eyes the Gazers strike' (canto 2, l. 13).

the lovely, the lively, but insensible: novelistic cant: 'insensible' contradicts 'lively', suggesting both 'void of feeling' and 'void of emotion or affection' (Johnson's *Dictionary*). There is a comparable joke in Elizabeth Blower's *Features from Life; or, A Summer Visit* (1788), in which Mr Needham sarcastically commends Lady Gaythorne's appearance: 'such a dress needs not the aid of animated, living, glowing beauty, to set it off; it needs but to be seen in a fashionable assembly on the body of an automaton to do a world of execution. How many men of fashion would be dying for the lovely insensible?' (239–40). In Jane Timbsury's *The Male-Coquette; or, The History of the Hon. Edward Astell*, 2 vols. (1770), the narrator recalls a career akin to that of Charles Adams: 'I have made an extensive devastation, a strange havock among the pretty creatures'. However, just as the Miss Simpsons are immune to Charles's power, so Edward finds one 'lovely *insensible*' who is strangely 'proof against every charm' (*The Male-Coquette*, i, 13).

like the great Sir Charles Grandison . . . Home: Harriet Byron praises Grandison for refusing to make his servants tell visitors that he is 'not at home' when he does not wish to see anyone (iv, letter 26).

13 *Bigamy*: another allusion to Grandison, who is torn between two potential wives. Cf. the double engagement leading to suicide in 'Frederic & Elfrida'.

out of spirits: a pun on 'spirits' in the double sense of alcohol and cheerfulness; the use of wine as a medicinal aid is also in play here. The same pun features in 'A beautiful description of the different effects of Sensibility on different Minds' (p. 64).

second attachment . . . serious consequences: the relative merits and dangers of first and second attachments are frequently discussed in 18th-century novels. In *Sir Charles Grandison*, Lady Grandison asks 'how few of us are there, who have their first Loves? And indeed how few first Loves are fit to be encouraged?' (vii, letter 43). Marianne Dashwood 'does not approve of second attachments', but thanks to her marriage to Colonel Brandon she lives 'to counteract, by her own conduct, her most favourite maxims' (*S&S*, ch. 11, ch. 50).

Life & Adventures: a phrase often used in the titles or subtitles of novels (e.g. Francis Coventry's *The History of Pompey the Little, or the Life and Adventures of a Lapdog* (1761)). The narration of 'life and adventures', frequently by characters in distress, was a stock device. In *The Female Quixote*, Lennox's Arabella repeatedly asks new acquaintances to recite their 'adventures'; towards the end of the work, a countess reprimands her for doing so: 'The Word Adventures carries in it so free and licentious a Sound in the Apprehensions of People at this Period of Time, that it can hardly with Propriety be apply'd to those few and natural Incidents which compose the History of a Woman of Honour' (bk 8, ch. 7).

sending me to School . . . Education at Home: JA herself attended school for several years, but she was primarily educated at home in Steventon Rectory—itself a sort of private boarding school, since her father took in a number of paying male pupils in order to supplement his income.

14 *Kitty*: pet form of Catherine; cf. Kitty in 'Edgar & Emma' (p. 26), and the heroine of 'Kitty, or the Bower'.

Winter . . . in town: the fashionable set spent winter in a London townhouse (in the West End, rather than in the City); the London season lasted until the king's official birthday on 4 June.

too much colour: cf. references to complexions and rouge in 'Frederic & Elfrida'; here, the excess colour may be natural, or due to cosmetics, or (as in Alice Johnson's case) to drink.

red in their Complexion . . . too red a look: JA revised 'too much colour' to 'too red a look' (see Textual Notes, p. 221), heightening the redundancy of the phrasing.

15 '*From Words she almost came to Blows*': JA here adapts a line from James Merrick's poem 'The CAMELION: A FABLE after Monsieur DE LA MOTTE', in which two men dispute the colour of a chameleon. The work appears in Robert Dodsley's *A Collection of Poems . . . By Several Hands*, 6 vols. (1758), v, 223–35. JA owned a copy of Dodsley's *Collection*; she sold it for 10*s*. in May 1801 (*Letters*, 92). See 'Ode to Pity', note to p. 66; 'Collection of Letters', note to p. 147.

Claret: red wine imported from Bordeaux; an expensive choice, drunk by gentlemen. In *Masquerades; or, What you Will*, 4 vols. (1780), Sir Charles

Montague is envisaged 'feasting on ortolans and quaffing claret and champaign' (iv, 79).

15 *Citron Grove*: a grove of citrus trees, not found in England. There is an orange grove in the Italian section of *Sir Charles Grandison* (iii, letter 22); a citron grove also appears in a much anthologized passage from Milton's *Paradise Lost* (bk 5, line 22). Groves of all kinds were popular settings in sentimental fiction and pastoral verse.

sensible: 'Cognizant, conscious, aware of something. Often with some tinge of emotional sense: Cognizant of something as a ground for pleasure or regret' (*OED*).

16 *fair Nymph*: stock sentimental and pastoral language, though in view of her other allusions to Pope's *Rape of the Lock* JA may again have Belinda in mind, this time with reference to her suffering, like Lucy, the hero's 'unresisted Steel': 'What wonder, then, fair Nymph! Thy hairs should feel | The conqu'ring force of unresisted Steel?' (canto 3, ll. 177–8). This episode and a beautiful character called Lucy have an afterlife in the person of *S&S*'s Lucy Steele.

your Life & adventures: JA may be recalling (among other things) an episode in Charlotte Smith's *Emmeline, the Orphan of the Castle*, 4 vols. (1788), in which the heroine and her friend, while out walking, happen to spot a melancholy young lady at a cottage window. When pressed, the beautiful stranger, Adelina, reluctantly embarks on her narrative of distress (ii, ch. 11). See also note to p. 13.

North Wales . . . capital Taylors: north Wales is a location celebrated for its wild, sublime mountain scenery rather than for its tailors; south Wales is the backdrop for the heroine's childhood in 'Love and Friendship'. See also 'A Tour through Wales' in 'Collection of Letters'.

accomplishments . . . Wales: the daughter of a tailor, adopted by a widowed innkeeper, would not be expected to possess skills such as those listed here (for criticism of female accomplishments, see *The Loiterer*, no. 27). JA's joke may partly allude to her brother Edward's adoption in 1783 by the wealthy but childless Knight family; in *MP*, Fanny Price is adopted as a child by the family of her mother's sister.

17 *rents . . . Estate*: a gentleman derived his income from the rent paid by tenants who farmed his estate; collecting such rents was usually the task of the estate owner's steward.

Mrs Susan: as a lower servant, Susan is known by her first name rather than by her surname.

her Place: employment or position as a servant.

pumping her: to pump is 'To subject (a person) to a questioning process in order to elicit information; to ply with questions in an artful or persistent manner' (*OED*).

offering him . . . hand & heart: JA may be recalling Lady Olivia's passionate offer 'to cast her fortune' at the feet of Sir Charles Grandison, and 'to comply with any terms he should propose to her' (*Sir Charles Grandison*, iv, letter 21). Cf. JA's apparent intention to have Eliza declare her love to Cecil in 'Henry & Eliza' (see Textual Notes, p. 223). For a woman to propose to a man was a thrilling breach of convention that went on to inspire radical novels of the next decade such as Eliza Fenwick's *Secresy; or, The Ruin on the Rock*, 3 vols. (1795).

18 *steel traps*: traps with jaws and springs of steel were laid in the grounds of private estates in order to catch poachers and trespassers (see *The Loiterer*, no. 50).

After examining the fracture . . . such a one before: in her highly unlikely resourcefulness and benevolence, Lady Williams resembles Lady Bountifull in George Farquhar's *The Beaux' Stratagem. A Comedy* ([1707]).

19 *I am very partial . . . real defects*: JA's revision of her original phrasing— 'I may be partial; indeed I believe I am; yes I am very partial to her'— changes a neutral comment into a snide, self-praising one (see Textual Notes, p. 221).

Bath: the well-known resort and spa town where JA lived with her mother and sister from 1801 to 1804 also features in 'The three Sisters' and 'Love and Friendship', as well as in her novels.

Jaunt: 'Ramble; flight; excursion. It is commonly used ludicrously' (Johnson's *Dictionary*).

20 *the Hero of this Novel*: Jack Johnson, who is named only in the title and barely features in the story.

my self unparalelled: Charles Adams, in delivering a lengthy eulogy on himself, takes to its logical conclusion the praise heaped on virtuous characters in Richardson's epistolary fiction. Harriet Byron's first description of Grandison is lavishly hyperbolic: 'Were kings to be chosen for their beauty and majesty of person, Sir Charles Grandison would have few competitors' (i, letter 36). Adams, however, prides himself on his looks and abilities, not on his charity or kindness. Charlotte Grandison says of her brother, by contrast, that he is 'valued by those who know him best, not so much for being an handsome man; not so much for his birth and fortune; nor for this or that single worthiness; as for being, in the great and yet comprehensive sense of the word, a *good man*' (i, letter 36).

21 *One freind I have*: that is, Mrs Susan, the cook. Friendship between a male employer and a female servant would be highly unusual, but 'freind' may in this context be a euphemism: in her first letter home, Richardson's Pamela excitedly reports that Mr B has offered to be a friend to her. Her parents are instantly alarmed (*Pamela*, i, letters 1 and 2). Cf. *OED* 'friend': 'A romantic or sexual partner; a lover'.

She flew to her Bottle . . . forgot: cf. Mrs Slipslop in Henry Fielding's *Joseph Andrews*, who on being rejected by the hero consoles herself with 'a visit to the Stone-Bottle, which is of sovereign use to a Philosophical Temper' (bk 1, ch. 9).

23 *raised to the Gallows*: hanging, usually in public, was the punishment for those found guilty of capital crimes, murder included.

some Prince . . . cheifly engaged: JA alludes to the notorious affairs and entanglements of the Prince of Wales, and of his younger brothers Frederick (Duke of York), William (Duke of Clarence), and Edward (Duke of Kent). The Prince of Wales had secretly married a Catholic widow, Maria Fitzherbert, in 1785.

great Mogul: the Muslim Mogul dynasty ruled most of India in the 17th century. During the next century, with the rise of the British Raj, its power swiftly declined, the Great Mogul being left in control only of Delhi and the surrounding area. He was recognized as the formal ruler and known by Europeans as the 'Emperor of Delhi'. Like sultans and sultanas, the Great Mogul often appeared in 18th-century oriental narratives; see e.g. Charles Morell, *The Tales of the Genii; or, The Delightful Lessons of Horam*, 2 vols. (1780).

EDGAR & EMMA

24 *a tale*: this generic designation (cf. 'Mr Harley', 'Mr Clifford', 'Amelia Webster', 'The Generous Curate', and 'A Tale') distinguishes the ensuing work from the typically longer 'novels' in JA's teenage writings. Probably composed in 1787, 'Edgar & Emma' is exceptional among the teenage writings in lacking a dedication.

Godfrey: an unusual name in the 18th century; it also appears in *The Amicable Quixote; or, The Enthusiasm of Friendship*, 4 vols. (1788). 'Godfrey's cordial' was a name given to 'various preparations containing tincture of opium mixed with treacle and often flavourings such as sassafras, ginger, or caraway, used as a sedative, esp. for children' (*OED*).

Market-town: the centre of a country area, a town permitted to hold regular market-days.

three pair of Stairs high: 'pair' here means a 'set' or flight of stairs. Sir Godfrey and Lady Marlow are living, anachronistically, as if they were tradesmen or merchants with rooms above the shop. Third-floor accommodation in town-houses was normally small and occupied by servants or lodgers of very modest means. In Robert Bage's *Mount Henneth, A Novel*, 2 vols. (1782), the narrator visits a patient 'who lodged in a garret up three pair of stairs, at a green grocer's. The room, and its furniture, were exceeding poor' (ii, 78).

Consumption: 'Originally: abnormality or loss of humours, resulting in wasting (extreme weight loss) of the body; such wasting; (*obs.*). Later: disease that causes wasting of the body, *spec.* tuberculosis' (*OED*).

25 *Marlhurst*: perhaps echoing the Whig aristocratic name of the Duke of Marlborough, this country seat combines the first syllable of the Marlows' name with 'hurst', meaning a wooded hill.

ninepence among the Ringers: major events in a community were traditionally marked by a peal of the church bells; the mere return of owners to their estate would not seem to merit such a celebration. In any event, nine-pence is a miserly amount to parcel out among a group of six or more bell-ringers. James Woodforde distributed money to the ringers in his village every Christmas, giving them 2*s.* 6*d.* as their 'annual Gift' on 26 Dec. 1786 (*The Diary of a Country Parson*, ed. John Beresford (Oxford: Oxford University Press, 1979), 291–2).

Villa: a smallish and newly built 'country seat' (Johnson's *Dictionary*), or any residence of a superior or handsome type, or of some architectural pretension.

Mr Willmot . . . the representative . . . Lottery: despite his 'very ancient Family' and the aristocratic associations of his name (echoing that of the dissolute poet John Wilmot, Earl of Rochester (1647–80)), Mr Willmot's money is new and far from genteel in origin. He owns a potentially very profitable share in a lead mine and has bought an expensive ticket in the national lottery that ran from 1709 to 1824. There is a cash-seeking Mr Willmott in *The Assignation. A Sentimental Novel. In a Series of Letters*, 2 vols. (1774); see also note below to p. 25. JA originally wrote 'a younger representative', but presumably revised her phrasing as only the eldest son could have inherited the 'paternal Estate' (see Textual Notes, p. 222).

their Coach: no private carriage of the type suggested here could in reality have accommodated as many people as nine children and two adults. JA's father's carriage, a 'chariot', had one row of seats for two or three people (see note to 'Sir William Mountague', p. 35).

Emma: a favourite name of JA's, it appears again in 'Mr Harley' and *The Watsons*, as well as in *E*, her only published novel to be named after the heroine. Many heroines in later 18th-century fiction are called Emma, perhaps thanks to the lasting popularity of Matthew Prior's verse dialogue 'Henry and Emma', first published in his *Poems on Several Occasions* (1709).

Edgar: an unusual name in the 18th century, not employed elsewhere in JA; it also appears in Prior's 'Henry and Emma'. In Burney's *Camilla: or, A Picture of Youth*, 5 vols. (1796), the heroine's suitor is called Edgar Mandlebert.

tremble: revised by JA from the original 'fear', and heightening the physical manifestation of Emma's feelings (see Textual Notes, p. 222).

Rodolphus: in a list of otherwise unremarkable male names, Rodolphus sticks out. A Rodolphus Vernon appears in Anna Maria McKenzie's *The Gamesters: A Novel*, 3 vols. (1786), as does the surname Wilmot (iii, 161); see note above to p. 25, and 'Lesley-Castle', note to p. 98.

sunk breathless on a Sopha: cf. 'Love and Friendship': 'We fainted Alternately on a Sofa' (p. 77). 'A long, stuffed seat with a back and ends or end, used for reclining; a form of lounge or couch' (*OED*), from the early 18th century onwards, the comfortable and relatively informal sofa became increasingly popular. It readily lent itself to fainting and posing as well as to relaxation. William Cowper's long blank-verse poem *The Task*, a favourite of JA's, appeared in 1785; Book One, 'The Sofa', commissioned by his female friend Lady Austen (no relation to JA), mentions the 'soft recumbency of outstretched limbs' afforded to women (l. 82). Lady Bertram makes the most of her sofa in *MP*, but Fanny Price gets scolded for idling there (ch. 2, ch. 7).

25 *confidante*: JA puns on the name given by the English designer George Hepplewhite (d. 1786) to a type of settee ('confidante', *OED*) and 'A person trusted with private affairs, commonly with affairs of love' ('confidant', Johnson's *Dictionary*). John Gregory's *A Father's Legacy to his Daughters*, 2nd edn (1774), warns against 'making confidants of your servants', as it would 'spoil them and debase yourselves' (71–2). Thomas the footman is, in any case, of the wrong gender and rank to be a confidante for Emma; cf. gender confusion in 'Frederic & Elfrida' and 'The History of England' (in which Lambert Simnel is imagined as the widow of Richard III). JA also changes the gender when quoting or alluding to other authors (see 'Jack & Alice', note to p. 15, and her allusion to Cowper's *Tirocinium: or, a Review of Schools* (1785) in *MP*, ch. 45).

26 *Parlour . . . social Manner*: the parlour in a private house was 'a sitting room; *esp.* the main family living room, or the room reserved for entertaining guests' (*OED*); Johnson's *Dictionary* describes it as 'elegantly furnished for reception or entertainment'. The more fashionable option for entertaining guests, by the 1780s, was a 'drawing room'. In Indiana Brooks's novel *Eliza Beaumont and Harriet Osborne: or, The Child of Doubt*, 2 vols. (1789), Eliza says that her house has 'only seven apartments . . . two best bedrooms, an eating parlour, and drawing room' (ii, 101); in another novel published that year, Lady Louisa refers similarly to 'an eating-parlour', as distinct from 'a drawing room' on the same floor (Richard Cumberland, *Arundel*, 2 vols. (1789), ii, 220). The circular seating arrangement described in 'Edgar & Emma' was also yielding to a more informal layout, as Humphry Repton observed in 1803: 'formerly the best room in the house was opened only a few days in the year, where the guests sat in a formal circle, but now the largest and best room in a gentleman's house is that most frequented and inhabited . . . in winter, by the help of two fireplaces, the restraint and formality of the circle is done away' (*Observations on . . . Landscape Gardening*, 185). The Austen rectory at Steventon had both a small parlour and a common parlour in which the family gathered.

Eton: Eton College near Windsor, the most prestigious public school for boys; in *MP*, the Bertram sons are sent there.

Winchester: Winchester College in Winchester, the cathedral city and county town of Hampshire, where JA died and is buried. As an adult, her primary association with Winchester College, another pre-eminent public school, was through her nephews: Edward Austen Knight's sons and James Edward, son of James Austen and JA's first biographer, were educated there.

Queen's Square: Queen Square, Bloomsbury, a fashionable address in London and home to a girls' school known as the 'Ladies Eton', at which Kitty is perhaps a pupil. The school was 'run by the Misses Stevenson exclusively for the daughters of the nobility and the gentry' and was attended by Elizabeth Bridges, who went on to marry JA's brother Edward (*Family Record*, 70).

convent at Brussels: the Willmots must be a Catholic family who have sent their daughters to be educated at a Belgian convent.

college: in view of Edgar's likely age, JA is probably referring to a school such as Eton or Winchester College, rather than to one of the colleges of Oxford or Cambridge.

at Nurse: that is, with a wet nurse or foster-mother, who is breast-feeding the baby and caring for it alongside her own offspring. The Austen children, like others of their class, were sent out to nurse; infants might not return home to their parents until they were two years old. The practice was falling out of favour in JA's lifetime.

HENRY & ELIZA

27 *Henry and Eliza*: JA's title combines the names of her fourth brother Henry (1771–1850) and her paternal cousin Eliza, Comtesse de Feuillide, née Hancock (1761–1813). In 1781, at the age of 19, Eliza had married a French soldier; he was guillotined in Paris in 1794. In Dec. 1797 she married Henry. A decade earlier, in Dec. 1787, they were flirting and acting together in family performances of Susanna Centlivre's popular comedy *The Wonder: A Woman Keeps a Secret!* (1714). The play sees the hero Don Felix (played by Henry) and the beautiful Violante (played by Eliza) contend with parental opposition, impish servants, and various misfortunes and misunderstandings before they are finally united for ever. 'Henry & Eliza' oddly predicts Eliza de Feuillide's widowhood and removal from France to England.

Miss Cooper: JA's cousin on the maternal side, Jane Cooper (1771–98), an early, close friend and regular participant in Austen family theatricals; also the dedicatee of 'Collection of Letters'. In spring 1783 she went to Oxford with JA and Cassandra Austen to be taught by a Mrs Cawley. Later that year, Mrs Cawley took the girls to Southampton, where JA and Cassandra succumbed to a putrid fever. Mrs Austen and her sister Mrs Cooper travelled to Southampton to take the girls home. Subsequently, Mrs Cooper caught the infection and died in Oct. 1783.

rewarding the industry . . . approbation: the standard reward for such labour would have been food and beer, rather than mere smiles. Haymakers were in high demand during the harvest and could expect reasonable salaries as well as board and lodging.

cudgel: 'A short thick stick used as a weapon; a club' (*OED*). To punish your workers in this way is comically disproportionate; but it may briefly register the reality that, from the 1750s onwards, farm labourers across the country were being offered less favourable and shorter-term contracts, losing their common land, and facing an overall deterioration in their circumstances. Their protests against such hardship culminated in the Captain Swing riots of 1830.

27 *Haycock*: 'A conical heap of hay in the field' (*OED*).

little Girl . . . 3 months old: Eliza thus appears to be a foundling. Her mysterious origins may allude to those of JA's cousin Eliza, widely believed to be the illegitimate child of her godfather Warren Hastings, later the first Governor-General of Bengal. 'Haycock' is tantalizingly close to Eliza's maiden name, Hancock. In Jan. 1788 another comedy was performed at Steventon, John Fletcher's *The Chances* (*c.*1617): one early scene features an abandoned baby (see also note to p. 31).

stealing a bank-note . . . inhuman Benefactors: this incident is echoed in 'Love and Friendship', a work dedicated to Eliza de Feuillide; Laura and Sophia repeatedly pilfer banknotes 'of considerable amount' from Macdonald (p. 85). Again, when they are caught the consequence is merely expulsion, although Macdonald (like Eliza's parents) is accused of being 'inhuman' (p. 91). Since stealing much smaller amounts of money was a capital offence, the response in both cases is relatively lenient, although expulsion from home could also be life-threatening.

28 *M.*: supposedly an abbreviation for the name of a real market town; JA is spoofing the convention in novels of only partly revealing names, places, and dates, as if shielding facts and protecting real identities. Cf. 'the Dutchess of F.' in this 'novel', and 'Miss XXX' in 'The three Sisters'. See also 'Love and Friendship', note to p. 72.

the red Lion: a common name for an inn or alehouse; the emblem would usually appear on the sign.

Humble Companion: usually a position for destitute gentlewomen, hired in exchange for room, board, and clothes to entertain and accompany another woman, such as a wealthy relative. The situation was rich in opportunities to humiliate the female dependent, as Jane Collier pointed out: 'The servant, indeed, differs in this; she receives wages, and the humble companion receives none: the servant is most part of the day out of your sight; the humble companion is always ready at hand to receive every cross word that rises in your mind: the servants can be teazed only by yourself, your dogs, your cats, your parrots, your children; the humble companion, besides being the sport of all these, must, if you manage rightly, bear the insults of all the servants themselves'. *An Essay on the Art of Ingeniously Tormenting; With Proper Rules for the Exercise of that Pleasant Art* (1753), 42–3. Mary Wynne endures a position as humble companion to Lady Halifax in 'Kitty, or the Bower'.

Willson: revised from 'Jones', perhaps because a Mrs Jones appears in 'Jack & Alice' (see Textual Notes, p. 222).

freindship for Mrs Wilson . . . reached the same Evening: a duchess would not be expected to befriend an innkeeper, let alone travel across the country to meet a future employee at the pub.

29 *a private union*: the Church allowed couples planning to marry to avoid the otherwise compulsory delay and publicity of calling banns on three successive Sundays by providing, for a fee, a common marriage licence. Those who wanted to marry in a private house or chapel had to pay a higher fee for a special licence from the Archbishop of Canterbury; because of the expense, such an arrangement was socially prestigious. There is another 'private' marriage in 'Sir William Mountague'.

dutchess's chaplain: without a licence from the bishop, a chaplain could not authorize a private marriage; this union is therefore invalid. The chaplain, having acted illegally, could expect to be imprisoned if caught.

the Continent: the mainland of continental Europe; here referring specifically to France.

18,000£ a year: revised upwards from £12,000 (see Textual Notes, p. 223) and therefore exceeding the annual income of the wealthiest character in JA's novels, Mr Rushworth of *MP*; in other words, this is an inordinate expenditure.

rather less than the twentieth part: what Eliza euphemistically terms a 'derangement in their affairs' means that the Cecil estate is generating less than £600 per annum.

30 *man of War of 55 Guns*: the odd number of guns is impossible; warships always had an even number. A fourth-rate ship carried between 50 and 60 guns and over 295 officers and crew; the man-of-war is therefore absurdly over-sized for a privately owned vessel. On the number 55, see also 'Jack & Alice' (p. 10) and 'Love and Friendship' (p. 69).

snug little Newgate: a private dungeon, named after the notorious London prison; 'snug' introduces the incongruous image of a cosy room. Newgate is also mentioned in 'Love and Friendship' (p. 79).

threw her Children after them: heroines in fiction sometimes escape captivity by ladders; see e.g. Sarah Fielding's *The History of Ophelia*, 2 vols. (1760), ii, ch. 7. JA may again be alluding to a scene in Centlivre's *The Wonder: A Woman Keeps a Secret!* in which Violante's friend Isabella jumps out of a window and is caught by a passing stranger who later marries her. Jane Cooper is likely to have played Isabella to Eliza de Feuillide's Violante in Dec. 1787. See also 'Frederic & Elfrida', note to p. 5.

gold Watch for herself: as an expensive, proverbially luxurious item, a gold watch purchased by someone in dire financial straits might indeed prove 'fatal'. In Agnes Maria Bennett's *Juvenile Indiscretions. A Novel*, 5 vols. (1786), Henry, recently facing starvation but now offered a share of his friend's 6 guineas, imagines for himself (among other gold and silver possessions) 'a very good gold watch, chain and seals' (iii, 86).

31 *walked 30 without stopping*: a woman was not expected to walk anywhere unaccompanied, let alone for 30 miles; Elizabeth Bennet raises eyebrows in *P&P* when she sets out on foot, alone, to reach her sister Jane at Netherfield (ch. 8).

31 *collation*: 'A light meal or repast: one consisting of light viands or delicacies (e.g. fruit, sweets, and wine), or that has needed little preparation' (*OED*); 'A repast; a treat less than a feast' (Johnson's *Dictionary*).

Junkettings: a colloquial term for feasting and making merry; Johnson's *Dictionary* defines 'To junket' as 'To feast secretly; to make entertainments by stealth', an activity which befits the other incongruous mysteries in this story.

receive some Charitable Gratuity: Eliza is cloaking a shabby truth in genteel euphemisms; she intends to beg for cash outside the inn.

our real Child: this turn of events parodies the endings of many 18th-century novels, including *Joseph Andrews*, *Tom Jones*, and *Evelina*, in which a foundling, illegitimate child, or orphan is suddenly discovered to be of noble parentage, often thanks to a coincidental meeting. See 'Love and Friendship', pp. 81–2.

Polly: pet form of Mary Anne.

the wellfare of my Child: a likely reference to Fletcher's *The Chances*, performed at Steventon in Jan. 1788: the heroine Constantia, fearing her brother's response to the birth of her child, secretly hands it over to a stranger, enclosing gold and a jewel for its care. Lady Harcourt, in giving birth to a girl, fears her husband's resentment at the child's gender and leaves her under a haystack.

MR HARLEY

33 *Francis Willm Austen . . . Perseverance*: this dedication to JA's brother Francis, like that which prefaces 'Jack & Alice', must date from between Dec. 1789 and Nov. 1791, when he served on the *Perseverance*. Le Faye suggests that both 'Jack & Alice' and 'Mr Harley' were 'probably written early in 1790' (*Family Record*, 69), but the dates of the dedications cannot help to establish the dates of the tales themselves. See Introduction, Chronology of the Teenage Writings, and 'Jack & Alice', note to p. 10.

Mr Harley: the name of the quiveringly sensitive hero of Henry Mackenzie's sentimental fiction *The Man of Feeling* (1771), itself perhaps a work of parody; the novel and its hero spawned a host of imitators. Noble characters called Harley feature in e.g. *Adeline; or the Orphan. A Novel*, 3 vols. (1790) and Agnes Maria Bennett's *Agnes de-Courci, A Domestic Tale*, 4 vols. (1789).

father for the Church . . . Mother for the Sea: the choice of an acceptable profession for younger sons who had to earn a living was generally between the army, the navy, the Church, and the law; such a debate must have occurred more than once in the Austen household. As a naval chaplain, Mr Harley unites the two Austen family professions, the sea and the Church.

half a year: a very short period of naval service, perhaps designedly abrupt in the context of this 'short, but interesting Tale'. Francis Austen spent almost three years, first as cadet and then as midshipman, on the *Perseverance*.

sat-off: that is, set off.

Stage Coach: a slightly faster, smaller, and better form of transport than the 'Stage Waggon' in which Roger and Rebecca travel in 'Frederic & Elfrida' (note to p. 8), a stagecoach ran daily or on specified days between two places for the conveyance of passengers, parcels, etc. (*OED*). It was usually drawn by four horses and could accommodate up to six passengers, as it does here. Cf. 'the Stage-Coach from Edinburgh to Sterling' in the last two letters of 'Love and Friendship'.

Hogsworth Green: this must be the country seat of Emma's father, rather than of Emma herself, who at 17 is too young to own property. The name and farmyard setting recall 'her Ladyship's pigstye' in 'Jack & Alice' (p. 15).

SIR WILLIAM MOUNTAGUE

34 *Sir William Mountague*: an echo of *Romeo and Juliet* (Montague is Romeo's family name) and of Richardson's *Clarissa. Or, the History of a Young Lady*, 7 vols. (1748–9), in which the villainous Lovelace is nephew and heir of Lord Mountague. Male characters called 'Mountague' also feature in e.g. Elizabeth Inchbald's *Emily Herbert. Or, Perfidy Punished. A Novel in a Series of Letters* (1787), Bennett's *Agnes de-Courci, A Domestic Tale*, and Charlotte Lennox's *Euphemia*, 4 vols. (1790).

unfinished performance: cf. the description of 'Frederic & Elfrida' as 'this little production' (p. 2); 'performance' (a word JA applied to no other teenage writing) may indicate a similar design for the work to be read aloud. It could further suggest that JA is completing the performance of a promise (albeit with an unfinished text), or the execution of a written work perhaps always intended for this dedicatee (cf. 'Lesley-Castle', note to p. 96). The story may have been composed in late 1788; one date mentioned in it, Monday 1 Sept., fell that year (*Family Record*, 66).

Charles John Austen Esqre: JA's brother Charles (1779–1852), youngest of the Austen siblings and four years her junior; he was about 9 when this tale was written and left home in July 1791 for the Royal Naval Academy in Portsmouth. 'Master' rather than 'Esqre' (Esquire) would be the usual way of addressing a child, but as in the dedication of 'Jack & Alice' to 'Francis William Austen Esq' JA is elaborately deferential.

inherited . . . from Sir Frederic Mountague: all are baronets, rather than knights, as the title is inherited. The pompous genealogical overload in this passage mimics the style of an entry in John Debrett's *A New Baronetage of England* (1769), as does the description of the Elliot family in the opening paragraph of *P*.

Park well stocked with Deer: a status symbol, deer were kept to be hunted and as an elegant, picturesque feature of a gentleman's estate; like groves, arbours, and summer houses, they were therefore also a standard feature of novelistic landscapes. In *Sir Charles Grandison*, Clementina 'diverts herself often with feeding the deer, which gather about her, as soon as she enters the park' (vii, letter 51).

34 *Kilhoobery Park*: despite the English location, the park has a spoof Irish name; cf. Crankhumdunberry in 'Frederic & Elfrida', note to p. 3.

equally in Love with them all: cf. 'The three Sisters', in which Mr Watts professes equal attachment to all the Stanhope girls, and Mr Collins in *P&P*, who is apparently indifferent as to which of the Bennet girls becomes his wife (chs. 19–22).

Lady Percival: an old English aristocratic name, Percival also features in JA's 'History of England' and in the revised version of 'Kitty, or the Bower'.

Vehemently pressed . . . first of September: cf. Elfrida's reluctance to name the day in 'Frederic & Elfrida' (p. 9); Lady Percival chooses the beginning of the partridge-shooting season, which ran from 1 Sept. to 1 Feb. (the day—Monday—for 1 Sept. is correct for 1788; see *Family Record*, 66). 1 Sept. is also mentioned in *P&P* (iii, ch. 9); see also Woodforde, *The Diary of a Country Parson*, 278.

a Shot: 'One who shoots; an expert in shooting'; *OED* cites 1780 as the earliest instance of the word in this sense (cf. *The Loiterer*, no. 21).

35 *Brudenell . . . Stanhope*: both names also feature in 'The three Sisters'; Stanhope appears in *Frederic & Elfrida*. A 'Brudenell' appears in *The False Friends. A Novel. In a Series of Letters*, 2 vols. (1785). Stanhope was the family name of Lord Chesterfield, and a popular choice in fiction (see e.g. *The History of Miss Delia Stanhope. In a Series of Letters to Miss Dorinda Boothby*, 2 vols. (1767)).

cruel Murder of her Brother . . . 14s: 'Murder' implies something other than death by duelling. Although to kill in the course of a duel was formally judged as murder, the courts were generally lax in applying the law. 14s. is an absurdly small amount of money to seek as recompense.

privately married: Sir William is seventeen at the beginning of the tale; it seems unlikely that he has by now reached the age of twenty-one and obtained a licence for a private marriage, in which case the union is invalid (cf. 'Henry & Eliza', note to p. 29).

Chariot: 'Applied in 18th c. to a light four-wheeled carriage with only back seats, and differing from the post-chaise in having a coach-box' (*OED*); it seated up to three passengers.

Brook Street: a fashionable London street, running from Hanover Square to Grosvenor Square. Like Portland Place ('Frederic & Elfrida', note to p. 6), it often features as a novelistic backdrop; in e.g. *The Assignation. A Sentimental Novel*, Edmond Harcourt writes: 'The morning after we arrive in Brook Street is to compose [my] happiness' (ii, 112).

MR CLIFFORD

36 *Charles John Austen Esqre . . . noble Family*: this 'unfinished tale', like the incomplete 'Sir William Mountague', was perhaps written in late 1788; 'patronage' and 'y^r noble Family' comically suggest that Charles, a younger sibling of the author, is in a position to offer her financial support.

Coach & Four: a large, closed carriage, drawn by four horses and seating up to six passengers.

Chaise: 'A carriage for travelling, having a closed body and seated for one to three persons, the driver sitting on one of the horses' (*OED*).

Landeau: 'A four-wheeled carriage, the top of which, being made in two parts, may be closed or thrown open. When open, the rear part is folded back, and the front part entirely removed. Also landau carriage' (*OED*). A landau carried four passengers.

Landeaulet: 'A small landau; a coupé with a folding top like a landau. Also called *demi-landau*' (*OED*); for two or three passengers. Cf. 'a very pretty landaulette' in *P*, ch. 24.

Phaeton: 'A type of light four-wheeled open carriage, usually drawn by a pair of horses, and having one or two seats facing forward' (*OED*); these vehicles were fast and expensive and driven by the owner.

Gig: 'A light two-wheeled one-horse carriage' (*OED*), fashionable in the 1790s.

Whisky: 'A kind of light two-wheeled one-horse carriage, used in England and America in the late 18th and early 19th c.' (*OED*). Relatively cheap and simple in construction, the whisky was named for its speed in 'whisking' past larger carriages.

italian Chair: a light, one-horse carriage without a top, used only for short jaunts.

Buggy: 'A light one-horse (sometimes two-horse) vehicle, for one or two persons' (*OED*).

Curricle: 'A light two-wheeled carriage, usually drawn by two horses abreast' (*OED*), more expensive and genteel than the gig; Henry Tilney in *NA*, Willoughby in *S&S*, and Mr Darcy in *P&P* all drive gigs.

wheel barrow: any sort of light, cheap carriage, or (as now) a small cart with a single wheel at the front, used typically for carrying loads in building work or gardening.

stud: 'An establishment in which stallions and mares are kept for breeding. Also, the stallions and mares kept in such an establishment' (*OED*).

Bays: reddish-brown horses with black manes, tails, ear edges, and lower legs.

poney: a small, inexpensive horse of any breed. JA's brother Francis apparently bought a pony at the age of seven and later sold him for a profit (*Memoir*, 36).

Devizes: a Wiltshire market town, about 22 (or 'no less than nineteen') miles east of Bath, and a staging post en route to London. In a coach and four Mr Clifford could easily travel the 110 miles from Bath to London in two days, but it takes him eighteen hours to travel just 22 miles.

Overton: a Hampshire town 3 miles from Steventon and a staging post on the main route between London and Exeter; JA's brother James became the curate there in Apr. 1790. It is about 50 miles from Devizes; Mr Clifford is travelling around 17 miles per day.

37 *Five months . . . celebrated Physician*: like everything else he does, Mr Clifford's recovery takes an absurdly long time. Overton's apothecary is listed in the *Universal British Directory of Trade, Commerce, and Manufacture*, 5 vols. (1790–8) as Robert Brookman (iv, 186); he is both 'celebrated' and unnamed by JA. She inflates his profession to that of a physician, who would have had a university degree. An apothecary, by contrast, dispensed medicines and learned his trade through an apprenticeship.

Dean Gate: the entry to Deane, 3 miles east of Overton; this was the location of Deane Gate Inn, at the junction of the lane to Steventon, which lay just over a mile and a quarter away. JA's brothers and other friends and relatives used this stop when travelling to and from Steventon Rectory.

Basingstoke: the largest and most important town near Steventon, 5½ miles east of Deane; Mr Clifford has taken four days to travel a mere 6 miles.

Clarkengreen . . . Worting: Clarken Green, a village about 2 miles east of Dean Gate; Worting is another village, about 2 miles closer to Basingstoke.

Mr Robins's: Thomas Robins was landlord of the Crown Inn and Post House at Basingstoke (*Family Record*, 63); in the *Universal Directory* he is listed as '*Post-master*' and the Crown is described as one of the two 'best inns' in town. *Universal British Directory*, ii, 316, 318.

THE BEAUTIFULL CASSANDRA

37 *Miss Austen*: Cassandra Elizabeth Austen (1773–1845), JA's elder sister and therefore known as 'Miss Austen'; JA was 'Miss Jane Austen'. The name Cassandra appears nowhere else in JA's fiction.

Phoenix: 'In classical mythology: a bird resembling an eagle but with sumptuous red and gold plumage, which was said to live for five or six hundred years in the deserts of Arabia, before burning itself to ashes on a funeral pyre ignited by the sun and fanned by its own wings, only to rise from its ashes with renewed youth to live through another such cycle'; figuratively, 'A person or thing of unique excellence or matchless beauty; a paragon' (*OED*), and novelistic cant. Cf. *All's Right at Last: or, The History of Miss West*, 2 vols. (1774): 'But she, forsooth, is such a nonpareil, such a phœnix of a woman!' (ii, 60).

38 *Millener in Bond Street*: milliners designed, made, and sold caps and hats, trimmings, accessories, and articles of female clothing. They were highly sought-after advisers on and arbiters of fashion, but those who worked in their shops also had a dubious reputation as flirts and gossips, perhaps even prostitutes (see e.g. John Gay's *Trivia; or the Art of Walking the Streets of London* (1716) (bk 3, ll. 267–84) and Charles Brandoin's prints 'A Modern Demi-Rep on the Lookout' and 'The Charming Milliner of——Street' (1771)). Milliners' shops were located in fashionable areas of London such as Bond Street (Willoughby stays here in *S&S*, ch. 29; Harriet's picture is framed here in *E*, ch. 7).

Pastry-cooks . . . six ices: the first record of ice-cream in England dates from 1667, but it was not widely available until the second half of the 18th century, popularized by French and Italian confectioners who set up shops in London in the 1760s. Ice-cream and water-ices were sold by pastry cooks, as in *NA* (ch. 15). They were pricey, due to the expense and complication of making them from ice stored in ice-houses all year round, and the need to keep them cool; in later life, JA boasted 'I shall eat Ice & drink French wine, & be above Vulgar Economy' (*Letters*, 144).

39 *Hackney Coach*: 'A four-wheeled coach, drawn by two horses, and seated for six persons, kept for hire' (*OED*).

Hampstead: a fashionable village around 4 miles north of Bond Street and with famously beautiful walks and views over London. Some key scenes in *Clarissa* are set here and their locations were visited by literary tourists. Cassandra, however, does not bother to look around.

demanded his Pay: the fare would have been about 5*s*. for a round trip of 8 miles.

She placed her bonnet on his head: an act of sheer defiance, but also a form of payment; the bonnet would have cost a great deal more than the coach fare. Difficulties in paying a coach fare preoccupy Burney's Cecilia (bk 10, ch. 7).

Bloomsbury Square: laid out in the 1660s and initially known as Southampton Square, this was one of the first London squares and a very fashionable address in 18th-century London. It fell out of favour with the upper classes in the early 19th century.

40 *her less window*: that is, a window smaller than the widow's head. Like Sir Godfrey and his Lady in 'Edgar & Emma' (see note to p. 24), the widow must be living in one of the cheaper upper-storey rooms of the house: these had narrower windows than the better rooms lower down.

AMELIA WEBSTER

41 *Mrs Austen*: Cassandra Leigh Austen (1739–1827), JA's mother, a fan of novels, who also wrote comic verse. This may be one of JA's earliest surviving stories (*Family Record*, 66).

Matilda: a name associated with the heroines of Gothic fiction, as in Horace Walpole's *The Castle of Otranto, A Story* (dated 1765 [pub. 1764]) and Matthew Lewis's *The Monk: A Romance*, 3 vols. (1796). Cf. also the imaginary heroine of Henry Tilney's Gothic narrative in *NA* (ch. 20).

Beverley: the surname of the heroine in Burney's *Cecilia* and of Captain Absolute in Richard Brinsley Sheridan's *The Rivals* (1775), a play performed by the Austen family at Steventon in July 1784; it has romantic and pastoral associations.

Maud: an alternative form of Matilda.

two thousand Pounds: a dowry which, assuming the usual 5% rate of interest, would yield £100 per annum. As this is a relatively modest amount,

Matilda's brother is on the defensive and keen to point out that Beverley himself is in line for money from other sources ('as much as you can get').

my paper will only permit me to add: like other formulas used in this exchange of letters, the phrasing is trite and banal—made more explicitly so by the fact that the letter is so short.

42 *Miss S. Hervey*: the initial distinguishes the younger from the elder sister; Matilda would be known as 'Miss Hervey'.

a very convenient old hollow oak . . . private Correspondence: hidden repositories for letters, allowing for the covert exchange of messages, were another stock device in 18th-century epistolary fiction, including *Pamela* and *Clarissa*. It would be reasonable to assume from this correspondence that Benjamin and Sally are engaged to be married (as the end of the tale reveals); in *S&S*, Elinor concludes from the fact that Marianne is writing to Willoughby that 'they must be engaged' (ch. 26).

my Paper, reminds me of concluding: another hackneyed conclusion to a letter; cf. Lucy Steele in *S&S*: 'My paper reminds me to conclude' (ch. 38).

lovely Fair one . . . telescope: cf. 'Lovely and too charming fair one' in 'Frederic & Elfrida'. Advances in the design and manufacture of telescopes brought them into popular domestic use in the late 18th century; they were heralded for their educational value and religious application, encouraging young people to admire the scope of divine creation rather than passing strangers of the opposite sex. However, the opportunities for such ogling were obvious and featured in contemporary fiction. In *The Summer-House: or, The History of Mr. Morton and Miss Bamsted*, 2 vols. (1768), a young gentleman 'increase[s] the pleasures of vision' when he trains 'his uplifted tube' on the passing Almeria, who in turn 'could not get the telescope out of her head' (i, 52–3).

THE VISIT

44 *Revd James Austen*: JA's eldest brother, James (1765–1819), was ordained deacon in Dec. 1787 and a priest in June 1789 (*Family Record*, 53, 71). From 1782 to 1789 he oversaw the Austen family's dramatic performances at Steventon, often supplying prologues and epilogues.

'The school for Jealousy' and 'The travelled Man': the titles recall many 18th-century plays, especially Richard Brinsley Sheridan's *The School for Scandal* (1777) and Oliver Goldsmith's *The Good-Natur'd Man* (1768)—Goldsmith also wrote a philosophical poem *The Traveller; or, a Prospect of Society* (1764), so 'The travelled Man' could be splicing the two works as well as referring to James's recent travels abroad. These two comic dramas may have been written by James Austen or by JA herself for family theatricals at Steventon; in the dedication, JA referred to 'they', subsequently altered to 'it', when describing the dramatic work 'composed by your Humble Servant the Author' (see Textual Notes, p. 224). 'The school for Jealousy' could derive from or relate to the libretto of Antonio Salieri's opera *La scola de' gelosi*, performed in London in Mar. 1786.

Curate: 'A clergyman engaged for a stipend or salary, and licensed by the bishop of the diocese to perform ministerial duties in the parish as a deputy or assistant of the incumbent; an assistant to a parish priest' (*OED*); Johnson's *Dictionary* defines a curate as 'a clergyman hired to perform the duties of another'. The reference here is either to James's curacy at Stoke Charity, near Winchester, which began in July 1788, or to that at Overton (near Steventon), beginning in Apr. 1790.

first composed: the phrasing suggests that the dedication was added after the play's initial composition.

Cloe: the name of a shepherdess, it originates in the Greek pastoral romance *Daphnis and Chloe* and became popular in later pastoral and mock-pastoral writing.

you found your Bed too short: alluding to the Greek legend of Procrustes, who offered his bed to strangers and then either lopped or stretched their bodies in order to ensure a good fit.

45 '*The more free, the more Wellcome*': probably alluding to a moment in James Townley's farce *High Life Below Stairs* (1759), performed by the Austen family in winter 1788. Kitty declares: 'Lady *Charlotte*, pray be free; the more free, the more welcome, as they say in my Country' (act 2); the aristocratic characters then announce their enthusiasm for the type of coarse food normally eaten by the poor. But the saying must also have been proverbial, judging by its use in the very different context of W. A. Clarke's meditative religious text *A Bed of Sweet Flowers; or, Jewels for Hephzi-Bah* (1778): 'You never need to apologize to me for your freedom; "the more free, the more welcome," you know, is my old motto amongst the friends of the Bridegroom' (125).

discovered: that is, 'revealed'; a stage direction indicating that the characters are already in place on stage when the curtain opens. The same word appears in 'The Mystery' (p. 50).

Truth: JA here deleted two more sentences in which Miss Fitzgerald praises her brother more lavishly (see Textual Notes, p. 224).

Exeunt Severally: a stage direction, indicating that characters leave the stage by different exits rather than together as one group.

46 *Chairs . . . row*: this arrangement suggests an old-fashioned and formal household, an impression compromised by the foreshortened beds, insufficient number of chairs, and vulgar food.

ought to be 8 Chairs . . . pretty well: cf. 'Frederic & Elfrida' (p. 6), which has a similar joke about chairs and men sitting in ladies' laps, alluding to *The Vicar of Wakefield*.

cherub . . . seraph: the seraphim are the highest, and the cherubim the second, of the nine orders or 'choirs' of angels. Cherubs were said to excel in knowledge, seraphs in love.

47 *Miss Fitzgerald at top. Lord Fitzgerald at bottom.*: the female and male hosts sit, as would have been expected, at the head and foot of the dinner table,

with their guests seated according to rank (the highest closest to the hosts, the lowest furthest away).

47 *fried Cow heel & Onion*: arrestingly coarse food to serve at a smart dinner party, this was the fare of those who could not afford any better (cow-heel or trotters would more usually be stewed to make jelly). In Thomas Bridges' *Homer Travestie: Being a New Translation of the Four First Books of the Iliad* (1762), the author recalls: 'I went on swimmingly, with hot tripe for dinner one day, and cold the next; hot cow-heel the third day, and cold cow-heel the fourth; and so on, with a fine pease-soup on Sundays, and a red herring boiled in it to give it a flavour' (30). Tripe, cow-heel, and pudding figure in subsequent, expanded versions of this comically degraded epic. At the Fitzgeralds' dinner party, JA reverses the premiss of *High Life Below Stairs*, in which servants impersonate aristocrats; here, as in 'Edgar & Emma', the wealthy live a comically straitened existence.

toss off a bumper: down a full glass of wine in one go, rather than sip it gradually.

Elder wine or Mead: inexpensive home-made alternatives to French wines, using elderberries in the first case and a fermented mixture of honey and water in the second. JA's family made their own wine.

warm ale . . . nutmeg: a drink for an invalid rather than for the young and vital Sophy Hampton, and in any case not to be served at a dinner party.

red herrings: herrings turn red when cured by smoking; they were considered less valuable than white or fresh herring. Red herrings were supposedly used by fugitives to put bloodhounds off their scent, hence the metaphoric sense of a false lead, which seems to date from the 1780s.

Tripe: 'The first or second stomach of a ruminant, esp. of the ox, prepared as food; formerly including also the entrails of swine and fish' (*OED*). Food eaten by the poor.

Crow: giblets (rather than crow, the carrion bird which was not eaten in England), typically fried with liver. Food eaten by the poor.

Suet pudding: a homely pudding made of flour and suet (animal fat), usually boiled in a cloth.

48 *Desert*: dessert, fruit and nuts, served after the pudding.

Hothouse: 'A greenhouse kept artificially heated for the cultivation of plants from warmer climates, and of native flowers and fruits out of season' (*OED*); here, grapes, oranges, and pineapples could be grown. In *NA*, General Tilney has 'a village of hot-houses' (ch. 22).

Come Girls, let us circulate the Bottle: a gender reversal. The women are hearty drinkers and pass the wine (probably claret, as favoured by Alice in 'Jack & Alice', note to p. 15) around the table, as men would normally have been expected to do after dinner, when the women had adjourned to the drawing room. Neither Stanly nor Arthur 'touches wine' in JA's playlet.

Gooseberry Wine: another simple, domestic, old-fashioned wine, inappropriate for smart formal gatherings. JA may have in mind *The Vicar of*

Wakefield, in which the vicar proudly mentions 'our gooseberry wine, for which we had great reputation' (vol. 1, ch. 1).

THE MYSTERY

49 *Revd George Austen*: JA's father, George Austen (1731–1805), rector of Steventon; this is the only one of the teenage writings dedicated to him. It may have been composed as an afterpiece at the family's 'private Theatrical exhibition' in 1788. James Austen's prologue to the main play performed at that exhibition survives (*The Complete Poems of James Austen: Jane Austen's Eldest Brother*, ed. David Selwyn (Chawton: Jane Austen Society, 2003), 26–7), but the name of the drama itself and the date of its performance are unknown.

Spangle: 'Any thing sparkling and shining' (Johnson's *Dictionary*); a bright metallic fragment usually attached to clothing to create a glittering effect. Popular with rich and fashionable men, it was further associated with the stage, trickery, and jokes. The name may echo that of the theatre critic Dangle in Sheridan's *The Critic*, a comedy partly based on George Villiers' celebrated satirical drama, *The Rehearsal* (1672) (see note to p. 50); both works contain famous whispering scenes. There is a Count Spangle, 'prodigiously well-bred . . . a most egregious coxcomb', in *The Legacy, or, The Fortune-Hunter*, one of the plays included in *The Comic Theatre. Being a Free Translation of All the Best French comedies*, 5 vols. (1762), iii, 35.

Humbug: a hoax, jesting trick, imposture, or fraud (*OED*); cf. Crankhumdunberry in 'Frederic & Elfrida', note to p. 3.

Corydon: a stock name for a pastoral singer-swain, it also appears in 'Frederic & Elfrida' (p. 8).

Daphne: the daughter of a river god, loved by Apollo, the mythological Daphne escaped his affections only to be changed into a laurel tree; like Corydon, her name was often used in pastoral verse.

50 *at work*: sewing or mending items for the family or others; needlework and embroidery were considered to be genteel female pastimes. There are references to this kind of 'work' in JA's correspondence (see e.g. *Letters*, 173).

whispers: cf. George Villiers' *The Rehearsal*, in which Bayes's play-within-a-play 'instead of beginning with a Scene that discovers something of the Plot' reveals nothing other than secrets uttered in 'a whisper', concluding with the stage direction '*Exeunt Whispering*' (act 2, scene 1). Whispering also features in Sheridan's *The Critic* (act 1, scene 1).

51 *RECLINED IN AN ELEGANT ATTITUDE*: cf. Caroline Simpson, who in 'Jack & Alice' adopts a 'studied attitude on a couch' (p. 11). Indolence was a fashionable affectation in the 1780s; for another caricature of the requisite 'lounging posture', see the description of Mr Meadows in *Cecilia* (bk 4, ch. 6).

THE THREE SISTERS

52 *Edward Austen Esqre*: JA's third brother, Edward (1767–1852), formally adopted by Thomas and Catherine Knight in 1783. On 1 Mar. 1791 he

became engaged to Elizabeth Bridges; that same year, her sisters Fanny and Sophia also announced their engagements. The story may have been written as a wedding present to Edward and Elizabeth, who married on 27 Dec. 1791.

52 *quite an old Man, about two & thirty*: cf. the joke about age in 'Frederic & Elfrida' (and note to p. 5). Colonel Brandon, whom Marianne considers 'exceedingly ancient', is 35 (*S&S*, ch. 8).

Settlements . . . very healthy: property or money legally settled by pre-nuptial contract on the wife and her children (if any); see 'Jointure' in 'Jack & Alice', note to p. 10. As Mary realizes, the longer her husband lives, the less will remain for her; she can in any case make no use of the settlement until after his death.

stingy: 'A low cant word' (Johnson's *Dictionary*); as such, it is involved in the definitions of several words in successive editions of Grose's *Classical Dictionary*, but has no entry of its own. The word appears again in Letter the fifth of 'Collection of Letters' (p. 144).

53 *blue spotted with silver . . . plain Chocolate*: Mary's preferences are extravagant, especially by comparison with Mr Watts's conventional choice of 'plain Chocolate', but they are not beyond the realms of possibility. *The Weekly Entertainer; or Agreeable and Instructive Repository* (Sherborne, 1792) reports as follows on the Hon. Mrs Lockhart's 'town coach': 'the ground of the body mazarine blue, highly varnished, and ornamented with silver; the lining pale blue, and trimmed with fancy lace; carriage crane-necked, elegantly constructed, and painted a light Chinese blue, relieved with dark blue and white. In appearance it is elegant without being gaudy; and the whole is finished in a manner that does credit to the taste and execution of the builder' (xxi, 82–3).

as low as his old one: high carriages were more fashionable and provided a better view, but they were less stable and less practical than the low models favoured by Mr Watts. *The Loiterer*, no. 32, includes a young woman who 'admired high Phaetons . . . to distraction' (13).

to chaprone: to accompany a young unmarried lady in public, as guide and protector. A chaperone was typically a married or elderly woman. The *OED* cites *S&S* as offering the earliest known example of the verb 'to chaperon' (ch. 20); cf. 'chaperon' in *P&P*, ch. 39.

Winter Balls: either private parties or public dances and assemblies, such as masquerades (see note to p. 10).

Mary Stanhope: on this surname see 'Sir William Mountague', note to p. 35. The character of Mary Stanhope may owe something to Nanny Johnson in Sarah Fielding's *Adventures of David Simple*. Like Mary, Nanny wants 'fine *Jewels*' and 'an *Equipage*', but cannot abide her old, wealthy suitor. Nor can she endure the possible sight of 'my Sister . . . in her Coach and Six, while I take up with a Hack, or at best with a Coach and Pair. Oh! I can never bear that Thought, that is certain; my Heart is ready to burst. Sure never Woman's Misfortune equalled mine' (bk 1, ch. 5).

54 *Law*: a colloquial euphemism for 'Lord' (cf. Mrs Jennings's use of it in *S&S*, ch. 30).

drinks Tea: tea was drunk in the late afternoon or early evening, several hours after dinner, and followed in due course by a light supper. Fashionable society favoured late dining hours, hence also later teas and night-time suppers. Life at Steventon did not follow such patterns, as JA wrote to Cassandra (18–19 Dec. 1798): 'We dine now at half after Three . . . We drink tea at half after six' (*Letters*, 28). In later years (9 Dec. 1808), however, writing from Southampton, she notes that 'we never dine now till five' (*Letters*, 164).

they should fight him: Mary hopes for a duel, which is not only unwarranted by the immediate situation but was a practice that by this period was becoming obsolete. Cf. 'Sir William Mountague', note to p. 35; *S&S*, ch. 23; *P&P*, ch. 48.

Miss XXX: a comic reference to the convention in 18th-century novels of abbreviating or withholding the names of characters as if they were real people; cf. 'M.' and 'F.' in 'Henry & Eliza'; see also 'Love and Friendship', note to p. 72.

56 *Three thousand a year*: a substantial rather than a vast income, as Georgiana notes; it may even be a threshold figure of sorts, at least in fiction of the period. Two or three thousand a year is said to be 'a neat income' in Burney's *Cecilia* (bk 9, ch. 4). There is a warning Mary would do well to heed in Agnes Maria Bennett's *Anna: or Memoirs of a Welch Heiress*—not to consider 'the riches of a man with three thousand pounds a year' as 'endless' (i, 63).

57 *your most obedient*: short for 'most obedient servant'.

pin money: 'A (usually annual) sum allotted to a woman for clothing and other personal expenses; *esp.* such an allowance provided for a wife's private expenditure' (*OED*).

58 *Saddle horse*: a horse used for riding, as distinct from the four bay horses needed to draw the carriage.

suit of fine lace: an expensive matching gown and petticoat; lace was a highly sought-after, luxury item. Samuel Johnson compared it with ancient Greek: 'every man gets as much of it as he can' (*Life of Johnson*, ii, 341 [1780]).

valuable Jewels . . . out of number: in a deleted passage (see Textual Notes, p. 225), Mary asks for still more fantastical jewels, alluding to those of the Princess Badroulbadour from 'The Story of Aladdin' in *The Arabian Nights* (trans. *c.*1706–21) and including 'Turkey stones' (turquoises) and 'Bugles' (tube-shaped glass beads).

Greenhouse: 'A house in which tender plants are sheltered from the weather' (Johnson's *Dictionary*). These constructions, another status symbol, were sometimes elaborate and costly. See also Mrs Peterson's greenhouse in 'Kitty, or the Bower' (and *S&S*, ch. 33).

58 *every Winter in Bath, every Spring in Town*: Mary wants to spend the fashionable winter season in the spa resort of Bath and spring in London (as well as the rest of the year away from home).

some Tour: a prolonged excursion in the British Isles or abroad, typically in pursuit of picturesque scenery; JA is perhaps recalling William Gilpin's accounts of his various 'tours' to the Wye and south Wales (1782), the Lake District (1789), and the Scottish highlands (1789). JA incongruously lists Gilpin among the 'first of Men' in 'The History of England' ('Edward the 6th') and alludes to his writings elsewhere in the teenage writings and published novels. Henry Austen remembered that his sister 'was a warm and judicious admirer of landscape, both in nature and on canvass. At a very early age, she was enamored of Gilpin on the Picturesque' (*Memoir*, 140–1). See also 'Love and Friendship', note to p. 70.

Watering Place: a spa town or seaside resort.

a Theatre to act Plays in: in the 1770s, it became fashionable for private theatres to be built in large country houses; the heroine of Frances Brooke's *The Excursion*, 2 vols. (1777) is promised such a venue in which to write and perform tragedies (ii, 257). From Dec. 1782 onwards, the Austen family used their barn or the rectory dining room for their performances. Cf. the makeshift arrangements for theatricals in *MP*, ch. 13.

Which is the Man: along with David Garrick's *Bon Ton; or, High Life above Stairs. A Comedy* (1775), Hannah Cowley's *Which is the Man? A Comedy* ([1783]) was considered for the Austens' Christmas theatricals in 1787; like Mary, Eliza de Feuillide seems to have fancied herself in the role of the heroine. According to James's additional verses for that year, the play eventually chosen (with Eliza in the heroine's role) was *The Wonder: A Woman Keeps a Secret!* (see 'Henry & Eliza', notes to pp. 27 and 30).

Lady Bell Bloomer: a lively, fashionable widow who is seeking to remarry, Lady Bell is pursued by the rakish Lord Sparkle. She is as demanding a character as Mary.

59 *silver Border*: probably silver plating; cf. the town coach 'ornamented with silver' (see note to p. 53).

Writings: these are the settlements to which reference has earlier been made in this story.

Special Licence . . . Banns: those wishing to marry in a private house or chapel had to pay for a special licence from the Archbishop of Canterbury; see 'Henry & Eliza', note to p. 29.

common Licence: a licence granted by the bishop, permitting couples to avoid the calling of banns from the church pulpit; see 'Henry & Eliza', note to p. 29.

60 *my appearance*: Mary's first entrance into the public arena as Mrs Watts (see note to p. 61).

provision: the sum of money left by Mary's father to his daughter, therefore presumably also to her sisters; perhaps each of them has, like their mother, £500 per annum.

Jemima: an Old Testament name (cf. Rebecca and Jezalinda in 'Frederic & Elfrida', Chapter the Second), it gained in popularity in the early 19th century.

61 *Entrée*: the action or manner of making a public entrance into a room (cf. *Letters*, 24, where JA jokes about her mother's '<u>entrée</u> into the dressing-room').

62 *Vixen*: 'The name of a she-fox; otherwise applied to a woman whose nature and condition is thereby compared to a she-fox' (Johnson's *Dictionary*). In *Classical Dictionary*, 'vixen' is synonymous with 'HELL CAT'.

Blackguard: 'A cant word among the vulgar; by which is implied a dirty fellow; of the meanest kind' (Johnson's *Dictionary*). In *Classical Dictionary*, 'BLACK GUARD' is 'A shabby dirty fellow, a term said to be derived from a number of dirty tattered and roguish boys, who attended at the horse guards and parade in St. James's park, to black the shoes and boots of the soldiers, or to do any other dirty offices'.

dressed: wearing evening dress for dinner.

[DETACHED PEICES]

To Miss Jane Anna Elizabeth Austen

63 *Jane Anna Elizabeth Austen*: JA's niece Anna (1793–1872), first daughter of James Austen, born on 15 Apr. 1793 and therefore not yet seven weeks old when this dedication was written. What JA refers to in the dedication as 'Miscellanious Morsels' might have been written some time before 2 June 1793; in the list of contents they are called 'Detached peices', but the group has no title in the text itself (cf. the 'Scraps' dedicated to Fanny Catherine Austen in *Volume the Second*). Anna grew up to become a writer of fiction and tried to finish *Sanditon*, left incomplete at JA's death.

trusting that you will in time be older: this sounds like a joke, but given infant mortality rates there was necessarily an element of trust in assuming a child would grow to maturity.

the care of your excellent Parent: revised from 'Parents', reflecting the fact that Anna's mother, Anne, died in May 1795, when her daughter was only two years old (see Textual Notes, p. 225). Anna was sent to be looked after and comforted by her aunts JA and Cassandra at Steventon (*Family Record*, 90–1).

these Treatises for your Benefit: a sly reference to the lucrative trade in sententious pedagogical works for teenage girls: e.g. James Fordyce's *Sermons to Young Women* (1766), John Gregory's *A Father's Legacy to his Daughters* (1774), and two works owned by JA herself, Ann Murry's *Memoria: or, The Young Ladies Instructor* (1780) and Thomas Percival's *A Father's Instructions to his Children* (1775). Mrs Peterson in 'Kitty, or the Bower' is keen on this kind of writing, as is Mr Collins in *P&P* (ch. 14).

A fragment—written to inculcate the practise of Virtue

63 *A fragment ... Virtue*: the shortest of all the teenage writings, the entirety
of this fragment was later deleted (see Textual Notes, p. 225). It contains
hints of emerging comedy: 'to study their wants, and to leave them unsupplied' could mean seeking out the unfortunate precisely in order to refuse
to help them; the vulgar image of 'those that perspire away their Evenings
in crouded assemblies' fails to present the anticipated contrast of the leis-
ured wealthy classes with the poor, who 'sweat under the fatigue of their
daily Labour' (cf. the collapse of upper- into lower-class characters in
'Edgar & Emma' and 'The Visit'). These aspects of the fragment suggest
that it may have been the beginning of a parodic treatise or conduct book
of the sort mentioned in the dedication to Anna.

A beautiful description of the different effects of Sensibility on different Minds

A beautiful description: striking and attractive 'descriptions' of scenes involving extreme states of being, emotional and physical, were meant to cultivate the sensibility and sympathy of those who read or heard them; they
are often mentioned in 18th-century fiction and pedagogical texts for young
people. See e.g. *Major Piper; or The Adventures of a Musical Drone. A Novel*,
2 vols. (1794): 'She listened with attention to my story, the particulars
of which I related to her, and attempted to raise her sensibility by an
affecting description of all my unmerited sufferings. I thought she began
to sympathize with me in my affliction' (ii, 22).

Sensibility: a key term in 18th-century philosophy, aesthetics, and literature, referring (broadly speaking) to the mind and body's susceptibility to
beauty and pathos. A touchstone throughout the teenage writings.

Melissa's: a highly unusual name in the 18th century, Melissa also appears
in Johnson's *Adventurer*, no. 34 (3 Mar. 1753).

book muslin: 'A fine kind of muslin owing its name to the book-like manner
in which it is folded when sold in one piece' (*OED*).

chambray gauze shift: an undergarment made of cambric, a fine white
linen imported from France. JA wrote a poem (1808) in praise of cambric
handkerchiefs.

french net nightcap: also known as a 'dormeuse', this type of large, elaborate, indoor cap was (despite its name) popular daywear in the second half
of the 18th century. It featured a ribbon-trimmed crown that fitted over
the head, with flaps called 'wings' at each side.

64 *hashing up ... old Duck*: 'hashing' means shredding, reheating and serving
with egg or a sauce; a cheap way of using up leftovers.

toasting some cheese: another cheap rather than refined meal.

Curry: introduced to England from India, this spicy dish is ill suited to the
delicate stomach of an invalid. JA reverses a joke made in 'The Visit' (act 2,
scene 2), in which a drink fit for an invalid is served to a young, healthy
woman (see note to p. 47).

cordials: cordial is 'A medicine that increases the force of the heart, or quickens the circulation' (Johnson's *Dictionary*).

The generous Curate

The generous Curate: this portrait may derive, in part, from that of Parson Abraham Adams in Henry Fielding's *Joseph Andrews*; he too is blessed and burdened with six children, strapped for cash, but cheerful and uncomplaining.

a moral Tale: a popular form of didactic fiction for children; see e.g. *Moral and Instructive Tales for the Improvement of Young Ladies: Calculated to Amuse the Mind, and Form the Heart to Virtue* ([1786]); Maria Edgeworth, *Moral Tales for Young People* (1801).

Clergyman: not the curate of the title (see 'The Visit', note to p. 44), but a rector with his own parish, responsible for executing or overseeing all official duties including those of his curate.

living . . . about two hundred pound: the clergyman's income, or 'living', derived from tithes paid by residents of his parish and from the rent paid to him by those who farmed parish land. He would also live in a rent-free house. £200 is not a large annual salary; JA's father's two livings (Steventon and Deane) brought in a total of £210 and had to be supplemented by tutoring and by income from one of his cousin's farms. JA's brother, the Revd James Austen, and his wife struggled to make ends meet on a yearly income of £300.

Royal Academy for Seamen at Portsmouth: the Royal Naval Academy, later the Royal Naval College, where JA's brothers Francis and Charles Austen began their illustrious careers. It took boys from the age of 11 to 17. Francis Austen entered in Apr. 1786, just before his twelfth birthday; Charles shortly after his twelfth birthday in July 1791. The Academy cost nothing for the sons of naval officers, but the Revd George Austen had to pay £75 per annum for Charles's tuition and expenses, a hefty slice of his income.

Newfoundland: the island of Newfoundland in Canada, Britain's oldest colony. A naval presence defended its valuable fisheries during Britain's many skirmishes with France, Spain, and Holland.

Newfoundland Dog: a very large breed of hunting dog, imported to Britain from the late 17th century onwards. Henry Tilney has a 'large Newfoundland puppy' (*NA*, ch. 26).

every Month: revised from 'every Year', thereby heightening the absurdity (see Textual Notes, p. 225).

65 *adopted by a neighbouring Clergyman*: perhaps another allusion to Edward Austen's adoption by the Knights in 1783. Here, the motive for such an adoption is comically lacking since this 'Benefactor' has scarcely any money and plenty of his own children to provide for.

Curacy of fifty pound a year: a very small income, a quarter of that earned by the clergyman.

65 *twopenny Dame's School*: a cheap, private, local school for young children, typically run by an elderly or widowed woman and offering lessons in basic reading, writing, and arithmetic. This is the earliest instance of 'dame-school' cited in the *OED*, though dozens of earlier texts mention the institution. Perhaps the best-known 18th-century work on the dame's school was William Shenstone's mock-Spenserian poem *The School-Mistress* (1737).

genius: 'Nature; disposition' (Johnson's *Dictionary*).

brickbats: 'Fragments of brick deployed as missiles' (*OED*).

ODE TO PITY

66 *Miss Austen*: JA's sister Cassandra; see 'The beautifull Cassandra', note to p. 37.

Ode to Pity: William Collins's well-known 'Ode to Pity' (1746) was included in Dodsley's *Collection of Poems* (1758), a copy of which JA owned (see 'Jack & Alice', note to p. 15). By the end of the 18th century, Collins rivalled Thomas Gray as the most popular lyric poet in the language; the works of both writers were frequently imitated. JA's poem does not attempt to replicate the rhyme scheme or other formal properties of Collins's 'Ode'.

pitiful: 'Melancholy; moving compassion' and 'Tender; compassionate' (Johnson's *Dictionary*).

Paths of honour: possibly echoing Thomas Gray's wildly popular *Elegy Written in a Country Churchyard* (1751): 'The Paths of Glory lead but to the Grave' (l. 36).

Myrtle: 'A fragrant tree sacred to Venus' (Johnson's *Dictionary*): Phaedra, besotted with her stepson, Hippolytus, pierced its leaves. Collins's 'Ode' includes the lines 'There first the Wren thy Myrtles shed | On gentle *Otway's* infant Head' (ll. 19–20).

Philomel: a poetic or literary name for the nightingale, alluding to the classical myth of the maiden Philomela's transformation into that bird (*OED*).

Gently brawling . . . Silent Stream: 'brawling' here means 'The confused din of a stream or torrent' (*OED*); the first citation supporting the word in this sense dates from 1837. JA's noisy scene poses a striking contrast to the 'soft notes' and soothing, muted atmosphere of Collins's 'Ode' (l. 23). There may be an echo here of *As You Like It*: 'an oak, whose antique root peeps out | Upon the brook that brawls along this wood' (act 2, scene 1); the last word of JA's poem is 'peep'. The incongruous pairing of a prosaic turnpike with a pastoral stream appears, too, in 'Love and Friendship': 'Before us ran the murmuring brook and behind us ran the turnpike road' (p. 86). Turnpike roads charged travellers at toll gates before they were allowed to proceed; money accrued in this way was supposed to pay for maintaining the roads.

The hut, the Cot, the Grot: poeticisms; the hut may recall Pity's 'Cell' in Collins (l. 21); 'Cot' is a small house or little cottage; and 'Grot' is grotto.

eke: 'Also; likewise; beside; moreover' (Johnson's *Dictionary*); a poeticism, often comically redundant. It is noted under the verb 'To eke' that 'our old poets . . . put *eke* into their lines, when they wanted a syllable' (Johnson's *Dictionary*).

the Abbey too a mouldering heap: ruined abbeys were a popular Gothic motif, especially in fiction of the early 1790s; cf. *NA*, ch. 17. The 'mouldering heap' echoes Gray's *Elegy*: 'Where heaves the Turf with many a mould'ring Heap' (l. 14).

Conceal'd by aged pines: on arrival at Mr B's Lincolnshire mansion, where she will be imprisoned, Richardson's Pamela is struck by the 'brown nodding Horrors of lofty Elms and Pines about it' (i, letter 31).

June 3ᵈ 1793: a day later than the dedication of the previous group of writings to Anna Austen, and the latest date JA gives to any of her teenage works.

VOLUME THE SECOND

67 *Ex dono mei Patris*: 'A gift from my father', a rare use of Latin in JA's writing. The notebook containing *Volume the Second* was a present from the Revd George Austen.

CONTENTS: JA inserted page numbers beside each of the items. 'Scraps' covers a number of different pieces whose individual titles are not listed here, nor are those pieces referred to collectively as 'Scraps' other than on the Contents page.

Friendship: corrected here from 'Freindship', although the 'ei' spelling predominates in the story itself (see Note on Spelling).

LOVE AND FRIENDSHIP

68 *Madame La Comtesse De Feuillide*: JA's cousin Eliza de Feuillide; see also 'Frederic & Elfrida', note to p. 3; 'Henry & Eliza', note to p. 27. She was probably at Steventon during the period including 13 June 1790, the date given at the end of 'Love and Friendship'. This is the only one of the teenage writings dedicated to her, although she clearly inspired 'Henry & Eliza'.

69 *Love and Freindship*: this titular pairing features in e.g. *Love and Friendship; or, The Lucky Recovery. A Comedy* (1754). Letter-writing manuals, popular throughout the 18th century, commonly offered advice on how to treat love and friendship, as noted on their title pages. Another possible source for JA's title and epigraph is the motto 'Amoris and Amicitiae' ('Of Love and Friendship') on a miniature portrait of Eliza de Feuillide (Deirdre Le Faye, *Jane Austen's 'Outlandish Cousin': The Life and Letters of Eliza de Feuillide* (London: British Library, 2002), 55–6, 96). Cf. also *The Loiterer*, no. 27, in which 'every Girl who seeks for happiness' is told 'to avoid love and friendship' (11–12). The heroine of Garrick's *Bon Ton*, Miss Tittup, announces 'Pooh, pooh, Love and Friendship are very fine names to be sure, but they are mere visiting acquaintance; we know their names indeed,

talk of 'em sometimes, and let 'em knock at our doors, but we never let 'em in' (act 1, scene 1). See also 'The three Sisters', note to p. 58.

69 *in a series of Letters*: a stock subtitle in fiction of the period, signalling the epistolary form of the ensuing novel and employed in Eliza Nugent Bromley's anonymous *Laura and Augustus, An Authentic Story; in a Series of Letters, by a Young Lady*, 3 vols. (1784), a major source for 'Love and Friendship'. Like JA, Bromley writes about female friends, tyrannical fathers, tales of adventures and life stories, wild emotions, the death of the hero, and a heroine who goes mad.

Deceived in Freindship & Betrayed in Love: the conclusion of a four-line glee for three voices, attributed to Colonel R. Mellish (1777–1817), a member of one of the glee clubs: 'Welcome the covert of these aged oaks, | Welcome each cavern of these horrid rocks, | Far from this world's illusion let me rove, | Deceiv'd in Friendship, and betray'd in love.' *The Poetry of Various Glees, Songs, &c. As Performed at the Harmonists* (1798), 109.

Isabel to Laura: Isabel was the original form of the popular name Isabella, later given to Isabella Thorpe in *NA* and Isabella Knightley in *E*; Laura, an unusual name with literary pedigree, gained new popularity in novels of the 1780s and 1790s, including Bromley's *Laura and Augustus*.

detail . . . of your Life: cf. 'Jack & Alice', in which Alice asks Lady Williams 'Will you favour me with your Life & Adventures'; the same question is later put to Lucy. See notes to pp. 13 and 16.

cruel Persecutions of obstinate Fathers: the best-known example of such paternal cruelty and obstinacy was Mr Harlowe, father of Richardson's tragic heroine Clarissa, who is fixed on marrying her to a man she detests. More recent epistolary treatments of paternal tyrants and persecuted heroines included Sarah Scott's *The Test of Filial Duty. In a Series of Letters between Miss Emilia Leonard, and Miss Charlotte Arlington. A Novel*, 2 vols. (1772); *The History of Miss Pamela Howard*, 2 vols. (1773); and *The Fatal Marriage: A Novel*, 2 vols. (1785). The heroine of Bromley's *Laura and Augustus* laments 'the tyranny of a parent! from him have originated all my sorrows' (iii, letter 47). Sir Anthony Absolute in Sheridan's *The Rivals*, a play in which JA performed, may also be an influence on the portrayal of supposedly despotic fathers in this tale.

70 *Marianne*: cf. Marianne Dashwood in *S&S*, a heroine embodying acute sensibility.

natural Daughter of a Scotch Peer by an italian Opera-girl: 'natural' means 'illegitimate', the offspring of unmarried parents. An opera-girl did not sing, but danced in the ballet interludes presented between the acts of an opera. The costumes of opera-girls were revealing; like actresses, they were understood to be sexually available to wealthy male patrons. Cf. *The Solitary Castle, A Romance of the Eighteenth Century*, 2 vols. (1789): 'Mr. *Le Fleur* was the fruit of an illicit amour, between an Italian opera girl, and an English peer' (i, 124).

a Convent in France: Eliza, illegitimate daughter of a duke, in *Laura and Augustus*, reports being educated at a French convent and that her mother is Italian (i, letter 4).

romantic: 'Full of wild scenery' (Johnson's *Dictionary*), a sublime landscape 'that fills the mind with a sense of overwhelming grandeur or irresistible power; that inspires awe, great reverence, or other high emotion, by reason of its beauty, vastness, or grandeur' (*OED* 'sublime', 9).

Vale of Uske: the river Usk runs through a picturesque river valley north of Newport in south Wales. For a description of its charms see William Gilpin, *Observations on the River Wye, and Several Parts of South Wales, &c. Relative Chiefly to Picturesque Beauty; Made in the Summer of the Year 1770* (1782); see also 'A Tour through Wales' (p. 156).

shortly surpassed my Masters: spoofing the conventional requirement that heroines in fiction must be superlatively accomplished; cf. Charlotte Smith's *Emmeline*, i, ch. 1. Looking back on JA's life, Henry Austen wrote that 'In the present age it is hazardous to mention accomplishments' (*Memoir*, 139).

Rendez-vous: a newly fashionable French word, meaning either a meeting or a favoured meeting place; Laura's use of the term is both affected and slightly odd. JA originally offered an explanation of the word, as 'place of appointment', then deleted it (see Textual Notes, p. 226).

tremblingly alive: possibly alluding to Pope's *Essay on Man* (1733–4): 'Or Touch, if tremblingly alive all o'er, | To smart, and agonize at ev'ry pore' (epistle 1, ll. 189–90), though the phrase appears so often in fiction of the period as to amount to novelistic cant. See e.g. Sophia Briscoe's *Miss Melmoth; or, The New Clarissa*, 3 vols. (1771): 'guard your expressions, she is tremblingly alive all o'er' (ii, 160, letter 55); Agnes Maria Bennett's *Anna: or Memoirs of a Welch Heiress*: 'The heart of Anna, naturally soft and tremblingly alive to sympathy and compassion, was now unaccountably hardened' (ii, 34); Burney's *Cecilia*: 'how fearfully delicate, how "tremblingly alive" is the conscience of man!' (bk 7, ch. 7).

Minuet Dela Cour: 'minuet of the court', a highly stylized dance for couples, associated with the French court and popular in England from the mid-17th century.

neighbourhood was small . . . eoconomical motives: cf. Sarah Fielding's *History of Ophelia*, in which the heroine is reared by her aunt in a similarly isolated cottage and Captain Traverse retires to Wales for reasons of financial constraint (i, ch. 2, ch. 28).

71 *one of the first Boarding-schools in London*: cf. 'Edgar & Emma', p. 26 and note. In the late 18th century, boarding schools were an increasingly popular choice for young girls from wealthy backgrounds.

Southampton: JA briefly attended boarding school in Southampton in 1783 (see 'Henry & Eliza', note to p. 27), where she and Cassandra were infected with typhus; the port was notorious for its dirt, bad smells, and poor air. Having 'supped' one night in Southampton is scarcely a claim to distinction.

JA originally wrote 'slept'; the revision heightens the joke in abbreviating the timespan (see Textual Notes, p. 226).

71 *Beware . . . the Metropolis*: cf. a similar joke about the city in JA's letter of 23 Aug. 1796: 'Here I am once more in this Scene of Dissipation & vice, and I begin already to find my Morals corrupted' (*Letters*, 5).

rustic Cot: a country cottage; poeticized and picturesque language. There is another 'Cot' in JA's 'Ode to Pity', p. 66.

We must not . . . partly convinced: JA here makes a substantial revision, deleting three lines and condensing the father's speech; the scene thereby becomes more focused (see Textual Notes, p. 226).

72 *I long to know who it is*: possibly echoing a protracted episode in *Tristram Shandy*, in which Walter and Toby Shandy discuss the activities of their visitors (bk 1, ch. 21; bk 2, ch. 6); cf. also Miss Tittup in *Bon Ton*, reflecting on 'Love and Freindship' that 'they are mere visiting acquaintance; we . . . let 'em knock at our doors, but we never let 'em in' (see note to p. 69).

Lindsay . . . Talbot: Lindsay is a noble Scottish name, Talbot an eminently English and heroic one. JA sends up the fictional convention of concealing the names of invented characters as if they were real people; see 'Henry & Eliza', note to p. 28; 'The three Sisters', note to p. 54; 'A Tale', note to p. 156.

Baronet: the lowest hereditary rank; see 'Sir William Mountague', note to p. 34.

Polydore . . . Claudia: strangers would not have been addressed by their Christian names; these names are also absurdly unrealistic, deriving in the first case from romance and drama and from a Roman matron in the second.

Deluding Pomp of Title . . . Lady Dorothea: 'Deluding Pomp' or 'Delusive Pomp' is a stock phrase in 18th-century literature, routinely applied to the supposedly hollow attractions of nobility, royalty, court titles, etc. See e.g. James Thomson, *The Seasons* (1730), 'Autumn', l. 1296. As a baronet, Sir Edward Lindsay would be eager to unite his son and Lady Dorothea, who in view of her title must be the daughter of a duke, marquess, or earl.

73 *Never . . . obliged my Father*: continuing the theme of children in conflict with their parents or guardians (see note to p. 69); however, the usual plot line is advanced to a new stage of absurdity here, with a son defying a father who wants him to marry the woman he loves. Cf. 'Frederic & Elfrida', note to p. 5.

Gibberish: 'cant language, pedlars['] French; or St Giles's Greek' (*Classical Dictionary*); 'Cant; the private language of rogues and gipsies; words without meaning' (Johnson's *Dictionary*).

studying Novels I suspect: a gender reversal; young women rather than men were usually criticized for reading novels. On the general scorn for novel-readers cf. *Laura and Augustus*: 'This comes of people suffering their children to read those ridiculous books called novels' (i, letter 11). Defending the novel, JA writes that 'no species of composition has been so much decried', while Henry Tilney declares that 'The person, be it gentleman or lady, who has not pleasure in a good novel, must be intolerably stupid . . . I myself have read hundreds and hundreds' (*NA*, ch. 5, ch. 14); JA noted that her family were 'great Novel-readers & not ashamed of being so' (*Letters*, p. 27, 18–19 Dec. 1798).

Bedfordshire . . . Middlesex: Bedfordshire is about 30 miles north of Middlesex; rather than travel this distance Edward has gone about a hundred miles west to the Vale of Usk.

never taken orders . . . Church: despite being 'bred to the Church', Laura's father has not been ordained a clergyman (he is also, apparently, a Catholic); Laura and Edward are therefore not legally married. Cf. other questionable or invalid wedding ceremonies in 'Henry & Eliza', 'Lesley-Castle' (Letter the Tenth), 'Collection of Letters' (Letter the second).

75 *Does it appear impossible . . . to argue with*: this dispute between a rational and an irrational character on love, sustenance, and practicality echoes that of *Laura and Augustus*: 'take yourself off with your beggar's brat, and see if love will support you: you will find it, Madam heroine, I fancy damned slender diet' (ii, letter 39).

76 *Sophia*: a common name for sentimental heroines, it means 'wisdom'. JA applies it ironically to vacant or fickle women; cf. 'Collection of Letters', p. 137.

77 *pathetic*: 'Affecting the passions; passionate; moving' (Johnson's *Dictionary*).

We fainted Alternately on a Sofa: cf. the comic use of 'alternately' in 'Frederic & Elfrida' (p. 3 and note) and 'Edgar & Emma' (p. 25 and note).

illiterate: 'Unlettered; untaught; unlearned; unenlightened by science' (Johnson's *Dictionary*), rather than unable to read or write. Cf. Laura's later reference to an 'illiterate villain' (p. 90).

78 *Clandestine Marriage*: Hardwicke's Marriage Act of 1753 prohibited the secret marriage of minors, and parents could prevent such ceremonies; the possibility of clandestine marriage (of dubious legality) often features in epistolary fiction. Cf. George Colman and David Garrick's *The Clandestine Marriage* (1766); the phrase itself pre-dates their play. See also 'Henry & Eliza', note to p. 29; 'Sir William Mountague', note to p. 35.

gracefully purloined . . . Escritoire: euphemistic language for 'stolen from his father's writing desk'.

blushed at . . . paying their Debts: among the wealthy it was fashionable to leave debts to tradesmen unpaid for as long as possible, putting many businesses in a precarious position. Cf. Charles Surface's remark in Sheridan's *School for Scandal* that 'paying' tradesmen 'is only Encouraging them' (act 4, scene 1).

79 *an Execution in the House*: the seizure of a debtor's goods by a sheriff's officers executing a writ; such an 'execution' would be ordered by the creditors. Goods would be sold and the proceeds used to pay off debts.

79 *the Officers of Justice*: the sheriff's officers.

Holbourn: a district in and route through central London. JA originally wrote 'Piccadilly', a more respectable area in the West End (see Textual Notes, p. 227).

Front Glasses: carriage windows that could be opened and closed.

Newgate: a notorious prison, featured in many 18th-century novels; cf. 'snug little Newgate' in 'Henry & Eliza', p. 30 and note.

80 *Annuity*: an annual payment or allowance, deriving from return on capital and ceasing on the death of the recipient. Cf. *S&S*, ch. 2.

travel Post: a rapid, expensive form of travel, involving a change of horses at each stage. Continuing day and night in this way, travellers could have reached Scotland in about three days.

81 *coroneted Coach & 4*: a coach that bears the crest of a peer's family; four horses indicate great wealth (cf. 'Mr Clifford', p. 36 and note).

82 *Acknowledge thee! . . . Grand-Children in the House*: this recognition scene is closely modelled on a famous example in Burney's *Evelina*, in which the heroine is finally, elaborately acknowledged by her father, Sir John Belmont, who already has one daughter and has just discovered a son (vol. iii, letters 17 and 19). There is another rapid-fire series of recognitions in Sheridan's *The Critic* (act 3, scene 1).

Janetta: a romanticized version of Janet, itself a Scottish form of Jane; JA is apparently toying with her own name.

83 *never read the Sorrows of Werter*: see 'Frederic & Elfrida', note to p. 7; cf. *The Loiterer*, no. 32, in which the narrator is asked by a young woman 'whether or no, I had ever read The Sorrows of Werter' (12). Goethe's wildly popular tale embodies the excesses of sensibility and hopeless, suicidal love.

Hair . . . auburn: red hair was fashionable in the 1780s.

84 *Billet*: note.

Gretna-Green: a town in southern Scotland, just across the border with England, where couples under the age of 21 could be married without parental consent (Hardwicke's Marriage Act did not apply to Scotland). Janetta and M'Kenzie already reside in Scotland, making the elopement unnecessary.

86 *we sate down . . . clear limpid stream*: alluding to a passage in Samuel Johnson's *A Journey to the Western Islands of Scotland* (1775): 'I sat down on a bank, such as a writer of romance might have delighted to feign. I had indeed no trees to whisper over my head, but a clear rivulet streamed at my feet. The day was calm, the air soft, and all was rudeness, silence, and solitude' (61). The parallel is noted by R. W. Chapman in *Minor Works* (459) and by Margaret Anne Doody in *Catharine and Other Writings* (318–19), but disputed by Sabor in *Juvenilia* (438).

murmuring brook . . . turn-pike road: see 'Ode to Pity', note to p. 66.

Eastern Zephyr: ignorant misuse of poetical language, since 'Zephyr' in classical mythology is the west wind.

87 *blue sattin Waistcoat striped with white*: striped waistcoats were popular in the 1790s, and thanks to *The Sorrows of Young Werther* blue was a fashionable colour (see 'Frederic & Elfrida', note to p. 7). Cf. also *Laura and Augustus*, in which the hero's 'waistcoat and breeches are white lustring, the waistcoat wrought in rose-buds, and fastened with bunches of silver' (i, letter 10). JA may also be recalling *Tristram Shandy*, in which Susannah, on hearing that Bobby is dead, finds herself thinking of 'a green sattin night-gown of my mother's' (v, ch. 7).

apropos: anglicization of *à propos* (French): 'apt', 'timely'.

fashionably high Phaeton: see also 'Mr Clifford', note to p. 36, and 'The three Sisters', note to p. 53. High phaetons were more unstable than low phaetons and therefore vulnerable to accidents.

Life of Cardinal Wolsey: Thomas Wolsey (1475–1530), cardinal and statesman during the reign of Henry VIII; his fall from royal favour was often taken to exemplify the dangers of ambition and pride. See e.g. the soliloquy of Shakespeare's Wolsey in *King Henry VIII*, comparing his downfall to that of a star (act 3, scene 2), of which Hugh Blair comments in his *Lectures on Rhetoric and Belles Lettres*, 2 vols. (1783), a work JA read, that it is 'at once instructive and affecting' (lecture 46). See also Johnson's *The Vanity of Human Wishes* (1749), in which readers are given an account of Wolsey's rise and fall and instructed to apply it to their own lives (ll. 99–128). Cf. 'examples from the Lives of great Men' in 'The female philosopher' (p. 152).

88 *sensible*: conscious, in possession of his senses; see 'Jack & Alice', note to p. 12.

Cupid's Thunderbolts . . . Shafts of Jupiter: Laura has things the wrong way round: Cupid, god of love, has the shafts or arrows as missiles; the thunderbolts belong to Jupiter, god of sky and thunder and ruler of the Olympians.

Leg of Mutton . . . Cucumber: cf. *Laura and Augustus*, in which the heroine is also given a mad speech after her husband's death (iii, letter 66); JA is further drawing on Tilburnia's wild speech in Sheridan's *The Critic* (act 3, scene 1), which features similarly absurd and incongruous ravings and is itself a spoof of Ophelia's speech in *Hamlet* (act 4, scene 5).

very plain . . . Bridget: cf. Richard Steele's *The Tender Husband* (1705), in which the quixotic heroine, Bridget, objects to her own name as nothing like that of a heroine (act 2, scene 2).

89 *a galloping Consumption*: rapidly developing tuberculosis, or any wasting illness. See 'Edgar & Emma', note to p. 24. Characters in sentimental fiction, including the hero of *Laura and Augustus* (iii, letter 49), often succumb to this rapid but supposedly pale and interesting disease.

91 *Coach-box*: an elevated seat at the front of the stagecoach, on which the driver sat.

91 *Basket*: a compartment hanging off the back of the coach, designed primarily for luggage; the cheapest and most uncomfortable place to sit.

92 *Gilpin's Tour to the Highlands*: William Gilpin's *Observations, Relative Chiefly to Picturesque Beauty, Made in the Year 1776, On Several Parts of Great Britain; particularly the High-lands of Scotland*, 2 vols. (1789).

Stage Coach: see 'Mr Harley', note to p. 33. This would not have been considered a genteel form of travel.

converted it into a Stage: a comically extreme drop from gentility into lower-class employment.

Edinburgh . . . Sterling: the ancient city of Stirling, known as the gateway to the highlands, is about 40 miles from Edinburgh. In a letter of 23 Aug. 1813, JA refers to this passage; another journey had put her in mind 'of my own Coach between Edinburgh & Stirling' (*Letters*, 270).

Postchaise: see 'Frederic & Elfrida', note to p. 6; 'Mr Clifford', note to p. 36.

93 *sentimental*: not recorded in Johnson's *Dictionary*, this was a key term in the language of sensibility, indicating a feeling response that engages the emotions and the heart, rather than reason and the mind.

Staymaker: a corset-maker; a 'stay' or corset is 'A laced underbodice, stiffened by the insertion of strips of whale-bone (sometimes of metal or wood) worn . . . to give shape and support to the figure' (*OED*).

nine thousand Pounds . . . principal of it: this is a blatantly foolish way to behave; Bertha and Agatha could live quite comfortably on the interest of their combined fortune, without touching the capital or 'principal'.

common sitting Parlour: see 'Edgar & Emma', p. 26 and note.

94 *Silver Buckles*: expensive fastenings for shoes, albeit not as expensive as this division of funds implies. £100 would have bought around thirty pairs of buckles.

strolling Company of Players: a travelling group of actors, offering proverbi- ally shabby and ill-rehearsed productions; often associated with vagrancy and infamy. See e.g. the Revd Vicesimus Knox, 'The Imprudence of an Early Attachment to Acting Plays. In a Letter', in *Essays Moral and Literary*, 2 vols. (1782), ii, essay 110.

eclat: that is, *éclat* (French): 'brilliance of effect', 'flamboyance'.

preferment: 'Advancement to a higher station'; 'A place of honour or profit' (Johnson's *Dictionary*).

95 *Covent Garden . . . Lewis & Quick*: William Thomas Lewis (*c.*1746–1811) and John Quick (1748–1831), celebrated comic actors and managers at Covent Garden, one of the two main London theatres.

paid the Debt of Nature: died—a clichéd euphemism.

June 13th 1790: this is the earliest date given by JA in the juvenilia, although several writings in *Volume the First* clearly pre-date 1790. JA deleted the day 'Sunday', before the date, 'June 13th', though it was not a mistake.

96 *Henry Thomas Austen Esqre*: Henry Austen (1771–1850), JA's fourth brother, took his BA at Oxford in spring 1792. JA may have dedicated this tale to him in order to mark the occasion: the last letter in 'Lesley-Castle' is dated '13 April 1792'.

I am now . . . Novels to you: B. C. Southam notes that the phrasing here is ambiguous. 'Novels' might refer to lost works by Henry, previously dedicated to JA; or JA could mean that she is only 'now' responding to Henry's repeated request that she dedicate one of her own works to him (cf. 'Sir William Mountague', note to p. 34); or that she has already responded many times to such a request, and that other 'Novels' dedicated to Henry once existed ('Jane Austen's Juvenilia: The Question of Completeness', *Notes and Queries*, new series, 11 (1964), 180–1).

Messrs Demand & Co: Henry assumes the role of patron by signing this note, purportedly ordering his bank to pay the author 100 guineas (£105). Cf. JA's reference to 'patronage' in her dedication to Charles Austen of 'Mr Clifford'.

Lesley Castle: on the name and setting of this tale, cf. JA's letter to her niece Anna, remarking on the latter's novel-in-progress: 'I like the scene itself, the Miss Lesleys, Lady Anne, & the Music, very much.—Lesley is a noble name' (*Letters*, 287).

Matilda: see 'Amelia Webster', note to p. 41.

97 *Louisa*: cf. Henry Tilney's vaunted 'knowledge of Julias and Louisas' in *NA* (ch. 14), stock names in 18th-century fiction.

stripling: 'A youth, one just passing from boyhood to manhood' (*OED*).

Perth: the ancient Scottish county town of Perthshire, located between Edinburgh and Aberdeen; celebrated in JA's lifetime for its picturesque beauty.

bold projecting Rock: echoing various descriptions of isolated, rock-bound castles in Johnson's *A Journey to the Western Islands of Scotland* and Boswell's *Journal of a Tour to the Hebrides* (1785). See e.g. sections on Slanes Castle and Dunvegan in *A Journey to the Western Islands* (36, 152). Boswell describes 'the old castle' of Rasay as 'situated upon a rock very near the sea. The rock . . . does not appear to have mouldered' (*Journal of a Tour*, 197, Friday 10 Sept.). On Saturday 18 Sept. (Johnson's birthday), he records a comic argument with Lady McLeod about the many inconveniences of life in such a castle, concluding with his urging her to 'keep to the rock: it is the very jewel of the estate' (269–70). On 25 Nov. 1798, JA mentions that her father has bought a copy of Boswell's *Journal of a Tour* (*Letters*, 22).

retired from almost all the World: perhaps alluding to a leitmotif in Boswell's *Journal of a Tour*, Johnson's supposed retirement to a remote Scottish island. Like the Lesley sisters, who live near Perth and see a wide circle of people, Johnson's fantastical visions of such retirement involved plenty

292 *Explanatory Notes*

of socializing. See e.g. his comments on Inch Keith (*Journal of a Tour*, 52, 168).

97 *M'Leods . . . Macduffs*: most of these are names JA would have encountered in Johnson's *Journey to the Western Islands of Scotland*: Macdonald, McLeod, and Mackinnon are listed in one sentence in the section on Skye (135); Shakespeare's McDuff and Macbeth are discussed by Johnson when he visits places associated with the Scottish king (see 'Fores Calder. Fort George'; 'Inverness'). Cf. also references to *Macbeth* in 'Love and Friendship': 'To say the truth this tragedy was not only the Best, but the only Play we ever performed' (p. 94). Mr Macpherson appears in the section of Johnson's *Journey to the Western Islands* on 'Ostig in Sky'. JA's 'M'Cartney' probably derives from Burney's *Evelina*, which includes a melancholy Scottish poet (resembling Young Werther) called Mr Macartney; he turns out to be the heroine's half-brother.

we work: see 'The Mystery', note to p. 50; 'work' here means sewing or mending.

bon-mot: 'A clever or witty saying; a witticism' (*OED*) (French).

repartée: 'Smart reply' (Johnson's *Dictionary*) (French).

entirely insensible . . . dwell on myself: cf. 'Love and Friendship': 'A sensibility too tremblingly alive to every affliction of my Freinds, my Acquaintance and particularly to every affliction of my own, was my only fault' (p. 70).

Rakehelly Dishonor Esqre [*footnote*]: the second of two notes JA added to her teenage writings, transforming the abstract 'dishonour' into a second male accomplice for Louisa and thereby magnifying her turpitude. A 'Rakehel' is 'A wild, worthless, dissolute, debauched, sorry fellow'; 'rakehelly' is 'Wild; dissolute' (Johnson's *Dictionary*) (cf. 'Rake, rakehell, or rakeshame' in *Classical Dictionary*). One of the dramatist George Farquhar's favourite words, 'rakehelly' appears in e.g. *Love and a Bottle. A Comedy* (1699), act 3; *The Inconstant: or, The Way to Win Him. A Comedy* (1702), act 4; *The Beaux' Stratagem*, act 1 (on which play, see also 'Jack & Alice', note to p. 18); *The Twin-Rivals. A Comedy* (1703), act 4; *The Recruiting Officer, A Comedy* ([1706]), act 1.

98 *these venerable Walls*: novelistic cant. Cf. 'These venerable walls, these gothic buildings, hollow groves, and awful tombs' in a letter from Olivia Wilmot, in Anna Maria McKenzie's *The Gamesters* (i, 49).

I live in Perthshire, You in Sussex: that is, at more or less opposite ends of Great Britain. Perthshire is in the east midlands of Scotland, Sussex on the south coast of England.

Tunbridge: Royal Tunbridge Wells, a spa town in Kent and smaller rival to Bath Spa (see note to p. 19); its popularity peaked under the patronage of Beau Nash, master of ceremonies from 1735 to 1762.

Peggy: pet form of Margaret.

Stewed Soup: stock made by simmering meat and bones in water; used for soup.

99 *as White as a Whipt syllabub*: cf. Israel Pottinger, *The Methodist, A Comedy* ([1761]): 'a Set of Teeth as white as whip'd Syllabub' (act 1, scene 2). A syllabub is a light, cold, frothy dessert made by whisking or 'whipping' together milk or cream, sherry, lemon or orange, and sugar; a popular dish in JA's day, as it was relatively cheap and easy to prepare.

Eloisa: the only instance of this name in JA; it has appropriately romantic and tragic literary associations, primarily with the heroine of Alexander Pope's *Eloisa to Abelard* (1717) and with Jean-Jacques Rousseau's sentimental epistolary novel, *Lettres de deux amans: habitans d'une petite ville au pied des Alpes* (1761), popularly known as *Julie, ou la nouvelle Héloïse*.

dressed: prepared for serving at the table.

100 *Decline*: 'Any disease in which the bodily strength gradually fails; *esp.* tubercular phthisis, consumption' (*OED*). See 'Edgar & Emma', note to p. 24.

Bristol: Bristol Hotwells, a resort on the outskirts of the port city of Bristol; cheaper and less fashionable than its neighbour Bath Spa. The last volume of *Evelina* is set there.

101 *those Jewels . . . always promised us*: a mother's jewels would traditionally be passed on to her daughter(s), but Margaret fears that Sir George has given them to his new wife.

Mother-in-law: that is, stepmother. In *Scoticisms, Arranged in Alphabetical Order, Designed to Correct Improprieties of Speech and Writing* (1787), James Beattie notes that 'Mother-in-law properly signals a husband's or wife's mother; in Scot. and in Eng. too it is often used improperly for step-mother'. The word does not appear elsewhere in the teenage writings, but in *E* Mrs Weston is described as Frank Churchill's 'mother-in-law' rather than as his stepmother (ii, ch. 5).

Matilda . . . Father's table: Matilda, as the elder sister, would in the absence of her mother have sat at the head of the table; the new Mrs Lesley takes precedence.

103 *Dunbeath*: a fishing village in the northern highlands of Scotland, though the immediate context suggests that this is the name of Lesley's estate near Aberdeen.

one of the Universities there: see Johnson's *Journey to the Western Islands*, in which he describes at length King's College in Old Aberdeen and Marischal College in the new town, noting the points of difference and resemblance between them ('Aberdeen').

I think and feel, a great deal: Sabor detects in JA's emphases 'a literary allusion' (*Juvenilia*, 448); Chapman thinks JA is echoing a note in Boswell's *Journal of a Tour* on the Pretender (*Minor Works*, 460). The phrasing, however, seems more generally derivative of sentimental writing than of a specific source.

healthy air . . . Bristol-downs: like Hotwells, the hills or 'downs' around Bristol were celebrated for their restorative properties.

104 *Chairwomen*: charwomen, 'hired . . . for odd work, or single days' (Johnson's *Dictionary*), rather than those regularly employed as live-in servants.

Jellies: leftover meats preserved in aspic or in clear, jellied stock.

rouges a good deal: cf. 'Frederic & Elfrida', note to p. 5; 'Jack & Alice', note to p. 14. By the 1780s, rouging was becoming unfashionable.

Brighthelmstone: Brighton, a popular seaside resort since the 1750s, patronized by the Prince of Wales. Lydia Bennet and Wickham elope to Brighton (*P&P*, ch. 39); Maria Bertram goes there for her honeymoon (*MP*, ch. 21).

105 *four thousand pounds*: Susan Lesley's capital sum of £4,000, assuming interest paid to her at the usual rate of 5%, would yield a yearly income of £200; however, as Charlotte points out, Mrs Lesley would like to spend almost £4,000 per year on clothes and socializing.

Curry: cf. the reference to 'making a Curry' in 'A beautiful description of the different effects of Sensibility on different Minds', see note to p. 64.

Cleveland: also the name of the Palmers' Somerset estate in *S&S* (ch. 20).

set her cap at him: a phrase described by Marianne Dashwood as 'commonplace' and 'odious' (*S&S*, ch. 9); cf. JA's use of it in a letter of 21 May 1801 (*Letters*, 88). Women commonly wore caps of white linen or muslin in the 18th and early 19th centuries. Any woman intent on attracting a man would, so the saying assumes, wear her best cap, probably decorated with lace and ribbons, and would set it at the most fetching angle. In Oliver Goldsmith's *She Stoops to Conquer* (1773), Kate Hardcastle tells her father: 'Well, if he refuses, instead of breaking my heart at his indifference, I'll only break my glass for its flattery, set my cap to some newer fashion, and look out for some less difficult admirer' (act 1, scene 1).

107 *Portman-Square*: a large, very fashionable square in London, completed in the 1780s. After the death of her husband, 'who had traded with success in a less elegant part of the town', Mrs Jennings spends 'every winter in a house in one of the streets near Portman-square' (*S&S*, ch. 25).

dismal old weather-beaten Castle: see note to p. 97.

a long rigmerole Story: 'rigmarole' is included in the second edition (1788) of *Classical Dictionary*, where it is defined as 'Roundabout, nonsensical. He told a long rigmarole story'. Boswell refers to 'that manner vulgarly, but significantly, called *rigmarole*' (*Life of Johnson*, i, 191 n. [1759]).

Scotch Airs . . . every thing Scotch: the craze for Scottish landscape and literature was fed by e.g. James Macpherson's cycle of 'Ossian' poems (1761–5), Johnson's *Journey to the Western Islands*, Sophia Lee's *The Recess; or, A Tale of Other Times*, 3 vols. (1783–5), Boswell's *Journal of a Tour*, and Ann Radcliffe's *The Castles of Athlin and Dunbayne. A Highland Story* (1789). Scottish poems, melodies, and songs (or 'Airs'), popularized by writers including Allan Ramsay and Robert Burns, are widely praised in late 18th-century fiction. In e.g. Miss Elliott's *The Portrait. A Novel*, 2 vols. (1783), Maria writes to Charlotte that 'I . . . sung a variety of songs, but found he was particularly charmed with the simple plaintive stile of the Scotch airs . . . I agreed perfectly with him on the subject (ii, 165). JA herself played and sang Scottish airs; in *P&P*, Mary Bennet plays Scotch and Irish airs, and Miss Bingley sings a 'lively Scotch air' (ch. 6, ch. 10).

toilett: toilette, dressing table, referring both to the table itself and to the acts of applying make-up, brushing hair, etc. The best-known 18th-century literary scene of a woman 'at the toilette' is Pope's *Rape of the Lock*, canto 1, ll. 121–48 (see 'Frederic & Elfrida', note to p. 5).

110 *Galleries and Antichambers*: long passages, a feature of medieval and Elizabethan houses and a frequent setting in gothic fiction; they were used to display paintings and for exercise in bad weather. Antechambers or withdrawing rooms, leading to adjoining bedchambers, could be used to receive guests (see 'Frederic & Elfrida', note to p. 4).

111 *Public-places*: in London, these would include pleasure gardens, theatres, operas, dances, concert halls, picture galleries, and museums.

Vaux-hall: on the south bank of the river Thames, Vauxhall Gardens—a 12-acre park featuring walkways, shrubberies, cascades, statues, and other attractions—remained a popular venue for public entertainment from the 17th to the 19th centuries. It had a reputation for being rowdy and seedy; Burney's Evelina gets into trouble in the 'dark alleys' there (ii, letter 15).

cold Beef . . . so thin: the slices of meat served at Vauxhall were famously thin; see e.g. John Dent's *The Candidate; A Farce* ([1782]): 'as easily seen through as a slice of beef at Vauxhall' (act 2).

Receipts: recipes.

drawing Pullets: eviscerating or gutting young hens, in preparation for cooking them.

112 *Country-dance*: here, the music accompanying 'A rural or traditional dance, esp. in England and Scotland; *spec.* one in which couples begin by standing face to face in long lines' (*OED*); a contrast to the formal, courtly minuet (see 'Love and Friendship', note to p. 70).

pidgeon-pye: pigeon pie, a dish (like other game pies) often served cold, popular in Scotland and England.

Malbrook: 'Marlbrough s'en va-t-en guerre' or 'Malbrook s'en va-t-en guerre' ('Marlbrough [or Malbrook] is off to war'), also known as 'Mort et convoi de l'invincible Malbrough' ('The death and burial of the invincible Marlbrough'), one of the most popular French folk songs. It is a mock lament on the supposed death of John Churchill, 1st Duke of Marlborough (1650–1722), after the Battle of Malplaquet in 1709. The melody is likely to pre-date the lyrics, and is used as the tune for two other songs, 'The Bear Went over the Mountain' and 'For He's a Jolly Good Fellow'. For years, 'Malbrook' was known only traditionally; around 1780, however, the song became a hit across Europe and lent its name to fashions, silks, headdresses, carriages, and soups. The subject of the song was printed on fire screens, fans, and porcelain, embroidered on tapestries, and depicted on toys and keepsakes.

112 *Bravo . . . Poco presto*: a hodge-podge of musical terms; the first three do indeed express admiration (as Charlotte and Eloisa claim): *Bravo* means 'excellent', *Bravissimo* 'outstanding', and *Encora* or 'encore' is a traditional, approving demand for more music or song. The other terms are descriptive and technical, directing performers on how to play: *da capo* means 'repeat from the beginning'; *allegretto* means 'brisk', but somewhat less brisk than *allegro*; *con espressioné* means 'with expression' or 'expressively'. *Poco presto* ('a little' and 'very fast') is an absurdly contradictory instruction.

Execution: the 'vocal or instrumental rendering (of a musical composition)' (*OED*). Ephraim Chambers's *Cyclopædia; or, An Universal Dictionary of Arts and Sciences*, 2 vols., 7th edn (1751–2) states that '*Execution* is particularly used in French music, for the manner of singing.'

Harpsichord: 'A keyboard instrument of music (resembling in appearance the grand piano), in which the strings were plucked and set in vibration by quill or leather points set in jacks connected by levers with the keys' (*OED*). By the early 1790s, the pianoforte was superseding it as the family instrument of choice; see *Letters* for references to JA's pianoforte (88, 168) and *Memoir*, 182.

satirical: cf. JA's explanation of why Lady Middleton dislikes the Dashwood sisters: 'because they were fond of reading, she fancied them satirical: perhaps without exactly knowing what it was to be satirical; but *that* did not signify. It was censure in common use, and easily given' (*S&S*, ch. 36).

114 *Grosvenor Street*: a very fashionable London address, running from Hyde Park to New Bond Street and boasting many titled inhabitants; a frequent setting in novels, including *Sir Charles Grandison*.

April 10ᵗʰ: The date on which Clarissa runs away with Lovelace in Richardson's epistolary novel, and the date she orders to be engraved on her coffin-plate.

115 *a proper size for real Beauty*: one of JA's running jokes, apparently reflecting her own height; cf. 'Jack & Alice', p. 10; 'Love and Friendship', p. 86; Jane Fairfax in *E*, ch. 20; cf. Henry Austen, 'Biographical Notice' (*Memoir*, 139).

116 *Toad-eater*: 'One who eats toads; *orig.* the attendant of a charlatan, employed to eat or pretend to eat toads (held to be poisonous) to enable his master to exhibit his skill in expelling poison'; hence, figuratively, a 'toady' or 'fawning flatterer, parasite, sycophant', or 'A humble friend or dependant; *spec.* a female companion or attendant. *contemptuous*' (*OED*). See 'Henry & Eliza', note to p. 28.

117 *celebrated . . . in Printshops*: images of actresses, celebrated beauties, and notorious criminals were offered for sale in printshops.

my Appearance as unpleasing . . . Small-pox: the disfiguring scars (or 'pock-marks') caused by smallpox were a cause of terror to many young women; since Margaret Lesley has already had the illness, she cannot suffer them now. Cf. the contrast between Jezalinda and Rebecca in 'Frederic & Elfrida', and Mary Tudor's pockmarked face, perhaps modelled on that of Mary Lloyd, in Cassandra's illustration of JA's 'History of England' (see note to p. 128).

Last Monday se'night: a week last Monday or Monday, seven nights ago.

Rout: 'rout' can mean 'A fashionable gathering; a large evening party or soirée of a type fashionable in the 18th and early 19th centuries'; however, given the context, JA is also playing on its popular, rowdy implications: 'A disreputable group of people; a violent or unlawful mob; a gang of criminals or ruffians; (also) a violent horde. Later in weakened sense: a disorderly, disorganized, or unruly group of people; a boisterous throng; a crowd, a mob' (*OED*).

Mrs Kickabout's: the name appears in an old nursery rhyme: 'Old Sir Simon the king, | And young Sir Simon the squire, | And old Mrs. Hickabout | Kicked Mrs. Kickabout | Round about our coal fire'. Cf. 'Frederic & Elfrida', note to p. 5.

on him depended . . . my Life: Cf. 'Love and Friendship': 'no sooner did I first behold him, than I felt that on him the happiness or Misery of my future Life must depend' (p. 72).

118 *Lady Flambeau's*: a flambeau is a wax torch, used to light the way to and from a carriage.

Pope's Bulls: papal edicts. In this case, the bull is required to invalidate Lesley's marriage; his spouse is Protestant (and has committed adultery), while he has become a Catholic. Cf. the complications of *Sir Charles Grandison*, whose hero is engaged to an Italian Catholic while being romantically involved with an English Protestant.

THE HISTORY OF ENGLAND

120 *Henry the 4th . . . Charles the 1st*: JA's title echoes that of Oliver Goldsmith's schoolroom text *The History of England, from the Earliest Times to the Death of George II*, 4 vols. (1771), itself based on David Hume's *The History of England from the Invasion of Julius Caesar to the Revolution in 1688*, 6 vols. (1754–62), which JA may also have known. Her copy of Goldsmith's *History of England* survives and contains more than 100 of her marginal comments; Sabor thinks they were probably made not long before she composed her own 'History of England' (*Juvenilia*, 316–55, 455). JA may also have read and drawn on Goldsmith's *An History of England in a Series of Letters from a Nobleman to his Son*, 2 vols. (1764) and *An Abridgment of the History of England* (1774).

partial, prejudiced, & ignorant Historian: gesturing towards the preface to Goldsmith's *History of England*, in which 'it is hoped the reader will admit my impartiality' (i, p. viii). JA tests this hope to instant breaking point, spoofing Goldsmith's transparently Whig and Protestant sympathies with her pro-Tory, pro-Catholic stance and her abuse of readers who might think or feel differently.

120 *To Miss Austen*: cf. JA's dedication to her elder sister of 'The beautifull Cassandra'. Cassandra is also the illustrator of 'The History of England', contributing thirteen medallion portraits and signing all but one of them 'C E Austen pinx[it]' ('C E Austen painted it').

very few Dates in this History: remarkably, the first of Goldsmith's histories of England (1764) includes no dates at all. The last word of JA's 'History' is a date: 'Saturday Nov. 26th 1791', but there are only four other dates in total. 'The History of England' also features very few battles (see note to p. 122).

121 *Henry the 4ᵗʰ*: Henry IV, known as Henry Bolingbroke (1367–1413), King of England and Lord of Ireland; only son of John of Gaunt, Duke of Lancaster, grandson of Edward III. The first of the Lancastrian monarchs, Henry IV reigned from 1399 to 1413.

the rest of his Life . . . Pomfret Castle: Richard died three months later, aged 33, having been forced to abdicate in Sept. 1399. He was imprisoned in Pontefract Castle, a remote Norman fortress in Yorkshire.

happened to be murdered: Goldsmith reports this royal assassination as among 'the most horrid crimes' (*History of England*, ii, 153); in *Richard II*, Shakespeare depicts the murder, and Henry's guilt thereafter (act 5, scenes 5–6). On the comic use of 'happened' to cover up a crime, cf. 'Love and Friendship': 'Sophia happening one Day to open a private Drawer in Macdonald's Library with one of her own keys, discovered that it was the Place where he kept his Papers of consequence & amongst them some bank-notes of considerable amount' (p. 85).

Henry was married . . . who was his Wife: Shakespeare's *Henry IV*, on which JA is presumably relying, does not mention his queen in *Part 1* or *Part 2*; Goldsmith, however, reports that 'by his first wife, Mary de Bohun, Henry IV had four sons . . . and two daughters. By his second wife he had no issue' (*History of England*, ii, 174).

long speech . . . still longer: see *Henry IV, Part 2* (act 4, scene 5).

beat Sir William Gascoigne: William Gascoigne (*c.* 1350–1419), chief justice of the king's bench. The incident reported by JA appears in Goldsmith's *History of England*: 'the prince was so exasperated . . . that he struck the judge in open court'; the magistrate 'immediately ordered the prince to be committed to prison' (ii, 171–2). It is also discussed in *Henry IV, Part 2* (act 5, scene 2). JA may be recalling *The Loiterer*, no. 43, in which a correspondent called Bluster writes that 'The brightest aeras of our History have been equally distinguished for Battles and Boxing Matches; for beating our Enemies abroad, and threshing our Friends at home. Henry the Vth, who afterwards gave the French so many *Cross-Buttocks*, first began practising against one of the Judges in England, and laid in a blow so neatly, that his Lordship, it seems, could neither *stop* nor *return* it' (5).

122 *Henry the 5ʰ*: Henry V (1386–1422), King of England and Lord of Ireland, eldest son of Henry IV and his first wife, Mary, reigned from 1413 to 1422. He is the only monarch whom Cassandra depicts in military dress, and Agincourt is the only battle mentioned in 'The History of England'. Cassandra's portrait resembles in style H. W. Bunbury's satirical military prints 'The Recruits' (1780) and 'The Relief' (1781), but Henry V is wearing the uniform of his namesake Henry Austen, then aged 21 and serving in the Royal Regiment of Artillery (see *Love and Freindship*, ed. Alexander, pp. xxiv–xxvi, 412 n.).

forsaking all his dissipated Companions: Goldsmith records Henry's renunciation of 'his former companions' (*History of England*, ii, 176), an episode that is famously dramatized in *Henry IV, Part 2* (act 5, scene 5).

Lord Cobham . . . burnt alive: John Oldcastle, Baron Cobham (d. 1417), soldier and rebel, executed for heresy and treason; he was probably Shakespeare's model for Falstaff. Goldsmith, narrating his execution, writes that 'He was hung up with a chain by the middle; and thus at a slow fire burned, or rather roasted, alive' (*History of England*, ii, 179).

turned his thoughts to France: cf. the king's words in *Henry V*: 'For we have no thought in us but France' (act 1, scene 2).

famous Battle of Azincourt: referring, briefly, to the momentous English victory over the French at Agincourt (JA uses the French spelling, 'Azincourt') on St Crispin's Day, 25 Oct. 1415; this battle lies at the heart of Shakespeare's *Henry V*.

Catherine . . . Shakespear's account: Catherine of Valois (1401–37), daughter of the French king Charles VI, was Queen consort of England from 1420 until 1422. On her multiply 'agreable' nature—she is likeable, kisses the king, and consents to marry him—see Shakespeare's *Henry V* (act 5, scene 2).

123 *Henry the 6ʰ . . . this Monarch's Sense*: Henry VI (1421–71), King of England and Lord of Ireland, the only child of Henry V and Catherine of Valois. He came to the throne as a 1-year-old in 1422, and ruled in person from the age of 16. Naturally unsuited to govern, in 1453 he suffered a severe mental and physical collapse and was left helpless. In Goldsmith's account, the attack on his health 'so far encreased his natural imbecility that it even rendered him incapable of maintaining the appearance of royalty' (*History of England*, ii, 223). Cassandra depicts him in clerical attire, perhaps signalling his lack of involvement in worldly affairs.

Duke of York . . . right side: JA backs the Yorkists in the civil war that raged across England in the latter half of the 15th century (the emblem of the Yorkists was the white rose, that of the Lancastrians the red). Henry VI was descended from John of Gaunt, Duke of Lancaster, the son of Edward III. JA sees his claim to the throne as weaker than that of Richard, Duke of York, who was descended from Lionel, Duke of Clarence, John of Gaunt's older brother. But her flagrant bias towards the Yorkists stems from her declared hatred of the Tudors, especially Elizabeth I.

123 *my Spleen*: variously regarded as the seat of laughter, melancholy, caprice,
jest, and anger (all of which are involved in JA's 'History'), 'spleen' in this
context refers primarily to the 'Violent ill-nature or ill-humour; irritable
or peevish temper' (*OED*) that JA, as a 'partial, prejudiced, & ignorant
Historian', plans to express ('vent') at will. Venting spleen was often associated with women; see e.g. *The Anchoret. A Moral Tale, in a Series of Letters*,
3 vols. (1773): 'I would vent a little female spleen' (iii, 181).

Margaret of Anjou . . . pity her: Margaret (1430–82), daughter of the Duke
of Anjou, who married Henry VI in 1445. This was the first of her many
'distresses & Misfortunes', which included the death of her only son, Prince
Edward, in the Battle of Tewkesbury (1471), when she was taken prisoner
by the victorious Yorkists. In 1475, she was ransomed by her cousin, King
Louis XI of France; she died in poverty aged 52. Shakespeare depicts her
as wicked, clever, and ruthless in *Henry VI*, *Part 1*, but in Goldsmith's
account 'this extraordinary woman' is said to deserve 'our pity' for 'her
courage and her distress' (*History of England*, ii, 246).

Joan of Arc . . . such a row: Joan of Arc (*c.*1412–31), a teenage peasant
girl who accompanied and inspired the French forces to a great victory
over the English in 1429. Captured by the English, she was tried for heresy and sentenced to burn at the stake in 1431. Shakespeare portrays
her in *Henry VI*, *Part 1* as rude, noisy, and unrepentant, qualities which
may have prompted JA to use the 'very low expression' (Johnson's
Dictionary) 'made such a row'. Cf. *The Loiterer*, no. 12 (p. 12), and Grose's
Classical Dictionary: 'ROW, a disturbance. A term used by the students at
Cambridge'.

The King was murdered—The Queen was sent home: see *Henry VI*, *Part 3*
(act 5, scenes 6–7).

*Edward the 4*th *. . . Picture we have here given of him*: Edward IV (1442–83),
King of England and Lord of Ireland, was born at Rouen, Normandy,
on 28 Apr. 1442, the second surviving child and eldest son of Richard, 3rd
Duke of York, and Cecily, Duchess of York. He reigned from 1461 to 1470
and from 1471 to 1483. JA echoes Goldsmith, who singles out Edward's
'courage and beauty' as his 'best qualities' (*History of England*, ii, 250);
Cassandra's portrait of a dumpy, ill-favoured man, comically at odds with
the text, seems to be inspired by H. W. Bunbury's caricature 'The Recruits'
(see note to p. 122), a source also for her image of Henry V. Christine
Alexander detects an additional likeness to the Austens' cousin Edward
Cooper (*Love and Freindship*, ed. Alexander, 415 n.).

marrying one Woman while he was engaged to another: in 1464, while his
council finalized arrangements for his marriage to Bona of Savoy, sister-
in-law of Louis XVI, Edward IV secretly married Elizabeth Woodville
(1437–92), widow of Sir John Grey. Cf. the double engagement in 'Frederic &
Elfrida'. Edward IV's namesake Edward Ferrars, in *S&S*, is engaged
to one woman (Lucy Steele) while hoping to marry another (Elinor
Dashwood).

poor Woman! . . . *Henry the 7th*: after Edward's death, Elizabeth was deprived of her estates and removed to Bermondsey, a monastery on the banks of the Thames where she died in 1492.

Jane Shore . . . *a play written about her*: in his highly popular *Tragedy of Jane Shore: Written in Imitation of Shakespeare's Style* (1714), Nicholas Rowe dramatizes the king's seduction of the beautiful young wife of a goldsmith. The play, still performed regularly in the 1790s, consists chiefly of domestic scenes and private distress: a repentant Jane Shore is forgiven; her husband is praised because he is merciful. Goldsmith echoes Rowe in his treatment of Shore as an 'unfortunate woman . . . deluded from her husband . . . the most guiltless mistress in [Edward's] abandoned court. She was ever known to intercede for the distressed, and was usually applied to as a mediator for mercy' (*History of England*, ii, 257–8).

124 *Edward the 5th* . . . *picture*: Goldsmith's *History of England* includes a portrait of Edward V (1470–83), eldest son of Edward IV, who succeeded his father in 1483 at the age of 12, but was deposed, imprisoned in the Tower of London with his brother, and disappeared in questionable circumstances two months later. The most favoured explanation for the brothers' disappearance, now as in JA's lifetime, is that they were murdered on the order of Richard III, late in the summer of 1483, to pre-empt a rising in their favour (see note below to p. 124). Cassandra may not have provided an illustration, but JA apparently expected her to do so as she left space for one in the manuscript, subtitling it 'Edward th' (subsequently deleted; see Textual Notes, p. 232).

Richard the 3d . . . *very respectable Man*: Richard III (1452–85), King of England and Lord of Ireland, was the youngest surviving child of Richard, 3rd Duke of York, and Cecily, Duchess of York, and reigned from 1483 to 1485. There was an Austen family joke about the respectability of anyone called Richard; in a letter of 15 Sept. 1796, JA writes: 'Mr Richard Harvey's match is put off, till he has got a Better Christian name, of which he has great Hopes' (*Letters*, 10); cf. *NA*: 'Her father was a clergyman, without being neglected, or poor, and a very respectable man, though his name was Richard' (ch. 1).

he did not kill his two Nephews: on the death of his brother Edward IV, Richard deprived his two nephews of their rights to the throne and had himself proclaimed king. Whether he was guilty of ordering the boys' murder was disputed in the 18th century; see e.g. Horace Walpole's defence of Richard in *Historic Doubts on the Life and Reign of King Richard the Third* (1768), a work that he went on to repudiate in 1793. Cf. 'Kitty, or the Bower', in which the heroine and Edward Stanley participate in a 'historical dispute' about Richard III's character (p. 198).

I am inclined to believe true: by swiftly gainsaying her own confident assertion that Edward V was murdered on his uncle's orders, JA contrives to endorse both Richard's supporters and his opponents.

124 *he did not kill his Wife*: in Shakespeare's *Richard III* (act 4, scene 2), and in Goldsmith's *History of England*, ii, 270, the king is described as plotting the death of his wife, Anne Neville, in 1485.

Perkin Warbeck . . . Duke of York: during the reign of Henry VII, Warbeck claimed to be Richard, Duke of York, one of the princes in the tower (see notes above to p. 124); in 1497, he confessed his imposture. He was executed two years later.

Lambert Simnel . . . Widow of Richard: during the reign of Henry VII, Simnel claimed to be Edward, Earl of Warwick, son of the Duke of Clarence and therefore the nephew of Richard III and Edward IV. JA's portrayal of Simnel as a widow is another instance of gender reversal; see 'Edgar & Emma', note to p. 25.

Henry Tudor E. of Richmond . . . getting the Crown: Henry, Earl of Richmond, derived his claim to the throne from his mother, Margaret Beaufort, great-granddaughter of John of Gaunt (third son of Edward III). Henry VII (1457–1509) reigned from 1485 to 1509; he was the first of the Tudor monarchs, whose line culminated in the reign of 'wicked' Elizabeth I.

battle of Bosworth: the last major battle of the War of the Roses, in Aug. 1485, in which Richard III was defeated and slain, and Henry VII took the throne. It is the climax of Shakespeare's *Richard III* (act 5, scenes 3–5).

125 *Princess Elizabeth of York*: Princess Elizabeth (1466–1503), daughter of Edward IV, was married to Henry in Jan. 1486, thereby uniting the two Houses of York and Lancaster. This, as JA recognizes, was a shrewd move; Henry's claim to the throne was tenuous and the marriage to Elizabeth gave him credibility.

happiness of being grandmother: parodying the tendency in Whig histories to look forwards, reading historical events in terms of their future significance. Henry VII's elder daughter, Margaret Tudor, married James IV of Scotland in 1503; their granddaughter and JA's great favourite, Mary Stuart, Queen of Scots, was born in 1542, a year after Margaret's death.

the D. of Suffolk: the Duke of Suffolk. Lady Jane Grey's mother, Frances Grey, Duchess of Suffolk, was the second child and eldest daughter of Henry VIII's sister Mary and Charles Brandon, 1st Duke of Suffolk.

amiable young woman . . . hunting: 'amiable' is a standard epithet for Lady Jane Grey (1537–54) in 18th-century history and fiction (also applied to Anne Boleyn in the next section of JA's 'History'); see e.g. Joseph Collyer, *The History of England, from the Invasion of Julius Cæsar, to the Dissolution of the Present Parliament*, 14 vols. (1774–5), vii, 146; Charles Coote, *The History of England, from the Earliest Dawn of Record to the Peace of MDCCLXXXIII*, 9 vols. (1791), v, 190; *Lady Jane Grey: An Historical Tale*, 2 vols. (1791), ii, 106; Thomas Gibbons, *The Life & Death of Lady Jane Grey* (1792), 13, 21, 56. See also 'Frederic & Elfrida', note to p. 4. Goldsmith describes Lady Jane as 'the wonder of her age', fond of 'reading

Plato's works in Greek, while the rest of the family were hunting in the Park' (*History of England*, iii, 36). See also note to p. 128.

taken into the Kings kitchen: cf. Hume's *History of England*: 'He was pardoned, and made a scullion in the King's kitchen' ('Henry VII', ch. 24); Goldsmith's *History of England* follows Hume's text almost exactly (ii, 286).

126 *Henry the 8th*: Henry VIII (1491–1547), King of England and Ireland from 1509 to 1547, the second surviving son of Henry VII and his wife, Elizabeth. Cassandra's image pokes fun at him, partly through his incongruous moustache and tasselled red nightcap, a fashionable daytime accessory in the 1780s (cf. 'french net nightcap' in 'A beautiful description of the different effects of Sensibility on different Minds', note to p. 63). The image may recall popular caricatures of the Whig politician Charles James Fox (see *Love and Freindship*, ed. Alexander, 417 n.).

a slight sketch of the principal Events: standard phrasing in historical narratives; cf. 'For the clearer understanding of the modern history of this country, . . . it is necessary to give a slight sketch of the principal events which occurred in the year 1787' (*The Historical Magazine, Or, Classical Library of Public Events*, 5 vols. (1789), i, 14).

come to lay his bones among them: see 'Love and Friendship', note to p. 87; in Goldsmith's *History of England*, the cardinal is said to have announced on his arrival at Leicester Abbey, where he died, 'Father abbot, I am come to lay my bones among you' (ii, 361). Cf. also Hume's *History of England*, 'Henry VIII', ch. 30, which gives this speech indirectly. JA combines the two, keeping Goldsmith's speech marks but using Hume's third-person voice.

Anna Bullen . . . Crimes with which she was accused: Anne Boleyn (*c.*1507–36), Queen of England, second consort of Henry VIII, and mother of Elizabeth I. She married Henry in 1533, but fell out of favour and was charged with adultery, committed to the Tower of London, and beheaded on 19 May 1536. Her name is given in the form 'Anna Bullen' in both Shakespeare's *Henry VIII* and Goldsmith's *History of England* (1771), but not in Hume's *History of England*.

6th of May: Goldsmith's *History of England*, following Hume's *History of England* ('Henry VIII', ch. 31), reproduces in full a letter from Anne Boleyn to the king in which she protests her innocence and concludes 'From my doleful prison in the Tower, this sixth of May' (ii, 384). JA draws attention to the fact that this date, one of only two included in Goldsmith's *History of England*, has no year attached to it.

Crimes & Cruelties of this Prince: see Goldsmith's *History of England* (1771): 'Henry was cruel from a depraved disposition alone; cruel in government, cruel in religion, and cruel in his family' (ii, 418). Cf. the more extensive catalogue of Henry's virtues and vices in Hume's *History of England*, 'Henry VIII', ch. 33.

abolishing Religious Houses: the dissolution or suppression of religious houses was carried out by a series of administrative and legal processes, set in train between 1536 and 1541, which allowed Henry VIII to disband Catholic monasteries, priories, convents, and friaries in England, Wales, and Ireland, appropriate their income, and dispose of their assets; see Goldsmith, *History of England*, ii, 373–4. Henry won the authority to do this in England and Wales through the Act of Supremacy, passed by Parliament in 1534, which made him Supreme Head of the Church in England, thus separating England from papal authority, and by the First Suppression Act (1536) and the Second Suppression Act (1539).

127 *infinite use to the landscape of England in general*: JA refers to the widespread contemporary enthusiasm for visiting and reading about medieval and monastic ruins, an enthusiasm stoked by the kind of gothic fiction that Catherine Morland enjoys reading in *NA* and by William Gilpin's accounts of his various tours (see 'The three Sisters', note to p. 58). Gilpin's definition of the picturesque was founded on an appreciation of ruined abbeys and monasteries. As he noted in *Observations, Relative Chiefly to Picturesque Beauty, Made in the Year 1772, On Several Parts of England; Particularly the Mountains, and Lakes of Cumberland, and Westmoreland*, 2 vols. (1786), 'In the ruins of castles . . . other countries may compare with ours. But in the remains of abbeys no country certainly can . . . the Gothic style, in which they are generally composed, is, I apprehend, unrivalled among foreign nations; and may be called a peculiar feature in English landscape' (i, 13).

5ᵗʰ Wife . . . led an abandoned Life before her Marriage: Catherine Howard (*c.*1521–42), niece of Thomas Howard, 3rd Duke of Norfolk and cousin of Anne Boleyn. She was executed less than two years after marrying Henry VIII. Goldsmith writes that Catherine 'confessed her incontinence before marriage, but denied her having dishonoured the king's bed since their union' (*History of England*, ii, 402).

noble Duke of Norfolk: Thomas Howard, 4th Duke of Norfolk (1538–72), son of the poet Henry Howard, Earl of Surrey, and grandson of the 3rd Duke of Norfolk; he was the wealthiest landowner in the country and for some years a favourite courtier of Elizabeth I. She imprisoned him in 1569 for scheming to marry Mary, Queen of Scots. Following his release, he was accused of involvement in the so-called Ridolfi plot of 1571, with Philip II of Spain, to put Mary, Queen of Scots, on the English throne and restore Catholicism in England. He was executed for treason in 1572. (See Hume's *History of England*, 'Elizabeth', ch. 41.) Southam suggests that JA may be covertly alluding to Sophia Lee's *The Recess*, in which Mary and Norfolk secretly marry (*Volume the Second*, ed. B. C. Southam (Oxford: Clarendon Press, 1963), 215).

The kings last wife: Katherine or Catherine Parr (1512–48), sixth consort of Henry VIII. Hume calls her 'a woman of virtue' (*History of England*, 'Henry VIII', ch. 33), Goldsmith 'a woman of discretion and virtue', who 'managed this capricious tyrant's temper with prudence and success' (Goldsmith, *History of England*, ii, 406). She 'contrived to survive' the king, as JA notes, only to die a year later after giving birth to a daughter.

Edward the 6ᵗʰ . . . during his minority: Edward VI (1537–53), King of England and Ireland, the first and only legitimate son of Henry VIII, came to the throne as a 9-year-old and died aged 15. Full power and authority during his minority—that is, until his eighteenth birthday—supposedly fell to a council comprising the sixteen executors of his father's will. Even before Henry VIII's death, Edward Seymour (*c.*1500–1552), Duke of Somerset and uncle of Edward VI, and Sir William Paget, the king's secretary, had decided to ignore the will and arrange for Somerset's preferment as protector of the realm and governor of Edward's person. Cassandra's portrait of Edward does not portray a child; Alexander argues that it is probably a likeness of JA's rich older brother Edward (see *Love and Freindship*, ed. Alexander, 419 n.).

those first of Men Robert Earl of Essex, Delamere, or Gilpin: Robert Devereux, 2nd Earl of Essex (1565–1601), was an English nobleman, general, and sometime favourite of Elizabeth I. Dashing and politically ambitious, he was placed under house arrest following a poor campaign in Ireland during the Nine Years' War in 1599. In 1601, he led an abortive *coup d'état* against the government and was executed for treason. Charlotte Smith's Frederic Delamere, hero of *Emmeline* (1788), with whom Essex is again compared in the next section of JA's 'History', is equally handsome, ardent, and doomed. William Gilpin, like Samuel Johnson, felt some of JA's passionate attachment to Mary, Queen of Scots (see *Observations, Relative Chiefly to Picturesque Beauty*, i, 92).

127–8 *He was beheaded . . . the manner of it*: see note to p. 125; here, too, JA parodies the Whig tendency to read past events in terms of their future significance.

the Duke of Northumberland: see Goldsmith's account of the jockeying for power between John Dudley, Duke of Northumberland and Somerset, whose downfall and execution Northumberland had engineered (*History of England*, iii, 25–9). He arranged for his son to marry Lady Jane Grey, whom he proclaimed queen against her will on the death of Edward VI. She and her husband were found guilty of treason and beheaded in 1554.

reading Greek . . . excess of vanity: Jane showed early promise of exceptional academic ability; sent to join the household of the widowed queen, Katherine Parr, in 1547, she benefited from educational opportunities then available in court circles for girls as well as boys. JA mocks this seeming paragon of virtue and learning—perhaps in part because she is called Jane (cf. the treatment of perfect Jane Fairfax in *E*). The word 'vanity' was originally the much lower, colloquial '*Cockylorum*' (also spelled 'cockalorum' and 'cockolorum'), meaning 'Little or young cock, bantam; self-important little man' (*OED*); 'cocky' means 'arrogantly pert' (*OED*) and can be applied to a man or a woman (see Textual Notes, p. 232).

conducting to the Scaffold . . . passing that way: Jane and her husband Guildford were executed on 12 Feb. 1554. Cf. *History of England*: 'the lady Jane was conducting to the place of execution'; 'she had just written three sentences on seeing her husband's dead body, one in Greek, one in Latin, and one in English, importing, that she hoped God and posterity would do him and their cause justice'. Goldsmith's handling of the executions is at once more lurid and more sympathetic than JA's, mentioning Guildford's 'headless body . . . streaming with blood' but seeing Lady Jane's lack of visible emotion as evidence of 'heroic resolution' rather than of indifference or affectation (*History of England*, iii, 49–50). See also Hume's *History of England*, 'Mary', ch. 36.

128 *Mary*: Mary I, also known as Mary Tudor (1516–58), daughter of Henry VIII and Katherine of Aragon, Queen of England and Ireland from 1553 to 1558. With her husband, Philip, heir to the Spanish throne, her chief objective was to restore Catholicism to England. Alexander suggests that Cassandra's 'rather frumpish image' of Mary could represent the Austens' friend Mary Lloyd (see 'Frederic & Elfrida', note to p. 2; *Love and Freindship*, ed. Alexander, 420 n.).

128–9 *Martyrs to the protestant Religion . . . not fewer than a dozen*: during her 5-year reign, Mary repealed the religious legislation that had been introduced by her half-brother, Edward VI, returning the English Church to Roman jurisdiction and resulting in the exile or execution of many Protestants. Parliament also restored the old heresy laws. Eventually, nearly three hundred Protestants were burned at the stake in the reign of 'Bloody Mary', as Goldsmith notes (*History of England*, iii, 62).

129 *Philip . . . Armadas*: Mary and Philip (1527–98) married in 1554; he became King of Spain in 1566. In 1588, when Elizabeth I was on the throne, the English defeated Philip's Spanish Armada—a fleet of more than one hundred warships—thwarting his planned invasion of the country to reinstate Catholicism.

Elizabeth: Elizabeth I (1533–1603), Queen of England and Ireland, only child of Henry VIII and Anne Boleyn. She reigned from 1558 to 1603. Hume credits her with 'vigour', 'constancy', 'magnanimity', 'penetration, vigilance, address' (*History of England*, 'Elizabeth', ch. 44); Goldsmith calls her 'prudent, active, and discerning', 'wise and good' (*History of England*, iii, 152–3). Cassandra's portrait of Elizabeth I has been identified as that of JA's mother Cassandra Leigh Austen; that of the young and beautiful Mary, Queen of Scots, on the facing page and also in formal attire, may be intended as a likeness of JA (see *Love and Freindship*, ed. Alexander, pp. xxiv–xxv). In his prologue to Susanna Centlivre's *The Wonder: A Woman Keeps a Secret!* (see 'Henry & Eliza', note to p. 27), James Austen mocked Elizabeth's 'ugliness & dress' (l. 27).

Misfortune of this Woman to have bad Ministers: a direct contradiction of Goldsmith, who writes that Elizabeth 'was indebted to her good fortune, that her ministers were excellent' (*History of England*, iii, 152). Cf. the dispute about Elizabeth in 'Kitty, or the Bower' (p. 175).

Lord Burleigh, Sir Francis Walsingham: William Cecil (1520–98), created Lord Burleigh (or Burghley) in 1571, served for two terms as Elizabeth's secretary of state and, for the great part of her reign, as her most trusted adviser. Sir Francis Walsingham (*c.*1532–90) was the queen's principal secretary and privy councillor, popularly remembered as her spymaster. Both men were heavily implicated in the death of Mary, Queen of Scots (1542–87).

130 *Mr Whitaker, Mrs Lefroy, Mrs Knight*: John Whitaker (1735–1808), historian and author of *Mary Queen of Scots Vindicated* (1787), which championed the cause of Mary and incriminated her enemies, particularly Elizabeth (a 2nd edn was published in 1790); Anne Lefroy, née Bridges (1749–1804), wife of the rector of Ashe, near Steventon, a close friend of JA and her family; and Catherine Knight, née Knatchbull (1753–1812), Edward Austen's adoptive mother. Gilpin comments in his *Observations Relative Chiefly to Picturesque Beauty* that Whitaker 'hath given the public some new lights on the history of Mary; and thrown the guilt on Elizabeth' (i, 92 n.). Differing interpretations of Mary persisted throughout the 18th century: historians such as William Robertson (in *The History of Scotland. During the reigns of Queen Mary and of King James VI. till his accession to the crown of England*, 2 vols. (1759)) and Hume (in his *History of England*, 'Elizabeth', ch. 42) argued that Mary was guilty of adultery and murder, charges hotly contested by John Whitaker and by William Tytler, author of *An Historical and Critical Enquiry into the Evidence Produced by the Earls of Murray and Morton against Mary, Queen of Scots* (1760), reviewed by Samuel Johnson in the *Gentleman's Magazine* and by Tobias Smollett in the *Critical Review*, and republished five times.

abandoned by her son: James VI and I (1566–1625) was King of Scotland as James VI from 24 July 1567—when Mary, Queen of Scots, was compelled to abdicate in his favour and to appoint her illegitimate half-brother as regent—and King of England and Ireland as James I from the union of the Scottish and English crowns on 24 Mar. 1603 until his death. He was the only son of Mary and her second husband, Lord Darnley. Reared a Protestant and anxious to safeguard his own right to the succession, he made only perfunctory efforts to save his mother from execution.

Fotheringay Castle . . . 1586: Fotheringay was a heavily fortified medieval castle in Nottinghamshire, in which Mary was imprisoned for nineteen years until her execution on 8 Feb. 1587 (JA gives the wrong year—1586).

Sir Francis Drake . . . now but young: Francis Drake (1540–96), the greatest sailor of his age, completed the second circumnavigation of the world in a single expedition, from 1577 to 1580, and was the first to undertake it as captain and leader throughout. Elizabeth I awarded Drake a knighthood in 1581; in 1588, he was second-in-command of the English fleet against the Spanish Armada. In another parodic treatment of historical events as a means to predict inevitable future occurrences, JA flatters her brother Francis, Drake's namesake, that he will equal such legendary exploits. Francis Austen went on to become Rear Admiral and Admiral of the Fleet, and to be knighted.

130–1 *Lord Essex . . . Delamere*: Essex, like Delamere, is daring and impetuous; both men could be viewed as the servants and tormentors of the women they purportedly love. Delamere pursues and abducts Emmeline, demanding that she marry him; when she breaks off their engagement, Delamere dies in a duel. Essex's reckless and treasonable behaviour culminated in a rebellion and his execution. See note to p. 127.

25ᵗʰ of Feb.ʳʸ: as with the letter from Anne Boleyn (see note to p. 126), JA omits the year—1601.

clapped his hand on his Sword: cf. *History of England*, in which Goldsmith reported that Essex 'turned his back on the queen in a contemptuous fashion' and 'she gave him a box on the ear'; Essex then 'clapped his hand to his sword; and swore he would not bear such usage even from her father. This offence, though very great, was overlooked by the queen' (iii, 139).

died so miserable: Elizabeth died in Mar. 1603, two years after Essex was beheaded; Goldsmith writes that, 'With the death of her favourite Essex, all Elizabeth's pleasures seemed to expire' (*History of England*, iii, 150).

James the 1ˢᵗ: Alexander suggests that the model for Cassandra's image of James as a well-dressed young gentleman may have been her brother James (*Love and Freindship*, 422 n.).

allowing his Mother's death: see note to p. 130.

Anne of Denmark: James married Anne of Denmark (1574–1619) in 1589.

died before his father . . . his unfortunate Brother: Prince Henry died aged 18 in 1612, 13 years before the death of his father. The fate of Henry's 'unfortunate Brother', Charles I, is recounted in the last section of JA's 'History', the 'evils which befell' him being a protracted and bloody civil war, imprisonment, trial, and (in 1649) a public execution.

I am . . . partial to the roman catholic religion: JA boldly reverses the Protestant bias typically displayed by 18th-century historians, and the expected allegiances of an Anglican clergyman's daughter.

Their Behaviour . . . very uncivil: alluding to the Gunpowder Plot (1605), in which a group of Catholic conspirators including Guy Fawkes (*c.*1570–1606) hoped to explode 'the king and both houses of parliament at a blow' (*History of England*, iii, 164). But the plan was exposed when the Catholic peer William Parker, 4th Baron Monteagle (1575–1622), received an anonymous letter, warning him not to attend Parliament on the intended day of the explosion, and passed it on to the secretary of state. JA follows Goldsmith in identifying the author of the letter as Sir Henry Percy (*History of England*, iii, 166–7).

132 *Attentions . . . Confined to Lord Mounteagle*: JA picks up on Goldsmith's description of Percy and Monteagle, which hints at a sexual relationship as well as a shared religion: 'his intimate friend and companion, who also was of the same persuasion with himself' (*History of England*, iii, 167).

Sir Walter Raleigh: Walter Raleigh or Ralegh (1554–1618), celebrated courtier, scholar, author, explorer, and favourite of Elizabeth I, knighted in

1585. He testified against his sometime ally the Earl of Essex at the trial that ended in Essex's execution; Raleigh himself was imprisoned for the first 13 years of James I's reign, set free to lead an expedition in search of gold in South America, and arrested, tried, and executed on his return in 1618.

the particulars of his Life . . . the Critic: cf. references to Sheridan's *The Critic* in 'Frederic & Elfrida' (see note to p. 3) and 'The Mystery' (see notes to pp. 49 and 50). *The Critic* features a rehearsal of Mr Puff's tragedy *The Spanish Armada*; Sir Walter Raleigh and Sir Christopher Hutton appear as characters in this absurd play-within-a-play.

amiable disposition . . . keener penetration in Discovering Merit: a bold *double entendre*, hinting at the king's sexual proclivities and tendency to promote good-looking young men to positions of wealth and status.

Sharade: or charade, 'A kind of riddle in which each syllable of a word, or a complete word or phrase, is enigmatically described, or (now more usually) dramatically represented (in early use often more fully *acted charade*), sometimes in mime (more fully *dumb charade*); a game of presenting and solving such riddles' (*OED*). Popular in JA's family, charades survive by her mother, sister, four of her brothers, and by JA herself. See also the charade in *E*, ch. 9.

My first is . . . my whole: another bold joke about the king's sexual preferences, this charade depicts Sir Robert Carr (1590–1645) as the favourite, or 'pet', of James I, hence 'car-pet'. The son of a Scottish nobleman, Carr was made Viscount Rochester in 1611, privy councillor in 1612 and Earl of Somerset and treasurer of Scotland in 1613.

Duke of Buckingham: the beautiful and corrupt George Villiers (1592–1628), who succeeded Carr as the king's favourite (James called him Steenie, a diminutive of Stephen, since St Stephen, according to the Bible, had a face like an angel). In 1619 he became Lord Admiral of the navy, exploiting his position to amass vast power and wealth for himself. His influence on the court persisted after the death of James I. He was impeached in 1626, accused of holding too many offices; of delivering English ships into French hands for use against the Huguenots; of selling honours and offices; of procuring titles for his relatives; and, finally, of poisoning James I. Rather than allow the impeachment to run its course, Charles I dissolved Parliament. Buckingham was assassinated in a public house in 1628. Writing about James I and Buckingham, Goldsmith notes cautiously that 'The history of these times . . . does not however insinuate anything flagitious in these connexions, but imputes his attachment rather to a weakness of understanding, than to any perversion of appetite' (*History of England*, iii, 178). In *The Ladies History of England; from the Descent of Julius Cæsar, to the Summer of 1780* ([1780–81]), Charlotte Cowley, by contrast, expresses some aversion towards James's 'peculiar weakness' and susceptibility to attractive young men (302, 304).

132–3 *Charles the 1ˢᵗ . . . his lovely Grandmother*: Charles I (1600–49), grandson of Mary, Queen of Scots, reigned from 1625 to 1649, when he was executed for 'high treason' following the victory of Thomas Fairfax and Oliver Cromwell's New Model Army over Royalist forces in the Civil War. JA's family remembered her vehement defence of Charles I (*Memoir*, 71, 173); her pro-Stuart marginalia in Goldsmith's *History of England* begin at the passage discussing the reign of Charles I, the rise of Cromwell, and the Civil War (see *Juvenilia*, Appendix B).

133 *Archbishop Laud . . . Ormond*: William Laud (1573–1645), Archbishop of Canterbury, accused of treason and imprisoned in the early stages of the Civil War, was executed in 1645, despite being granted a royal pardon. Sir Thomas Wentworth (1593–1641), 1st Earl of Strafford and leader of the House of Commons, attempted to strengthen the royal position against Parliament and was executed in 1641. Lucius Cary (1609/10–43), politician and author, sat in the House of Commons from 1640 to 1642, fought on the Royalist side, and was killed in action at the First Battle of Newbury. James Butler (1610–88), 1st Duke of Ormonde, commanded the Royalist forces in Ireland. Sir Thomas Wentworth was a remote ancestor of JA's mother, Cassandra Leigh; the surname Wentworth is given to the sailor hero of *P*.

Cromwell . . . Pym: cf. hostile references to Cromwell and Hampden in JA's marginalia to *History of England* (see *Juvenilia*, Appendix B). Oliver Cromwell (1599–1658), Parliamentarian and supporter of the regicide, governed the republican Commonwealth of England, Scotland, and Ireland as Lord Protector from 1653 until his death. Thomas Fairfax (1612–71) commanded the parliamentary forces in the Civil War; John Hampden (1594–1643), politician and Parliamentarian colonel, was killed at the Battle of Chalgrove in June 1643; and John Pym (1583–1643), politician, created the administrative machinery to run the Parliamentarian war effort.

[COLLECTION OF LETTERS]

134 *Collection of Letters*: a popular title in the 18th century, attached to works of epistolary fiction, to letter-writing manuals, and to historical and biographical anthologies of letters. In its preoccupation with young ladies' innocence and experience, the need for instruction, their entrances into the world, and with names and namelessness, 'Collection of Letters' seems to be recalling Burney's *Evelina* (see also note to p. 138).

Miss Cooper: Jane Cooper, JA's cousin (see 'Henry & Eliza', note to p. 27). Given the use of her maiden name, this must pre-date her marriage in Dec. 1792 to Captain Williams.

Clime: 'Contracted from *climate* and therefore properly poetical' (Johnson's *Dictionary*).

Curious: 'Exquisite, choice, excellent, fine' as well as 'Deserving or exciting attention on account of its novelty or peculiarity; exciting curiosity; somewhat surprising, strange, singular, odd; queer' (*OED*). JA's alliterative list recalls other *Collections of Letters*: see e.g. 'a curious collection of letters on compliment, business, and several other occasions' in Thomas

Wise, *The Newest Young Man's Companion, Containing a Compendious English Grammar*, 9th edn (1773); *A Curious Collection of Genuine and Authentick Letters* ([1750]); *Elegant Epistles: Or, a Copious Collection of Familiar and Amusing Letters, Selected for the Improvement of Young Persons, and for General Entertainment* ([1790]). Cf. the comic use of alliteration in 'Frederic & Elfrida' ('Patches, Powder, Pomatum & Paint'; and see note to p. 5), and in JA's letter to Cassandra of 9 Feb. 1813: 'Candour & Comfort & Coffee & Cribbage' (*Letters*, 213).

at that age . . . become conversant with the World: JA refers to the rite of passage for genteel young women known as 'coming out', typically occurring in their mid- to late teens. Whether a girl was 'out', taking her place in society and therefore becoming available on the marriage market, was not always clear. See 'Kitty, or the Bower', p. 194; cf. *P&P*, ch. 29; *MP*, ch. 5. See also JA's comment to her niece Anna on 'the madness of otherwise sensible Women, on the subject of their Daughters coming out' (*Letters*, 281).

entrée into Life: here, 'entrée' means the formal entrance into polite society in general (cf. 'The three Sisters', note to p. 60).

drink tea: see 'The three Sisters', note to p. 54.

Morning-Visits: short, formal, pre-dinner social calls (*OED*), made from around noon to 3 p.m. ('morning' was the period between breakfast and dinner).

135 *presided over their infancy*: cf. Louis Mayeul de Chaudon's *Historical and Critical Memoirs of the Life and Writings of M. de Voltaire* (1786): 'Apollo appears to have presided over the infancy of M. de Voltaire' (2). Similar phrasing about a mother appears in another work translated from the French, M. Florian's *Gonzalva of Cordova; or, Grenada Reconquered*, 3 vols. (1793): 'Never could the tenderest of mothers do more for a beloved child. To no one would she confide the care of my earliest infancy; she alone presided over my education' (ii, 72). Although in JA's fictional letter the mother appears to be babying her teenage offspring, 'Civil infancy', as Johnson notes, was 'extended by the English law to one and twenty years' (Johnson's *Dictionary*, 'infancy').

136 *Willoughby . . . Crawfords*: the names at either end of this list are given to major characters in JA's novels: Willoughby in *S&S*, Crawford in *MP*.

Melancholy: 'Sadness, dejection, esp. of a pensive nature; gloominess; pensiveness or introspection; an inclination or tendency to this', with an implication of 'Tender, sentimental, or reflective sadness; sadness giving rise to or considered as a subject for poetry, sentimental reflection, etc.' (*OED*). In the late 18th century, melancholy was increasingly associated with women. Cf. 'Kitty, or the Bower': 'tender and Melancholly recollections . . . at once so sorrowful, yet so soothing!' (p. 170).

Dashwood: another name to appear in JA's mature fiction: the Dashwoods are the central characters in *S&S*.

136 *Sister*: here, sister-in-law.

137 *I am advised to ride by my Physician*: riding was recommended as beneficial
to health, partly because it involved plenty of fresh air. Fanny Price depends
on riding to feel well (*MP*, ch. 7).

'*Ride where you may, Be Candid where You can*': freely adapting Pope's *Essay
on Man* (epistle 1, l. 15): 'Laugh where we *must*, be candid where we *can*'.
To laugh is 'ridere' in Italian and 'rire' in French, which may have encouraged JA to turn 'Laugh' into 'Ride'. In any case, Pope's aphoristic line was
often rewritten, by authors including Oliver Goldsmith in the Epilogue to
The Good-Natur'd Man; George Crabbe, in *Inebriety, A Poem* (1775), pt 3;
and Arthur Murphy, in the prologue to *The Upholsterer; or What News?
A Comedy* (1786).

fighting for his Country in America: that is, fighting on the British side in
the American War of Independence, or the Revolutionary War (1775–83)
between the rebel colonies and the British army.

138 *I could not prevail on myself . . . no right to that of Annesley*: in failing either
to adopt her husband's name or revert to her maiden name, Miss Jane
casts doubt on the validity of her marriage and suggests she may be illegitimate (in which case she would not be entitled to use her father's surname).
Burney's Evelina encounters similar problems, caught between a father
who will not acknowledge her and an invented surname, 'Anville'. Miss
Jane's solution of 'bearing only my Christian [name]' is adopted by Evelina,
who signs herself in letters to her guardian by that name alone.

139 *honour of calling for me in her way . . . sit forwards*: Lady Greville is on her
way to the ball, so the 'honour' costs her little; sitting 'forwards' means
facing the direction of travel. This confers 'a great obligation' on Maria
Williams as it is considered the preferable position.

you know I always speak my mind . . . old striped one: cf. Lady Catherine de
Bourgh in *P&P*, an equally insulting character, who also says 'You know
I always speak my mind' (ch. 37). Lady Greville and Lady Catherine fur-
ther agree on the matter of dress; Mr Collins tells Elizabeth that 'Lady
Catherine will not think the worst of you for being simply dressed. She
likes to have the distinction of rank preserved' (*P&P*, ch. 29).

Candles cost money . . . extravagant: candles made of beeswax rather than
tallow (animal fat) were expensive; cf. Miss Bates on 'the comfort and style'
of having 'Candles every where' at a ball in *E*, ch. 38.

140 *white Gloves*: gentlemen wore white gloves at formal dances.

hop: 'A dance; a dancing-party, esp. of an informal or unceremonious
kind' (*OED*); Lady Greville is belittling Maria, since 'hop' was considered
a vulgar term.

a Grocer or a Bookbinder: both are tradesmen and therefore excluded from
polite society. As a wine-merchant and a wholesaler, Maria's grandfather
would be a cut above a retailer selling directly to individual customers, but
Lady Greville brushes such niceties aside.

broke: became broke, or bankrupt.

as poor as a Rat: a more offensive version of the proverbial phrase 'as poor as a church mouse'.

141 *Kings Bench*: King's Bench Prison in Southwark, south London, took its name from the king's bench court of law, in which cases of defamation, bankruptcy, and other misdemeanours were heard; primarily a debtors' prison.

too saucy: JA revised several parts of this exchange, perhaps because of the uncertainty Maria herself expresses about her possible 'impertinence' (see Textual Notes, p. 234).

umbrella: an insult, since umbrellas were used by those unable to afford carriages, who were therefore compelled to walk in the rain.

shews your legs: altered by JA from 'shews your Ancles'; the revised version involves more flesh and is therefore more offensive (see Textual Notes, p. 234).

142 *the history of her Life . . . what had befallen her*: there is a similar appetite to discover the lives and adventures of strangers in 'Jack & Alice' and 'Love and Friendship' (see notes to pp. 13, 16, 69).

a relation of Mr Evelyn . . . her name was Grenville: the names are reminiscent of Burney's heroine Evelina, and her invented surname Anville (see note to p. 138).

a whispering Conversation: cf. the whispering scene in JA's 'The Mystery', and note to p. 50.

Essex . . . Derbyshire . . . Suffolk: Essex is much closer to Suffolk than it is to Derbyshire, hence Miss Grenville's surprise.

a good dash: a sudden stroke or blow (Johnson's *Dictionary* and *OED*), perhaps with the added implication of 'cutting a dash', or making a showy appearance in company (see also *OED*).

143 *Perfect Felicity . . . uninterrupted Happiness*: commonplace moralizing that often surfaces in novels; see e.g. 'To complain, therefore, that man is not capable of a more perfect felicity, is . . . unreasonable' (Richard Graves, *Columella; or, The Distressed Anchoret. A Colloquial Tale*, 2 vols. (1779), i, 82); 'mortals are not born to perfect felicity!' (*He is Found At Last: or, Memoirs of the Beverley Family*, 2 vols. (1775), i, 89); 'it is not in this life that we are to be truly happy; it is a state of trial, and inconsistent with perfect felicity' (*The Ill Effects of a Rash Vow; A Novel, in a Series of Letters*, 2 vols. (1789), ii, 121). Cf. JA's comment in *NA*: 'we are all hastening together to perfect felicity' (ch. 31).

144 *Musgrove*: A name that reappears in *P* (in which Anne Elliot's sister has married into the Musgrove family), and very similar to Musgrave, which appears in *The Watsons* (Tom Musgrave); the 'T. Musgrove' in this letter also turns out to be called Tom.

Sackville St.: a fashionable London street that branches off Piccadilly. In *S&S*, Marianne and Elinor Dashwood visit 'Gray's', a real jeweller's in Sackville Street (ch. 33).

144 *toasted*: a society beauty could expect to be toasted; that is, to have her health drunk and beauty praised at male gatherings. To be celebrated in this way sometimes compromised a woman's reputation.

You are Venus herself: a ludicrously exaggerated compliment; sentimental and novelistic cant. See e.g. *Cleanthes and Semanthe. A Dramatic History*, 2 vols. (1764): 'The duke declared, he should have supposed Venus herself might have tempted him in vain' (ii, 95); *The Phœnix; or, the History of Polyarchus and Argenis*, 4 vols. (1772): 'O maid, to whom in beauty's bloom would yield | Venus herself' (iii, 72); *Blenheim Lodge, A Novel*, 2 vols. (1787): 'throwing himself gracefully at my feet, swearing by all the gods and goddesses I was ten times more beautiful than Venus herself' (ii, 255). Cf. JA's dedication of 'The beautifull Cassandra': 'You are a Phoenix' (p. 37).

Abandoned: having given oneself up 'without resistance or restraint *to* a passion, emotion, unreasoning impulse, etc.' (*OED*), rather than having been deserted or forsaken.

improvable Estate: here, an estate that might yield more revenue if better managed or cultivated, rather than 'improved' in the sense that Mr Rushworth intends when he considers paying a landscape gardener to alter the appearance of his grounds (*MP*, ch. 6).

145 *a pattern for a Love-letter*: referring to collections of model letters such as those mentioned in the above notes; see also Samuel Richardson's *Letters written to and for Particular Friends on the Most Important Occasions* (1741), a volume reprinted throughout the 18th century which includes many love letters.

unfeigned Love in one Sheet: suggesting Musgrove's straitened circumstances; since paper was expensive, even the most lavish expressions of unfeigned love were prudently confined to no more than a single sheet.

I believe I shall run mad: cf. Sophia's advice in 'Love and Friendship' to 'Run mad as often as you chuse; but do not faint' (p. 90).

Yours for ever & ever: Henrietta should not be answering the letter at all, let alone in such explicit terms; cf. 'Amelia Webster', note to p. 42.

dab: colloquial term for an expert or 'an adept' in any field (*Classical Dictionary*), as in 'a dab hand'. Johnson's *Dictionary* notes that it is 'low language' and 'not used in writing'.

146 *I would give a farthing for*: proverbial language expressing the little value placed on something by the speaker. Henrietta suggests that she would not give even a farthing for any love that was not true (a farthing is a quarter of a penny). Grose cites 'the common expression, I do not care a dam, i.e. I do not care half a farthing for it' (*Classical Dictionary*, 'DAM').

an estate of Several hundreds an year: not an impressive income, especially not for a man hoping to marry an heiress. In *S&S*, the Dashwoods have to live on £500 per year, a figure that (as Fanny Dashwood notes with relish) precludes not only luxury but many home comforts (ch. 2). In 1805, after the Revd George Austen's death, the widowed Mrs Austen and her two daughters had around £450 per annum to live on.

147 *Yes I'm in love I feel it now . . . has undone me*: alluding to the opening lines of William Whitehead's song, 'The *Je ne scai Quoi*': 'Yes, I'm in love, I feel it now, | And CÆLIA has undone me; | And yet I'll swear I can't tell how | The pleasing plague stole on me'. The same verse is referred to in *MP* (ch. 30). It appears in Robert Dodsley's *A Collection of Poems*, ii, 265–6. JA owned a copy of this work (see 'Jack & Alice', note to p. 15; 'Ode to Pity', note to p. 66).

150 *make the pies*: well-to-do young ladies would not be expected to make pies; in *P&P*, Mrs Bennet contrasts her own daughters with Charlotte Lucas, who helps with the mince pies: 'For my part, Mr Bingley, *I* always keep servants that can do their own work; *my* daughters are brought up differently' (ch. 9).

[SCRAPS]

To Miss Fanny Catherine Austen

151 *Fanny Catherine Austen*: Fanny Catherine (Austen) Knight (1793–1882), JA's first niece, eldest daughter of her brother Edward. The writings dedicated to her are called 'Scraps' in the table of Contents for *Volume the Second*, but not in the text itself (cf. the 'Detached peices' dedicated to JA's niece Jane Anna Elizabeth Austen in *Volume the First*).

Rowling & Steventon: Rowling was an estate in east Kent which the Knight family gave to Edward and his wife Elizabeth on their marriage; it was around 100 miles away from JA's home in Steventon, Hampshire.

Opinions & Admonitions on the conduct of Young Women: cf. JA's description of her writings to another niece, Jane Anna Elizabeth Austen, as 'Treatises for your Benefit' containing 'very important Instructions, with regard to your Conduct in Life'. Conduct books or works of advice for young women were popular throughout the 18th century; JA was not the only writer implicitly to criticize or overtly to ridicule them. See e.g. Robert Bage, *Hermsprong; or, Man as He is Not. A Novel*, 3 vols. (1799): 'indeed, it was not necessary for any one to talk but Mrs. Sumelin, whose collection of admonitions, to render young women prudent, is certainly inexhaustible. Oh! could I but call them to mind just at the time of need, there would not be such another discreet girl in all these parts' (i, 154).

The female philosopher

female philosopher: for many writers of the period, the notion of a female philosopher was inherently absurd; the phrase is deployed scornfully and fearfully in some novels and conduct book literature for women. See e.g. *The Exemplary Mother: or, Letters between Mrs. Villars and her Family*, new edn (1784): 'A female philosopher! Defend us from petticoat innovators!' (i, 98). Those who supported advances in education for women, however, used the term 'female philosopher' without satiric or critical intent; see e.g. David Fordyce, *Dialogues Concerning Education*, 2 vols., 4th edn (1755), ii, 95–6. The target of JA's work seems primarily to be epistolary and educational collections for young women such as *Ideal Trifles. Published by a Lady* (1774), in which the commonplace and superficial moralizing of a would-be 'female Philosopher' is represented as novel, elegant, and striking, combined with reflections on the fashionable habits of the '*beau monde*' (90–1).

151 *Sallies, Bonmots & repartées*: lively, bold witticisms and clever retorts; a 'sally' is a 'Flight; volatile or sprightly exertion' (Johnson's *Dictionary*); see 'Lesley-Castle', notes to p. 97.

Sentiments of Morality: moral reflections, typically those expressed in writing and of a proverbial nature, therefore ready to be extracted and repeated (cf. Mary Bennet's fondness for such 'sentiments' and 'sensible reflections' in *P&P*, ch. 2). In *The History of Women, from the Earliest Antiquity, to the Present Time*, 2 vols. (1779), William Alexander observes that the education of Roman girls 'had always a tendency . . . to inspire them with sentiments of morality' (i, 40).

152 *social Shake, & cordial kiss*: a handshake, or 'social shake', was usual between male friends; a cordial kiss would be overstepping conventional boundaries, at least between English gentlemen. There are comparable excesses of male affection in 'Love and Friendship' (p. 77) and 'The History of England' ('James I', p. 132).

instability of human pleasures . . . examples from the Lives of great Men: for the pat use of such celebrated 'examples', cf. Laura's remarks in 'Love and Friendship': ' "What an ample subject for reflection on the uncertain Enjoyments of this World, would not that Phaeton & the Life of Cardinal Wolsey afford a thinking Mind!" said I to Sophia as we were hastening to the field of Action' (p. 87).

amiable Moralist: cf. John Langhorne's *The Correspondence of Theodosius, and Constantia: From their First Acquaintance to the Departure of Theodosius* (1765): 'is it in my power to return those rich lessons in kind, by which I have been so much delighted—I hope, profited?—Exalted Moralist! amiable and excellent Philosopher! What a loss would CONSTANTIA suffer, if deprived of your friendship! To you she owes every valuable sentiment, and almost all the little knowledge she can boast' (80).

five or six months with us: a ludicrously extended visit.

Arabella: a fashionable name that reappears in JA's 'A Tale'; also the name of the heroine in Lennox's *The Female Quixote*.

The first Act of a Comedy

Popgun: 'A gun with which children play, that only makes a noise' (Johnson's *Dictionary*); by extension, something ineffectual, a joke that misfires (*OED*). There is a Mr Popgun in Charlotte Smith's *Ethelinde* (iv, ch. 2).

Postilion: see 'Frederic & Elfrida', note to p. 6.

Chorus of ploughboys: the chorus suggests that JA's drama is a musical comedy or comic opera, a genre that became popular in the late 18th century.

Strephon: a name conventionally given to pastoral lovers and shepherds (see 'Frederic & Elfrida', notes to pp. 4 and 8). Strephon is traditionally paired with Chloe, the last of JA's cast list, as his female beloved; the couple had already been sent up in e.g. Jonathan Swift's scatological poem 'Strephon and Chloe' (1734).

Pistoletta: the female form of pistolet or pistoletto: a small gun.

153 *the Lion*: the inn's public rooms have names such as 'the Lion', 'the Moon', and 'the Sun'; the bedrooms have numbers.

bill of fare: menu.

I wull, I wull: Cook might be Scottish; 'I wull, I wull' could therefore be alluding to popular Scottish songs such as 'Lord Thomas and Fair Annet', in which 'will' is 'wull' throughout. See *Ancient and Modern Scottish Songs, Heroic Ballads*, 2 vols., 2nd edn (1776), ii, 24–8. But JA may simply be rendering phonetically an unspecified dialect, or mimicking the comic rusticity of 'I wull, I wull' as it appears in e.g. Farquhar's *The Recruiting Officer* (act 2).

My Girl . . . Strephon: parodying the dramatic convention of relaying necessary information to the audience, information which the characters themselves must already well know.

it wants seven Miles: there are 7 miles to go.

Hounslow: a village west of London; the adjacent Hounslow Heath, once used as a military encampment by Oliver Cromwell, was reputedly the haunt of highwaymen and thieves. *Novellettes, Selected for the Use of Young Ladies and Gentlemen*, 2 vols. (1784) includes a tale by Elizabeth Griffith, 'The Dupe of Love and Friendship: Or, The Unfortunate Irishman' which mentions robbery, gambling, Hounslow Heath, pistols, and a woman called Maria (i, 49–91).

Stree-phon . . . that will be fun: hyphenated and drawn out in order to stress the rhyme scheme, which is both laborious and imperfect, possibly as a hint to the performer. 'Fun' is described as 'A low cant word' in Johnson's *Dictionary*; Grose defines it as 'a cheat, or trick' (*Classical Dictionary*).

154 *stinking partridge*: game birds were hung for at least a few days before being consumed, in order to enrich their tenderness and high, gamey flavour. This partridge has presumably been left too long.

Staines: another village west of London; a regular staging post with coaching inns.

bad guinea: a guinea was a gold coin, worth 21*s.*; a 'bad' guinea was counterfeit. Forgery was a capital offence.

pawn to you an undirected Letter: a letter without an address, lacking in any obvious or commercial value and therefore little use as security for the fee of 18*d.* (1*s.* 6*d.*). Cf. difficulties in paying the coach fare in 'The beautifull Cassandra' (see note to p. 39).

A Letter from a Young Lady, whose feelings being too strong for her Judgement led her into the commission of Errors which her Heart disapproved

155 *feelings being too strong . . . her Heart disapproved*: the language of conduct books and sentimental fiction; cf. 'he is hurried away by every storm and start of passion, to the commission of a thousand errors. Reason and religion, in vain, exert their voices to bring him back to the path of wisdom' (*The Man of Experience: A Sentimental History*, 2 vols. (1780), i, 144); 'a repentant sinner, one who has been led into the commission of his errors by very bad advice and profligate examples, but whom misfortunes and painful experience have restored to reason' (Eliza Parsons, *The Errors of Education*, 3 vols. (1791), ii, 127).

Ellinor: the spelling is close to that of Elinor in *S&S*.

twelve Years: 'Years' originally read 'months' (see Textual Notes, p. 235): JA's revision makes Ellinor a far more precocious perjurer.

Horseguards: the cavalry brigade protecting the royal household; specifically, the elite third regiment of this body, known as the Royal Horse Guards.

Anna Parker: the surname appears again in *Sanditon*, which opens with Mr and Mrs Parker's carriage toppling over.

A Tour through Wales

156 *A Tour through Wales*: JA probably knew Gilpin's *Observations on the River Wye* (1782), a work that helped to popularize Wales as a destination for those seeking picturesque scenery; on Gilpin, see 'The three Sisters', note to p. 58; 'Love and Friendship', notes to pp. 70 and 92; 'The History of England', notes to pp. 127 and 130. In 1774, four years after Gilpin, Samuel Johnson also undertook a 'tour to Wales', with his friends the Thrales, a tour that is discussed in letters reprinted by Boswell in the *Life of Johnson* (1791), i [1774].

on the ramble: engaged in rambling, walking or wandering, on a journey or by way of recreation. Johnson published his journal *The Rambler* from 1750 to 1752.

last Monday Month: a month ago last Monday.

galloped . . . fine perspiration: a comically inappropriate way for three women to travel, sharing one pony between three and forced to run alongside the rider. To mention 'perspiration' is inherently very indecorous, so that 'fine', attached to a highly unrefined observation, gains in comic force. Cf. 'those that perspire away their Evenings in crouded assemblies' in JA's deleted work 'A fragment—written to inculcate the practise of Virtue' (Textual Notes, p. 225).

capped & heelpeiced: repaired with toe-patches and replacement heels.

Carmarthen: a town in south-west Wales.

blue Sattin Slippers: delicate, formal footwear, designed for the evenings; highly inappropriate for galloping or hopping across the countryside.

hopped home from Hereford: alliteration is similarly deployed in 'Frederic & Elfrida' and 'Collection of Letters' (see notes to pp. 5 and 134). Hereford, a cathedral city on the river Wye, lies about 16 miles east of the border with Wales.

Elizabeth Johnson: Samuel Johnson's wife's name was Elizabeth (he called her 'Tetty'); for other allusions to Johnson, see e.g. 'Jack & Alice', note to p. 10; 'Love and Friendship', note to p. 86; 'Lesley-Castle', notes to p. 97.

A Tale

A Gentleman . . . I shall conceal: cf. similar conventional mystifications in 'Henry & Eliza', 'The three Sisters', and 'Love and Friendship'.

Pembrokeshire: a seaside county in south-west Wales.

Closet: 'A small room of privacy and retirement' (Johnson's *Dictionary*), usually adjoining a bedroom.

Wilhelminus: a comic, latinized version of Wilhelm, itself a German form of William; 'Robertus', his brother, is a latinized Robert.

157 *Genius*: see 'The Generous Curate', note to p. 65.

VOLUME THE THIRD

159 CONTENTS: as in the Contents for *Volume the First* and *Volume the Second*, JA inserted page numbers beside each of the items.

Kitty: JA refers to the heroine as Kitty, occasionally varied by the use of Catherine; Catharine is the later revised form. See Introduction, pp. xxii–xxiii, and Textual Notes, pp. 236–7.

160 *Miss Mary Lloyd*: see 'Frederic & Elfrida', note to p. 2. The Lloyds, who had rented Deane Parsonage from the Austen family since spring 1789, had to give up the house in Dec. 1792 in order to make way for the new curate of Deane, James Austen, and his wife, Anne, a situation that is echoed in the departure of the Webb family to make way for Mr Gower and his new bride in 'Evelyn'. JA also gave Mary Lloyd a sewing bag containing a poem, 'This little bag', dated 'January 1792'.

EVELYN

161 *Evelyn*: an imaginary village, echoing the name of Burney's heroine Evelina and perhaps recalling the idealized 'Sweet Auburn' in Goldsmith's 'The Deserted Village' (see 'Frederic & Elfrida', note to p. 3). Only Evelyn and Crankhumdunberry are hailed as 'sweet village' in JA's teenage writings.

any house to be lett: the situation parallels that of 'A Tale', the final item in *Volume the Second*, in which Wilhelminus finds a Pembrokeshire cottage advertised 'To be Lett' in a newspaper.

threw up the sash: opened the window; the 'sash' is a sliding wooden frame, part of a sash window, that can be raised and lowered (*OED*). Such windows were popular in the late 18th century as they allowed more light and air into a room than leaded casement windows did.

161 *would I form myself by such an example!*: stock language in 18th-century novels, which often present their characters as positive examples on which readers might model their own conduct—as, indeed, do other characters within the fiction itself. See e.g. *Female Stability*: 'I often think, when I am going to do any thing material, would Augustus have acted thus? and endeavour to form myself by his excellent example' (iii, 158).

best of Women: like the phrase 'best of Men' (which appears three times in 'Evelyn'), this hyperbolic praise echoes that of *Sir Charles Grandison* (see e.g. i, letters 19, 26, 37, 39). Unlike the helpful Mrs Willis, Mr Gower is comically undeserving of the tribute, being selfish, greedy, and opportunistic, where Sir Charles is noble, self-sacrificing, and generous.

162 *their house*: JA originally wrote 'the remainder of their Lease' (see Textual Notes, p. 236), suggesting that the family does not own but rents the house; there is a similar confusion in 'A Tale', in which Wilhelminus is initially said to have 'bought a small Cottage in Pembrokeshire', but proceeds to rent it.

circular paddock: a paddock offers enclosed pasture to horses, sheep, and cows; making it circular is a joke aimed at Lancelot 'Capability' Brown (1715–83), a landscape gardener known to favour the circle, and his followers. Under Brown's influence, straight avenues, canals, or walks converging on the ceremonial spine of the house disappeared in favour of a circular layout, enlivened by cleverly placed temples, obelisks, seats, pagodas, rotundas, etc.

paling: a fence made of pales, or pointed lengths of wood arranged closely together and driven into the ground.

Lombardy poplars: the Lombardy poplar is a tall, columnar variety, brought to England from Italy in the 18th century; a staple feature of the landscape in gothic fiction (see also the 'Grove of Poplars' in 'Frederic & Elfrida', p. 3). Travelling through France in 1789, Hester Lynch Piozzi noted that 'the rage for Lombardy poplars is in equal force here as about London: no tolerable house have I passed without seeing long rows of them; all young plantations, as one may perceive by their size' (*Observations and Reflections Made in the Course of a Journey through France, Italy, and Germany*, 2 vols. (1789), i, 9). Cf. JA's letter from London on 17 May 1799: 'The Drawing-room Window . . . commands a perspective veiw of the left side of Brock Street, broken by three Lombardy Poplars in the Garden of the last house in Queen's Parade' (*Letters*, 42). Lombardy poplars were commonly planted in a long line in order to mark a boundary or to screen something unattractive from view (as is the case in *S&S*, ch. 42), rather than (as here) in a circle around the entirety of a house, where they would block the view and obstruct the light.

alternatively placed in three rows: cf. the orchard in *Sir Charles Grandison*, offered as evidence of the 'peculiar taste' and fanciful character of Sir

Thomas Grandison: 'planted with three rows of trees, at proper distances from each other; one of pines; one of cedars; one of Scotch firs, in the like semicircular order' (vii, letter 5). For JA's jokes about 'alternately' in the teenage writings see 'Frederic & Elfrida', note to p. 3.

Shrubbery: 'A plantation of shrubs' (*OED*); it usually featured a winding, irregular path rather than a straight gravel walk. Cf. the shrubberies in JA's early epistolary work *Lady Susan* (letters 15–17; unpublished until 1871—the title is not JA's) and in *MP* (ch. 6, ch. 22).

four white Cows . . . at equal distances: flouting Gilpin's picturesque 'doctrine of grouping *larger cattle*' in his *Observations, Relative Chiefly to Picturesque Beauty, Made in the Year 1772, On Several Parts of England; Particularly the Mountains, and Lakes of Cumberland, and Westmoreland*, where he insists that two or four cows are inferior to three and that they must not be placed 'at equal distances' (ii, p. xii). Elizabeth Bennet cites the same doctrine when she refuses to join Miss Bingley, Mrs Hurst, and Darcy on a walk: 'The picturesque would be spoilt by admitting a fourth' (*P&P*, ch. 10).

gravel road without any turn or interruption: like the straight gravel walk through the shrubbery, this gravel road affronts the picturesque requirements of a winding approach and a variety of striking prospects en route to a country house (see *P&P*, ch. 43; *S&S*, ch. 42).

a very elegant Dressing room: see 'Frederic & Elfrida', note to p. 4.

Chocolate: hot chocolate, a luxurious drink made by dissolving a paste or cake of cacao seeds into milk and sweetening it with (e.g.) vanilla.

venison pasty: a pie stuffed with deer meat, a luxurious dish.

163 *a handsome portion*: a substantial dowry. Cf. Lady Williams in 'Jack & Alice', who has 'a handsome Jointure & the remains of a very handsome face' (p. 10).

164 *ten thousand pounds*: far from being 'almost too small a sum to be offered', £10,000 is a very large dowry; Mrs Elton's in *E* is 'so many thousands as would always be called ten' (ch. 22).

the next day, the nuptials . . . were celebrated: this is an invalid marriage (see 'Henry & Eliza', notes to p. 29; 'Sir William Mountague', note to p. 35; 'The three Sisters', notes to p. 59); no banns have been read or special licence obtained, and there is no clergyman to conduct the ceremony.

a rose tree . . . pleasing variety: the rose trees, like the grazing cows, contravene Gilpin's advice to shun groups of four and pursue a 'pleasing variety' (see e.g. 'that pleasing variety, which we admire in ground', in *Observations on the River Wye*, 63).

Carlisle . . . Sussex: the city of Carlisle is in Cumberland, near the Scottish border, around 350 miles away from Sussex on the south coast of England.

Isle of Wight: a small island off the Hampshire coast, popular with tourists in the 18th century, the Isle of Wight clearly does not merit the title of a 'foreign Country'. Fanny Price is mocked for being overly impressed by the Isle of Wight; she calls it '*the Island*, as if there were no other island in the world' (*MP*, ch. 2).

164 *Family Chaplain*: in the late 18th century, only a very wealthy, old-fashioned family would have its own domestic chaplain. See Fanny Price's regretful comments on the lost relationship of a great house to its chapel (*MP*, ch. 9).

165 *wrecked on the coast of Calshot*: Calshot is on the mainland, opposite the Isle of Wight; the Solent—the narrow channel between the Isle of Wight and the mainland—is not known for storms or shipwrecks. In 1539, Henry VIII built Calshot Castle to protect the south coast from potential invasion from French or Spanish forces; it was part of a chain of coastal defences that remained important throughout the 18th century.

166 *gout*: 'A specific constitutional disease occurring in paroxysms, usually hereditary and in male subjects; characterized by painful inflammation of the smaller joints, esp. that of the great toe, and the deposition of sodium urate in the form of chalk-stones; it often spreads to the larger joints and the internal organs' (*OED*). The condition is associated with over-indulgence in eating or drinking, such as that displayed by Mr Gower.

favourite character of Sir Charles Grandison's, a nurse: Grandison (an accomplished nurse himself) recommends marriage to his uncle Lord W., who suffers from gout, because women shine in the 'sick chamber', where 'they can exert all their amiable, and, shall I say, lenient qualities' (iii, letter 11).

irregularity in the fall . . . enliven the structure: the castle, with its commanding coastal position, beautiful views, ancient pedigree, and rugged irregularity, answers Gilpin's exacting requirements of the picturesque; the paddock would certainly offer a contrast, albeit one that breaches Gilpin's rules.

winding approach, struck him with terror: unlike the straight gravel paths of Evelyn Lodge, this meandering route meets Gilpin's requirements; it also echoes the 'winding' and fear-provoking layout of castles in gothic novels; see e.g. Ann Radcliffe's *The Castles of Athlin and Dunbayne*: 'Alleyn was conveyed through dark and winding passages to a distant part of the castle, where at length a small door, barred with iron, opened, and disclosed to him an abode, whence light and hope were equally excluded. He shuddered as he entered, and the door was closed upon him' (ch. 3).

168 *Gipsies or Ghosts*: a juxtaposition that is comic, even though gipsies as well as ghosts were feared in the period—see the terrified Harriet Smith's encounter with a group of gipsies, 'loud and insolent', in *E* (ch. 41). Boswell recorded Johnson's view that, as far as the existence of ghosts was concerned, 'All argument is against it; but all belief is for it' (Boswell, *Life of Johnson*, ii, 190, [1778]).

gallop all the way: cf. 'A Tour through Wales': 'my Mother . . . galloped all the way' (p. 156). JA's 'Evelyn' ends abruptly here; her nephew James Edward and her niece Anna both wrote continuations of the tale (see pp. 205–8).

KITTY, OR THE BOWER

169 *Miss Austen*: JA's elder sister Cassandra; 'The beautifull Cassandra' (see note to p. 37), 'Ode to Pity', and 'The History of England' were also dedicated to her.

a place in every library in the Kingdom: JA is echoing the terms in which contemporary fiction was advertised. The title page of *Edward and Harriet, or The Happy Recovery; A Sentimental Novel*, 2 vols. (1788), states that the work 'may be had at every Circulating Library in the Kingdom'; Charles Dibdin's *The Younger Brother: A Novel*, 3 vols. (1793), includes a bookseller, Mr Allen, who boasts 'look at this drawer: full, chuck full—all novels—I supply every library in the kingdom' (iii, 138). Cf. later references in 'Kitty, or the Bower' to Mrs Peterson's 'Library' and to the 'kingdom' (p. 199).

threescore Editions: sixty editions, an impossibly high number even for the most successful works of fiction; JA's teenage writings are in any case unpublished. The figure of 'threescore' features on the title pages of some 18th-century novels and may contribute to JA's dedicatory joke; see e.g. Daniel Defoe's *Memoirs of a Cavalier . . . Written Threescore Years Ago by an English Gentleman* ([1720]); *The Fortunes and Misfortunes of the Famous Moll Flanders, &c. Who was Born in Newgate, and During a Life of Continu'd Variety for Threescore Years, besides her Childhood, was Twelve Year a Whore* ([1721]).

Kitty: here and elsewhere in the text (but not throughout), 'Kitty' has been deleted and 'Catharine' inserted above the line (see Introduction, pp. xxii–xxiii, and Textual Notes, pp. 236–7).

as many heroines have had . . . very young: the orphaned heroine is a stereotype of gothic and sentimental fiction; see e.g. the opening letter of *The Orphan, A Novel*, 2 vols. (1783), where we learn from the heroine that her 'parents . . . left me at an age when happily I was too young to feel the misery of my helpless situation' (i, 5–6).

Bower: 'An arbour; a sheltered place covered with green trees, twined and bent' (Johnson's *Dictionary*), associated with solitude and with medieval romance. William Cowper's *Hope* (1781), like many other 18th-century poems, refers to 'bow'rs of bliss', alluding to Edmund Spenser's Bower of Bliss in *The Faerie Queene*, bk II (1590), which may also be an influence on Kitty's bower in this tale (*Poems by William Cowper, of the Inner Temple* (1782), 149).

infantine: 'Not mature' (Johnson's *Dictionary*); see 'Collection of Letters', note to p. 135.

170 *tenure*: tenor, or habitual state of mind.

enthousiastic: enthusiasm was both a positive and a negative attribute in this period. Johnson defines enthusiasm (negatively) as 'A vain belief of private revelation; a vain confidence of divine favour or communication' and 'Heat of imagination; violence of passion; confidence of opinion', but also (more positively) as 'Elevation of Fancy; exaltation of ideas'. In her 'warm' rather than heated imagination, and in her cultivation of 'Fancy', Kitty seems to hover between the second and third senses of the word. JA's niece Anna Austen used the working title of *Enthusiasm* for one of her novels; when it was abandoned, JA wrote regretfully that '"Enthusiasm" was something so very superior that every common title must appear to disadvantage' (*Letters*, 280, 18 Aug. 1814).

170 *equip her for the East Indies*: that is, furnish her with all the necessary provisions for a journey to the East Indies, where young women could expect to find husbands among the numerous single young men employed by the East India Company. JA may have in mind her aunt Philadelphia Hancock (1730–92), the Revd George Austen's elder sister, who in 1752 sailed to India, disembarking at Madras, and married Tysoe Saul Hancock, an East India surgeon, in Feb. 1753; he was seven years her senior. Like Kitty, Philadelphia and George were orphaned early.

Maintenance: 'Supply of the necessaries of life; sustenance' (Johnson's *Dictionary*); here, as afforded to an impoverished young woman by marriage to a wealthier man.

Bengal: the British name for a province in north-east India, where the East India Company was based.

171 *Dowager*: 'A widow with a jointure'; 'The title given to ladies who survive their husbands' (Johnson's *Dictionary*).

companion: see 'Henry & Eliza', note to p. 28.

Chetwynde: the name of a village in Gloucestershire, though this one turns out to be located in Devonshire.

Peterson: this Anglo-Saxon surname was later changed, here and elsewhere in 'Kitty, or the Bower', to the courtly-romantic name 'Percival' (see Introduction, pp. xxii–xxiii, and Textual Notes, p. 237). Of the many small revisions made to the story, this is the most consistent alteration. A Lady Percival appears in 'Sir William Mountague'.

Dudley . . . younger Son of a very noble Family: this unpleasant character and his insolent, high-born relatives are probably named after Robert Dudley, Earl of Leicester, and his family; as the earliest favourite of Elizabeth I, Dudley would be a natural target of JA's antipathy (see 'The History of England', 'Elizabeth', note to p. 129).

tythes: that is, tithes, 'The tenth part of the annual produce of agriculture, etc., being a due or payment (orig. in kind) for the support of the priesthood, religious establishments, etc.' (*OED*). Landowners were meant to make such payments to the rector of a parish; the amounts of money involved varied considerably and were the subject of much public debate. In her spoof 'Plan of a Novel' JA followed the advice of James Stanier Clarke (*Letters*, 320) and included a clergyman who offers 'his opinion of the Benefits to result from Tythes being done away'.

parade: 'Shew; ostentation' (Johnson's *Dictionary*).

172 *Stanley*: a name with Elizabethan pedigree; Henry Stanley (1531–93), 4th Earl of Derby, participated in the trial of Mary, Queen of Scots.

Working: see 'The Mystery', note to p. 50.

173 *Establishment*: the domestic staff who run the household and prepare for the reception of visitors. Cf. William Combe, *The Devil Upon Two Sticks in England: Being a Continuation of Le diable boiteux of Le Sage*, 6 vols. (1790–1): 'she is such an excellent manager, that she lives in a very elegant house—keeps a very handsome equipage—possesses an ample establishment of servants—is never without company' (ii, 192).

sweep: 'A curved carriage drive leading to a house' (*OED*). The earliest example the *OED* gives of the word in this sense comes from *S&S*.

Music of an Italian Opera . . . hight of Enjoyment: by the 1790s, at least as much deprecation as enjoyment of Italian opera is expressed in fiction, though Burney's heroines Evelina and Cecilia both delight in it (*Evelina*, i, letter 12; *Cecilia*, i, ch. 8).

half the year in Town: that is, during the London winter season, from New Year until the king's official birthday on 4 June. See 'Jack & Alice', note to p. 14.

174 *Modern history*: Western historical study traditionally divides history into ancient, medieval, and modern periods. Although these have no definite chronological limits, ancient history is usually thought of as ending with the fall of the Western Roman Empire in AD 476, and medieval history, when considered as separate from modern history, with the discovery of the Americas in the late 15th century (see *OED* 'history', sense 2). In her *Letters on the Improvement of the Mind*, 2 vols. (1773), Hester Mulso Chapone cautions against 'mixing *ancient* history with *modern*' (ii, 183).

Mrs Smith's Novels: by Aug. 1792 Charlotte Smith had published *Emmeline, the Orphan of the Castle*, 4 vols. (1788), *Ethelinde, or the Recluse of the Lake*, 5 vols. (1789), *Celestina. A Novel*, 4 vols. (1791), and *Desmond. A Novel*, 3 vols. (1792). She had completed six more novels by 1798.

Emmeline: see note to p. 129, on 'Delamere', hero of Smith's first novel, *Emmeline*, and among the 'first of Men' listed in JA's 'History of England'.

Ethelinde is so long: like Kitty, JA may not have minded how long a well-written book was, but she joked about the protracted nature of multi-volume works such as Smith's novels. In one letter to Cassandra, alluding to a character in Burney's five-volume novel *Camilla*, she passes on her love to 'Mary Harrison, & tell her I wish whenever she is attached to a young Man, some <u>respectable</u> Dr Marchmont may keep them apart for five Volumes' (*Letters*, 9).

Descriptions of Grasmere . . . the Lakes: Smith's *Ethelinde* begins with descriptions of 'the small but beautiful lake called Grasmere Water' (i, 1), a popular destination in the Lake District for tourists in search of picturesque and sublime landscapes. Elizabeth Bennet and the Gardiners plan a 'tour of pleasure' in the region (*P&P*, ch. 27).

174 *Sir Henry Devereux*: Devereux is a name with Elizabethan associations (see 'The History of England', note to p. 127); a Sir Francis Devereux and his daughters appear in Smith's *Emmeline* (i, 59). JA's niece Anna Lefroy used the name Devereux Forester for a character in her unpublished novel *Which is the Heroine?*, on which she was working in 1814.

travelling Dress: a woman's 'travelling dress' usually consisted of a riding habit (a tailored jacket with a long skirt); this could be worn as a practical and durable everyday dress, not only for travelling or riding. In *Beatrice, or the Inconstant. A Tragic Novel* (1788), Charlotte gets married in a travelling dress, 'the model of simple elegance' (ii, 43); JA's mother, Cassandra Leigh, wore her red riding habit when she married George Austen in Bath in 1764.

Matlock or Scarborough: Matlock is in the Peak District of Derbyshire; Scarborough is on the east Yorkshire coast and on the opposite side of England from the Lakes, indicating Camilla's uncertain command of geography.

175 *such a horrid Creature*: Camilla's language resembles that of Isabella Thorpe in *NA* (and, to a lesser extent, that of Catherine Morland); 'horrid', as applied to thrilling books and tedious people, is a favourite adjective (chs. 6, 10, 12, 21).

the whole race of Mankind were degenerating: cf. Henry Mackenzie, *The Lounger*, no. 19 (11 June 1785): 'There are a set of cynical old men, who are perpetually dinning our ears with the praises of times past, who are fond of drawing comparisons between the ancients and moderns, much to the disparagement of the latter, and who take a misanthropical delight in representing mankind as degenerating from age to age, both in mental and corporeal endowments'. *The Lounger*, 3 vols., 3rd edn (1786), i, 73–6 (at 73).

all order was destroyed over the face of the World: hyperbolic language recalling that of Edmund Burke in his *Reflections on the Revolution in France* (1790), in which he warned of the dangers posed by the French Revolution: 'The usurpation which, in order to subvert antient institutions, has destroyed antient principles, will hold power by arts similar to those by which it has acquired it'; 'destroying at their pleasure the whole original fabric of their society; hazarding to leave to those who come after them, a ruin instead of an habitation' (*Reflections on the Revolution in France, and on the Proceedings in Certain Societies in London Relative to that Event. In a Letter intended to have been sent to a Gentleman in Paris* ([1790]), 116, 141).

said her Neice: here and later in the story, Kitty's replies have subsequently been toned down by selective deletion (see Textual Notes, p. 238).

if she were to come again . . . she did before: Kitty's alarm at the prospect of a resurrected Elizabeth I echoes JA's verdict on that queen, who died at the age of 69, in 'The History of England'.

176 *Harpsichord*: see 'Lesley-Castle', note to p. 112.

sweetest Creature in the world: comparable saccharine overstatements appear in *The Loiterer*, no. 52 (7) and *NA* (ch. 6), in which Isabella Thorpe describes 'a particular friend of mine' as 'a sweet girl, one of the sweetest creatures in the world'.

in Public: that is, in places of public assembly; see 'Lesley-Castle', note to p. 111.

177 *Brook Street*: see 'Sir William Mountague', note to p. 35.

find her in Cloathes: supply her with clothes; a phrase applied to servants and impoverished dependants. In *The History of Emily Willis, a Natural Daughter*, 2 vols. (1768), Mrs Languish tells the heroine, who has applied to be her companion, 'I must find you in Clothes and Pocket-Money, but I shan't fix any particular Sum, till I see whether you will suit me' (ii, 14).

two or three Curacies: a clergyman might have more than one 'living', or curacy, and employ curates on low wages to carry out his clerical duties; see 'The Visit', note to p. 44.

Cheltenham: like Bath, a fashionable spa resort in the west of England.

sent to Sea: subsequently changed to 'got into the Army' (see Textual Notes, p. 239). The author of this alteration forgets it later in the tale, when Kitty again refers to the bishop sending 'Charles Wynne to sea' (see Textual Notes, p. 239). On the choice between these professions, cf. 'Mr Harley', note to p. 33.

School somewhere in Wales: Welsh schools were cheaper and less highly regarded than their English counterparts; because they were relatively remote from England, many wealthy patrons liked to send their dependent charges there. In Agnes Maria Bennett's *The Beggar Girl and her Benefactors*, 7 vols. (1797), Horace Littleton, 'the object of Sir Solomon Mushroom's charity', is 'got rid of for a few years at a free grammar school in Wales' (i, 222).

178 *Ranelagh*: Ranelagh Gardens in Chelsea, a more expensive and upmarket version of Vauxhall Gardens (see 'Lesley-Castle', note to p. 111). Like Vauxhall, Ranelagh features in Burney's *Evelina*.

Bengal or Barbadoes: an alliterative pairing that makes little geographical sense; Miss Wynne has been sent to Bengal in the East Indies. Barbados was another British colony, but in the West Indies.

179 *extremely nice*: that is, betraying a 'culpable delicacy'; 'Fastidious; squeamish' (Johnson's *Dictionary*).

Draws in Oils: sketches or draws in oil paint rather than in watercolour or crayon; considered to be a technically superior accomplishment.

180 *Gold Net*: a fashionable cap, with a hairnet woven from golden thread.

181 *receipt book*: a book containing both culinary and medical recipes, including prescriptions for common ailments such as toothache. Martha Lloyd's handwritten receipt book, owned by the Jane Austen House Museum, Chawton, Hampshire, is a compilation of remedies and recipes made in a stationer's quarto notebook akin to that of JA's *Volume the Second*.

Mortality: 'Mortals collectively; mankind' (*OED*).

182 *have a tooth drawn*: have a tooth extracted, without the aid of anaesthetic.

183 *Pierrot*: 'A kind of sleeved, close-fitting jacket or bodice, worn by women in the late 18th cent., having a low neck and basques extending slightly below the waist' (*OED*). A later insertion of 'Regency walking dress' was made after Feb, 1811, when the Prince of Wales was proclaimed regent in place of his incapacitated father, George III (see Textual Notes, p. 240). A walking dress had a shorter hem than an evening dress, making it more practical for everyday and outdoor wear.

   a Jacket and petticoat: later revised to 'Bonnet and Pelisse'; a pelisse is 'A woman's long cloak, with armhole slits and a shoulder cape or hood, often made of a rich fabric; (later also) a long fitted coat of similar style' (*OED*). See Textual Notes, p. 240.

183–184 *Kingdom . . . flourishing & prosperous a state*: Mr Stanley, a member of William Pitt the Younger's Whig government, voices a general mood of optimism about Pitt's leadership, at least during his first decade as Prime Minister. Pitt took up office in 1783 and proved far more popular than his predecessor, Lord North, who was the first British Prime Minister to be forced out of office by a motion of no confidence (on account of a British defeat at Yorktown, Virginia, in the American War of Independence).

184 *at sixes & sevens*: 'in confusion, commonly said of a room, where the furniture &c. is scattered about, or of a business left unsettled' (*Classical Dictionary*). In the revised 4th edition of his *Dictionary* (1773), Johnson refers to it as 'A ludicrous expression that has been long in use'.

   scotch Steps: in Elizabeth Pinchard's *Dramatic Dialogues, For the Use of Young Persons*, 2 vols. ([1792]), Matilda and Harriot also practise their 'scotch Steps' and Matilda exclaims 'I love the Scotch reels, and they are very fashionable now' (ii, 13). Scottish reels and quicksteps were indeed a popular feature of public dances in the 1790s, but they were not entirely proper (in *P&P*, Elizabeth assumes that Darcy's invitation to dance a reel is made in order to mock her bad taste (ch. 10)). On the fashion for all things Scottish, cf. 'Lesley-Castle', note to p. 107.

   Nanny: this name was later changed to the more formal 'Anne', in line with the shift from 'Kitty' to 'Catharine' (see Introduction, pp. xxii–xxiii, and Textual Notes, p. 240).

   Lavender water: 'A perfume compounded, with alcohol and ambergris, from the distilled flowers of lavender' (*OED*); also used as a stimulant. (Later deleted; see Textual Notes, p. 240.)

   Chaise and four: a light, elegant carriage drawn by four horses; a fast and glamorous mode of transport.

185 *his hair is just done up*: hair powdered, curled, and elaborately arranged to resemble a wig.

   Livery: 'the characteristic uniform or insignia worn by a household's retainers or servants (in later use largely restricted to footmen and other manservants), typically distinguished by colour and design' (*OED*).

hack horses: hackney horses, hired from a stable, implying a lower rank in those who hired them than that of a guest who arrived with his own horses and servants.

187   *go to the door . . . comes*: answering the door was usually a servant's responsibility.

188   *travelling apparel*: for men, this would probably be a riding outfit with boots and an overcoat—highly inappropriate as formal wear for a ball.

 linen: that is, shirts and other items of clothing made of linen.

 powder & pomatum: items to assist Stanley in dressing his hair. There are 'Patches, Powder, Pomatum and Paint' in 'Frederic & Elfrida' (see p. 5 and note).

189   *monthly Ball*: that is, a public ball, funded by subscription, rather than a private event.

191   *Hunter*: 'A horse used, or adapted for use, in hunting' (*OED*) and therefore often an expensive thoroughbred.

 Express: a messenger sent on horseback to deliver news as quickly as possible.

192   *Brampton*: a village in Cambridgeshire.

 led her to the top of the room: Stanley and Kitty have taken the place of honour, leading the way in the dance; neither of them has the rank or social standing to justify such an action.

193   *did not know who her grandfather had been*: this was a 'boast' of Johnson's, who said to Boswell 'I can hardly tell who was my grandfather' (*Life of Johnson*, i, 423 [9 May 1773]).

 only a tradesman: Kitty's father, like Camilla's, is in fact a merchant; Camilla, as an heiress, has the superior claim to 'consequence', but her birth is no more aristocratic than the heroine's.

 Mr Pitt or the Lord Chancellor: William Pitt the Younger (1759–1806), Prime Minister (see note to pp. 183–4) and Lord Chancellor, who from 1778 to June 1792 was Lord Thurlow (1731–1806). His duties included presiding over the House of Lords and the judiciary.

 her partner during the greatest part of it: to dance with the same partner for more than two consecutive dances was a breach of etiquette.

 Address: 'Manner of addressing another; as, we say, a *man of an happy or a pleasing address; a man of an aukward address*' (Johnson's *Dictionary*).

194   *come out*: see 'Collection of Letters', note to p. 134.

196   *impudent*: 'Wanting in shame or modesty; shameless, unblushing, immodest; indelicate' (*OED*); a serious slur on female character.

197   *tremblingly alive*: see 'Love and Friendship', note to p. 70.

198   *temper*: 'Calmness of mind; moderation' (Johnson's *Dictionary*).

 Richard the 3ᵈ: Stanley's warm defence of this monarch goes well beyond that of 'The History of England', where JA is 'inclined to suppose him a very respectable Man' (p. 124).

199 *Profligate*: 'Abandoned; lost to virtue and decency; shameless' (Johnson's *Dictionary*).

Blair's Sermons: the Revd Hugh Blair (1718–1800), a Scottish minister of religion, author, and rhetorician, was best known for his *Sermons* (1777–1801), a five-volume guide to practical Christian morality, including strictures on the modesty and filial obedience of the young, and *Lectures on Rhetoric and Belles Lettres* (1783), a prescriptive guide on composition with which JA was also familiar.

Seccar's explanation of the Catechism: Archbishop Thomas Secker's popular and influential *Lectures on the Catechism of the Church of England* (1769) were published after his death. In his *Liberal Education: or, A Practical Treatise on the Methods of Acquiring Useful and Polite Learning* ([1781]), the Revd Vicesimus Knox noted that: 'The number of books written on purpose to introduce young people to religious knowledge, is infinite: I would confine the attention of the scholar to the Catechism, Secker's Lectures, and the Bible' (316). The reference to Secker was later updated to *Coelebs in Search of a Wife*, Hannah More's didactic novel of 1809 (see also *Letters*, 179). See Introduction, p. xxiii, and Textual Notes, p. 242.

my own Library: this may refer to a bookcase or to a private room full of books.

overthrow the establishment of the kingdom: see note to p. 175 ('all order was destroyed over the face of the World'); JA again alludes here to the perceived threats to England resulting from the French Revolution, and employs the language of Edmund Burke and his supporters. See e.g. Burke, *Reflections on the Revolution in France*: 'instead of quarrelling with establishments, as some do, who have made a philosophy and a religion of their hostility to such institutions, we cleave closely to them. We are resolved to keep an established church, an established monarchy, an established aristocracy, and an established democracy, each in the degree it exists, and in no greater' (135–6)); John Bowles, *Farther Reflections submitted to the Consideration of the Combined Powers* ([1794]): 'It is the nature of this Revolution not merely to subvert all Government, but to overthrow every establishment, civil and religious' (3). For such writers, female modesty and chastity were bound up with resistance to sudden and violent political change.

202 *Oh! what a silly Thing is Woman! How vain, how unreasonable!*: a parodic debasement of Hamlet's celebrated speech, 'What a piece of work is a man! How noble in reason, how infinite in faculties' (act 2, scene 2); another instance of gender-switching in JA's teenage writing.

203 *nice*: not in the sense of 'extremely nice' (for which see note to p. 179), but in the emerging sense of the word, as deplored by Henry Tilney: 'Oh! it is a very nice word indeed!—it does for every thing. Originally perhaps it was applied only to express neatness, propriety, delicacy, or refinement . . . But now every commendation on every subject is comprised in that one word' (*NA*, ch. 14).

[FAMILY CONTINUATIONS TO VOLUME THE THIRD]

[Continuation of Evelyn, by James Edward Austen]

205 *Family . . . Austen*: for the relation of the various 'continuations' to the main body of JA's notebook see Textual Notes, p. 243.

he rang the housebell . . . as little success: this scenario—a protracted description of someone's failure to have the door answered—echoes a comic interlude, narrated from the other side of the threshold, in 'Love and Friendship' (pp. 71–2).

observing the dining parlour window open he leapt in: on characters leaping in and out of windows, see 'Frederic & Elfrida', note to p. 5; 'Henry & Eliza', note to p. 30.

Maria's Dressingroom . . . the servants assembled at tea: for servants to assemble for tea in their mistress's dressing-room is comically and startlingly inappropriate, as is registered in Mr Gower's extreme reaction. On JA's dressing rooms, see 'Frederic & Elfrida', note to p. 4.

Hungary water: a restorative named after the Queen of Hungary, 'made of Rosemary Flowers infus'd some Days in rectify'd Spirit of Wine, and thus distill'd' (Ephraim Chambers, *Cyclopædia; or, An Universal Dictionary of Arts and Sciences*, 2 vols. (1728)).

the order of the procession: Mr Gower arranges the funeral procession so as to exclude himself from it, a highly irregular move for the chief mourner.

to give vent to his sorrow in the bosom of his family: novelistic cant; see e.g. *The History of Miss Melmoth*: 'Lady Evelin tenderly pressed her to her maternal bosom . . . She went, I believe, to give vent to a sorrow which I observed rising to her eyes' (iii, 250, letter 91).

saved her from sinking to the ground: this conduct and language echo 'Frederic & Elfrida', 'A beautifull description of the different effects of Sensibility on different Minds', and 'Love and Friendship', all of which feature sinking and fainting heroines.

——Castle: a comic reference to the convention in 18th-century novels of abbreviating or withholding the names of locations and characters (and sometimes dates), as if they were real, a practice mockingly echoed in JA's 'The three Sisters', 'Henry & Eliza', and 'Love and Friendship'.

offering me his hand . . . married yesterday: for other precipitate and probably invalid unions, see 'Henry & Eliza' and 'Sir William Mountague'.

206 *a pot of beer*: sinking beneath the conduct expected of a man of his social station, Mr Gower is drinking a tankard of beer in a public house.

more grateful to him than Nectar: 'grateful' here means 'pleasing' or 'welcome' (*OED*); nectar is, in classical mythology, the drink of the gods.

an offer of his hand & heart . . . condescended to accept: an echo of 'Jack & Alice': 'offering him with great tenderness my hand & heart' (p. 17); on condescension in the teenage writings, see 'Frederic & Elfrida', note to p. 6.

206 *the Anchor*: a popular name for an inn.

*Westgate Buil^gs^*: Westgate Buildings, towards the lower end of Bath, where the Austen family considered taking lodgings and where Mrs Smith lives in *P.* Sir Walter Elliot associates the address with 'low company, paltry rooms, foul air' (ch. 17).

207 *the White horse Inn*: like 'the *Anchor*', a popular name for a public house.

[Continuation of Evelyn, by Anna Lefroy]

round-Robin of perpetual peace: 'A document . . . having the names of the signatories arranged in a circle so as to disguise the order in which they have signed. Later more generally: any document of this type signed by many people, freq. in alphabetical order to indicate that responsibility is shared' (*OED*, 'round robin', sense III.8.a). The Austen family may have considered it a nautical term: the 'round robin' was apparently invented by sailors. (The modern sense of a letter of news, sent in multiple copies to friends and relatives on a special occasion, seems to begin in the 1870s.)

enjoyment had no End, and calamity no commencement: on JA's comic alliteration, see 'Frederic & Elfrida', note to p. 5; 'Collection of Letters', note to p. 134; 'A Tour through Wales', note to p. 156.

Did she not dart . . . gracefully reclined . . . precipitate herself into his arms?: novelistic cant; cf. JA's 'The Mystery', in which Sir Edward Spangle is 'reclined in an elegant Attitude' (p. 51) and 'Love and Friendship', in which Augustus 'gracefully purloined' a large sum of money from his father (p. 78). See also e.g. *The Unfortunate Lovers; A Story Founded on Facts*, trans. George Wright (1798)—an abridgement of Goethe's *Sorrows of Young Werther*—in which a female 'stranger to virtue' is said to be willing to 'precipitate herself into the arms of another' (59).

breathe forth as it were by installments: such jokey exchanges of book time with real time are an Austen family idiom; cf. JA's letter to Cassandra of 5 Sept. 1796: 'Give my Love to Mary Harrison, & tell her I wish whenever she is attached to a young Man, some <u>respectable</u> Dr Marchmont may keep them apart for five Volumes' (*Letters*, 9).

Ah, Who? Vain Echo! vain sympathy!: novelistic cant, hence the vain echo of a vain echo; see e.g. 'ah! how vain, how still less satisfactory are riches! She made many more reflections of the same nature' (*The History of Miss Pamela Howard*, i, 12); 'Vain, vain delusive hopes, whither, ah! whither are you fled?' (*The History of Miss Melmoth*, i, 264, letter 33).

a mahogany ruler: in the early 19th century, most rulers were made of wood; some were carved from bone or (the most expensive kind) from ivory. This is hardly a surprising or fatal item to discover on a writing desk.

a curl paper: 'A piece of soft paper with which the hair is twisted up for some time, so as to give it a curl when the paper is taken out' (*OED*). This example from Lefroy is the earliest included in the *OED*.

a skein of black sewing silk: a skein is 'A quantity of thread or yarn, wound to a certain length upon a reel, and usually put up in a kind of loose knot' (*OED*); silk could be sold in the form of a thread or twist for sewing.

208 *Laudanum*: 'a name for various preparations in which opium was the main ingredient' (*OED*); also a staple ingredient of gothic fiction.

'Tantôt c'est un vide; qui nous Ennuie; tantôt c'est un poids qui nous oppresse': 'Sometimes it is a void that wearies us; sometimes it is a weight that oppresses us'. The book in question must be Samuel de Constant's *Laure, ou lettres de quelques personnes de Suisse*, 5 vols. (1787). Vol. i includes the following passage, which differs slightly from the quotation given by Lefroy: 'tantôt c'est un vide qui l'on éprouve, une autre fois c'est un poids qui oppresse' (3, letter I: 'sometimes it is felt as a void; at other times it is a weight that oppresses').

Rolandi—Berners Street: Pietro Rolandi, an Italian bookseller whose shop at 20 Berners Street, Soho, was a meeting place for the Italian community in London. For his name and business address to be imprinted on the cover of a book is, in view of his profession, far from 'strange'.

a Bravo or a Monk: a 'bravo' is 'A daring villain, a hired soldier or assassin; "a man who murders for hire" (Johnson); a reckless desperado' (*OED*). Monks were a staple feature of gothic fiction; Lefroy's continuation of 'Evelyn' post-dates Matthew Lewis's scandalous *The Monk: A Romance*, 3 vols. (1796) and Ann Radcliffe's *The Italian, or The Confessional of the Black Penitents*, 3 vols. (1797).

monitory finger . . . interdicted speech: Maria's cautionary gesture is interpreted as prohibiting speech.

only these—Search—Cupboard—Top shelf: here and throughout her continuation of 'Evelyn', Lefroy is sending up such gothic novels as Ann Radcliffe's *A Sicilian Romance*, 2 vols. (1790); see esp. i, ch. 1, of that novel for a far more protracted version of Lefroy's terrifying search through a house full of secrets.

the Rush light was expiring in the Socket: candles made from the pith of a rush, dipped in tallow or some other grease, gave off a proverbially weak and feeble light (see *OED* 'rush candle', 'rush light'). The dim candle, as well as other details of this scene, resemble JA's gothic parody in *NA*, chs. 21–2, in which a mysterious trunk, apparently containing a secret manuscript, turns out to yield nothing more exciting than a laundry list and other items relating to household expenditure.

[Continuation of Kitty, or the Bower, by James Edward Austen]

hot house of Vice . . . wickedness of every description was daily gaining ground: see 'Love and Friendship', note to p. 71.

indulge in vicious inclinations: conduct book and novelistic language; typically, a euphemism for sexual misconduct. See e.g. *The Accomplish'd Letter-Writer: or the Young Gentlemen and Ladies' Polite Guide to an Epistolary*

Correspondence in Business, Friendship, Love, and Marriage (1787): 'all manner of precepts are useless where the inclinations are vicious' (32); *The Auction: A Modern Novel*, 2 vols. (1770): 'no Man ever professed a greater Love for Variety, nor no one ever gave a more unbounded Scope to his vicious Inclinations' (i, 86).'

209 *Mrs Lascelles*: in *Catharine and Other Writings* (359 n.) it is suggested that the name may derive from the Whig Thomas Lascelles (1670–1751), quartermaster-general during the War of the Spanish Succession. But it features in late 18th-century fiction, too; a Miss Lascelles appears in Sophia Briscoe's *The Fine Lady: A Novel*, 2 vols. (1772), i, 18; there is a Lady Lascelles in *Fashionable Infidelity, or the Triumph of Patience*, 3 vols. (1789), i, 71.

departure of her Brother to Lyons: this picks up on JA's earlier reference to Lyons, the city in east-central France through which Sterne's Yorick passes in *A Sentimental Journey through France and Italy* (1768). Earlier in the tale, Stanley says 'I was in such a devil of a hurry to leave Lyons that I had not time to pack up anything but some linen' (p. 188).

panegirge: panegyric; an encomium.

many Officers perpetually Quartered there . . . infested the principal Streets: officers were lodged in private houses (as in *P&P*), a situation rich in opportunities for pleasure and disaster that is mentioned in e.g. *Masquerades; or, What you Will*, i, 137; *Anna: A Sentimental Novel. In a Series of Letters*, 2 vols. (1782), i, 86.

strolling players . . . Neighbouring Races: cf. the disreputable 'strolling Company of Players' in 'Love and Friendship' (see note to p. 94); such players often put on shows at race and fair meetings, boisterous occasions of which Mrs Percival would not approve.

necessity of having some Gentleman to attend them: this 'new difficulty' is perhaps a hint as to why the text ends here.

APPENDIX

214 *Non venit . . . Ovid*: 'This complaint will not appear to come before its day' (Ovid, Epistles, no. 2). The use of classical epigraphs as a way to introduce the ensuing essay was common in periodical writing throughout the 18th century.

The following letter . . . our capacity as authors: female characters and invented female correspondents regularly featured in *The Tatler* (1709–11) and *The Spectator* (1st series, 1711–12; 2nd series, 1714); a number of spin-off journals were written by female contributors. In *The Rambler*, Johnson did not specifically address women as often or as directly as had his predecessors, a fact that did not go unnoticed by his correspondents (see e.g. Richardson's *Rambler*, no. 97), though he, too, regularly adopted female personae. *Rambler*, no. 62, picking up on similar strains in *The Tatler* and *The Spectator*, offers a precedent to Sophia Sentiment's letter of complaint. An impatient Rhodoclia begs for up-to-date information about 'the entertainments of the town' and threatens to stop reading the journal if Mr Rambler does not comply with her demands (*The Rambler*, ii, 225–33 (at 232–3).

Tatler and Spectator . . . Microcosm and the Olla Podrida: Joseph Addison and Richard Steele, founders of and chief contributors to *The Tatler* and *The Spectator*, were the most 'celebrated periodical writers' throughout the 18th century, as JA suggests in a reference to *The Spectator* in *NA* (ch. 5). More recent journalistic success had been achieved by schoolboy George Canning and his associates in the Eton journal *The Microcosm* (1786–7), and by the *Olla Podrida* (1787). The title of the latter, alluding to a Spanish stew, means 'A diverse mixture of things or elements' (*OED*); it was edited by Thomas Monro of Magdalen College, Oxford, and published in book form in 1788.

a periodical work . . . not too long: periodical papers were typically no longer than 2,500 words.

215 *Eastern Tale . . . the Loiterer*: oriental tales, fables, and allegories were a staple ingredient of 18th-century journals; see e.g. Addison and Steele's tale of Abdallah and Balsora (*The Guardian*, no. 167 (1713)); Addison's 'Vision of Mirza' (*The Spectator*, no. 159 (1711)); and Johnson's essay on Obidah and the hermit (*Rambler*, no. 65 (1750)).

dismal chapels . . . two days afterwards: Fanny Price visits Oxford in 'the dirty month of February', but misses out on the typical highlights of the tour as listed here—college chapels, libraries, and halls—and is able to 'take only a hasty glimpse of Edmund's college as they passed along' (*MP*, ch. 28). 'Vapours' are 'A morbid condition supposed to be caused by the presence of such exhalations; depression of spirits, hypochondria, hysteria, or other nervous disorder' (*OED*).

retiring to Yorkshire, he might have fled into France . . . some great person: the conjunction of Yorkshire retirement with flight to France and a possible affair with a French '*Paysanne*', or peasant woman, sounds as if the author has Sterne's *A Sentimental Journey through France and Italy* in mind. Sterne was a parson in rural Yorkshire, and mentions his retired, out-of-the-way situation in the dedication of *Tristram Shandy*, i, [10–11].

set fire to a convent . . . more interesting: Catherine Morland entertains similar hopes of an 'interesting' story: 'she could not entirely subdue the hope of some traditional legends, some awful memorials of an injured and ill-fated nun' (*NA*, ch. 17).

if you thought, like the Turks, we had no souls: cf. Samuel Johnson, 'Life of Milton' (1779): 'His family consisted of women; and there appears in his books something like a Turkish contempt of females, as subordinate and inferiour beings. That his own daughters might not break the ranks, he suffered them to be depressed by a mean and penurious education. He thought woman made only for obedience, and man only for rebellion'.

Samuel Johnson, *Prefaces, Biographical and Critical, to the Works of the English Poets*, 10 vols. (1779), ii, 144.

215 *never conversed with a female, except your bed-maker and laundress*: bedmakers and laundresses, unlike most women, were free to come and go on college premises; 'conversed with' may be an innuendo in this context, given that many female bedmakers and laundresses were 'Objects of . . . Gallantry' (see Graham Midgley, *University Life in Eighteenth-Century Oxford* (New Haven and London: Yale University Press, 1996), 84–6).

no more of . . . your Homelys and Cockney: 'H. Homely' (in no. 8) and 'Christopher Cockney' (in no. 3) were two of the identities assumed by *The Loiterer*'s contributors.

two lovers . . . just as they were going to church: possibly alluding to Pope's epitaph 'On two lovers struck dead by lightning' (1718), as well as to countless scenes of sentimental love and distress in 18th-century fiction.

a great deal of feeling, and . . . very pretty names: cf. Mary's hope for a duel in 'The three Sisters' (p. 54); death, running mad, a great deal of feeling, and a stress on pretty names all feature in 'Love and Friendship'.

216 *the pastry-cook's shop . . . a bachelor . . . a maiden sister to keep house for you*: cf. the pastry cook in 'The beautifull Cassandra' (p. 38); a proverbially dreadful fate for literary works was for them to end up as wrapping paper in a pastry-cook's shop.

SOPHIA SENTIMENT: this name appears in William Hayley's *The Mausoleum; A Comedy* (1784), a copy of which JA owned.